Night Flight to Shoebury

A Memoir

David Taplin

ISBN-13: 978-1547249824
ISBN-10: 154724982X

"From now on I'm thinking only of me."
Major Danby replied indulgently with a superior smile:
"But, Yossarian, suppose everyone felt that way."
"Then," said Yossarian, "I'd certainly be a damned fool
to feel any other way, wouldn't I?"

- Catch 22. Joseph Heller

With countries, just like with people, it's easy to let the
best of yourself slip away.

- Bruce Springsteen

INTRODUCTION

The good thing about the flight to Mallorca is it only lasts two hours. The bad thing about it is that it only lasts two hours. Two hours in which to contemplate my short but eventful life - along with it's imminent conclusion. Never have arrivals and departures felt so close together.

I'm travelling 'scheduled' on account of Big Patsy picking up the tab, which is nice. But bearing in mind the fact that he will have me killed as soon as we land and are away from any crowds, I figure this is the least he can do. He wouldn't want me showing up for my own assassination hot and flustered from cattle class. Yeah, nice touch. I've even got a window seat.

Ironic too, the Mallorca thing. Bringing me back one last time. If I hadn't been over there chasing dreams in the first place none of this would be going on.

Last call. Don't want to be late for my own murder now. No, that most certainly wouldn't do.

What isn't traceable back to here probably isn't worth tracing. Captain Francis for instance, that salty old sea dog. Vicky Patterson too. Hot Vicky, emerging from the surf like every straight bloke's dream. All curves, smiles and dancing blue eyes, leaving nothing to my imagination, then looking me over after my insipid approach and taking her time before deciding I was OK. If it hadn't been for Vicky then I wouldn't have met Ishy.

If I hadn't met Ishy I wouldn't have become an E dealer of choice and if I hadn't done that then Masters and Chalmers wouldn't have told me to take a walk, and if they hadn't done that... Ah, screw it. I could trace it back as far as it went and it still wouldn't make any sense. You can follow all the world's troubles back to someone or something.

Then, of course, there is Lauren Chetkins. Apparently I did her a big favour once and her father was in my debt; now here I am getting on a plane to meet him again. But far from patting me on the back and buying me a cold one, he is going to take me to a quiet, unexplored corner of the island where he will make a practised effort to impinge negatively upon the status of my well-being by adding a few grams to my body weight by way of a thirty-eight bullet fired directly into my ear from obscenely close range. Funny way to repay a debt of gratitude, but then that isn't the whole story.

The whole story involves me losing a fifty kilo load of Patsy's finest Bolivian in a service station at the side of the M2. It also involves me being relieved of a suitcase full of his cash following the Deutschmark scam in a field over in Surrey. So yeah, I can understand his ire. I helped his little princess out once, but you don't get to maintain his kind of villainous pomp by being sentimental.

OK I could run - but with what? I'm cleaned out. It's all gone: the cars, the warehouse flat, the dosh, the drugs, the girls, the lifestyle… All gone. And where would a screw-up like me go to get away from someone like Patsy? He has an address book a tabloid hack would kill for. He could arrange a murder with one phone call, and dinner with a foreign diplomat with the next. He's got ex-army men along with the legendary Georgie Harper on the payroll, together with cops, councillors and members of parliament of at least two different governments that I know about. Patsy is a businessman and a gangster and he's very good at being both.

On top of everything, it's all gone so wrong: I've fallen so far and from such a great height that I really can't be arsed carrying on. I'm so tired I really don't care anymore, and if Patsy isn't going to do the job then somebody else will. I'm carrying the scars and still feeling the impact of - what is it now - four recent beatings? Five? Not forgetting a certain torture session which I doubt I'll ever get over.

My only hope is that Patsy does it quick. Quick, clean and with minimal suffering. Surely he'll do that much for me. For old times' sake, surely he'll do that much.

PART ONE

CHAPTER ONE

There isn't really a lot to know about me growing up. In fact, the only relevant thing about my upbringing is that it provided me with no excuses whatsoever to do what I would later do. So I'll cut to it. We moved out from Stepney to Essex in 1971. I was twelve and I suppose you could say that was the beginning of the end right there, because, in a certain way, to get on in that place you had to *be* a certain way, and that way involved greed and selfishness on unparalleled levels. Before the end of the decade I was a fully paid up member of the Me Generation; part of the Thatcher-inspired gold rush. Problem was, while everybody around me was cracking on making piles of dosh, I quickly discovered I bore an unfortunate handicap: I was rubbish at it.

I went to a decent school – Coopers in Mile End and then Upminster - and scored a couple of less than vocational A levels (French and Geography) and squeezed into a Polytechnic Business Studies degree which I blew out after less than a term because my pal Colin Mason got a Jag. There I was: nineteen years old, staying in at night doing homework in these poxy digs in Ealing. Skint. And Colin bought a Jag.

So I figured the big bucks were in the Stock Exchange. I got two jobs but got my arse fired from both: - Wedd, Durlacher, Mordaunt and then Buckmaster and Moore. Remember them? Of course you don't. Apparently I had an attitude problem, but I knew that wasn't the whole of it. The problem lay with their old school inability to accept the likes of me into the hallowed portals. This was still the late seventies and the revolution had not quite happened. I wanted to talk to them the way I talked to my pals down the pub, and they couldn't handle that. It would only be a few short years before Essex lad was making himself rudely heard, dropped aitches and all. But not then.

So I got a job working for a mate called Greasy Roy, the son of an old friend of my dad.

Roy was running his own company storing and repairing cargo containers. The three years I spent with him opened up my eyes for the first time to another way: not necessarily crime as such, but what Pete Chalmers would later call 'our own left handed version of ordinary life'.

Roy's company rented space in the old King George the Fifth dock in North Woolwich. It had all started out as a perfectly legit operation, but it didn't take long for Roy to crack on that there were all manner of juicy bonuses to be made.

Half the containers that came in didn't need any repairs, but they didn't stay that way for long, because we had hours of juvenile fun gouging huge holes into their sides and roofs with the blades of the fork lift truck. The silent, rusted cranes hung their long necks in shame at our deceitful industry but, boy, was it ever lucrative. I talked my way into a percentage and we all started coining it. That was pretty basic hit and run stuff but we refined the process into some half decent fraud and corruption.

The shipping companies had M&R (maintenance and repair) departments who employed roving inspectors to check each individual container and it's respective repair estimate before allowing work to begin. Obviously these were the boxes we needed to bash up first. Other companies were daft enough to trust our honesty regarding the damage we assured them their containers had suffered on their previous voyage, and gave us free rein to repair them up to a certain limit - normally two hundred pounds worth of damage repair for each box. This meant that we could submit an estimate for repairs and an accompanying invoice at the end of each month for 'damage' that did not exist. Just so long as the container was out of the depot and away on it's next trip before anyone from the shipping company came around to check it out, we were golden. To smooth the running of this scam, I knew for a fact that Roy had at least one and quite possibly all of the M&R inspectors on the payroll. All those boys ever inspected was the contents of the plain brown envelopes Roy slipped them down the pub on Friday afternoons.

For a wide-eyed kid like me it was heady stuff. The system had been corrupted in a way that made the entire coup practically foolproof. Dishonesty pays. Crime, come on down. I would suffer from the occasional pang of conscience as I was writing out ever more elaborately descriptive repair estimates, but I knew I had to rise above all that guilt shit. And rise above it I did, because soon enough pay day would come around - and pay day, as I found out soon enough, justifies everything.

Nineteen, twenty, twenty one. I rode the wave but eventually that old relativity angle caught up with me. Sure I was doing fine, but it wasn't long before I noticed that some of my peers were doing better. I was used to having more money, nicer cars, faster motorbikes than all the others and I railed when people started edging past me in that odd, ego-fuelled race in which we were all entered, whether we had asked to be or not. Having ten grand in the bank was no good to you at all if everybody else had twenty. Promotions: advancements: company cars. Tax breaks: directorships. My pals were no slouches. All you had to do was relax for just a while and you were back at the bottom of the pile. I needed more. Yeah, I had to be scoring more.

But in the scramble to keep up, I made a mistake.

I answered an ad in the Standard. You've seen them and thought only a mug would fall for such garbage: 'Smart, self-motivated trainee broker required. If able to work on own initiative, earning potential unlimited'. Yup - I was that mug.

A smooth-talking bastard in an RAF moustache and an Austin

Reed suit told me I could make a fortune, if only I did what he said.

"Which is...?" I was more than keen to know.

"That's it. Whatever I say. You do what I tell you to do and you'll clean up. Think you can manage that?"

I gave him my cocky stare - the one I used to let people know they weren't dealing with a fool. "When do I start?"

Now if he had told me I would be cold calling people trying to flog life insurance, I would have told him what to do with his unlimited earning potential - but he'd sold me already. I'd told Roy I was leaving and I'd told my parents and all my friends I was going back into the City, and that was that. I knew had to give it a shot and so I did.

A year is a long, long time to have people consistently tell you to fuck off and not bother them anymore. As my section manager kept reminding me, I had to stay positively motivated because it was *me* that was doing *them* the favour by giving them the chance to get in on all the investment opportunities and tax havens I had access to. Few of them saw it like that. They just saw me as yet another chiselling little life salesman interrupting their busy day and urged me in no uncertain terms not to do so again.

I stuck it out for two reasons. Firstly my mum was worried about me. Dropping out of college and then getting blown out of two decent jobs in the space of six months had converted the few remaining auburn hairs she had left to shiny silver. Also, I did enjoy the occasional success. I would call someone up and they would concede that what I was saying did make sense; I would invite them into the office, give them the script and they would take out a life policy or a savings plan. There was money there.

There was another reason I stayed on too. I had the feeling, bless me, that this was my last chance. I was twenty three.

So I'd cold called this real poz bloke. (poz being an early eighties buzz-word for positive, self-motivated etc.) I gave him the mumble and he went for it. Next morning he came in and nodded in all the right places and by the time he left I had insured his car, his life (a whole life plan with Cornhill) and arranged a ten year savings plan with Trident Life into which he kicked thirty quid a month. My commission on that was three hundred quid. When it happened like that – Yowzah! Top of the world, ma.

And it was Friday.

So I skipped out at lunch time, rammed my Number Of The Beast album into the Walkman and headed to The Elephant in Fenchurch Street for a few swifties. A couple of chaps I knew rolled in but before things got out of hand I bounced and caught the four-sixteen out of town. I was asleep before the train pulled out and - not for the first time or the last - I stayed on board all the way down to the sidings at Shoeburyness. The Night Flight to Shoebury we used to call it. Twat. I scampered woozily across the bridge and down onto the westbound platform. We were tanking into Upminster before I realised the bastard thing wasn't stopping there and all I could do was watch in gnawing frustration as we belted through, all the way back to Barking. By the time I was back on the right platform and getting on the right train I was wedged in with all the plebs I was trying to avoid in the first place. Hey ho.

Friday night back then - even now for all I know - was Boys' night and Boys' night meant The Essex Yeoman next to the station. Believe me, this place surely was a sight to see. All the BBC had to do was get a film crew in there and it would have made the best documentary ever screened - assuming, of course, that we let them out alive. Get down the Yeo and learn about life. Essex man in his natural habitat.

The last time I had been there it had gone. Well, not gone actually - but gone in spirit. Knackered and middle aged. Like me. The eighties' hurricane had blown itself out and the Yeo, that last bastion of wealthy, suburban yobbery, had proved unable to hold on. I heard they sell food in there now.

Then, though, it was springtime - literally and metaphorically. The evenings were mild and getting longer with each day, and everywhere you went and everyone you spoke to gave truth to the rumour that there really was something happening.

Something was going down. If talentless pricks like my mates were cracking, it then surely I could.

I hoofed it down the hill from the station, grabbed a quick shower at the parents' bungalow and began the mile and a half hike all the way back up there to the pub in a cloud of cheap aftershave and optimism.

We were blessed with many really average boozers back then - the Broker and Artichoke being another haunt, but the Yeoman was the favoured choice of the discerning pisshead. The logic being that the shittier the pub, the fewer people will go in there and the easier it will be to get up the ramp.

The proprietor of our den of gluttonous and flatulent activity was one Brian 'Sugar Ray' Robinson. Like many a landlord in those days Brian had done a bit of boxing in his time. It was obvious. What was equally obvious was that he had not been any good at it. Nonetheless he was a fine sort and a top drawer guv'nor, not at all averse to a spot of the old 'apres' every now and then. This was the Yeoman and the Yeoman was our drinker.

I deliberately made myself walk all the way back up the hill as part of the thirst building exercise. Half way there I spotted the shuffling figure of Gow Renson. Gary was a top bloke and since he practically lived in the pub he was something of celebrity in the Yeoman subculture. I jogged over to him.

"Micky boy," he said by way of acknowledgement. "What's new?"

"Not a lot, mate. Got a thirst on. You're leaving this a bit late aren't you? It's after seven."

He mopped a lake of sweat from his quivering jowls and grimaced. "My guv'nor innit? Bastard's got it into his head that we have to work until four if we want to claim overtime 'til seven. 'Sbollocks."

"Bastard." I concurred sympathetically, remembering that Gary was a printer.

"I've been thinking about this all day," he said.
"What?"
"Drinking."

We plodded on.

"Hard day slaving over a hot press was it?"

"Not really. Oi look. There's The Stomach."

He pointed along the pavement to a huge bear of a man who was eating directly from a Kentucky Fried bargain bucket. He looked like he was wearing a nosebag. This was The Stomach. I won't mention his real name but I think everyone - including his mum who had the unenviable task of cooking for him - had forgotten it a long time before anyway. The Stomach was my pal; my mucker. Apart from family there was no one I had known longer or more closely. I loved the bloke. He was stocking up on the protein. Lining that legendary gut in preparation for the coming onslaught.

Now there were three of us and it was calling to us all. We spread out gunfighter-style across the trail under a blazing sun; striding manfully onwards back up the hill towards our prized and deserved goal.

For blokes like us at that time, it didn't get any more crucial. Grim-faced, we powered on remorselessly until eventually we were up the step and bursting through the doors with dramatic force; out of the sun and, almost sprinting by then, into the shocking cool of the inner sanctum.

I stormed into the home straight, only stopping when the bar rammed me under the ribs with a poleaxing jolt that all but knocked the wind clean out of me. I was kneeling at the alter of beer, begging for the priest's blessing. I motioned to the staff but I was so thirsty and so agitated I lost effective power of speech, mustering only a series of obscene, gummy sucking noises. Luckily Sugar Ray was on duty, and was shrewd and experienced enough to assess and appreciate the urgency of the situation.

"How many?" Was all he needed to say. All of us drank Holsten back then, the old German groin gouger. I held up six fingers and waggled them excitedly.

But it took so long. It came out of the tap in a useless, pathetic dribble. It was all happening so *slowly*. Jesus, was that a bucket he was filling down there?

Not only was the Holsten tap at the far end of an already busy bar, but a horrifying panic overcame me when I realised that in spite of his initial professionalism, Brian intended to fill *all six glasses* first before transporting them down the other end to me and the chaps. Bar keeping of such staggering naiveté that could easily mean an added delay of some two, perhaps two and a half minutes. A treacherous light-headedness overcame me but then I saw that the big boy - my Stomach - had anticipated the problem and was already moving down to the far end of the ramp. Utilising his superior height and reach he leaned across and, through a ring of unknown blokes, waving a very aggressive armpit under their noses in the process, secured the golden gift from Sugar Ray. My heart swelled with the glow of human fellowship. Then the fat bastard stood there, smiled at me and scoffed the whole pint down in one.

I felt my knees go and clung desperately to the driftwood of the bar. Gow must have seen that I was in trouble as I felt arms around my waist, strong arms lifting me upwards and forwards so that I was practically lying on the counter. It is possible, through a combination of dehydration and fear, I passed out, but then I heard and felt a resounding, wooden DONK on the bar near to my head. I managed to stir myself and look up and... there it was. Sugar Ray muttered some kind of financial threat which sounded more like a ransom demand than the price of a round, so I waved a score at him and he left me alone.

The chill of the glass practically fused it to my palm. You seen that film *Ice Cold In Alex*? John Mills? I braced myself and took my time. As strung out as I was, I knew I had to take things easy, for this was truly an emotional moment. I knew that if I rushed it and cocked it up it would be another entire week before I'd have the chance to get it right again. I savoured the smell and the sight and then in a swift, practised and - if I say so myself - accomplished movement, it was up to the lips; angle the glass, head tilted slightly back. One, two, three, four, five long, slow swallows until it started to bite at the back of the throat. Then ease that last mouthful down and ...

'Ecstasy' is a word bandied about a lot these days and most people still don't know what they are talking about. Back then a happy, life insurance-selling oik and his mates knew what it meant. Times change. Fashions, fads, drugs, tastes, they all come and go, but back then there was nothing but nothing to compare with the thrill and the satisfaction of slinging that first pint down with your mates on a Friday night at the end of a hot, nerve-jangling week. Sheer exhilaration. My thirst was quenched so perfectly that tears of joy and gratitude sprang to my eyes. Beer was good for you. It didn't make us fat, diseased or turn us into alcoholics. That would come in time, but it didn't back then. It was as close to a religious experience as I would get until little Jenny sold me my first Dove and Romanov made me go to that illegal warehouse party over in south London that time.

After the initial euphoria and with a pint and a half of liquid gold at my disposal I relaxed, turned and supported my weight through my elbows on the bar and surveyed the situation.

The Yeoman was no more than a large, square room with a bar at one end, a juke box and two dart boards. That was it. The place was approximately sixty feet by sixty, maybe less. They had an orange, nylon carpet laid years before, most of which was still as fresh as it had been on the day it was installed. Running along the bar and some four feet out from it was a strip of brown, industrial strength lino. This was so consistently pummelled and eroded by the shuffling feet of clamouring piss-heads that it needed to be replaced, on average, once a month. The carpet could have come with a lifetime guarantee but it would never be used because no bastard ever stood on it.

I have no concept of what the place may have looked like from the far end of the room. I had never seen the bar without at least one of my limbs being firmly secured to it. I certainly had never sat down in the place, although I understand facilities for doing so were allegedly provided. I had *laid* down in there many times, but sit? Why? There were no bar stools in there either, because, although the place was less than ten percent full even when it was busy, there was no room for any.

Women? Forget it. Occasional sightings of dubious examples of the opposite sex had been the stuff of rumour, but why would any woman wish to go in a place like that? With the likes of us?

No. No women. It was a sanctuary in which a man nurtured the special relationship he enjoyed with his beer.

I slung down what was left of mine. The Stomach was in the corner yakking away to someone. Gary seemed to have disappeared. Then I did one of those things I instantly regretted.

"Anyone want a drink?" I yelled. I was kind of hoping not too many people would hear.

I got caught for four pints of bitter, three gin and tonics, a Bacardi and soda, three bottles of Pils, six pints of Holsten and a creme du menthe with scotch. This Irish fella - never knew what his name was - always insisted upon a drink with something green in it. I had no idea I had so many bastard friends. Sugar Ray gave me his renowned mono-toothed grin as he lifted what felt like the average weekly wage from my rapidly shrinking wad, although I was comforted in part by the thought that it was unlikely I would be called upon to buy another drink all night. Or hopefully for the rest of the month.

But why did I do that? Appearances, pure and simple. Sheer vanity demanded that I at least tried to maintain the image of prosperity and advancement that everyone else appeared to be enjoying. But why? Did it really matter? Was being not so well off really such a crime? You bet your arse it was. Back then anyway. As we cruised inexorably towards our mid-twenties, some of us were starting to make big money. The fact that I wasn't one of them made things doubly worse. It was like the greatest party in history was being held next door but I wasn't invited.

Once I had recovered from the shock of the mega round and people started reciprocating, I felt fully able to relax and partake of some jolly banter, saucy recollection and advanced political and philosophical discussion. Yeah right. Me? My lot? Basically, we all tended to agree with what each other said because we were all mates and none of us wanted to fall out. Apart from that we all had precious little idea of what we were talking about anyway.

Beer flowed, views were expounded, promises made, friendships cemented. I even recall a brief fracas; a furious bout of punches and boots at the far end. Strangers? What were they doing in there anyway? They must have been from out of town otherwise they would have known not to have taken up so much valuable room at the bar. At *our* bar.

At one point that Irish bloke handed me a pint. " 'Ere you go, Mick. Get that in your head."

"Ah cheers, mate."

"So, look. What's happening with this 'oliday? Me and The Stomach want you to come but we're running out of time. How's it looking?"

Good question, and the truth was it wasn't looking too clever. Aside from the occasional score like the one that very day, sales were generally down. A fortnight away with those two animals would put a substantial dent in my already diminished savings. I made a mental note to find out what his sodding name was.

"I won't piss around any longer, son," I told him. "I'll let you know by next Monday evening."

"Fair enough. 'Ere. Did you know there was a bloke in here looking for you earlier?"

"No."

"Yeah. Big geezer. Said he'd be back later. Big geezer he was."

"Did he leave a name or say what he wanted?"

"Nah. Big geezer he was though."

I was well on the way by then and, as I figured it could well have been after nine o'clock, I hit turbo-drink mode. I drained the half pint I was holding in my left hand so that I could concentrate on the fresh beer in my right. However, because it was getting pretty crowded in there I found myself stranded some distance from the bar, so I decided to pass my glass to Sugar Ray whom I spied lurking furtively at the far end of the ramp.

"Oi, Brian." I called above the noise and the music and the smoke and the beer. He looked up and I threw the glass at him. Not nastily of course - but for him to catch. I had played fly half for the district so I knew what I was doing. The spinning receptacle flew neatly, noiselessly and harmlessly two feet above the heads of the swarming mob. Sugar Ray caught it too. He caught it smack on the forehead. I was a tad embarrassed at this unexpected turn of events, because it would have looked really cool if he'd fielded it with his hands as opposed to his eyebrow. I scurried over to explain things. He aided me in this endeavour with an outrageous demand for a large vodka and orange. What could I do?

"Late one tonight, Bri?" I asked when I was sure he wasn't going to hit me.

"Dunno, son. Got Plod coming in later. Have to see how it maps out."

"Plod? What for?"

"Just a social visit. Just so they can see there's no ag' going on. Lucky that little handbag session just then didn't go off in a few hours' time. They want to see that things are quiet and peaceful and everything is above board."

"Do they know you do afters?"

"Yeah, course. You were in here at about four last Saturday morning talking to one of them so you should know."

"Do they cost you much money?"

"Starting to get that way, greedy bastards. Not like back up Befnal Green a few years ago when they were content with a couple of free piss ups a week. This lot want to be yuppies. Sign of the times I suppose. But it's all sorted. Bit of a doddle really."

Course it was. A doddle. A right Glen. Bit like Essex life in general was back then. Booze, women, cars, bikes, holidays... Yeah, a right Glen Hoddle.

I left Sugar Ray once more apologising for the blue egg that was already growing out of his forehead and rejoined a group of the others. The Stomach came bulldozing across from somewhere too, scattering people to either side like a plough through human snow. He was clearly fully aware of how time was marching on too, because clutched in his mighty mitts were two half empty pints of lager and two short glasses filled to overflowing with clear, sparkling liquid.

A word about The Stomach and his line; money broker. He bought money with money and sold money for money. For these tricky endeavours he was rewarded with vast amounts of... yeah sure, money. There has always been this joke doing the rounds about those currency cruisers and junk bond junkies in that they are like double cream: rich and thick. The Stomach was certainly both - and then some. I used to help him with his homework when we were at school together, but by the Yeoman days he was rolling a company BMW and had been in the highest tax bracket since any of us could care to remember. Sure, he worked like a dog for it but basically he had it cracked. His dreams were coming true. I often felt like asking him what that was like. How does it feel? Does it make you happy every day? All the time?

He had promised me he would do a savings plan and maybe some life cover when I needed a big month for my next promotion push. We knew each other too well for him to be just bullshitting me, but it sounded like he thought he was doing me a massive favour and my ego didn't like that too much. But I needed the money.

"You look happier," I told him.

"I feel it."

"How's the diet going?"

"Very well. This Fat Fast one I've discovered seems to suit me. Hey, how does an Essex girl turn the lights off after she's made love?"

"I can't wait for this."

"She closes the door of the Cortina."

He chewed his way through one of his beers so aggressively I thought the glass was going to go down as well.

Back then the Yeo, slap bang next to Upminster station, was not the kind of gaff where you would be likely to see Harry Normal and his missus sit down for a pint of Mild and a Sherry. Joe Average would be unlikely to pop in for a Light and Tankard and a packet of pork scratchings on the way to the Conservative Club. No. It was our boozer. It was where we went to booze. The clientele, particularly on a Friday night, were highly likely to be in the place giving the guv'nor his living well before most people were even thinking about leaving the house for the night. If we weren't in there hard at it before seven, we were either out of town, out of the country or just plain out of it. It was like what Tombstone must have been like when Wyatt Earp was on holiday. Our standards of behaviour were often so appalling even *I* got embarrassed.

Upminster was, and probably still is, commuter central. It was one of the places out in the Home Counties to where the more successful East Enders flocked during the explosion of prosperity during the sixties and seventies. Then, during the late seventies and early eighties, their offspring moved back westwards into town. But they had their eyes on different sorts of markets. Same people as their parents, same market traders. Same voices and attitudes, just different opportunities, calls and options. No fruit and veg. No ladies' handbags and blouses. It was more like: What are you making in ICI? Dollar-Yen. Tom-next? Three month Sterling? What are you in ten million for *me*?

Still early risers like their dads, they were at the dealing desks by seven in the morning. Lunch crammed down in ten minutes - assuming there was any time to eat at all. Either that or the boys were out talking shop to clients or other dealers or money men, which naturally involved getting slaughtered in The Monument or The London Stone or wherever. Then it would be back to the phones, woollen headed and bleary eyed, where a price could easily be misquoted or misheard, and before you could say 'quarterly trade figures' you could be down a hundred K, thus blowing the Christmas bonus for the entire section. An unholy verballing from the management would ensue, assuming they were still interested in retaining a chap's services. Suitably chastened, it would be down the pub at the close of business: get seriously loaded.

Onto the last train home from Liverpool Street or Fenchurch Street, where enforced standing was a timeless necessity because if you sat down on those warm, comfortable seats and closed your eyes for just a second... Bollocks! Done it again. Screeching seagulls and the whiff of salt in the air. Yes, another Night Flight crashed out by the coast.

No time to go home for a shave and a shower though. No coffee. No breakfast. Furry tongue, itchy teeth, blurred vision. The hangover wins the right to be called 'Your Lordship'. One foot in front of the other. Hit the buttons and quote the prices.

More cock ups, more bollockings. Hair of the dog, gallon of coffee, kilo of toast. Make the money back. Square the position. Thank God we're young and strong. Make it through the week. Make it to the pub. To the Yeoman.

But those Friday night sessions weren't so much about getting over a rough week or drowning sorrows. No - they were about celebration. Most of the time the boys were hitting record profits and were in receipt of the attendant bonuses, in which case the carnage down the pub would be even worse. Moreover, there was a fabulous mix of people in that place. There were obviously loads of suits like us, but there was an equal number of concrete-clad manuals with whom we got on famously. Printers like Gow, plumbers, self employed. There was no snobbery, no discrimination. So long as you were a success that is. The only thing that wasn't tolerated was failure. Failure, as the lady would say, was not an option.

It was heady stuff back in those halcyon, pre-recession days. You could feel the optimism like it was the first evening the clocks changed at the start of summer. As the sixties were the decade of love, so the eighties, it was clear even then, were the decade of the love of money - and somehow us bunch of thick, ignorant berks had found ourselves at the sharp end of the whole thing. How the hell had *that* happened? We were living that way light years before all those stupid Essex jokes came out. Loud, proud and with far too much money, although the money aspect seemed to apply less and less to me as time went on. The world was fizzing with opportunity but my life appeared to effervesce with all the sparkle of a pint of last week's Tuborg Gold.

Yet the reason my lot was so good at it all? The knack? The boys were on monster mazuma not in spite of the fact they were loud-mouthed, mindless yobs but *because* they were loud mouthed, mindless yobs. I have seen it and so have you. When the trade figures or economic indicators were out and Sterling or the Dollar was taking another kick in the nuts, the television crews were right there in the dealing room. The boys were apoplectic, bug-eyed with crazed delirium, two phones crammed into each ear, bottle of brandy under the table and a gram of

Charles pre-racked on the shelf of the third cubicle in the khazi. I know those lads. I could have been a part of that.

Market traders, just like their dads. Nothing much changes apart from technology and attitudes. Even up to the mid-seventies, a City worker wore a bowler hat, was called Jeremy, Henry or Cyril and lived in places like Hampstead or Weybridge. Separated by education and accent, working class people either feared them, suspected them or downright loathed them. Then, in nineteen seventy nine, something happened. For better or for worse the Tories got elected and suddenly the City was taken over by Pete, Ron, Tony and Dave - the living example of what Margaret Thatcher's Britain was supposed to be all about. Myself and countless others of my oikish, suburban ilk were tearing at the invisible walls that had been erected over the centuries to keep the money and the privilege in and the threatening, interloping riff-raff out. We were the new self-preservation society. Rampant Cockney hordes. The Huns of the Home Counties at the gates of the castle. Open the door or we'll just kick it right the fuck in anyway.

Standing there at the bar that night, I already knew I needed to rethink my part in the glorious crusade because I knew the life selling thing wouldn't work for me, and I was losing time. Every day you're not rich you're poor, and every day you're poor is a mistake not worth repeating. The race was well and truly under way and I'd been left at the start line. All in all I was just another brick in the wall.

There had to be something I could do well enough to make some proper money, and I knew - I just instinctively knew that I wouldn't care what it was. I had never broken the law in my life, well - not seriously anyway, but I just felt that if I could do so safely and profitably, then I would go straight ahead and do it without hesitation. Maybe even without remorse. I was selling life insurance for Christ's sake, and there aren't many people in *that*.

CHAPTER TWO

Once more I am waiting.

I am used to it now. It has become part of my way of life. Things must be done in a certain order. So I wait. I wait for the call.

I am at my father's bungalow - or rather I am at the bungalow that my father used to own but now does not. This is where I live. My last refuge.

He sits quietly by the window, my father, or sometimes on his bench in the garden. He reads, all day every day. Sometimes I watch him as he reads and as he dozes. I am so concerned for him that at times I feel myself becoming drawn in and entranced; made part of him by the measured rhythm of his breathing.

I scan his face for memories; for reports and milestones of happiness and joyful occasions in his life. The footprints that pleasure must surely leave; traces in the sand of his features of experience and good times past. But no. There are none. The lines in his handsome face are not the work of happiness and contentment but of pain and worry. Despair has cut and scratched him cruelly. He is tattooed by misery; scarred by betrayal and hardship.

Things are better now than they were. He has not mentioned suicide for some time and we are adjusting, but the heartache has done its foul work and is irredeemable, and I feel, as I watch him breathe, that his soul may have already died. I know that from time to time when the depression returns to haunt and to punish him, he wishes he could join it. But he is too strong to get away with it just yet.

I finger the plaster covering the thin slice along my temple as I wait. And then the call comes.

"It's done. Come now." Professional.

I am curiously relaxed in spite of the circumstances because I know this is some kind of watershed. A unique achievement even for me. All the time my father was suffering, I wanted to tell him I was hurting too. I wanted to tell him my own horrors and demons and doubts. I wanted to tell him to recollect how good things had been for him when he had been in his early thirties in comparison with mine. But I didn't.

The journey was brief. Through the lanes to the service station at the northern end of the Dartford river crossing. The forecourt. They would approach me. I pull over to the car wash and park up behind an old panel van. And wait again.

I watch every car arrive and leave, wondering what kind of vehicle they would be driving and what kind of people they would be. What were people like that could do these things for a living?

Then, having been there for nearly ten minutes, the rear door of the van opens from the inside and a man in his mid-thirties gets out. He looks like an ordinary kind of bloke, well dressed, tidy hair. Respectable. This is why I pay him no mind. Then he walks right up to the door of the car and looks in at me. But he doesn't speak.

"Can I help you?" I ask.

"It's me."

I am surprised and my heartbeat zooms, but I open the door and he slides in next to me. He gets straight to it. Professional.

"I was told there were a few options but we did everything that was suggested. They were both there. We were thorough."

He reaches inside to his jacket pocket and pulls out two small, white plastic bags. The kind the butcher wraps up the meat in, which is appropriate. Without further comment or warning, he hands them to me and as I take them the full impact of what I have done comes home, for the bags are warm.

"Check it. Check them. I don't want any mistakes. You have to be satisfied or I don't get paid."

I want to tell him that I am satisfied. I want to tell him that he and his work are OK by me and that I will tell this to whoever he wants me to, just so long as he gets the fuck out of my car and away from me, but.... I place the bags onto my lap and feel the moist warmth oozing through onto my thighs. I open the first one and count one, two, three, four, five. There is no nausea as I expected; only pain and regret, and I fight hard to keep back the tears. I close the first bag and pull the knot on the second. I peer in, not wanting to see, but there it is, staring right back up at me.

"OK?" I hear him say.

I nod and breathe deeply.

"Alright." He digs into the back pocket of his jeans. "Here's the Polaroids."

I take them from him and move to put them straight into my coat pocket.

"Check them." He is so strong and so compelling I have to look.

There is no mistaking him. Gained some weight since I last saw him but there is no mistaking who it is. I nod slowly.

"Are you happy? The job has been done and you are happy with it, is that correct?"

"Yeah. I'm happy," I tell him wishing that he would leave me alone.

"OK now what you have to do is go back home and phone the man and tell him that everything is sorted out and that you are happy. I only get paid when that has been done. Yeah?"

I say nothing.

"Is that clear?"

"Yes. Yes it's clear. I understand." I say, nodding a lot.

"Good. Then I'm gone." He gets out of the car.

"Did they suffer? Did he suffer?" I ask urgently.

"Did you want them to?" He closes the door behind him.

"What about these?" I call out, opening my palms to show him the bags still nestling on my lap. He smiles an undeniably pleasant smile. He looks like anyone. He looks like the bloke standing next to you in the pub, in the cashpoint queue. He looks like me. He looks like you.

He makes a little saluting motion with his right hand and says - like he's doing me a favour or something: "On the house." Then he is gone.

It takes me long minutes to compose myself. Then I put the bags and the photographs into my jacket pocket and walk to the garage shop, where I buy a bottle of mineral water and a plastic cigarette lighter. Back in the car, I take slow sips until I feel able to continue, able to retake my place in normality. Such as it is.

After three wheezing attempts, the old Fiesta fires and I drive out onto the bridge itself. At its highest point I pull over and snap on the hazards. Knowing a patrol vehicle will be with me in minutes, I hop over the Armco barrier to the railings at the very edge, where I pull out the two bags. I quickly squeeze out the slimy little nobbles. One two three four five toes. Oh Jesus, the nail on the big toe is snagged on the inside of the bag. I look up at the sky and squeeze them out by touch alone. If I look, my stomach will be down there in the Thames as well and I'm only halfway through the job. I feel the toe release and fall.

Then the other bag. Like a lychee in syrup, I can feel the soft sphere inside. As it clings momentarily to the soggy bag before dropping, I notice with gory interest how the iris, formerly deep brown, is now practically colourless. Then it too is gone. Food for the fishes.

Later I pull over at the side of the lane at a spot I know and walk into the trees. I hold the flame steady and scan the photographs one last time, trying to imagine what it had been like. The pain, the suffering. The fear. The screams. A pang of remorse, which I chase away with thoughts of my father. With thoughts of me. Poor Dad. Poor me.

On the drive back I'm in that weird mood you sometimes get into at funerals, when you suddenly become flippant or inappropriately amused by what's going on. Her nylons used to go big toe first. I can see them now. No wonder, with toenails as sharp as that. Suddenly I'm giggling hysterically over the un-funniest joke in the world that I'll never be able to share with anyone.

At home, Dad is pleased to see me back as he is peeling potatoes for tea. Whilst he is in the kitchen, I take the telephone into the bedroom once more.

"It's done," I tell the man. "Thanks. It's perfect. Just what I was looking for."

"Good," he tells me. "If you're pleased then so am I. When can you come and see me?"

"As soon as you like. No reason to hang about."

"Good boy. The restaurant. Tonight."

CHAPTER THREE

Years ago when every summer seemed to be long and warm me, and Andy Thompson used to race motorbikes together. Just club level. Knee out and pretend to be Barry Sheene.

Because deep down I suspected I was never going to realise my dreams by flogging life insurance, he and I had been hatching an alternative plan. A contingency caper. That was why he had been looking for me down the Yeoman that night. He was the big geezer the Irishman had told me about and he had something for me.

Long before Sky One had hijacked the Club Rep experience and turned it into the tabloid tit fest it would become, Andy had worked in Mallorca for the 18-30 company. He was a pioneer for that whole scene. Christ, his grandkids are probably going there now, throwing up against the same walls, shagging his old birds' granddaughters on the same rubber covered mattresses. Yeesh.

I digress. Andy had been sacked from 18-30 the previous season when he got caught fiddling the tickets for the excursions he was selling. He had secured similar employment with another holiday outfit called Twenties or Teenies or Bonkies, something like that - but he had been given no choice but to sling the job on account of his new employers making, what he considered, unfair demands upon his time and his energy by asking him to do certain things. Such as work. Moreover, they were wise to all the scams before he had even tried to pull any. That was no good to him, he explained forlornly, when I finally caught up with him. No good at all.

However, from that recent doomed jaunt he had brought back a copy of the Mallorcan Bugle, the classified section of which made interesting reading. Businesses, particularly bars and restaurants, were up for grabs by the tower block. Failed dreams manifested themselves in the form of ludicrously cheap leasehold deals. Neither of us once thought to ask why it had all gone wrong for so many people. Today, instead of packing it in, they'd be selling their lives to a daytime docusoap called Cocking It Up In The Sun.

Andy pointed out that I had unchallenged use of a phone. He gave me the newspaper and, for once, I put that phone to some sensible use. My own bar in Spain. Now there *was* a thought.

What I came up with was a bloke called John Durridge. He told me the bar he was selling was a winner but he was working on his emphysema by smoking forty a day. He couldn't hack it anymore; he could just hack.

What he had on the table was the last four years of a renewable lease for eight and a half large which me and Andy could raise between us without needing to borrow. He described the whole set up; the lease, the rent, bar, building, piazza, location, everything - and it all sounded pukka.

The coincidences and opportunities were piling up, which made the whole venture seem like some kind of destiny calling for me because The Stomach and the Irishman were due to hit Ibiza within days, and were bugging me to go with them.

My boss at work expressed his concern at my taking any time off, pointing to my somewhat dismal recent sales figures as reason to buckle down and hit that phone. I didn't give a monkey's about figures or phones. I'd had enough of both. I was off to the sun with the chaps, aiming to come back not just with a new tan, but a new life.

Ibiza ('82, '83? I really can't remember too well) was in essence the same as it is now. Get out there, get wrecked, try to get laid, have a good time. Take out the raves, the Es, the superstar DJs and the bloody camera crews and there it was. Essex boys on tour.

We had been on the island for less than three hours and the Irishman - who turned out to be called Aiden - had already managed to get sick, get his end away and get arrested. He languished comatose in San Antonio nick for a whole night because me and The Stomach weren't there to help him and *that* was because we were both unconscious on the beach at the time. It cost us three hundred quid of our hard earned folding to spring him, but he promised to pay us back as soon as we got home.

Another potential problem was the flight from Ibiza to Mallorca left dangerously early every morning. To bypass the horror of getting up at the crack of eight o'clock we went for the preferred option and stayed up all night getting pissed.

The journey between the two islands is so brief that by the time we got on the plane and sat down it was time to get off again. Easier said than done. It was like the night train to Shoebury all over again. With no little hollering and shoving the stewardesses managed to rouse Aiden and I, but they had to call in the airport authorities to help with The Stomach because we needed a luggage transporter to haul him through the airport terminal and a qualified doctor to declare him still alive.

From the airport we bundled into a fast black and belted over to the address that the bar owner had given me in a place called Portals Nous and that was the first time I clapped my eyes on John Durridge. And what a sorry, old, knackered out individual he turned out to be.

"If this is what running a bar does to you," Aidey whispered as we awaited refreshments on the bloke's cramped terrace. "Then maybe you should stick to flogging insurance."

This decrepit, north London sleazebag coughed and wheezed his way through the pitch. He had bought the place a couple of years previously, hoping that a move to the dry air of Spain would help his condition. Far from that his galloping lung rot meant that he now barely had the strength to pick up his pack of Fortuna and fire up another cancer stick. He was heading home to die. As a stop-gap measure prior to finding a buyer, he had sublet the bar to a Spanish friend who was paying well over the odds for the privilege. The rent payable on the official lease was fifty thousand pesetas; the sublet pulled in seventy-five. My brain was whirring like the groaning overhead fan. If Andy was in, we would buy the place without delay and keep the Spanish bloke in there, so by the following spring we would have a nice few quid already banked to get us on our way. The Spaniard had no voice in it whatsoever, as he had only a verbal agreement and was out on his ear whenever he was told.

Into his car and we were off. Portals Nous became Palma Nova which became Magaluf. High-rise low life. Then onto Santa Ponsa.

By yet another delightful coincidence, it was in Santa P. that Andy had worked when he had been out there with 18-30. He'd made contacts and as we arrived at the outskirts of town I was already imagining how things would take shape. In my head I was already living out there: working, prospering.

On the face of it Santa Ponsa seemed to be as much of a khazi as the rest of the Bahia de Palma. In the sweatbox of Durridge's pre-aircon Seat we chugged past Mrs. Murphy's kitchen, Joe's Tartan bar. Past Kitty O'Shea's music bar and the Caramba disco. Past The Rising Sun pub and up a hill through canyon-like ranks of massive apartment blocks. It seems almost quaint now. Andy had told me that Santa P. was a touch up-market from the rest of the resorts, on account of the relative lack of our trouble making countrymen. This appealed to me. I couldn't stand yobs.

What also appealed to me was that the bar, my bar, was called Bugsy's, and had a gangster theme featuring posters of Bogart and Cagney and the like. Under a five-story block, it was sandwiched between a Spanish restaurant called Paco's and an English owned eatery called The Pepperpot. The interior was around twenty-five feet square and was divided up into cushion seated booths. There were eight bar stools and a bar. There were two toilets and a tiny storeroom. That was it but that was all there needed to be. I took one look around and fell in love with the place. Running a pub in Spain was what I wanted to do.

During the afternoon hop back to Ibiza, while the others zonked out again I was awake and buzzing. What a deal. What a coup. I could scarcely believe it. Nowadays you could watch a channel four documentary to suss the pitfalls of such a life, but back then it was all unchartered territory. It was like going to the moon.

Back in London, I was demob happy. Me and Andy scored a couple of bucket shop flights and returned to the island within the week, staying with an old pal of Andy's in Cala Mayor. Then we got pissed quite a bit and topped up our tans.

We made our way around and looked up a few of Andy's old 18-30 buddies who all made lots of encouraging noises about bringing coach loads of thirsty punters around to Bugsy's the second we opened. Things were sounding so good the dream machine in my mind was blowing fuses.

Once we had established the place was a winner, we went to see John Durridge. He showed it to Andy, who loved it as much as me, and there then followed some serious haggling which resulted in us agreeing a price of seven and a half grand. This included all the booze that was in stock at that time plus the sound system and a couple of fridges. We shook on it.

Durridge declared that he was so pleased his pride and joy was going to such a nice pair of Essex boys he volunteered to collect the rent from the Spaniard for us and bank it in the account he helped us open. Things just kept getting better and better.

He introduced us to his bilingual lawyer, Nick, whose offices constituted two crummy rooms above a gift shop in an arcade in Magaluf. He seemed a reasonable sort and assured us that the lease and its sale were legal and proper and that he could expedite the transaction with all speed and safety for the normal fee. Not for a second did we doubt anyone's word. Not for a second did we think we would have a solitary problem.

Andy only had one reservation about the whole thing and that was his girl. He and Suki had been together for about eighteen months or so, and now he was going away again. But he was professional about it and she was the trooper he needed her to be. He would let her come out to see him during the season, just as long as she didn't ask him what went on the rest of the time. In return she would live a simple life, stay in, and presumably take up knitting. Everyone's a winner.

As a single man I had no such worries. The only loose end that needed tying up was the job, and that kind of took care of itself. I was sitting around one afternoon listening to Dial a Disc on the phone (Cuba by The Gibson Brothers, I seem to remember) when Ali, my boss, caught me. He called me a wanker and accused me of still being 'mentally' on holiday.

"I wish I was still 'actually' on holiday," I told him. "And don't call me a wanker."

"How many lives have you got lined up for this month? I want to see some projection figures."

I was more than pleased to tell him there was no point in providing him with any figures because I had no lives whatsoever lined up.

"What's happening with the cold calling?"

I sighed heavily. "Actually, Ali, nothing's happening with the cold calling."

He made the mistake of calling my bluff. "How would you like it if you didn't work here anymore?"

"I think I'd like that just fine."

That was that. He sat there doing a passable impression of a red-gilled goldfish while I grabbed my box of client cards, put on my jacket and walked.

We sent John Durridge a cheque for a thousand pounds as a deposit and six weeks later Andy and Suki went over to pay the balance, sign the necessary forms and meet the freeholder. After that, all we had to do was keep in touch with Durridge to make sure our rent was being paid on time and just kick back until the following spring. Suhweeeeeeeeet!

I had a little clear out to raise funds. I sold my Cortina mark IV for fourteen hundred quid and out went my Canon camera, my Aiwa ghetto blaster and a couple of leather jackets. I bought a reasonable Yamaha RD400 and went despatch riding. It was far from ideal particularly with summer overlooking autumn and handing directly over to the winter of 1983, but it gave me the regular income I needed. Then something happened.

One evening I was putting through my monthly call to John Durridge to check on things.

"Hi, John. You alright?"

"Excuse me?"

"John? Micky Targett."

"I'm sorry, I think you have the wrong number."

"That is 695216, yes?"

"695216. Yes. Yes that's right."

"54, Apartamentos Deya?"

"That's us."

"So is John Durridge there?"

"Oh, Durridge. Now I've got you. The funny little chap with the cough we bought the lease from. I am sorry. My wife dealt with most of that you see. He's moved out."

"Moved out?"

"Yes, about two weeks ago."

"Ok, who is this?"

"My name is Turner. Giles Turner."

"Right. Listen, Giles, have you got a forwarding number or address for him?"

"Actually as I say my wife dealt with most of that and she is not here, but I believe he has moved to Enfield."

"Enfield? Jesus where's that? That's not on the south west side of the island is it?"

"Actually I believe it's in north London."

Trussed up like a chicken and with someone ramming stuffing up my arse.

"Hello. Premier Motors."

"Hi. Andy Thompson please."

"Putting you through."

"Spares."

"Andy? You sitting down?"

"Tell me."

"John Durridge has skipped the island."

Andy and I held a crisis meeting at which it was decided I should go to Mallorca on my own to suss the situation and check the bank account. Remember this was still the time of traveller's cheques and postal orders. I was self-employed and could get the time off when I wanted, and Andy was employed and couldn't. That was fair enough I suppose, but what seemed unfair was that apart from the time I had taken him over there to look at the place initially, his entire hands-on involvement consisted of having a nice week in the sun with the pneumatic Suki and handing over six and a half large of our dosh. When it was November, however, and there was suddenly shit to be sorted out, it was equally clear that it was down to me to do the sorting.

Then I was lying to my parents. It had been a while since I had made them proud. My adult life had been highlighted by such noteworthy achievements as winning the annual yard of wine drinking contest down the Broker and Artichoke, and coming second two years running in the Margate beano pig pulling contest. I told them I was dashing over merely to make the necessary connections with suppliers, get some information about apartments and to count money. Who wouldn't be proud?

By the time the cab pulled up outside Nick's office the sun was down, and the dark, along with a genuine chill in the air, completely unnerved me. I had never seen *that* Spain. No balmy night air, no thronged avenues. I pulled my denim jacket tighter around me, to word of the sense of foreboding that seized me as much as the cold. Something was very wrong, and I cursed myself for not insisting Andy come with me.

Nick was doing some typing for a Spanish woman who slung an elegant bag over her shoulder, ignored me and left. He was starting to look less and less like one of the island's top briefs that John Durridge had described.

"Evening, Mick. Good flight?" he asked.

"Not bad, Nick, but judging by the way the bloke brought the thing down I'd figure him for a trainee or something..." I stopped and looked at this scrawny, Woody Allen lookalike and thought about what I had just said. That was it. I had said the word. He was the char waller. *He* was a *trainee*. I was suddenly very scared.

"You got the keys John Durridge left?"

"Certainly." He plonked a bunch down onto the cracked

Formica of his desk. "What are your plans?"

"I'm going over to the bar to have a chat with the Spanish bloke that's in there, to explain the situation. What's his name again?"

"Luis. Luis Martinez. What situation?"

"I'm going to tell him that he can stay in the bar if he continues paying the rent, but come next April he's out, because that is when me and Andy are out here to open up."

"What rent?"

I felt my heart pounding. "He has been paying John Durridge an agreed rent which John has been banking for us. Out of that he has been paying the landlord."

"That reminds me. I need to speak to John myself. I have been getting some pressure from my directors about his bill."

It was and still is very rare for me to take an instant dislike to someone. I enjoyed giving Nick the bad news.

"When was the last time you saw John, Nick?" I asked.

"About three or four weeks ago. I saw him in a restaurant in Palma. Seemed to be celebrating."

"I can imagine. Your company was picking up the bill. John has jumped ship. He's left the island." I was gratified to see he didn't have a clue.

"But that's impossible. How do you know?"

"Because I spoke with the man who now lives in his house. Wasn't difficult."

He placed one hand on his hip and the other to his forehead and strutted around behind his desk. "This is most unseemly. My superiors will be very concerned. He has quite an outstanding bill."

I leant towards him and with all the menace I could muster, which probably wasn't a lot, I told him, "My partner and *I* will be most concerned if it transpires there has been any negligence at our expense. What your superiors will say and do will be a stroll in the park compared to what we will say and do if it turns out there is a squatter in our bar, or if we have any problems with our work permits."

"Now," I added, shoving his jotter pad towards him across his desk and selecting a fat, felt tipped pen from a collection of vertical plastic tubes. "In big, clear letters I want you to write the word 'Closed' in Spanish."

I watched the word CERRADO squeak its way across the page, as the smell of the ink teased my nostrils.

"What's this for?"

"I'm going over to the bar now. Depending upon what this bloke tells me, I may close the place tonight and put this on the door to warn off any customers."

"I don't think that is a good idea."

"Listen. There is someone in my bar and if he doesn't tell me what I want to hear then he's out on his arse. Apart from that I haven't booked a hotel and I may choose to crash in the bar. I'm the kind of bloke who gets thirsty during the night, know what I mean?"

Hands on hips, he drew breath over his jagged, little teeth as he shook his head. "I really don't think this is a good idea, Mike."

I hated people calling me that.

"Nick, I'm not out here to piss around and make friends. Durridge has skipped the island without a word and that stinks. Me and Andy are liable for the rent and there is someone running his own business from our premises, and it occurs to me I don't even know what the bastard looks like. Now I'm going to see him, and if he comes out with a single word that I don't like I'm going to boot his arse all the way down the street and I know I can do it because this Luis bloke has no legal recourse whatsoever."

He made to say something but quickly changed his mind.

"I am correct in thinking he doesn't have a leg to stand on, right, Nick?"

He sweated and breathed and winced. "Yes. Yes of course. That is the legal position but this is not the Spanish way. You are in a foreign country now and you are the foreigner. Calm down and let's see what can be done in the morning."

He was right and I knew it, but I was both scared and angry. Yob instincts were coursing their way through me like raw amphetamines. I wondered how my dad would have dealt with the situation. Nick would already be lying in the corner holding his jaw for starters.

"No!" I shouted petulantly. "I've heard all about that manana shit and that isn't how things are going to go. You're right about this not being the Spanish way. I'm from Essex."

Fuelled by pure, ignorant jingoism, I grabbed a roll of sellotape, along with the CERRADO sign, chucked them in my bag and stormed out. I cabbed it to Santa Ponsa and had the driver drop me at the entrance to Paco's some thirty yards from the door to the bar. It was all so quiet. So quiet and so terribly cold and I can remember feeling small and afraid and thinking that, at that precise moment, I would have paid good money - not that I had any - to be back at my desk working my way through the ritual abuse of a cold calling session. Then I looked up to the illuminated pub sign hanging from the awning. It had the same comedy gangster logo, but now it read: – Bugsy's Topless Bar.

As I neared the front door, I heard muted music and saw low lights inside. Before I'd left Upminster I'd borrowed Sugar Rays' Louisville Slugger baseball bat and I made sure it was visible to whoever might open the door. I reached for the handle, but was forced to watch transfixed as it moved by itself and the door opened inwards.

Bad teeth and acne aside, the teenaged Spanish girl who had opened it was quite pretty. I looked down to see that she was wearing white, high-heeled shoes and a white bikini. That was shocking enough in itself but what really threw me was that it didn't take a gynaecologist to appreciate she was at least six months pregnant; the gleaming dome surging towards me like an offensive weapon.

"Hi. Is no open now," she informed me brightly. How did she know I was English?

"Is Luis here?"

She told me he wasn't and I was glad. I didn't want a public scene. No punters. No hookers. Just one on one.

"When does he get here?"

She shrugged. "Maybe ten."

Well that was my element of surprise blown. It was November and there was an Englishman in town looking for him. Carrying a baseball bat. Smart. Depending on what John Durridge had told him he would have a pretty good idea who I was and what I wanted.

I checked into Caesars apartment block across the street. Then, with a lot less than nothing much to do I pulled my jacket up around my ears and hiked down the hill into town. Santa Ponsa was dead. Andy and I had discussed the possibility of running the bar all the way through the off season. A five minute recce told me that idea was a non-starter.

Eventually I happened across a murky old boozer that kind of reminded me of The Yeoman. Half a dozen desperate looking geezers huddled together for warmth and companionship periodically toking upon elixirs of all manner of sizes and colours. All sound ceased as the wind blew in behind me like a scene from a B Western. I scored a San Miguel, although a cup of tea would have been better.

Time passed. No one spoke to me and I spoke to no one but the frustration of the situation along with half a dozen or so beers saw me desperate to do something about it once more. I hoofed it back up the hill to the bar. OK, I told myself: no helpful concessions. No hard luck stories. Just do the business.

I didn't get to speak to Martinez but at least it wasn't the hooker. Second time around I got a child instead. Fresh into his teens and as lairy as you like.

"Si?" he snapped instantly knowing who I was and what I wanted. More than that, he had back up. I knew because I could hear voices from within.

"Where is he?" I growled, knowing he would understand English.

"He is not here."

An almighty surge of indignation swept over me bringing home the foul unfairness of what was happening. Those fuckers were on *my* property, drinking *my* drinks, burning *my* electricity. The humiliation released an anger within me, which I hadn't dared think I was capable of.

I hunched my ruddy face down to within two inches of his cute, little, olive- skinned boat. Spunky and mature beyond his years he may have been, but one swift flick of my neck would have seen my forehead brought down hard into the middle of his face and that would have been his peachy, Latin looks ruined for life. And he knew it. "When?" I sneered.

"I don't know," he whispered, now unable to hold my stare. "Maybe later tonight. Maybe no. I don't know, Mister. Please."

I stared into him, searching for clues. Martinez may even have been inside, hiding behind a boy and a young whore. My plans of meeting him one on one lay in tatters.

"Your name? Tu nombre? Tu?" I demanded.

His eyes, bright and defiant a second before, now darted with nervous evasion. He did what I would have done. He lied.

"Fernando."

I scored a horseburger from some dingy tuck shop and retired for the night but, unsurprisingly, with my ruck enzymes and yob neurons on overload, sleep was elusive. I pushed out a few sets of press-ups and then swung the bat around the apartment trying to imagine how it would feel to bring down on someone's knee. A shoulder. A head. Could I go through with it? Was I up to this? I tried to keep calm. Nick was right: I was the foreigner: the outsider.

The following morning I made my way across the street and let myself into the deserted bar. I had no intention of being greedy. Fairness was all I was after. I had John Durridge's inventory and all I wanted to do was separate our stuff, down to the last bottle of beer, from the Spaniard's. Then I would call Nick, arrange a meeting and lay it all out for him to choose. He could be pay rent and stay in the bar until the following spring when he would leave. If he was unhappy with that he was perfectly free to take the second option; he could fuck right off right now.

Then I got some reality.

I was placing all his booze on the counter ready for him to move out when I heard footsteps. Unfortunately they were not those of my hitherto unseen adversary. And Spanish police come in threes, carrying guns.

Somewhat taken aback, I was prepared after a fashion and produced the inventory to which I was working and the agreement of sale. I smoothed both out on the bar and, in my best Spanish, I attempted to explain.

"Yo el heffe," I told them, gesturing to the bar, the seats, the lights, the drinks. My life. "Esto is para mi."

I pointed to my name on the contract. "Yo Senor Targett. Soy el proprietor. Esto caballero is Senor Thompson, mi amigo."

Clearly satisfied I was no burglar, they busied themselves studying the paperwork. I relaxed. I was even of a mind to make them my very first customers. Keep in with the local plod, I thought. Sugar Ray would have been proud. Then he bundled in. Scurrying, panting, sweating. Stinking. He took in the situation and then rounded upon me. I knew it was him.

"Who the hell *are* you?" he demanded in perfect English.

I was cool. I rested an elbow on the bar, content in the knowledge I had the law both on my side and *by* my side. "You know who I am," I told him. "I'm the man who owns this bar and I'm here to collect some rent." To the point, but not impolite.

"John Durridge owes me money," he shouted.

"Then get it from him. That's your problem. You owe *me* money."

Then I got my first taste of what a foreign country can do to you if it doesn't like you. Martinez switched to Spanish and started talking to the cops and all I could do was stew in my own impotence. A stranger in a strange land. I felt waves breaking over my head. I felt hands, weeds and tentacles around my ankles, dragging me under.

Martinez had his hands together, beseeching, almost in prayer, the words lilting, cajoling, pleading. My frustration was total. All my interjections, all my arguments were either not understood or were ignored altogether. Then everything screeched to a halt and Martinez turned to me.

"We go now," he said.

"Hey, not me, old son. I've got work to do in my bar."

"Listen, my friend. The police are busy. They have much to do today. Your contract is not completely legal. I am telling you this for your own good. If you stay they will arrest you for trespassing. Do not make them anymore angry than they already are. When do you leave?"

"One week." Shit. Why did I tell him that?

"OK. You go to see Nick. Arrange a meeting."

That did seem fair enough especially when I noticed boss cop fingering his holster.

"Alright," I finally relented, giving him plenty of eyeball.

I reached between the cops to retrieve my papers from the bar, I picked up my bag and ambled confidently to the door, aware that all eyes were on me. Then I stopped and turned.

"Bring plenty of money," I said, trying not to sound like the frightened kid I truly was.

Checking on our account was a task I really did not want to perform. And yes, there it was. We had opened it with five thousand pesetas (about twenty five quid) and that's all there was. Nothing had been paid in so even if Durridge had been collecting from Martinez he'd stuffed us for that. We owed months in rent to the freeholder and were responsible for it throughout the winter as well.

Martinez was shrewd enough to suss that me and Andy were young and inexperienced and all he had to do was wait until I was back on a plane to England, then freely enter the premises with zero fuss and open up his knocking shop again. Surprise surprise, Nick wasn't able to contact him at all during the week of my stay.

I would meet a lot of lying, cheating people over the coming years but John Durridge and Luis Martinez were the first. Had my life to that point really been so sheltered and protected? Answer: yes.

Throughout that winter Martinez did not pay a single penny. As a consequence me and Andy had to work our nuts off to save the rent in order to stop the bar somebody else was making a living in from being repossessed from us. Work that one out. All we could do was continue shelling out and cling to the blind hope that once we got out there it would be OK. Twice I'd bought a duff dream from the classifieds. I just hoped there was a slow, painful death waiting for Durridge and that the frisky gentlemen of Santa Ponsa would all stay true to their wives and girlfriends, pushing Martinez out of business. And a pox on his whores.

CHAPTER FOUR

Lessons. Yeah right.

Learning lessons is something that you can do with hindsight. Hindsight is perhaps something you can develop once you learn your lessons.

If I had possessed a sliver of talent at either, I would not be where I am today - which is sitting on an aeroplane on the way to my own execution. I can see it all now, obviously. Of course I can see it all *now*. But now it's too fucking late, isn't it?

I listen, incandescent with indifference, as the pilot kindly draws our attention to the fact that there is a fine view of the Pyrenees, should those people with a window seat on the left of the plane care to press their faces up against the scratched plastic and take advantage of it. Sod the Pyrenees.

I can remember making the same journey eons ago and the pilot said the exact same thing. You would think these blokes would vary their act, although, in their defence, I don't suppose there are too many things you can look out for between London and Mallorca at thirty three thousand feet.

That time it was me and Andy boy making the trip. It should have been a thrilling, joyous event but that too was tainted by a dark foreboding.

Suki had run us to Gatwick and I recall kissing her in dreadful silence before leaving the two of them to it and making my way through into the departure lounge. I copped a litre of Courvoisier in duty free. In the time Andy had managed to extricate himself from Suki's smothering embraces I'd got through two inches of it. It was six thirty a.m.

Dewy-eyed he mooched around the shop before buying a bottle of Teachers. Noticeably glum and irritatingly silent he shuffled through in front of me towards the boarding gate.

"Let's go get 'em, big boy," I urged, jauntily thumping him between the shoulder blades.

Looking like a kid on his first, horror laden journey to school he turned to face me and said, "I'll see how it goes. I'll give it the first season and then I think I'll definitely let you buy me out."

Nothing like loading on the last straw first.

I declined the cardboard breakfast on the plane, opting only for intermittent sips of the brandy. The sleep-deprived excitement I had envisaged when we struck the deal with Durridge the previous summer had been replaced with sleep-deprived dread. I felt woefully out of my depth. There was so much that could go wrong and so much that already had, and, not for the first time, I felt the enormity of our task begin to crush me like a diver a hundred fathoms down.

A friendly tail wind barrelled us in ahead of schedule, when what I really wanted was for the plane to develop some kind of technical difficulty so we would have to divert to another airport, or possibly ditch in the sea. No such luck.

Mallorca welcomed me and Andy with howling winds and pissing rain. That kind of set the tone.

We had two hopes: one, Martinez had operated throughout the winter and had cut and run before we had got there. Or two, he had left it until the very last minute, when we had actually arrived in town, at which point he would seek to incur our wrath no longer and move out. It didn't take us long to learn the truth.

I can still see the look on Andy's face as we lugged our cases to the door of the bar. He had the keys and he tried them all, and then he tried them all again. Not only had the locks been changed but there was a security bar across the door. He wasn't going anywhere.

Weird to think this will be my last ever trip to Spain. I give the snow-capped mountains one last look anyway. What the hell. I'll never see them again and it is an impressive sight. Settling into tourist mode I hit the bell and order up a few gin and tonics. It's on Patsy anyway.

I gulp from the plastic glass, lean my seat back as far as it goes and close my eyes. Only a few hours now.

But of course it wasn't always thus. One time I had this scene in the back of the only Cadillac stretch limo in Mallorca. Not one but two Spanish stunners. A fridge full of Bollinger and a bag full of top grade Charlie. I've been there. That was me.

I remember this time when, because of where they were tied, my arms were beginning to ache, but that was quite alright. The blindfold was irritating but served its seductive purpose. Hee hee! I felt like peeking to discover whose mouth was where and whose fingers were doing what but decided not to because it's more fun trying to guess. One of them was my girlfriend and the other was her best chum. Now how had that delightful little set up come about? I suppose I should mention the drugs.

There are other times, other experiences. Not all so cosy though. Industrial warehouses all over London. Relentless, merciless fifty thousand watt boosted bass beats for hours upon hours. One 'tune' indistinguishable from the next and it was the most harmonious, most moving sound I have ever heard. Staring into blinding, stroboscopic lights. Multi-coloured, flickering laser beams flashing frantically across my field of vision. Sweaty bodies jostling me constantly, yet all around was beauty and understanding. Why was that so good? Drugs is why.

Then there was me, Masters and Romanov in a car repair shop in Hackney, East London. I observed with detached, almost serene curiosity as Romanov sat on the proprietor's chest while Masters sliced through the webbing between the bloke's fingers with his own jig saw. He made a sound like a Fender's feedback burning through a stack of Marshalls. The twanging tendons; the strangled, agonised screams all had a distant, eerie quality that I found fascinating. Then he screamed too loudly and Masters stamped on his face. With commendable attention to detail, he fished out the shards of broken teeth from his mouth and freed his tongue from his throat.

"Wouldn't want anything *baaaaad* to happen to this man now would we?"

So we waited. Waited for timeless, drifting moments until he regained consciousness. Then we started with the questions all over again and Masters got to work on the other hand.

How do I stand this? How do I watch and retain my sanity? Drugs is the way.

Ah yes, narcotics. Where do I start? Where else? All roads lead to Mallorca.

CHAPTER FIVE

Our first task on arriving in Santa Ponsa was to hand over some fifteen hundred quid's worth of pesetas to the landlord, Bernado, for the rent due over the winter months. Understandably he was pleased to see us.

"Boys. Boys. How are you? What happens?"

Andy had told me he had learned quite a lot of Spanish during his previous trips.

"Problemos with el bar," he explained lucidly. "Pero toto will now be bueno." He whipped his hands around in front of the portly Spaniard, leaving him as bemused as me. If Andy was our spokesman and interpreter then we were in worse shape than I had feared. However, if his Spanish wasn't quite top drawer then his talent for abuse had certainly not been dimmed by the miles. Riding a bad mood, we elected to go straight to Magaluf to see the hapless Nick.

"Oi, you foreign cunt," Andy hailed jovially from across the room. "We want a word with you."

So we sat down and had a nice chat – but, as affronted as we were, there was a certain desperate inevitability about what we heard.

"You should not have taken on a lease when there was a third party on the premises."

"Bollocks. You were the one who told us we were safe." That

was me. "You said he had no legal rights."

"So it is."

"Let's get him out then." That was Andy.

"Have you spoken to him?"

"We can't even find the fucker."

"So you don't know what his intentions are?"

"We don't give a shit what his intentions are," I declared, beginning to lose my rag. "Our intentions are that he vacates the place immediately, if not sooner. We're not here on holiday you know."

Plain speaking appeared to faze him as much as any other kind.

"So what do you want me to do?" he asked.

I think I actually saw steam coming from Andy's ears. I cut in.

"Nick, look. This man has changed the locks and reinforced the door. He's not planning on leaving. He is running his own business rent free and me and Andy are the berks picking up the tab. We need him out of the place at minimum cost and delay. What are our options?"

As he was telling us, telling us about Spanish litigation and court procedure, and about how long that court procedure might be likely to take, I became aware of the sounds of the tourists down in the street below. The clouds had cleared and although it was still only April it was warm, and the buzz - that tangible something that constituted a holiday atmosphere was in the air. But it made me feel sick because, at that moment, more than anything else in the world, I wanted to be a part of it. More than money, more than success. More than anything I wanted to be a number; an ordinary face in the crowd. I wanted to close my eyes and make it all go away. My dream had become a nightmare. Nick was still talking but I cut him off.

"So optimistically, Nick," I began as I massaged my eyeballs. "How long are we looking at for a legal eviction bearing in mind that, under ideal circumstances, we would prefer to be in there and working..." I swung my arm around and looked at the space my recently flogged watch used to occupy, "...in about three hours."

"If the circuit judge in Palma deals with the case himself, as I think he will, then we can hope for a final judgement in nine or ten weeks with a further fortnight for the official eviction procedure."

"Jesus wept," Andy said.

"And if it has to go to Madrid?"

Nick shrugged the pathetic walnuts of his shoulders. "Anything. Impossible to say. A year? Anything."

We trudged wearily back to the bus stop. We could have taken a cab but we weren't exactly in any rush to get anywhere.

"Jesus." I heard Andy say. "Lucky we didn't have a big leaving do."

Never in my twenty-five years had I felt so lost and lonely. How had it all gone so wrong? Why had I built my dreams up so high instead of just staying put? I could have stuck with flogging insurance or easier still just got some job in a bank or something. Anything. Every moron was cracking it back then and I had to aim so high.

Nick said he would try to arrange a meeting between us, Bernado the landlord, his lawyer and Martinez, if he would come, in the hope that we could thrash something out without resorting to litigation. Andy was already talking of Martinez buying us out. He wanted minimum damage, home and Suki.

It turned out that Martinez was a notorious liar; a pimp with police and underworld connections, and it was fairly clear that the meeting Nick proposed, should it ever take place, would constitute little more than an opportunity for me, Andy and our representatives to ask ever so nicely if this man would kindly vacate our premises so that we could move in. That, it seemed, was our best shot.

"Jesus wept."

"Easy."

"Easy? Christ! What are we supposed to do now?"

I was suddenly *very* awake. "Easy, Jen. Stay calm." I tried to free my thoughts from scrambled senses.

"Stay calm? Mick are you kidding me? How the fuck am I gonna stay calm?"

Through the dark and the haze and the sleep and the drugs - and that massive brutal punch I'd taken from Farmer, came the reality.

"Jen, where are you? You're not still in custody are you?"

"Of course I am. This a bit more than copping a parking ticket. I had two large, about three hundred caps, loads of trips and six grams of wiz on me. I'm in deep shit here. Of course I'm still in custody."

"You're calling me direct from a police station? What have I always told you?" I felt Jade stir next to me.

"Fucking right I am. Christ, what do you expect me to do? There's dozens of the bastards all over me here. They think they're onto the big time."

"Jenny I gave you the number of a brief to call if anything like this ever happened."

"I know, I know - but I never thought anything like this ever *would* happen did I? I'm sorry. I lost the number and you're all I've got."

"So now the old bill have my number in connection with a drug dealing offence. Thanks a bunch, Jen."

"You selfish cunt. This is the end of my life here."

Oops. And the gold medal for saying the wrong thing at the wrong time goes to… I mess this up now and she'll be leading Plod round to mine like the Pied Piper before I've got my shoes on.

I heard a tremor in her voice as she fought to hold back both the tears and the fear.

"Come on now, darling. It ain't that bad. Don't forget they've got to prove it."

She sniffed and swallowed and bit down hard on her swirling emotions.

"You hang on. We'll get this sorted and we'll get you out of there. You're connected, don't forget that. Now, answer me as briefly as you can. Try to stick to yes and no. You've been out selling in the clubs, yeah?"

"Yes."

"Where? The Ministry?"

"Yes."

"Is that where you got caught?"

"No."

"Where then? The Marquee? The Fridge?"

"No."

"Don't tell me you were in The Roller Express, Jen."

"I was."

"Shit. I thought we'd agreed to leave that out. You know it's all sewn up by the spades on the door. And where was Rick while all this was going on?"

"I don't know. It all happened so fast. Plain clothes."

"Look, is there anyone standing around listening to this?"

"Of course not. I'm not an idiot."

She knew she was in deep and so did I. Even as a first offence that amount of gear saw her looking down the barrel of at least two years. And even if she was a good girl and kept her mouth shut I was still looking at losing one of my best earners. But worse than all of that, I was running the risk of having Masters and Chalmers down on my head when I was supposed to be towing the party line and steering clear of selling Ecstasy.

A distraction.

"Mick?"

"Go back to sleep, darling."

"What time is it?" Jade murmured.

"Jen, what time is it now?"

"'Bout four."

"Going well, was it?" I asked with deep regret and a slice of unavoidable pride.

"Like a dream. Everyone knows. Everyone knows how good they are. Half the problem. Buzzing around me like bees around a jam pot."

"OK. Now just take it easy and I'll have a brief there as soon as I can. Tell me, have you been charged with anything yet?"

"No, but they are going to interview me in a minute."

"No. No way. Don't you say a fucking word, alright?" I launched clear out of the bed

"Christ, Mick, who is that? What's going on?"

I ignored Jade. "You tell them nothing, right? Until you see the brief you say nothing, and even then all you say is 'hello'. Got it? Now get your nut down and get some kip."

"Not a lot of chance of that. I dropped a couple of Stingers about half an hour ago. Only place I'm going is into orbit."

"In that case we can wait until morning because nobody is going to want to go near you in that condition. Keep schtum and enjoy the ride. Got anything stashed at home?"

"No. It's all plotted up safe."

"Good girl."

"Mick?"

"Yeah, darling."

"I'm scared."

"I know, love. I know. But you're not alone. You're part of a family. Don't forget that. We look out for each other."

"Good," she sniffed. "I'm pleased to hear it."

"OK. Jen, one more thing?"

"Yeah?"

"You still on the dole?"

"Yeah. Why?"

"We'll be able to get legal aid."

"Jesus wept," Andy kept saying, over and over again.

Neither him nor me were the kind of blokes that enjoyed roughing it and 'getting by'. I for one was far from happy about sharing a cockroach ridden, ten feet by twelve feet sweat box with another man and the largely dysfunctional shower and toilet facilities with twenty seven other people, who all seemed to be unconcerned whether the bog was flushed after use or not. But it was either that or scuttle off home skint and defeated to our mums.

Thus the Dunkirk spirit rose, and in order to conserve our

rapidly disappearing funds we shoplifted whatever food we could from supermarkets and discovered that if we surreptitiously mingled with other hotel guests we could sneak into dining rooms at meal times and sit down for free munchies. We both put on weight. We were a couple of Essex lads on the wrong end of a fairly nasty situation and consequentially we didn't give a toss. Spain wanted to play rough? Bring it.

During those early days out there I deliberately left the phone calls back home vague. I described one or two teething problems and left our opening date as 'imminent'. Meantime I would busy myself praying for a miracle. Weirdly enough, something akin to a miracle actually happened because Nick had somehow managed to arrange a meeting between all of us - including Martinez. We were to call again in a day for details of where and when. My fingers were crossed so tight they went numb.

Because we were getting up early to slither into the Magaluf Sol hotel for breakfast we were routinely in bed by eleven or so. Occasionally; however, when sleep was elusive, I was to be found, come the witching hour, hunched in a solitary prowl through the streets of Magaluf.

By mid to late May, although the resort was still only half full, most of the bars were open for the season's business. This anomaly fortunately gave rise to that glorious invention; the happy hour. And so it was that a down at heel, sun-seeking, wannabe bar owner such as yours truly could stretch a few hundred Pesetas through half an evening or so, thus whiling away a few therapeutically distracting hours. It was on just such a night - with Andy tucked up in bed exercising his wrist with lurid thoughts of Suki - that I met Lauren Chetkins and quite possibly the most fateful piece of my life's jigsaw slipped into place.

Lauren was a 'propper': helping with the propaganda advertising a bar. This meant that it was her job to stand outside Dicey Riley's pub in Magaluf in a short skirt and drag people inside. My job was to let her.

"'Ello. You look like you need a drink. Why not try Dicey Riley's? Bar snacks, five different types of lager and draught Guinness that really is Guinness. Also, there's a happy hour on tonight that lasts all night."

I had to smile as I looked past the cute, freckled button of a nose and into her bright, hazel eyes. "Where you from? I asked as an opener.

"Essex."

Bingo.

"Yeah? Me too. Whereabouts?"

"Grays."

"No shit. I'm from Upminster."

Her turn to look me over. "You know I think I might have seen you before."

"Yeah, well," I shrugged. "Probably in some magazine or other."

She grinned widely as she hooked her arm into mine. "Thought so. It was one of those reader's husbands features wasn't it?"

I gladly let her steer me towards the bar.

"Go and get a drink," she instructed confidently. "I get a break later on and I'll come in and have a chat then."

The barman told me that the deal was not half price drinks, but two for the price of one. Fair enough. Let's relax a little. From my vantage point at the end of the bar I could look out onto the street and see that the girl was very friendly with the Spanish boy with whom she was working but, true to her word, she came in to join me as I was halfway through my second bottle.

"What can I get you?" I asked as she slipped onto the stool next to me.

"San Mig', please. Cheers. 'Ere, what's your name? I really do think I might have seen you before somewhere."

I scored two more bottles and paid the barman in coins.

"Well I normally go out in Romford or Upminster. Sometimes we go into the East End but it's always to blokey kind of places. I'm not much of a disco type and besides..." I leant forward keenly and gave her some cheeky chappy eyeball. "... I'm sure I would have remembered meeting you."

She threw her head back with a girlish giggle. "Oh per-lease.

Save it for the tourists. The lines I haven't heard already aren't worth hearing."

I laughed too and clinked our bottles together. "I'm Micky. Micky Targett."

"Hey, cool name. Good to know you, Mick. I'm Lauren Chetkins."

"Hi, Lauren. Now tell me. Things still seem a bit slow. How's business?"

"It's always like this until the first week in June. Quiet like. Then the whole place just explodes. Wall to wall punters. No real need for proppers then, so I'll probably be behind the bar helping with the rush."

She shifted her weight on the stool and crossed her legs. Her skirt, already a good foot above the knee, rode up even higher. The chill of the night air had left her thighs sprinkled with goose bumps. I tried not to stare.

"So you're out here for the season then?" I asked.

"Yeah. I've been over since February. You think it's quiet now, you should see it then. Deadsville Arizona."

"I was actually here in November so I know what you mean. Not Magaluf, but the next town - Santa Ponsa."

"You were in Santa Ponsa in November? Funny, that's where I live. I'm out here for the season but I come here a lot anyway. My dad owns an apartment in Santa Ponsa. He knows Robbie, the bloke who owns Dicey's, and he gave me the job."

Interesting.

"Whereabouts is your family's place? I normally stay in Caesars. Anywhere near that?"

"Yeah, not far. Caesars is a bit touristy. Ours is down the hill on the right. Privately owned. Bit snotty but it's nice and quiet."

Yeah, very interesting. What *do* we have here? Apartment, contacts, money. The shoes, the leather, the suede. This was no cheap, tacky, spoilt, little Essex girl. No, this was a *rich*, tacky, spoilt little Essex girl.

"So you reckon you'll be working here all summer?" I asked.

"Yeah. What about you? A fortnight is it?"

I shook my head and grinned. "This is really coincidental. Me and a mate have got this place over in Santa Ponsa. Our own bar which we are due to be opening soon. It's a right shame you're stuck over here for the season because one of the things we need to sort out straight away is a girl propper who looks the business. Be ideal. Two minutes walk and you're there." Laying it on a bit thick?

"Really? Oh that's brilliant. Fantastic. I've always said there ain't enough English places in town. But which one? What's it called?"

I knew a little about body language from my selling days with Ali and it was all there: the uncrossing of the legs which she swung down and aimed in my direction, the knees nudging into the right side of my thigh. A hand on my forearm.

"Just up the hill from you, between two restaurants called Paco's and the Pepperpot."

"Gotcha." She snapped her fingers loudly in the air. "Stewart and Doreen, the couple who own The Pepperpot, are friends of the family. But that place, that bar. I mean, it's a knocking shop innit? A real dive."

"Yeah, sure is. I *like* dives, but we are going to clean it up a bit."

"So why are you sitting here talking to me Why ain't you open?"

I rolled my eyes. "Bit of legal ag' at the moment. The previous tenant is just winding his business up, so we are using this quiet period before the season kicks off to make all our contacts. You know - booze suppliers, wholesalers. People like yourself. Introducing ourselves to the island."

"Great. I've been on at my dad to buy me a little pub for ages. I'd love it."

Flipping marvellous. I feasted upon the possibilities this fluke encounter might yield. Could I wangle myself and Andy a room in her apartment? Could her father or any of his contacts give us any help in shifting Martinez from the bar? Would Daddy be interested in buying Andy's half as a pressie for his little girl? Was there any chance of her getting the next round in? And, of course, there was the perennial leg over situation. What a worthwhile evening stroll it was turning out to be.

"Your father," I enquired casually. "Sounds like an influential kind of bloke. What's he into back home? Maybe I've heard of him."

"Ah he's got his dabs in all kind of pies. Owns Chetkins Transport. Seen any of our lorries flying around? Blue and white paint job?"

"Oh yeah, right. I know," I lied.

"That's one. I expect you've heard of Clacton Pier too?"

"Don't tell me he owns that."

"Kind of. He leases it from the council. Every ride, every game of bingo, every cup of tea, every penny that rolls into a slot..."

I whistled appreciatively. Talk about landing on my feet. Then this sparky, happy young girl landed on *her* feet and was screeching in her tinny, Essex howl at someone down at the far end of the bar.

"Oi. Oi, Robbie. Down 'ere. Want you to meet a friend of mine and bring some more beer too."

A moment later, shuffling down behind the bar with a fistful of beer bottles clanking away, came a portly, middle-aged man. Clearly Brylcreem's most loyal customer, he sported an old, green T-shirt which, in white letters, proclaimed: 'Dicey Riley's Irish Bar'. Underneath that was written: 'I don't have a drink problem - I drink, get drunk, fall down. No Problem'.

"Rob, this is my mate Mick from Essex. He's in the trade. He's just bought a pub over in Santa Ponsa. Mick, this old wheezer is Robbie Piper otherwise known as Mister Dicey Riley."

"Hey, Rob. Good to know you. How's it going?" I offered my hand across the bar. Instead of shaking it, he filled it with a bottle.

"Hello, son. How's yourself? What place is it you have?" He handed Lauren a bottle and took a swig from a third.

"It's called Bugsy's. Up at the far end in the Princessa block."

"Not the topless place?"

"Yeah."

"You going to keep it that way?"

"No. No way. It's going to be a straight place. You know - lively disco type bar."

"Ah now that's a shame."

"Yeah? Why's that?"

"They have some of the best hookers outside Palma. I was hoping you might be able to swing me a discount."

Then, I was in familiar territory. I was lying in bed feeling awful and my mother was making her usual valiant attempt to get me up. Thank Christ for that. It had all been a bad dream. Hoo-bloody-ray. All that had happened was that I had caned it big time down the Yeoman or the 'Choke and it was getting on for Saturday afternoon and my dear old mum wanted me out of the way so that she could change the sheets. What a relief it was to know I hadn't bought that stupid bar in Mallorca and didn't have a ton of aggravation with some spic who was trying to rip me off. I was so happy I forgot about the hangover. As soon as I was up I'd call The Stomach to see what jolly scrapes we'd got into the previous evening.

"Come on. Hurry up."

"Yeah. I'll be there in a minute."

"Look, I'm not missing it. I'll go without you."

"Why?"

"I'm not missing out just because you can't handle your booze."

Oh dear.

"Don't matter to me. You can go hungry today."

Oh deary, deary me. With a massive effort I hauled myself upright in bed. I unglued my tongue from the roof of my mouth just as my hangover kicked in with pulverising force.

"Wassertime?"

"Half eight. You coming or not?"

Like a wounded, sleazy lizard I eased out from between the sheets and onto the cold hardness of the lino. Finding a precarious perpendicular, I listened with mournful fascination as the soles of my feet sucked luridly on the tiles as I padded to the bathroom down the hall.

"I was getting on really well, " I recalled as I downed my

twelfth thimble sized glass of OJ at the hotel breakfast buffet. "It was going great. She's got this rich dad and she lives in this flash gaff in Santa Ponsa and I'm sure she said we could crash there if we wanted. She works at this place just around the corner from here and she introduced me to the owner and he got loads of beers in. And there was something about Clacton pier."

"'Scuse me?"

"Don't ask me, mate," I told him, sniffing the salami. "Christ knows where it all fits in."

"So then what?"

I shrugged gormlessly. "Dunno. I can't find an address or a phone number or anything, but if she works at this place around the corner all I've got to do is go back there tonight."

Of the nine hard-boiled eggs Andy had grabbed he was unable to eat three. These he stuffed into his bag along with butter, jam, bread rolls, salami, ham and some very sweaty cheese. He looked at his watch. "OK let's go."

"What's the rush?" I asked, noting he had limited himself to just four cups of coffee.

"The solicitor's office is open. We have to phone to see when that fuckwit has arranged the meeting for. It's alright acting the tourist, but we're supposed to be here on business."

Dealing with Nick was Andy's department because he had developed this fantastic talent for being sensationally rude to him. In the phone box outside the hotel he scribbled an address and slammed the phone down, looking quite upset that Nick had managed to do something right for a change.

"Friday at four at this place in Palma. Shit. Another week of doing fuck all."

During that period 'fuck all' was not an entirely accurate description of what we were up to. We ate. We stole from shops. We watched countless videos in a number of hotels and, as June approached, we sat around on the beach a lot getting brown but feeling like a couple of languid, left out lotharios. We also wrote a lot of letters. With pens on pieces of paper. By that time I had dispensed with the charades and come clean with my mother about what a mess we were in. I tried the unusual step of telling the truth, and not only found that I felt a lot better for it but, with each note, I sensed a bridging of the gaps that had widened between us throughout the preceding years. She wrote back saying that I had her and the old guy's full support, using many phrases such as 'Learning from my mistakes' and 'Making the best of a bad lot'.

She told me other things too. She told me she loved me and urged me to think about that, relative to my problems. She also told me that she and everyone else were very proud of me for having the guts to follow my convictions and go after what I wanted. I made sure Andy was never around when I cried my heart out.

The night after I'd met her I went to see Lauren again, but as in all good mysteries, and to compound my frustrating memory block, she had disappeared. If only I could remember. Christ, I must have been sooooo pissed. We were all getting along famously. Then, for some reason, I was behind the bar. And there was an arm wrestling contest. I think. Then cocktails. Then in a file at the very depths of my subconscious I retrieved the memory of kissing someone, although I had no inkling if it had been Lauren or not. In that condition there was every chance it had been Robbie.

As I tumbled into Dicey's I got a hale and hearty 'buenas tardes' from all the staff including Robbie who was wearing a grin that held a thousand secrets. He cracked a couple of bottles and handed me one. As I took it I felt the dull ache in my right hand that had been troubling me all that day.

"Hey, son, how's it going? How was the head this morning?"

"Not so bad, mate. Yourself?"

"Ah now I've been doing this too long to get hangovers." He tapped his temple with a gnarled, warty forefinger. "Nothing left in there to damage."

"I didn't see Lauren outside, Rob. What time does she get on?"

"She's late already. She's normally very good like that but I just haven't seen her. You did make sure she got home alright last night, yeah?"

Whoa. Hold up. She and I left together? Shit.

"Yeah, mate. Fine. We were fine. No worries."

"Good thing, son. I'd hate to think anything happened to her while you were looking after her. Her father, big Patsy, would be round."

I kept out of Dicey's from then on. I didn't know what had happened that night but I knew - I just knew it hadn't been good. I skirted by the pub every evening on the lookout for Lauren but there was no sign of her, nor of the young Spanish kid with whom she had been working that first night.

But there were other things on my mind.

We arrived at the lawyer's office with time to spare. Bernado was next followed by the reluctant, shrew-like figure of Nick. Ten minutes late the fat, pale, sweating Luis Martinez deigned to favour us with his presence.

Bernado's lawyer - a clean cut, handsome man in his late thirties named Antonio conducted the meeting with commendable efficiency, switching between Spanish and English at will.

"You arranged this contract between Mr. Durridge and the two boys?" he asked Nick in all politeness, holding aloft our legal documents.

"Yes." Nick replied.

"And what about the contract between the two boys and Bernado Mayol?"

"What contract?"

"Exactly!" He slammed the papers down onto his desk. "Now the boys are in no position whatsoever. If Bernado decides he does not wish to do business with them what then? They have an agreement with Mr. Durridge but until they have one with Bernado they have bought something which as yet does not exist."

"Yes but I thought that..."

"It does not matter what you thought. You had to bring Mr Durridge, Bernado, the boys and..." He looked at Martinez like he was some kind of paedophile, "...this man together to my office *all at the same time.* In this way all difficulties can be examined first and we do not have the trouble we have now."

Nick was speechless. A chastened boy. His pipe cleaner arms hung miserably from his short sleeves as he looked down at his shoes. One of the island's top briefs was how John Durridge had described him. What a joke.

"Antonio," I quickly said. "Can you confirm that Bernado would be willing to grant us the same kind of contract he had with John Durridge?"

"In essence, yes. We have already spoken. He likes you and he wants you to succeed. First there is the problem of access to the bar."

"Indeed," I replied. "Please thank Bernado with his help in all this."

"Of course, of course," he said with a dismissive wave of the hand. "Now tell me, how much are you willing to offer Snr. Martinez?"

I expected him to say something more at the end of the sentence, such as the punch line.

"I beg your pardon?"

"Money. What are you able to offer?"

"Antonio," I told him with all humility, "the only money we have is money which we need to live on and to stock our bar when it opens." I jerked a contemptuous thumb in Martinez's direction. "It is he who should be paying us."

"Good. I am pleased you say this. He asked me to ask you and this is a good reply." Then he turned to Luis and basically got straight to it.

"What are you doing? This is so bad of you. You are making things very difficult for everyone."

We all hung on his word like he was the Pope. I wanted to see him squirm, to wriggle like a low worm impaled on the hook of Antonio's interrogation. Far from it.

"Is no my problem," he said.

The words bounced off the office walls, and I saw Andy turning beetroot and practically starting to climb the walls and I finally appreciated what kind of scumbag we were up against.

Antonio stared him down.

"No. This is no way to behave. You have taken advantage. You have the business in the bar since last year and all the time they have paid the rent for you. You must be fair. If you leave now I will advise them not to bring the action against you in court."

I liked him. I liked this boy. Dynamic yet sensitive. A Spanish James Stewart. Problem was Martinez then launched into a blazing monologue of Spanish that took even the redoubtable Antonio by surprise. There then ensued a ferocious argument which had me and Andy and the other two gawping at each other.

The row boiled for long, worrying moments until Antonio, clearly gagging with contempt, collected his papers and shuffled them into a neat pile before slamming them back down onto his desk.

"It's the girls. It's the girls," Martinez protested, returning to English for some reason.

"Forget the girls. Give them a holiday. They can still earn money. What is the problem?"

The question was meat and drink to him, for he smiled his horrible, sickly smile that we all wanted to punch into the middle of next week, shrugged and said, "I don't know but I know that it is not *my* problem."

With commendable professionalism, Antonio held onto the gobful of spit I sensed he wanted to launch at Martinez and addressed the rest of us. "Gentlemen. Thank you for coming. The meeting is now ended."

"Hold on," said Andy. "We haven't sorted anything out yet."

Everybody was on their feet, collecting their belongings and readying to leave whilst Andy and I wanted to rewind the whole thing. Rewind the meeting. Rewind our lives.

"Young man," Antonio said. "I don't think anything will be sorted out today."

He shook hands with Bernado and bade him farewell, but simply stood with his hands upon his hips as Nick and Martinez left. When the three of us were alone he spoke.

"This is a bad man. It is bad that you come to our country to try to work and you meet someone like him. I am very angry."

"So...Err... What did he say?" Andy asked.

"Well it is not so bad. He has agreed to leave the bar, if his word is to be trusted. Of this I am not so sure, but there you are."

We brightened immediately at this.

"When? When?" Andy jabbered. "Did he say when?"

"Well, he does not know exactly. The thing is he is having a new bar built for himself in Santa Ponsa and he will leave your bar only when the construction for the new one is completed."

Me and Andy swapped puzzled glances. "He's building a new bar?" I said.

"Yes, but it is not as bad as it sounds. The building exists already - at the moment it is a supermarket but he is having it changed and will be having his new bar there."

"So how long will it take?" I asked not really knowing if I wanted to hear the answer.

"He does not know for sure. Many weeks. Months. At the end of June, maybe the beginning of July. *He* say. But remember this is a man you can*not* trust."

I leant forward and held my head gently in my hands and heard Andy say, "Jesus wept."

"I am sorry. This is the fault of Nick. Also - don't forget this Durridge man. It seems clear he was trying to deceive you too. It is very bad luck that you have met three bad men as soon as you come to my country."

"So if we go through the court, how long will that take?" I asked.

"I am sorry, but again I can give you no clear answer. One month, maybe two. The courts are slow as they are in London."

Oddly enough that didn't seem too bad.

"Would you like me to begin the court action?"

"Yes," I said.

"What's the fucking point?" Andy snarled.

"Because we don't give up," I told him. He sighed and turned away from me.

"Good," Antonio said. "This is good. We need the positive attitude. Dealing with the court will be a nuisance for him. If we keep up pressure it will make him move quicker."

His generosity and allegiance warmed me.

"To do this we must first get the new contract with Bernado. I will call him later today and arrange a time when we can come back here. Will you call me later today and I will tell you when it is?"

"Sure," I said, standing and offering my hand.

"The cost of the contract is thirty thousand pesetas. Is OK no?"

We didn't have much more than that and the rent was due again. Back out on the street Andy asked the question.

"Where the fuck is that going to come from?"

"We'll have to send home for some more. It's all we can do."

We plodded away on leaden legs through the swarms of tourists I loathed from the pit of my stomach. I wonder how many of them knew the agony, that little death inside that comes with the realisation that a dream, that has been nurtured and cherished, is breathing its last.

Back at the room, I changed into my Speedos. Andy grabbed his copy of the Mallorcan Bugle. He said, "I'm just going out for a bit."

Our hovel might not have been up to much but at least it was a hovel smack on the beach. I padded barefoot down the stairs, through the alley and right onto the sand and walked to the spot where all the British workers, bums and hippies out for the summer usually gathered. I spotted a bloke I'd bumped into a couple of times called Simon. Apart from a predilection for West Ham United Football Club, he was alright.

"Hey, Si," I said, laying my towel down next to his.

"'Ello, Micky. What's happening?"

"Nothing that's going to make me a fortune, I know that."

"Know the feeling, mate."

"Still no sign of any work?"

"Nah. I've been around every pub and disco in town and they all have their proppers organised for the summer already."

I thought about asking Robbie in Dicey's on Simon's behalf, but decided it would be more grief I didn't need. "Ah, bad luck. What's the moolah situation?"

"Running on empty, mate. Looks like I'll have to sling it in even before the season gets going. Didn't think there'd be this many people chasing jobs."

"So, what's your move?"

"I've got an uncle coming out who owns his own apartment. I'm going to stay with him for a fortnight and if nothing turns up in that time then I'll have to go home."

Well, I saw the keeper off his line, what could I do? "Hey - I don't suppose he has any room does he? Me and Andy have to leave our place at the weekend and we still don't have anywhere sorted yet."

"Yeah. You might be alright there. It's a nice three bedroomed place and he's a good bloke. Always up for a laugh. I'll mention it to him. It's over in Santa Ponsa."

I couldn't wait to tell Andy. I went back via a call box, where I phoned Antonio who had arranged our contract signing meeting with Bernado for the following Wednesday. But Andy had news for me.

"I've just bought a ticket," he announced as I bundled through the door.

"I see."

"We need to get some more money and I can do that safely. The ticket was only thirty quid. Daft both of us sitting out here doing nothing."

"Thing is, I've just called Antonio. He's set up that meeting with Bernado for next Wednesday afternoon."

"Perfect. The flight is Thursday morning."

Something wasn't right. Something just didn't seem right.

"Cool. Listen - I've just been talking to that Simon geezer, you know, the one with the daft perm. He reckons he's moving to Santa Ponsa in a few days and there's a good chance we can crash there too."

"Nice one."

"Innit. So what I'm thinking is, we can give the runaround to the old git we owe rent to on this place for the next few days, and then jump on a bus over to SP."

After the run we'd had, even small victories assumed major importance.

For Andy, things were simple. He needed to keep his head down until the Thursday morning, whence he would be back in the lap of luxury and, more importantly, back in the lap of the luscious Suki. Once again I drew the short straw. I had no money, nowhere to stay, a ton of gear to look after and an irate landlord on my arse.

The Wednesday meeting was straightforward, and for thirty thousand Pesetas (a hundred and fifty pounds) we had a legally binding contract with the landlord of Bugsy's.

Motivated by sheer sympathy I felt sure, Bernado and Antonio offered to buy us lunch. This was something of an error of judgement because, using little known eating skills honed to perfection at the tables of the Magaluf Sol hotel dining room, Andy and I made a concerted effort to eat back our thirty thousand in its entirety. At our prompting, soup was followed by snails which was followed by Paella. Then we had Steak Tournedos followed by ice cream and then loads of cheese. We also disappeared four bottles of San Miguel and a bottle and a half of Rioja. Each. We rounded things off with loads of minty, choccy things and enough coffee to alter the price of Brazilian beans.

The following morning I saw Andy off at the bus stop. The obvious defeat in his eyes made me wonder if he'd be back.

Shooting defensive glances all around for the prowling landlord, who had already left two notes pinned to our door, I decided to hit the beach early. The guy who owned the bar near where we all congregated solved all my problems in one hit.

"Hey. You are Micky, yes? You have a friend from London called Simon?"

"Yes. Have you seen him?"

"He go. He leave yesterday."

My heart sank. The shit just kept getting deeper. Then he turned and plucked something from the noticeboard on the far wall of his bar.

"He gave me this for you."

I read the note. 'Mick. Sorry I missed you. My uncle was delayed but he finally made it. If you still need to crash somewhere you're very welcome. We're at Appt. 3C, Edificio Las Rocas, Avenida de la Playa, Santa Ponsa. If we are not there, we are either in the bar or in the pool. Hammers rule OK.'

As I feverishly packed both my stuff and what Andy had left behind, I was singing *I'm Forever Blowing Bubbles* as quietly as I could. Less than two hours later I was dangling my feet in the pool drinking cold beer. Get in. I had graduated directly from an insect ridden sauna the size of a car boot to a comfortable bed with clean sheets, my own bathroom, a TV with video, a laundry room and a private pool. Simon and his uncle Frank turned out to be good company too. And it was free.

"So how come you were over in Magaluf slumming it when you had this little lot tucked away?" I asked Simon as I glugged down half a bottle of the Spanish nectar.

"Frank rents it out. He comes over for two or three breaks a year but the rest of the time it's always rented. Make the most of it Micky boy. Here comes summer."

We clinked bottles.

He was right too, and just as Lauren had predicted, in the first week of June the whole place just exploded. Saturday, June the fourth. 1984 was changeover day and the beach - and indeed the whole town was a different place to the day before. The buzz in the air was tangible. There was youth, there was glamour, there was fun and there were girls. Packs of them. It was what I had come for in the first place, and as Two Tribes belted out from every bar every night I made the most of it. And I got a job.

Ricardo - the bouncer on the door of Caramba Disco hired me - on a commission basis to flog tickets for the beach party he was running. It wasn't a lot but at least I could buy the chaps a beer now and then and feed myself without stealing. It was like having a really nice two week holiday. And when I was in with Ricky, entry to everywhere in town was gratis. And he introduced me to Randall P. Schnipper III.

The first time I ever clapped eyes on Randy was down in the bowels of Caramba. I edged towards the back bar and heard that great song:

> *A businessman is caught with twenty four kilos*
> *He's out on bail and out of jail and that's the way*
> *it goes. RAAAH!'*

Totally choice when I think about what happened next.
"Hi, Randy," I said, showing him my palm.
He nodded thoughtfully. "Beer?" was all he said before foisting a cold one onto me.

Randy and a few of his pals that lived in and around town were oilfield workers. Riggers, roughnecks, roustabouts.

What they did was work twelve hours a day, seven days a week for the duration of their spell on their particular rig literally anywhere on the planet. Nasty places like the cholera infested flatlands of Turkmenistan, freezing Norway, sweltering Venezuela or the kidnap centre of the world, Nigeria. For their efforts, they were rewarded with unseemly bundles of tax free cash - and if they worked a month on the rig in those conditions then who would begrudge them a month away to blow off steam and have some fun?

For some reason Santa Ponsa was home to quite a few of them, and those boys had the dosh to insist on the best of everything. Randy, for example, would always call for Glenmorangie whisky. As I got to know him I felt this to be an example of outrageous snobbery though, as Glenmorangie rendered him as violently ill as any other brand surely would.

He was a kindly faced, good looking kind of bloke, but his straight, brown hair, drooping moustache and brown eyes gave him the air of a lugubrious bloodhound. Or possibly a reluctant seventies porn star. I loved him immediately.

We shot the shit, during which I told him about the bar and the problems we were having with it. In the time it took to tell him my story of woe, he managed to buy me five bottles of beer. When I began to protest at his generosity he assured me that once I was in the bar I would be given every chance I desired to return it. In the meantime, perhaps I should just shut the fuck up and drink.

We surveyed the sweaty, moiling pit that was the sunken dance floor as *Against All Odds* by Phil Collins drew the dancers into swaying pairs like a magnet teasing iron filings towards each other.

Then he said, "Can you get the keys to the office?"

"Nah. I don't think so. Helmut the owner caught someone smoking dope in there last week so he's the only one that uses it now."

"Hmmm. Well they got a shitter in here, don't they?"

"Something that passes for one."

Then he said something that I suppose changed my life.

"So. What say we do a line of coke then?"

My heart slipped a beat. Now then. This was indeed a step up. I'd been a piss-head since I could remember but I knew nothing of illegal substances. The idea thrilled me. The absolute bloody naughtiness of it all.

"You got some onya?"

"Well whaddya think we're talking about?"

Randy's generosity was legendary but I still felt the need to clarify. "Listen, man. I'll have to owe you. You know how things are for me right now."

"Fuck you, asshole," he said by way of clarification, before grabbing a fistful of my T shirt to drag me off.

Two grown men crammed into a tiny, stinking, Spanish bog cubicle, ankle deep in tourist piss is no way to imbibe expensive medicine, but everybody who has partaken of a bit of chop will know that sooner or later such circumstances need to be endured. Having mopped copious amounts of urine from the toilet seat (how does it get on the *seat*?) we kneed and elbowed each other half a dozen times as we sank to our haunches. Randy then pulled a tiny paper envelope from his shirt pocket and managed to hack the powder into four lines some three inches in Length with the encrusted edge of his chromium American Express card.

With a rolled up ten thousand Peseta note shoved up his right nostril and his little pinkie applied to his left, he snorted noisily and aggressively. A swift changeover saw both of his rails, to the grain, disappear. He handed me the note. Baby's first line.

I had got pretty near to the end of the first line when it suddenly felt like my left nostril and half my head were jam packed with a mixture of snot, mustard and curry powder.

"Tell me something, son," he said; his big, handsome face creasing with amusement. "This the first time you done any of this shit?"

"Well yeah," I confessed. "But that don't make me a wimp you know."

"Well there's one golden rule in snorting coke; never ever sneeze. That would be an extremely expensive thing to do."

"I'm not going to sneeze."

"Good."

"My head is going to explode, but I'm not going to sneeze."

"Get the rest on up there. Don't waste any. This is primo. We're talking mucho puro here."

"My schnozz is full already."

"Bullshit. The size of that motherfucker you should be able to get half a kilo up there."

"Bitch."

I tentatively sniffed what was left of the first line, fuelling the red hot poker that seemed to be wedged up my nostril already. After a moment of snorting, sniffing and fingering I was fairly sure nothing was going to fall out, including my brain.

"Good boy. Now get the other one up the other side."

If the sound I was making was anything to go by, my friends in the Mallorcan Police force would be kicking the door in any second. Two boisterous rhinos with flu, copulating and eating dinner all at the same time would have made less noise than me endeavouring to enjoy my first taste of the champagne drug. Eventually the hard part was over.

"Fuck me backwards, Randy," I warned him with all conviction. "This shit better be good."

He was licking his finger and dabbing at the stray flakes I had left.

"No problemos, boy. You gonna be able to drink the place dry tonight and still stick it to the babes 'til sun up. Word is you got a drinking contest going on."

Getting out of the bog was funny. Picture the scene; you're on holiday, in the toilets of the local disco minding your own business, checking out the tan lines or whatever. Then two smiling blokes with watering eyes and looking a tad flustered emerge from the same trap shooting wary glances all over the place. These days you wouldn't think twice but it was virgin territory back then.

Back out in the club I was bobbing and weaving with trembling excitement during that period of delicious danger between absorption and effect. To add to the thrill, my drinking opponent had arrived.

I'm not sure how it had come about but I had met this really gorgeous Dutch girl a few nights before, and had started giving her all kinds of nonsense. Getting on really well we were - until her fella showed up. It was cool, though. He knew she was always going to get attention like that from blokes like me so we had a drink. Then we had another. Before you could say 'mine's a large one' he'd challenged me to a glugging match. Well, I could hardly refuse could I? Young, stupid and happy. Those were the days.

Not only had they and their contingent turned up but most of the English workers I knew were arriving too. It seemed like everyone knew what was about to happen. In addition Ricardo, the doorman who had mysteriously taken a liking to me, drifted down from the entrance and told the barman to give me and the Dutch bloke whatever we wanted.

Pete the DJ even made an announcement over the PA that the evening's entertainment was about to start at the back bar. That'll be me then.

The girl was there too. That girl. She couldn't have been more than eighteen, and at around five feet ten and wearing half a vest and a quarter of a skirt, she was the embodiment of pre-AIDS European sexual liberation. She looked sex. She *was* sex. She skipped and glided all around the place like a catwalk model flirting outrageously with everyone, but mostly me.

Her boyfriend didn't seem to mind this. In fact her boyfriend didn't even seem to notice - and this, I soon realised, was because even before we had sunk the first drink, he was already astonishingly pissed. I warmed to him immediately. In fact I found myself warming to everyone - boys as well as girls, and the nervous anticipation that had been gnawing away at my gut had been miraculously replaced by a warm, affable anticipation. Suddenly I couldn't stop myself thinking what a wonderful bloke this mullet-haired nutter was. Fancy taking on a complete stranger in a drinking match. What a guy!

Then I was looking around at his bunch of chums and I was in love with all of them too. Friendly, chatty, happy... Terrific value. But then all Dutch people were like that, weren't they? Intelligent, progressive. That is one sussed country. All the fellas liked a drink and all the girls liked a fella. I made a mental note to get over there as soon as I could.

Then I can remember chiding myself for limiting my exploration to Holland. How lucky I was to have been born into such an advanced and cosmopolitan continent. So many great people in so many great places. Potentially I had millions of friends. And of course there was the rest of the world, and what a world! So what if I was locked out of my own bar? Sure I was in danger of blowing my life savings, but was that so important in the great scheme of things? Considering everything in a broader sense, I couldn't believe how fortunate I was. I looked around the mad, buzzing throng of my new friends and was blown away by how wonderful my life could be. Santa Ponsa was turning out to be my kind of town after all. Maybe I really could settle there. And everybody was so good looking.

Whilst I was absorbing the splendour of my surroundings a weird blast of deja vu swept by me; something I hadn't felt since my last visit to the dentist years before. It was like I'd had one of those injections in my gums because, for some bizarre reason, my teeth were going numb.

I'm not sure how long me and everybody chewed the fat for,

but interestingly it was the girl - this statuesque Sylvia, who called time on the socialising and got us to our marks at the bar and then it was another of those preciously rare moments of pure definition for a little Essex yob who had come a long, long way. I was the centre of attention, this stunning woman had the undisputed hots for me and I just felt so fucking *good*. I was in love with everyone and everyone was in love with me. What else could I have asked for?

Ricardo had introduced me to tequila slammers (tumbler sized) only the previous week so I knew what to expect. Raul the barman poured, and Randy and Ricardo smashed the glasses down to the sound of two rifle shots. I got mine inside me like it was milk. That loony was only a second behind but the glazed, swivelling eyes told me the good news. He smiled and so did I.

"Hey, man, you're fucking crazy," he howled. We grabbed the other's thumb in boozy kinship and shook vigorously.

"But what a life eh, Freddie? What a fucking life?"

"Is it finished?"

"No way. We keep going."

"Oh, man," he whimpered, resigned to his fate. "When will it be finished?"

"When one of us is."

"Oh, man."

He was dead in the water and we both knew it, but what a sport to keep bashing away like that. Me? I was flying and sporting a winner's grin all the way down the finishing straight. It was easily the best night of my life. Between the belts of Tequila people kept handing me beers like I was some kind of star, and all the while there was big Randy looming at my shoulder smiling and whispering, "Always pays to have an edge, my man. Always pays to have an edge."

I couldn't lose. I couldn't lose ever again.

Then, there she was. Shimmering and shining between us like some kind of dazzling prize, and her bloke was flat on his back midway through the fourth round. Some people carried him out shoulder-high like the fallen hero he truly was and dumped him on the beach for the night - and to the victor goes the spoils.

An almighty groping and tongue lashing session ensued in one of the upstairs booths for the remainder of the evening but - and rightly so - she had no desire to humiliate her bloke further by taking me home, and that was fine by me.

What I learned from that episode was that ordinary life - the life that ordinary people live is only a fraction of what there truly is. There is another way, and that other way has a myriad of options and avenues leading to it, through it and away from it. One of those had been shown to me when Randall P. Schnipper III asked me if I wanted a line of his coke, but that was all preamble. That was just training. Good training, but mere training. The whole world is full of drugs and they would all demand my company.

CHAPTER SIX

Andy was ten days late getting back and I was doing my nut. I hate to bang on like it was war time or something, but it's easy to forget what things were like before email, penny flights on Ryanair and mobile phones. I couldn't get hold of him but was reluctant to send up any distress flares by calling Mum. It was lucky I had an income of sorts from Ricardo's beach party ticket sales, but that was offset by being homeless when Frank and Simon left and rented their place out.

Ricardo put me in touch with a local kid called Modesto who was looking after his parents' flat while they were away for the summer. The problem was he wasn't looking after it very well. His mates were in and out twenty-four hours a day, nobody had any money and none of the bills ever got paid. Consequently the electricity and the water had been cut off. I swear you could smell the place on the other side of town. They would crap in the bog, throw a litre of something down after it and walk away thinking it was fine. Even though it was free it was outrageously overpriced.

I had been living like that for longer than I wanted to think about when Andy finally showed up. He had the money with him but that wasn't all he had. Grinning, pouting and almost liquidly nubile was the one and only Suki out for a week long holiday too. They were booked into Caesar's and I hated him for that. A week with his girl, clean sheets and running water and there was me, stuck two miles out of town in another heaving, bug-ridden cess pit.

Although I had the money Mum had lent me, which Andy had brought out, I decided to stick it out at Modesto's because it was free and I was painfully aware that nothing was certain. We were into July, the bar rent was due again and I knew we would have to stock the place from absolute scratch. The construction work in Martinez's new bar was progressing but slowly.

Filtering through from back home was news of the ever escalating problems of the miners' strike, which peaked with a day of astonishing violence at a place up north called Orgreave. It was of little comfort to me that mine wasn't the only life falling apart, but by that time I was lucky enough to be forming strong friendships with a few cool people. As well as myself, Ricardo employed two Finnish girls who were out for the summer to sell his beach party tickets. Gitta and Ingrid were lively, intelligent and a hell of a lot of fun. They knew I was in a jam and suggested the idea of pooling all our sales. That gesture put money in my pocket which would come out of their own, but they were insistent and I was very touched by that.

I was also pretty tight with the Caramba DJ, Pete, and his mate Paul. They were both from Manchester but the interesting thing about Paul was that he was a rich kid. His father was a genuine millionaire and each spring Paul would fly out and stay in his Dad's villa at Costa de la Calma and do the summer. He had no need to work but got himself a job propping for Caramba, simply to enjoy the added kudos and celebrity that came with being a worker in a holiday resort. He was a lucky, spoilt bastard whose dreams came true every day he woke up and opened his eyes. But he knew that was exactly what he was, so he was OK by me.

The day Suki, left I watched as Andy visibly shrank before my eyes. That evening he moved into Modesto's too. He spotted a cockroach the size of a Shetland pony and that was it.

The next day we were just hanging around on the beach when he said what I knew he was going to say. "I'm out of this, Mick.

You can buy me out at the end of the season. I can't do it anymore. If I had a buyer right now I'd be on a plane this evening."

My initial panic gave way to flaming indignation. Me pay him? If he was out I'd rather it be without delay. I found Paul cooling off in the crypt like gloom of the Caramba.

"Hey, Mick," he called. "What's going down?"

"The price of a half-share in my bar by the looks of things. Andy has just told me he wants out."

"You're on." He seemed to be running towards the door even before he'd stood up.

That night, as Paul and Andy haggled furiously, a good looking kid with long blond hair hair, a set of pink dungarees and no shoes gave me a propping ticket for a rival disco. We got talking.

"How much are you on here?"

"A thousand a night plus two bottles of beer."

"How much could you drink in a night?"

"You give it to me and I'll drink it."

"Do you have a place of your own?"

"Yeah, it's the big sandy thing between the sea and the town."

"What's your name?"

"Brad."

"Tell you what, Brad. You come and work for me and you'll get no hassle from the cops. It's five hundred a night but you can drink whatever you can handle and I'll provide somewhere to crash for nothing."

He beamed a delighted, handsome smile. "Where do I sign?"

Paul gave Andy a grand with a promise of a further three to come, as soon as he could find his dad and tap him for the balance. Andy bought a one-way ticket out of the place. I wasn't sad to see him go because a cloud of gloom lifted from us.

Then one day I was walking past old Bernado's cafe when he caught sight of me and called me over, palming me a couple of keys and shaking my hand. I didn't understand a word he was saying but I knew what he meant. I saw his smile of congratulation and there was suddenly a massive lump in my throat.

I sprinted up the hill and dived through the door. He had taken everything that was not part of the structure, including - as I suspected he would - every single bottle of drink in the place. But it didn't matter.

We had no draught beer so I simply stopped the Skol delivery lorry in the street and bought ten cases of bottled larger from the driver there and then. Then me, Paul and Brad went down to the supermarket and bought a couple of bottles of each spirit and as many mixers as we could carry.

Then, because Martinez had made it his business to take ours, we embarked on a massive minesweep of all the poolside bars and restaurants in town and nicked as many glasses as we could. We blitzed the beach with hundreds of propping tickets that I had designed and brought out just for that purpose, some marked 'FREE DRINK' and signed by me. Then I buttonholed all the holiday reps that I had met over the previous three months or so and told them to have their clients ready to ship in, because anyone with one eye and half a brain would see straight away that Bugsy's was the best place in town.

We swarmed everywhere like coked up Jehovah's Witnesses on commission and finally opened on July twenty seventh, nineteen eighty four. Over half the summer had gone, but as the man was singing, it was indeed a nice day for a white wedding.

All the pain. All the worry. All the heartbreak. All the money. Losing Andy. Leaning so heavily on Mum. Being made to live like gypsies, tramps and thieves. Was it worth it?

The evening began with three German guys coming in. They asked if it was OK for them to have free drinks and whilst they had no freebie tickets, I figured Brad and Paul had steered them in off the streets to get things moving so I dished out a Tequila slammer each along with one for me just to ease the old opening night nerves. Then they sat there and looked at me.

Then an old Spanish geezer came in, sat down in the corner and pulled out a magazine. Brad bundled in, grabbed two beers for him and Paul and dived back out onto the street.

The three Germans called for more slammers. I lined them up.

"That's three hundred, boys."

"You said they were free," one of them said.

"Only the first one," I told them formally, suddenly aware of the odds and feeling quite vulnerable.

Then two girls came in straight from the beach, lugging their lilos and towels and snorkels, depositing several gallons of sea water and half a yard of sand on the floor. It was almost dark.

"Two cokes, please. Lots of ice," said one, chucking a screwed up five hundred note on the bar. I felt like keeping that note framed.

I gave them the drinks and the change. The girl spoke again. "We are staying upstairs and we hadn't noticed this place before."

"First night, darling. Make sure you get yourselves back in here when you've changed. It'll get lively later on."

With awful, inhuman, guzzling sounds they both downed their cokes in one and smacked the glasses back down on the counter. The quiet one belched.

"Are *you* going to be in here later?" the first one said.

"Certainly am."

"Alright then. See ya." They both smiled, collected their gear and were gone. Get in!

I cracked myself a beer. I'd taken one pull when the three krauts tried hitting on me for more slammers, but feeling valour to be the better part of discretion on that occasion I fucked them off and, although it reduced the potential paying clientele by seventy five percent, I was pleased to see the back of them.

I sat around trying out different tapes for a couple of hours trying not to get depressed because nobody else had come in. After everything it was a flop. A non-event. To cap it all the old Spaniard who was still sitting in the corner pulled out a flask and a sandwich.

Then a fat, greasy Spanish bloke came in but immediately halted dumbstruck in his tracks. He shot worried looks all over the place, as though he had lost something important. Somehow he knew I was English.

"What has happened? Where are all the girls?"

I sighed and pointed, for it was actually possible to see

Martinez's new topless place across the street. He thanked me and left.

The terrace tables of the two adjoining restaurants had not only filled but were by then emptying. I guessed it to be around midnight. I would have looked at my watch to check but of course…

Brad popped back in. I figured he was after a couple more beers so I got them.

"You're gonna need more than that," he said.

I looked across to see him holding the door open for the first of at least two dozen young blokes who turned out to be an Irish amateur football team on tour with wives and girlfriends. Brad dived behind the bar to give me a hand. I knew next to nothing about bar work or what we were supposed to be charging and he knew less than me but, Keystone Kop stylee, we got through it.

Then the two girls from upstairs walked in and with them were two others from the next apartment. Don't people scrub up well? I had to ask one of them what a Lumumba was but that was OK..

Paul came in from propping duty. With him were Pete the DJ and a few of their friends. I whacked on the long version of The Crown by Gary Byrd - and suddenly the place was jumping. Then the Irish lot began calling for more booze which included, for some reason, drinks for me, Brad and Paul and I noticed something that both thrilled and astounded me. No one knew. None of them. About the problems and the fact that all I had behind me in terms of experience was about three and a half hours. And all the resources I had was in the till and on the shelves. No one knew that and they didn't care. They were having a good time in a decent bar and I had made that happen. I allowed myself a moment of contented pride and a brandy to help with my simmering emotions.

Then Randy walked in with six of the biggest, ugliest blokes I had ever seen in my life.

"Hey, bud," he called, noting the buzzing throng. "Things looking pretty good in here."

"Just warming up, Randy. Just warming up, mate," I grinned as

I pumped his hand. "I'm really pleased to see you. I've got something here for you."

I reached down below the counter, very grateful that Andy had managed to do the shopping I had asked him to while he was back in the UK. I held aloft the Glenmorangie like it was a trophy. I swear I saw a tear in his eye.

"Your favourite brew. Now listen, first drink on the house for you and your boys, and for you the first drink is always on me, OK? I won't forget how good you were to me when I needed it. I'll leave the bottle with you."

He looked at me like I had just saved his life and leant across the bar to envelope me in a huge bear hug. Amid mucho macho real man back slapping I saw Ricardo, lithe as a panther, stroll in, the wet oak of his eyes glowing with warmth and friendship. Randy saw him too.

"Okay, Mick," he called. "I need to start a tab in this place and I need to christen it by buying you and Ricardo a drink."

"The girls are here too," Ricardo said.

"Girls? What girls? Mick, get the girls a drink," Randy hollered.

I looked past Ricardo and there were Ingrid and Gitta with two other beautiful Scandinavian women I had never seen before.

I had always had something for Gitta. Just one of those indefinable chemical conspiracies, which I knew she felt too. She walked straight behind the bar, threw her arms around me and submerged me in the most sublime, stupendous kiss. The whole place erupted in applause. She eventually released me and grinned in my face. "I'm so glad everything is okay for you now, Mick," she said. "You are a good boy. You deserve this night."

"Thank you, Gitta," I said, feeling every cent of the million dollars she had planned. "I'm glad you are here to share this with me."

I got loads more drinks in and plonked it all on Randy's bill, which was already looking like the national debt of a small South American country. Things just couldn't get any better.

Then Brad elbowed me in the ribs.

"Listen, the old trout who lives upstairs wants to know if she can buy you a drink. The minute I told her you own this place she couldn't believe it. Give her the chance and she's going to eat you, mate."

When I was a small boy I wanted to be Dave Mackay. (If you don't know, look it up) Then, when I hit my teens, I wanted to be Richie Blackmore, and when I got into my twenties I wanted to be Barry Sheene. Call it lack of self-esteem, but there was an unmistakable pattern. I didn't just want to be like them; I wanted to *be* them. Famous; talented; admired. I had never been overly impressed at being me. But that night, back there in that little pub there were great looking girls rowing over who was going to buy me the next drink, and there were top blokes - men I truly respected - making a point of shaking my hand. And I had done it all.

I was me and I was proud to be me. Things had turned out so well, why the hell would I ever want to be anyone else?

All the worry, all the expense, all the heartbreak? Was it worth it? Of course it was. Such is the power of dreams when they come true.

But the wave, as all waves will, broke, crashed and ebbed. That kind of high - at least not without an inexhaustible supply of class As - just isn't sustainable.

There were other highlights of course but equal amounts of lows came with them.

The first thing that went wrong was Paul, who turned out to be an alcoholic coke-head who cared very little for the reality of having to work for a living. Come to that, he wasn't all that keen on reality in whatever form it came. He got in a fight one night and stabbed a Spanish kid in the arm. The cops knew it was him so he skipped the island on the first flight out and nobody ever saw him again. That meant I inherited the bar in its entirety.

Andy was therefore down three grand and came looking to me for it when I got back to England at the end of the first season. The winter rent wasn't going to take care of itself, so if I had paid him I would have dumped myself right back in the shit through no fault of my own. The bar just wasn't producing those kind of profits.

"I haven't got the money, mate," I told him, genuinely fearful of how upset he would be. "Your deal is with Paul. Or you can come back out there and work with me next season."

But he didn't do that.

One of the things that gave me great satisfaction was designing my own T-shirt. It was a piss take of the old drink problem gag that had been doing the rounds since the invention of tourism. Beneath the Bugsy's logo of the crossed pair of Thompson sub-machine guns, it read: "I DO have a drink problem... But at least I haven't got one of those poxy, fucking T-shirts" We had to print hundreds.

And I regained my self-esteem out in Mallorca. The relative failure of the insurance sales and the early season problems with Durridge and Martinez had left me drained of the life blood of a sense of my own value. The modest success of the bar returned to me my confidence and my belief in myself. I stood taller. Brad put it down to being in the sun a lot and watering myself with all that beer. Tall and tanned and young and lovely … Yeah, I *was* that boy from Ipanema.

And all the time the cast list was growing.

One afternoon when Brad was propping the beach and I was cleaning up, the door opened and this little bloke walked in. He had a receding hairline, incredibly bright blue eyes and a huge grin. Dressed in over-sized dungarees (a weird holiday fad of the time, Brad even let me wear his) he looked like a thirty-two year old baby.

"Hi," he called, sliding through the door. "I'm looking for Mick."

This was back in the days when I had no reason to hide from people who asked for me by name.

"That's me."

I was behind the bar at the time and in need of a break myself, so I reached down into the fridge bin and grabbed a couple of bottles. Problem was, that was the day after the horrendous drinking match between Preston Jack Rafter and Dutch Piet, when they had both slung back too much too soon, and in a simultaneous exertion of pyrotechnic quality, heaved up what looked like their previous week's consumption of both food and drink. Now behaviour like that was not entirely unknown in my little place, but what was disturbing to me personally was that they were both facing the bar at the time. What didn't slosh violently all along the counter spilled over into the *open* fridges, and what didn't cascade down into them gushed forward onto me. At the time I was sporting my customary garb of shorts but no shoes or socks. I thought I'd seen it all. The spectacle and the stink emptied the place in a minute. Apart from Piet and Jack, who continued with the contest.

I was so appalled I couldn't bring myself to clean out the fridge for fear of what I might find in there, which was bad news for our beer drinkers because I had just restocked that afternoon. For the next two nights we would be selling beer to people with extra peas and carrots, but I didn't care and no one else seemed to either.

So I looked down at the two bottles I had brought out, uncapped them and handed one straight to this bloke.

"Have a beer," I told him. "Tell me all about it."

He took it in his right hand and immediately transferred it to his left, looking at his palm the way you might look at your shoe when you step in something nasty.

"Bit of a night last night," I informed him by way of a casual explanation. "What did you say your name was?"

"I'm Randy Schnipper's boss. I'm considering moving out here. He told me to look you up. I'm Tony Francis. Most people call me Franny – or, to those who have security clearance, Captain Francis."

I held out my hand to shake. He took it and the mighty smile of pleasure he gave as he ground that lump of potato into my palm told me that we would be mates forever.

So by mid-August things were cool and we were established as the cool place for all the cool kids in town to hang out. None of them ever seemed to have any money to shove over the bar, but were we ever jumping.

During the day, when the cleaning and propping had been done, me and Brad would join everyone and we would hang out at Dutch Piet's shack of a beach bar, kick back and enjoy our notoriety and fame.

I had noticed her a couple of times. Always on her own. Always topless. Always gorgeous. One day someone was celebrating something so there was plenty of that Pomagne stuff flying around. I took a deep breath, grabbed two plastic cupfuls and waited for her to emerge from the surf. She looked like Ursula Andress, but with bigger tits.

"Hi," I said. "Want some shitty Champagne?" Smooth or what?

She eyed me coldly. She was foreign. She was gay. She was not in the mood for a smart-arsed prick like me.

"Oh yeah, great. Cheers, sit down."

Get in.

"Hi. I'm Mick. I've seen you here a few times. What's your name?"

"Hi, Mick." She offered me her hand, which was a mistake because I pumped it enthusiastically, and when a woman built like that has her hand shaken like that when she's topless... You catch my drift?

"Nice to meet you," she said. "My name's Vicky. Vicky Patterson."

At the end of that first season when things would really begin to slacken off I would let Brad wander around town at his leisure, just chatting to people. There really wasn't much for him to do but he had earned his keep ten times over during the scorching chaos of the summer.

One evening in October around nine, I was alone in the bar reading a book and sipping a beer. I was wearing jeans, shoes, socks and a jumper. It really was the end of something. Murray Head was singing about one night in Bangkok.

I can feel the devil walking next to me.

So the door opened and a big fella in his fifties walked in. The ring of hair that remained around the back of his head was the colour of rust and his pale face was littered with freckles. Big fella too. Heavy. He looked swiftly around the room and, satisfied we were alone, closed the door. You knew it was something he'd done before.

He approached the bar and rested massive hands upon it. I pushed the book to one side, suddenly concerned. I looked up to the concealed rack above the bar where I kept our bat.

"Looking for Mick." London accent.

I took a deep breath. "Yeah. That's me. What can I do for you?"

"A while ago, earlier this year, you did a wonderful thing, son. I'm here to thank you for it."

Well that sounded fairly poz.

He cleared his throat, looking hard for the right words. "You've probably forgotten about it, son, but I haven't and I never will. A while ago you met up with my little girl. You spent time together and she told me you were the perfect gentleman, unlike a lot of these yobs around nowadays."

My eyes flicked to the door. Brad would not be back for an hour.

"She told me how you were seeing her to her car and as she was getting in you were jumped from behind by that spic bastard. Apparently you took a hell of a clump, so much so that she thought you were out for the count. Then he started on my baby, my little girl."

I watched as his eyes glazed over and a thin film of saliva formed on his pink, fleshy lips.

"But you knocked that bastard sideways with one swing and sent him on his way with a couple more. Got her home. None of us, not even her, knew she was pregnant at the time. If it hadn't been for you, young man, my little girl might have died that night, and the nipper too of course. I wouldn't be a proud granddad if it weren't for you and your bravery, my son."

I was just about to tell him that he definitely had the wrong bloke when, for the first time, he mentioned her name, and with her name came the answer. The solution to the mystery.

"This is the first time any of us have been back to the island since then. We obviously had to get Lauren to hospital in

England that night and we've been busy looking after her and running businesses ever since. This is the first chance I've had to come and find you. The baby was born over two months early, a week ago. If it hadn't been for you, Mick, he may never have been born at all."

With melting eyes he held out his right paw to me, and I saw at last. As he crushed my hand in gratitude I noticed he even looked like her and I sussed what must have happened. I was a hero and I hadn't even known about it because I was so pissed.

"I owe you more than I can say, son. I owe you more than money can buy. I'm Lauren's daddy. I'm Patsy Chetkins."

PART TWO

CHAPTER SEVEN

My return from Spain didn't go as I imagined it would. Despite all of our hard work and endeavour, the place was simply too far from the beach and the centre of town to pull in any real passing trade - the life blood of any bar. Sure, it was packed with friends and strangers alike on occasion, but for every night that made money I had two that did not. During the winter, when I was back in London freezing my nuts off riding despatch, the rent on the bar still needed to be paid. Even my enthusiasm was being sorely tried.

Young Brad stuck with it the following season but it wasn't the same. Ricardo wasn't there and neither were Randy and his boys, although Captain Francis made his home in Santa Ponsa as he said he would, and during his months off we would hang out. I knew the friendship we formed would be a lasting one.

Whilst I had no trouble from wankers like Martinez, the problems in the second season came from local residents who, needing to be up for work at seven in the morning were enraged at us lot still ripping it up at four. Maybe word got out somehow that all my permits were not in order. Whatever it was it started to feel like I was holding back the tide and something had to give.

Throughout the second half of the second season we were plagued by visits from the cops following complaints from local residents. Just imagine the scene: there you are on your holiday, slinging back a few, rapping away with whoever, and generally getting into the swing. Next thing you know there are a couple of big, horrible coppers with shooters lumbering around scowling at everyone. Not good for the ambiance.

Then, one night in September, this bloke I'd never seen before walked in. He knew who I was and, in excellent English, called me across to the end of the bar nearest to the door. He smoothed out a sheet of paper onto the counter.

"Turn the music off, get everyone out and close the bar. This is a court order closing you down."

I looked past him out into the cul-de-sac and saw two uniforms glaring back at me. Past them and out on the street proper, I saw a meat wagon. They were clearly not about to take any votes on the matter. And no joke, I can still remember the lyrics to the song that was playing at the precise moment I turned the stereo off:

And I can tell you my love for you will still be strong
After the boys of summer have gone

That was how it happened. The Spanish - don't forget this was pre their membership of the Union - were closing ranks. They wanted my bar shut and if I had managed to stay the execution until the following spring, they would have found something else to hang me for. I sold everything that was legally mine, had three weeks on the piss, bounced a few cheques and skipped the island.

I landed at Luton on a horribly cold morning in October nineteen eighty five with three and a half thousand pounds worth of Pesetas crammed into my pockets: my total return on an initial investment of over four grand, and of over two years of blood, sweat and no few tears. It had been a hell of a party but what did

I have to show for it? A nice tan that was fading fast - that kind of summed things up. In a visit to the barber rich in ceremony I even trimmed the mullet.

My brother Nigel picked me up in his Escort and I crashed at his. That night, as I counted the cost of my little adventure, rather than the anticipated rewards, I was moved (not for the first time) to give consideration to the *relativity* of everything. I'd been away and had my fun, but now what? I was no better off and I was two years further down the road. No job, no career, no skills, no prospects. And what about the others? What was The Stomach earning? The lads from school? The boys from the Yeoman? What kind of houses were they living in now? What cars were they driving? Suddenly that all seemed so important. The eighties rollercoaster was clattering ever faster down the track and I hadn't even bought a ticket for the ride yet.

And Nigel. My brother. This rotund and irretrievably inept wearer of cheap suits and bad haircuts. What about him?

There had always been a friendly rivalry between us and I was clearly giving him a peach of a head start too. From modest beginnings - namely the back of his car and some business cards - he had expanded his insurance brokerage to the point where he had a shop on the high streets of both Bromley *and* Sidcup. He employed six staff, had established agencies with all the top insurance companies, had Building Society arrangements and had developed useful contacts everywhere. In the proverbial right place at the right time, he was seriously riding the mid-eighties boom. I begrudged him nothing. There was no schadenfreude. Quite the opposite - I could always tap him for a loan.

His boast was that his credibility was such, there was no amount he could not borrow from any financial institution any time he liked. He was already into buying up and renovating local properties - a bandwagon half the country would leap upon a few years down the line.

But this five feet seven inch, fourteen stone lardy-arsed berk was by then already under insane pressure; driven to keep up with his peer group the same way I was. This was a fact that would blight all our lives before too long.

"Looks like you're back from your wanderings just in time, old son. What are you doing tomorrow night?" he asked me.

"Dunno. I've just got back haven't I? I haven't even seen the old dear yet."

"You can do that on Sunday. You playing rugby this year?"

"Can't you ask me any easier ones. I've been back in the country ten minutes."

"You'll be coming to the player's supper tomorrow night though."

"Ah no. No way. Not after last time."

"No problem," he assured me, chuckling at the memory. "Just stay up the back away from the stage when the strippers come on, that way they won't drag you up there."

Just thinking about it made me shiver.

"Where is it?"

"Down the 'Cod obviously."

"I'll think about it."

"Don't do that or you'll never get anywhere. Here y'are."

He pulled two crudely printed squares of purple cardboard from his pocket and flipped one across at me.

"Ticket only. On me. My welcome home treat. Someone there you should meet."

"Oh yeah? 'Oozat?"

"Bloke who is propping for the firsts. Top East End villain. Could be right useful to us."

If things were rolling so well for Nigel, I failed to see why he needed a 'top East End villain', but at the same time I was pleased to hear him say 'us' as opposed to 'me'. So I went, and that was when another piece of the jigsaw fell into place.

The evening itself lived up to its normal debauched standards. The 'Cod - The Duke of Marlborough's Codpiece in Shernall Street, Walthamstow - was the customary venue for the highlight of our rugby club's season. Drinking, eating, singing, screaming, vomiting, public defecation. Strippers with scars, stretch marks, puckered bums and saggy tits. Fifteen quid a go hookers in the upstairs toilets. Ollie the Bastard, for the third year running, won the pint of urine drinking contest. One of the Colts was rushed to hospital with suspected alcoholic poisoning. There were two fights. And there was Terry Farmer. Big, bad, brooding Terry Farmer.

During a break in the artistic entertainment when a small but orderly queue of Colts was forming at the gents' to take on Big Gertie as part of their initiation ceremony, I collared Nigel at the bar. "Get us another one," I told him.

He obliged without comment but then somebody thrust a glass thimble over my shoulder towards him. At least it looked like a thimble in those hands, but I watched as it miraculously changed back into a normal sized pint glass as soon as Nigel took hold of it. I turned and there he was.

"Fill that one for me, Nigel, would you? Strictly beer please..."

The voice was a dark, velvet rumble. I turned and looked into a perfectly trimmed black beard flecked lightly with premature grey, then up at a fleshy head that was squashed atop massive shoulders.

"...And whatever you two likely lads are having."

I still hadn't been introduced so I thought I would do it myself - and with the spunk that I had plenty of back then.

"Don't interrupt him when he is up the ramp, mate. My brother buying a round is rarer than Terry Farmer scoring a try."

Then it was like a scene from a bad film. Everyone within earshot fell silent to see how he would respond. It was the big fella's move but I'd got it just about right.

"For once in your life, Nigel, you have not exaggerated. Your brother really is a lairy little cunt."

The following Monday Nigel called me.

"Well, what do you think?"

"About what?"

"Don't be a prick. Farmer."

"Seems like a nice bloke."

"Do you reckon he can be trusted?"

"Jesus, what do I know? I've only just met the geezer."

Silence. Then... "He's got some unbelievable scams. I think we should get involved."

As intrigued as I was I was suddenly a little unsure of this 'we' business, so for the time being, I gave them both a wide berth.

In the meantime, after my mum had fed me back up to my normal weight, me and Brad went on tour.

I had an absolute volume of names and addresses but I should have known that the harder we chased those warm, summer memories the further away they got. Husbands and boyfriends materialised and weren't too happy about two loonies showing up with stories that invariably started: "Hey do you remember the night when…?" It wasn't just a different country, it was a different world. The party was over. It was time to call time.

However, before I did so completely I hit Preston to meet up with Jack Rafter. His family had property interests in Santa Ponsa and he had spent most of that last summer out there too, just hanging around, doing the season and we had got on really well. He told me to look him up.

Aside from the place in Santa Ponsa, Jack and his family seemed to own half of Preston, including a car site, and one time he told me that if I wanted to buy cheap cars he could help me do it. So I grabbed a grand and bought a one way ticket. By the Sunday morning around two hundred and fifty of that had gone on beer, speed and curry, so the profits of that first trip are debatable - but by the evening I was chugging back down the M6 in a neat little Cortina mark 5.

An advert in the Exchange and Mart brought a hail of calls and before you could say 'dodgy second hand car dealer' I was four hundred notes to the good. In return for Jack's help in the deal I got the Vindaloos in next time around. It was an excellent system.

To prove my commitment to the tireless Essex work ethic that appeared to have swept the entire country, I bought a Honda four hundred Super Dream from another bloke I had met in the bar called Steve, who sold bikes in Eddy Grimstead's showroom on the A127 near Romford. I went despatch riding again. Getting through that first winter and into the spring was tough but I was gratified to see a nice little stash reforming in the bank. Although a stash back then would probably only fund my monthly drug intake in a few short years, it was a start.

All was well with the cars and I'd worked my way up to a decent XJS. The original V12 5.3 - not one of the crappy little 3.6 things. Then something happened.

Since coming back from Spain the previous October, I'd been staying out at the Upminster home with my parents. I missed the independence and freedom, but the place was handy for work and for the Yeoman, and it was good for selling cars from. But the best thing about it, and I don't care how naff this sounds, was that I got to see my mum all the time. Having missed her so much over the previous summers, it was great to be back close to her. Then she turned orange.

None of us paid it too much mind. She was commuting from Upminster to the West End everyday so we assumed she was fit. Looking back I can see that she was tired a lot of the time, but in all honesty and to my eternal shame, I can hardly remember her being any other way.

Looking like she had spent a week too long on a cheap sun bed she eventually went to see the doctor who told her she had some kind of jaundice. He put her on a special diet but after three weeks of living on rabbit food she was no better, so she was booked into hospital for some tests.

I was at home the evening Dad came back with the results. I met him in the hallway as he closed the front door but hardly recognised him. For a start he looked like he was wearing someone else's coat. But it was his sheepskin - he'd just shrunk. He looked like a lost little boy. Then I saw his eyes: bewildered, beleaguered, frightened. He was crying. He was crying and I knew.

"Tell me," I said anyway.

"Mum's got cancer."

We stood there looking at each other and we both understood the same thing. We both understood that from that point on our lives would be effectively meaningless.

Spain helped me through the experience of that night and for that alone I was grateful. Spain was the first time I had ever had to stand on my own two feet and cope with a tough situation. Dad falling apart that night was the second. He crumbled in front of me and I held him together. I hugged him, I kissed him. I soothed him. I gave him lots of brandy. Then I had plenty myself.

Around three I managed to get him to bed but I knew neither of us were going to sleep. I lay awake all night listening. His sobs, his cries. His screaming of her name in his grief. I felt I lost a part of me that night. The last of my innocence perhaps. Nobody ever deserved to suffer as much as he did, and I didn't deserve to be there to witness it and be so totally helpless. His pain and my inability to do anything about it hardened me.

We gave up trying to sleep around eight. He went to the hospital and I went to the supermarket where I bought more brandy. Then I walked all the way up the hill towards the station and sat on the front doorstep of the Yeoman drinking until they opened. Then I went inside.

I called Nige from there but he was out. I told his wife Nicolette I'd be needing some help with the old fella and she came over that evening. She told the old man they were making tremendous strides in cancer care: drugs, radiotherapy, chemo. He was inconsolable. She was going to die, he knew it. And he was right.

She was riddled with it and if they'd cut out all the affected parts there would have been nothing left, so she came home to die. Dad dosed her up with painkillers and never left her side.

Curiously it was a blissful time; the three of us together like that. Each morning I would stop outside her bedroom window on my way to work to wave to her. It could have been the last time I saw her.

I asked the courier firm's controller to give me all the jobs they had. Early starts, late finishes, long runs. Anything to keep my mind off the situation. When I came home each evening I would go straight to see her and she would be older and thinner and weaker.

During her last few days it was difficult to tell if she had died or not. Her legs were like arms and her arms were like twigs. Skin hung from her in folds. Her face, once so beautiful, kind and open, was tortured and barely recognisable.

You don't know how good things are until they aren't good anymore. You don't know what you've got until it's gone. Was I a bad person? Was I an idiot? Was I normal? Whevs. No excuses.

Soon after she died I was belting along in the XJ with The Stomach, demonstrating its remarkable handling characteristics. I must have been going some because even that mad fucker was telling me to slow down. I lost it on a greasy curve and wiped out a line of parked cars. Luckily I had just sobered up.

Five points on the license plus a oner fine were annoying enough, but at least all the victims of my stupidity were compensated. Except me.

"What do you mean I've only got third party insurance?"

"That's all you asked for," Nigel replied, a weird shrill of defensive indignation rising in his voice. "As soon as some arsehole makes a mistake, it automatically becomes my fault does it?"

He was lying and we both knew it, and I'm not sure why I let it slide. Maybe it was because he was older and wiser and more successful than me and therefore he clearly knew best. I was just the mad little brother who drank too much, fell off motorbikes and smashed up cars. I found him intimidating.

He flatly denied that I'd asked him for full comp and I started thinking that it was me who had messed up again. Either way I just accepted what he said.

Fortunately he came up with the perfect solution, and the perfect solution involved both Terry Farmer and crime.

Firstly we needed to get the Jag out of sight so Terry came around to Upminster in a recovery vehicle, lugged it to Nige's place in Bromley where we stashed it in the old garage behind his shop. Then Terry came up with some very authentic repair bills for work done on the car from a couple of workshops that he knew, authentic enough and indeed verifiable should some dogged loss adjuster wish to check them out. A fortnight later he came back for the wreck and relieved me of two hundred quid, assuring me that the thing, bound for a reliable crusher, would never be seen again. We then waited for three weeks.

Nigel drove over to Upminster to collect me and together we

drove back through the Dartford tunnel into Kent and had a couple of beers in his local. Refreshed and prepared we drove directly to the nearest police station to report my gleaming, newly repaired Jaguar stolen.

"I can't believe it, officer. I saw some kids looking at it when I parked it up at the pub."

Nigel bollocked the insurance company for an early settlement, reminding them of all the business he was putting their way. Before you could say the words 'sweet little insurance fiddle', a cheque for five thousand two hundred flopped onto the mat. A grand and four hundred more than I had paid for it.

Nigel was so jubilant I had to check to see that it was my name on the kite and not his.

"You see? You see what can be done. If you've got the know-how, the bottle and the right people you can do anything. It's *all* doable."

Unfortunately, the worst thing about what he was saying was that he was right. I could see it and that was when I truly gave up caring whether what I did was right or wrong. It would be easy to say I went off the rails because of the way things had gone for me in Spain and my mother dying, but that wasn't it. I have no excuses and I seek none. All I wanted to do was get ahead, to be a winner, and when me, Farmer and Nige worked that scam I knew I'd found the way in.

But in my confusion and excitement I missed a lot. Maybe I was just being the younger brother but I really should have seen the signs because Nige had been bitten by something that hadn't yet come anywhere near me. He started to see himself as some kind of robber baron. He thought he was Al Capone. Reggie Kray. Suddenly he wanted to start bribing cops, beating up competitors, burning out rivals. He was *an insurance man* for Christ's sake. You didn't get the man from the Pru carving up the Sun Alliance rep did you?

If I'd had half a clue what he would do when the whole paper palace began collapsing in around his ears, I swear I would have killed him myself.

.

CHAPTER EIGHT

I had a premonition. That's actually a bold statement because I was asleep at the time, but I know it was much more than any dream or nightmare. I woke up not with a start but with a whimper and I could tell, even before I had touched the sore, gummed lids of my eyes, that I had been crying.

This was no terror ride, though. No nocturnal journey of horror through the dark, haunted canyons of my mind. I hadn't been frightened by what I had seen - in fact it had been something of a relief to know I would be put out of my suffering by a third party. Almost comforting to know, in fact, that the end of my life would be in the hands of professional men of violence.

So if the tears were not of fright or dread then why cry at all? For the simple, sad loss, that's why. It's such a shame, this loss of a life and this loss of a *way* of life. Why had it all happened to me? Did I choose it? All I wanted to do was be someone and not hurt anyone in the process. That was my business plan and I had always tried to stick to it.

Oh yeah, now I can see. There's Jonesy the printer. Even though he's wearing a ski mask I can tell that he's the man with the big gun, and he is ordering me off the road and into a field over near the M25. At least I know what happens and why, and I'm grateful for that.

Watch out, Micky boy. Here it comes now. Any second.

"Good boy," someone says, and for a split second I am confused. Then I hear the crack of the gun and I feel a surprisingly pleasant warmth. Somehow I know I'm gone, even before I hit the ground.

    I settled into a comfortable groove. I reinvested my insurance pay out up in Preston and carried on working hard on the bike. On the face of it, everything was as OK as it had any right to be, even though I missed Mum terribly. Apart from one thing. Whilst Dad was pleased with the success that Nige and I were enjoying, he would still lapse into terrible, maudlin troughs of crippling sadness that would tear him apart before my eyes. Sobbing uncontrollably, he would swear that if he couldn't be with her in this life he would go to join her wherever she was. There was nothing anyone could do.

    Nigel was up to his ears in it running his little empire, but I leaned on him to get over to share some of the load. Fortunately he needed to be around to some extent anyway to attend to the financial peculiarities that Mum's death had thrown up. The bungalow in Clayton Avenue (at that time some two hundred grand's worth) was now the sole property of Dad. Mum's modest savings also passed to him. Thanks in part to my pathetic badgering, her life was well insured - (Ali had been right after all: life cover really was a good idea). She also had a substantial pension which obviously passed to her next of kin upon her death.

    Suddenly the old guy was pretty wealthy. Having worked down the Royals and then Tilbury docks all his life, there he was with dosh coming out of his earholes. Without Mum, of course, it was just paper. To compound an already uneven equation he opted for early retirement and copped a severance pay-out of another thirty odd grand. Although retirement meant he simply had more time in which to sit around thinking about what he'd lost.

    Rising star and financial super hero that he was, Nigel handled the whole thing. He invested all the monies in a combination of bank and building societies for liquidity and safety, and unit trusts and insurance bonds for growth. The whole bundle was growing nicely as it yielded Dad a good income.

I suggested diverting money into a car deal Preston Jack and I had discussed. I wanted to hire a transporter and buy up the six car fleet of a company he'd heard of that had just gone belly up.

"Who is this geezer?" he demanded. "How do you know you can trust him? They could be nicked motors and then you'd be giving the old man's dosh away to some northerner you met on holiday. Forget about it. Leave it to me."

Well God forbid *I* might come up with a good idea but he knew what he was doing. As well as that Dad wasn't overly chuffed about people phoning up all the time to buy cars anyway, so he would have gone ballistic had I turned the front drive into a dealership forecourt.

It also occurred to me that I was potentially quite wealthy. Well it would, wouldn't it? There was the bungalow and about eighty large which was growing by the minute. Dad appeared to have no intention of making inroads into any of it and when he pegged out I'd cop for half. These mercenary thoughts were brought into sharp focus one Sunday lunchtime when Dad told Nigel that he wanted the bungalow put into Nigel's and my name jointly. He scared the shit out of me when he said that.

"In case something happens to me."

"What's going to happen to you?" I asked.

"I don't know, but if it does there will be a lot of tax to pay, right Nige?"

Nigel concurred and got to it.

The more time I spent over at Nigel's place in Kent, the more intrigued I became by the whole set up. He was obviously doing great, you could tell that just by the way he lived, but things just didn't add up. He seemed to spend half his time arguing with bank managers and the other half down the pub. And even though Nicolette had long since given up teaching at the local primary school in order to join in the family quest for fame and fortune, I never understood what her role was in things. They were both great talkers and great administrators but I knew as well as anyone how difficult it was to sell a policy.

Helping them were two salesmen. One was a spotty kid of twenty they picked up at the Jobcentre. The other was an ex-Spitfire pilot of seventy one. They both had a company car, into which they diligently climbed each morning and (I suspected) drove around all day long visiting family and friends, before going home. As reward for this tiger-ish endeavour they were paid one hundred and twenty pounds per week plus petrol plus commission, which they never got. They were both clearly as happy as could be with the arrangement as they were both able to live comfortably enough without ever having to do a stroke of work. Nigel couldn't see they were taking the piss. If he'd hired two blokes with families and mortgages they would have written plenty of business.

Since they'd been working they had actually pulled a few bits and bobs in. The old guy had sold a policy to the couple who'd bought his house when he'd moved, and one to his sister and one to his wife. The kid had sold a savings plan. To his mum. He'd also knocked out four other plans each to men of around his age who all cancelled their policy within the statutory fourteen day cooling off period. So he'd got his mates to sign up and then renege to make it look like he was doing some work. I knew this because I had done it a couple of times when I worked up town.

To support this astounding commercial enterprise, Nige and Nicolette had a personal secretary. Each. There were two other employees who essentially hung around the Bromley office drinking coffee and talking on the phone to their friends. Their official title, I discovered, was 'in-house sales'.

Baggy-eyed and with premature grey hairs weaving their treacherous way around his ears, I wasn't overly concerned about Nige's ever present irritability. He knew what he was doing. He was riding Maggie's wave. We both were. I had been back from Spain for a year and I'd really turned things around for myself. There actually appeared to be some degree of truth in the rhetoric for once: if you wanted it badly enough it was there for the taking. Work hard and any prat could do well.

Then I slipped off the bike and badly sprained my wrist. It was no big deal - a few weeks rest and some physio, but I was stuck with little more than sod all to do. Then I did something for which I can give no explanation. I called up Terry Farmer and started hanging around with him.

OK, so I was doing alright with the cars and I made reasonable dosh on the bike, but there was a ceiling on how far I could go and I certainly didn't see riding despatch as any kind of career move. By the time I would be fit enough to ride again the winter of nineteen eighty six would be on its way, and the more I thought about it the less appealing the idea was of getting my leg back over the Honda that side of spring. If at all.

The success of the Jag dodge had me curious. I wanted to know more. Brains, bottle contacts. Hmm.

Terry, apart from everything else, was a fence. He knew an absolute army of thieves, robbers and housebreakers who, having plied their own particular trade, needed to unload their booty as quickly as possible. He was always holding folding.

One time he and I were eating in his favourite Greek restaurant - the Yaksak in Walthamstow, when an oily thief oozed in and approached our table. Not only did he pull up a seat while we were still eating, but he poured himself a glass of wine from our carafe.

"Thing is, Tel," he explained as soon as Terry told him it was OK to talk in front of me. "I think I may have been clocked driving away and I'm in my brother's van. So I want to unload, like - now."

"Watchergot?" he asked as the man looted a slice of pitta bread and scooped a huge dollop of taramasalata into his mouth.

"Two videos, two tellies, a Walkman, a stack stereo system with one of those new CD systems in, about a hundred CDs, a watch, few clocks. The normal crap. I also picked up a couple of credit cards and some cheque books. Couple of driving licences. Bit of ID, phone and gas bills. I know you like all that."

"Have the books got guarantee cards with them?"

"Yeah and the people are on holiday so you'll have a bit of

time with them and the plastic."

"Are they in blokes' or women's names?"

"One is a joint account, the other is just a bloke."

"You got it all here?"

"I'm in the car park, but like I say, Plod might already be on this. Got to get an alibi sorted, report the van stolen and all that old malarkey."

"Tell you what, son," the big fella said, lumbering to his feet. "If you get nicked tell them you were in here with us. Young Micky here and me'll back you up."

With that he was out into the night, buying the swag from the bloke there and then. When he came back in... Well, when he came back in he made me an offer that changed my life.

"This could be a bit of you, young Mick. Fancy working the plastic and some kites? I'll run through the whole thing on Monday morning. I'm already thinking of someone I might be able to partner you up with."

I wanted him to think I was one of the chaps. For some reason I craved his acceptance, having become as dazzled as Nigel had a year before. But no, this was real crime.

"I'm in."

Monday morning saw me nursing my Opel Manta through the rush hour to arrive at Terry's 'office' in Walthamstow. It was a two storey brick and wood affair with an office downstairs and warehousing to the side and above. As a cursory nod to the ethic of security he did some legal car repair work but what he and his oppoes were into was stealing cars, breaking them for saleable spares or ringing them. They also stored weapons, drugs and tons of stolen goods. I felt sick before I got there and prayed no one would show. Terry had told me to be there for nine, sharp. I resolved to be on my way by one minute past but at ten to, Cut Throat Jimmy Mulroney turned up.

Jimmy was Terry's cousin and he was a touch unbalanced on account of seeing his father stabbed to death in front of him three years before. Terry told me this in the strictest confidence as the subject was completely taboo. To compound Jimmy's suffering the bloke who did it had got off on some technicality and Jimmy was lining him up for an equaliser. I didn't want to know.

"So why is he called Cut Throat?" I had asked Terry.

"'Cos he carries one of those old barber's razors in his sock. Ain't slow in using it neither."

"He worries me. The way he looks at me sometimes. I haven't upset him or anything have I?"

"You'd already know if you had. Don't worry. He quite likes you as it goes."

"Jesus. How can you tell?"

He scared me to my boots, that nutter, with his dead, shark eyes and his hot, ragged looks. He ignored me completely as he snapped on the kettle and the radio. Don't Leave Me This Way by that little Scottish gay guy was still getting airplay.

He placed two saucers and a hub cap on the work bench which ran down the length of the warehouse wall. Into the them he poured a clear fluid from a five litre can. I thought he was leaving something poisonous out for an unwanted cat.

"You working some plastic and cheques today?" he asked without looking at me.

"Yeah."

"Got 'em here. Driving licences too. Just cleaning them off."

I approached to peer over his shoulder and saw him pull two cards from a wallet. He placed one in each saucer, signature side up and prodded them until they were totally submerged.

"What's that, Jim?"

"Brake fluid. It breaks down the ink and lifts the signature clean off. Don't take a minute. The strip will be completely clear and you can use your own handwriting to write the name back in. Look."

I gazed in wonder as the ink began to loosen and float away like wispy trails of black smoke. We heard a car pull up.

He cocked his head and knew who it was from the sound of the engine alone.

"Your partner."

I wasn't looking forward to meeting whichever bozo Farmer had in mind as my partner but then...

"I bet he's not here yet, is he, Jimmy?" she said as she stepped daintily over the frame of the walk through door. In time, the only things she and I didn't do together wouldn't be worth doing, and if they were we'd be too knackered to do them anyway. Holy shit.

She was dressed very tastefully in a dark blue, pinstriped suit. The skirt hem was pitched dangerously high for such an elegant outfit, but her body made perfect sense of it. Black tights and black, suede, high heels. Bobbed blonde hair. Five feet four, I guessed. She looked a couple of years older - no, a couple of years more *experienced* than me, and on the day I met her I was precisely three months short of twenty eight. My partner indeed.

"Oh 'ello there," she said, noticing me at last. "Didn't see you. Got the kettle on? Good boy."

"Yeah. I'm on duty. How do you want it?"

"White with three please."

"Jim?" I called.

He turned from his vigil over the cards and licences and squared up to me with surly disinterest.

"What?"

Did I need this? "How do you want your coffee?"

"Black."

"Any sugar?"

"No."

I made the drinks as the woman went out back to the toilet.

"What time's Terry normally in, Jim?"

"Depends. Should be here soon."

"Who's that?"

"Who's what?"

"That woman?"

His mouth made a shape that I suppose was as close to a smile as I had seen since I'd known him, but then gave up when it was almost there.

"That," he said as we strolled through to sit in the office. "Is Juliette Dixon. Dixie she's called. She's famous around here."

"Oh yeah? Famous for what?"

"Carding and kiting. One of the best in the business. This

110

must be a special occasion or something. She don't normally get out of bed for anything less than a gold Amex card."

The big fella finally rolled in at twenty to ten.

"Morning, everyone. Morning."

Jimmy vacated Terry's seat immediately and went to make his Lord and master coffee.

"Morning, young Mick."

"'Allo, Tel."

"Morning Dixie."

"'Ello, Terry. 'Ow are you today?"

"Full of the joys, darlin'. Full of the joys. What have you been up to lately?"

She smiled. "Doing my best to keep out of trouble, matey, but I don't seem to quite make it."

"That's what I like to hear, someone deeply committed to their chosen profession. You met Micky Targett, have you?"

"Between the time you said you were going to get here and the time you actually managed to drag your fat arse out of bed, yes, I did get the chance to say hello. Seems like a nice young man. What's he doing hanging around with the likes of you?"

She flashed a sensational smile and made mincemeat out of wrapping him around her little finger. I could tell Terry was at least as hot for her as I was.

"Don't start, Dix. Just don't start. Let's not forget you still hold the world record for turning up late."

She turned to me. "Don't listen to him, Mick. He's always 'aving a go at me. Just don't listen, sweetheart."

Terry was loving it. He threw back his fat, grizzly head and let out a deep peel of laughter.

"Mick you wouldn't believe it. Check it out... Three days! Three days this one was late for a date."

"Yeah, but there were... how do they say it? Insinuating circumstances."

They were clearly using me as a sounding board for their little game, and the longer it went on the more relaxed I felt. If only we could stay there all day talking.

"Insinuating circumstances? I'll say there was. She was coked out of her nut in a hotel room in Glasgow at the time and missed her flight. That's fairly insinuating I suppose."

She sighed and rolled her huge, hazel eyes to the ceiling. "How many more times? I was not coked out of my head."

"Speed and Jack D then was it?"

The history between them was obvious.

"He's always trying to show me up, Mick. I don't know why I bother sometimes. I don't have to do this you know. I'm supposed to be retired."

"Yeah yeah. Many a tale eh?" Terry chuckled indulgently. "Anyway, you seen the cards?"

The mood changed in an instant. To business. Jimmy was coming back in with Terry's coffee.

"Everything's off," he said. "They're just drying. The driving licences may take a bit of time."

"Turn the heater on, Jim. Stick 'em near that," suggested Terry.

As the space heater exploded into life back out in the warehouse, Terry gave me the form.

"What I thought would be good, Mick, would be if you went around with Juliette. To begin with anyway. There are two cheque books. One is in a bloke's name, which will obviously be you, and the other is in a couple's names which Dixie's having. There is also a Barclaycard which she'll have. Fortunately there is a driving license for each of you so it should be a doddle. I think it'll be best if you stick together and follow each other to the counters just to watch each other's arse."

"Fine by me," Dixie said. "I'll watch his arse all day long."

We signed our new ID and there was me feeling like the new kid at his Saturday job. This is your locker, this is how you work the till, this is how you commit credit card fraud.

We headed first to the Wood Green shopping centre as Dixie said she hadn't hit the place for a while. What the fuck was I doing? By way of encouragement, Dixie said: "Strap your skates on, handsome, you're going in."

I was so nervous, the first cheque I flopped down looked like it had been written in Sanscrit. I was almost embarrassed to hand it over. I expected the sales assistant in the electrical goods shop to say one of a number of things: "Pardon me, sir, you have to be kidding" was one of them. "Sir, do kindly have a seat while I send for the police" was another. But not a bit of it. What he did was compare the signatures on the card and the cheque for a cursory microsecond, shove the cheque in the till and give me my camera. Have a nice day.

I stared back at him and felt like saying, "What, you mean that's it? It really is that easy?"

I spun on a sixpence and swept past the watching Dixie. We met at a bus stop down the street as arranged and she arrived swinging her own plastic bag.

"Well done. Wasn't too bad, was it? What you have to remember is that all they're really interested in is a match of the signatures. Salespeople don't want any trouble. What do they care? You only have to worry if they reach for the phone. Then you know you've got a problem. If that happens don't hang about. Grab what you can and leg it and keep your face away from the cameras. Remember the old kite floppers charter: If in doubt, get the fuck out."

Who was I to argue with such sage wisdom? Emboldened by early success, it was green lights all the way. An hour ago I was looking for a way out. Now I suddenly discovered I *loved* shopping. Word of advice to blokes who hate being dragged around the shops on Saturday: try nicking the stuff and you'll be chuckling all the way to the football results.

We went into the same places separately, taking it in turns to make a purchase while the other pretended to browse. High value - small dimensions. Electrical goods, cameras, watches, alcohol, cigarettes, tapes and CDs. And Dixie was just so cool it was ridiculous. During that first morning she got asked out on six dates by slobbering salesmen that I saw. Either side of the law, she would have been a success at whatever she had chosen to do. She was *so* good-looking and *so* nice to everyone. The fuck was she doing hanging around with dodgy villains? Halfway through the day we drew breath.

"OK let's go to Sainsbury's now. Time to get the shopping in.

The good thing about Sainsbury's is if you have proof of ID they let you go over the fifty pound limit."

She directed me to the supermarket and, as we pulled up in the carpark, she removed her jacket. "Time to look more like a housewife."

"So what do we get in here?" I asked naively, failing to comprehend the resale value of a tin of peas.

"Anything. Supermarkets are the best places to go because you can get so much. Everybody needs shopping. Don't you know any families? Do you know the price of nappies these days? You must know someone with a kid."

"Yeah I do actually."

"There you go. Get some nappies and sell them on."

"How much for?"

"Whatever you can get away with. Half price sounds reasonable. You get the cash, Mum gets the nappies cheap and the kid gets something nice and clean to dump in. Everyone's a winner. As well as that the checkout girl will suspect a family man less than an ordinary, single, non-nappy-buying bloke. Know what I mean?"

"Yeah, but isn't Terry going to be buying all this anyway?"

"He didn't explain the deal?"

"Deal?"

She rolled her eyes again but I could tell she was enjoying our teacher-pupil roles.

"Out of each book, Terry lets us keep a couple of cheques for ourselves - three hits on the plastic if it's a card. What we get off those we keep. Terry buys everything else and gives us a third of face value. I always get my stuff in a supermarket because, like I say, they let you go over fifty quid and I need to get some shopping in anyway. 'Sup to you what you get though. Have you ever been *in* a supermarket?"

She may have had a point. I'd never seen a place so big that sold so much. Along with the nappies I scored for an old schoolfriend, I got loads of stuff for home: light bulbs, washing powder, that sort of crap. Then I hit the meat counter and got a couple of cows' worth of steaks. Then I zipped down a few aisles, virtually chucking stuff in at random - and then I hit the drinks section. Beers, brandy and vino for me and Dad, vodka for Nige and gin for Nicolette. I hadn't appreciated what expensive tastes I had until I had the chance to get something for nothing. Well, what was I going to do? Get the home-brand shit instead of the real thing? Chablis, Bollinger, Remy Martin. Outrageous fun.

As I joined the queue of lunchtime mums I saw Dixie wheeling away a load that would have fed the Coldstream Guards for a month. Piece of piss. Soon it was my turn and the sweet old darling on the till gave me a friendly smile.

"Lot of drink," she commented as the stuff bleeped across the disco light of the bar code gadget.

"Yes. It's my parents' anniversary," I blabbed without thinking, instantly flooding with shame at using my mother for such a low purpose.

"Oh lovely. How long?"

"Er, thirty years."

"Lovely. What's that one called?"

Now what was this all about?

"Do you know, I have no idea. I suppose I'll have to find out before I buy the card."

I was bagging and stashing the gear as fast as I could. Eventually it was done and I pulled the cheque book out. The total was one hundred and twenty three pounds and ninety nine pence. Quite a shopping bill back in the mid eighties.

"Now I only have a fifty pound card, but I understand that's alright here."

"Oh no, young man. I can only take a cheque to the value of the card."

Bum info from Dixie. A shame, but it didn't really matter. I'd just back loads of it and start again.

"Unless of course you have some other form of identification."

"Of course," I said, reaching for my wallet.

Now I'd noticed that the license looked fine just so long as it remained in its little plastic folder - remember those? Removed and examined closely, it was possible to make out the rightful owner's original signature imprint. So what did she do? She pulled the thing out of the plastic and held it up to the light. My heart exploded in my chest. The people in the gathering queue behind me edged forward curiously. I saw a security guard looming near the exit.

"What is your date of birth, sir?"

Wise to that one Farmer had already worked it out from the coded information on the licence. I told her. She looked through me. The Terminator of the tills. Jesus.

"Is there a problem, madam? We seem to be causing a queue here."

"No, Mr. Perryman," she said with a smile, repackaging the licence. "My son is a police officer you see and he tells me what to look out for. I was just checking the watermark in the licence. I'm sorry to delay you."

She tilled the kite and gave me back the card.

"Enjoy the party," she said, as I broke into a gallop.

"Keep up the good work."

Dixie was waiting by the car.

"You took your time."

"Phwoar!" I exclaimed, blowing out my cheeks. I told her about it as we loaded up the car.

"Bit odd but it couldn't have been too heavy because you're alright. Coming through again?"

She wasn't joking either. "Are you mad?"

She grinned. "What's the problem? All you do is go through a checkout further down the line. They won't notice. The place is mobbed." She reached into her bag and pulled out a pink cardigan and a baseball cap. She was serious.

"If it's all the same to you, Dix, I'll sit this one out. Watch out for Miss Marple on till seventeen."

Ten minutes later she was back with another groaning trolley load, clicking on her expensive heels and smiling beautifully.

Luckily I had a sheet in the car because our stuff had filled the boot and we needed to cover up what we put on the back seat - easy meat for a carpark break in. Over afternoon tea and cake

Dixie gave me the benefit of her experience and her philosophy.

"This game is dying. Everyone's at it. Amateurs. Burglars. Druggies. Soon enough every outlet will have direct links to Access and Visa and Amex and every transaction will be checked by computer. Already some smaller, family businesses just refuse to take cheques, guarantee card or not."

She looked out of the cafe window towards the street as if to bear witness to the sad passing of some special, longed for era. A golden age when the sun always shone and people left their doors unlocked, presumably enabling opportunistic shysters like her to stroll in and walk out with armfuls of whatever they wanted. I remember feeling fascinated by what she was saying and beguiled by the woman herself.

"Technology," she mused prophetically. "It's going to screw everything."

After the hiccup at Sainsbury's I was tensing up again and she sensed that.

"Look. You're a motorcyclist so I hear, right? So what are you supposed to do when you fall off?"

I nodded to concede the point. "Get straight back on."

"Exactly. Now try a nice little Threshers offy. Always a pleasure to do business with, they are."

I did and she was right. If you knew what you were doing it was just too easy.

"How long you been doing this, Dixie?" I asked as I shouldered the sagging Manta off the packed North Circular, around the Crooked Billet roundabout (when it was still a roundabout) and in towards Walthamstow at the end of that first memorable day.

"Too long. Gets to be like a drug. I've given up a couple of times but I've got a little boy so I can't really hack a full time job. I can earn more in an afternoon doing this than I can in a week working straight. I'm not trying to justify anything. I know it's wrong but... Well, it's what they call a victimless crime isn't it? Banks and finance companies? Screw 'em."

Back at Farmer's, the Escort Turbo I'd seen in the lock up next to the office that morning had been magically reduced to a hundred pieces. Jimmy was loading the Reccaro seats and dashboard into a Transit van as we pulled up. Terry was helping and sweating buckets.

"Did you get any beer?" he asked, even before I had got out of the car.

"Yeah."

"Good man. I'm gasping. In fact, Mick, drive your car right in now. We'll have a sort out behind closed doors."

He opened the gates and I eased the car inside while Jimmy took off in the Transit. I grabbed a beer each for me and him and Dixie put the kettle on.

"Looks like a fair day," Terry said as the car spilled its guts all over the floor. I made a note to look at buying a larger car next time I was up in Preston. Or possibly a lorry. "Did you get all the receipts?"

In the office we did the money thing. I had written twenty one cheques; the proceeds of two - the goodies from Sainsbury's and a very attractive Rotary watch that had caught my eye - were for me. The value of the nineteen others was eight hundred and fifty-five pounds. Once agreed, Terry reached into his back pocket and counted out two hundred and eighty five notes in cold blood. The average weekly wage back then was a hundred and sixty quid.

Wielding the more lucrative Barclaycard as well as a cheque book with all the cool accomplishment of an ambidextrous gunslinger, Dixie copped nearly five hundred quid cash, plus about four hundreds' worth of groceries and miscellaneous stuff. Not bad for a day's work. Farmer would fence it all on and I figured he would make about two hundred quid on the day - this at zero risk to himself, and for nothing more than knowing the thief who nicked the stuff in the first place, and me and Dixie. Then he would shove the cards and the licences away, to be pulled out at a time when he needed extra ID for another scam. Maximum utilisation of resources.

Whilst Dixie was wrong in saying it was a victimless crime, at least everyone was covered. The victims of the theft would be compensated by their insurers and all the retailers would claim payment from the banks and Barclaycard. They in turn would work in extra charges the following year, which everyone probably wouldn't even notice. Yeah, everyone's a winner.

She and I hooked up regularly after that, and we became a good team. The Bonnie and Clyde of the shopping mall, as Farmer christened us.

I also found out that flopping down moody kites and plastic wasn't the only way she made money, and at the same time it became clear how she kept such a terrific figure. Topped up Dixie was a speed freak and part-time dealer. Who was her supplier? Big Tel of course.

Speed was quite respectable back then - not the cheap 'can't afford the real thing' kid's drug it was to become. I liked it with a beer, and scored mine from a bloke down the Broker and Artichoke in Hornchurch, or the 'Choke as we called it, but at the usual tourist rate of a tenner a gram. Farmer turned things around and let me have really strong stuff at eighty quid an ounce. Soon my mate from the pub was scoring from me, and I was off and running. It was that easy.

One time I was down at the warehouse to cop for another ounce when I casually enquired as to the likelihood of Dixie accepting, should I ask her out on a date. The atmosphere became instantly and markedly envenomed.

"Do yourself a favour, son. Forget about that. Don't even think about it."

"Yeah but I just thought..."

"Well don't. She's trouble. You go with her, you'll regret it."

It wasn't like he was warning me off her because I was stepping on his toes. It sounded like he meant what he was saying and that he was really worried about me. I was confused and concerned.

"You want this or what?" he said dumping one of those bank change bags half full of white powder on the desk between us.

"Yeah right." I peeled him off four twenties.

"Now I was thinking, if you're dealing wiz you might as well play like a big boy." He opened the top drawer of his desk and flipped a paper wrap across at me.

"What's this?"

"Grade one Columbian flake, my man. A gram, on the house. Use it for samples, see what you can get going. To you it comes at eleven hundred on the oz. If you don't touch it and gram it out at sixties that pulls in seventeen hundred quid. But it's good enough to wear a third stomp, easy. Think about the numbers."

I thought about them alright. Problem was I did the whole gram myself so I was unable to think about much else - but I knew, I just knew that everything from then on was going to be fine. It all made sense, and when I saw that it was all gone and when, for some weird reason the clock told me it was seven a.m., I crawled happily into bed, and, with the help of a stolen bottle of Courvoisier, was able to drift into a soft, warm place where I knew I would be able to live my life in comfort and luxury for the rest of my days.

CHAPTER NINE

While things were going well for me with Farmer, Dixie and those early, fledgling drug sales, the opposite was true for life at home. I had sold the bike back to Steve at Grimmo's and whilst the old guy appreciated that riding despatch was a mug's way to make a living, he was constantly on my back. When was I going to get another job? Did I think my mother would be proud of me?

The thing was, I was the first real criminal in my family, as far as I knew anyway. Dad had been a genuine tough guy in his younger days, but there was no way I could tell him what I was into, that I was enjoying it and that it looked like I could be successful.

Me and my ilk were the offspring of the generation that had got out: out of urban depravation, out of relative poverty. Out. And we were expected to continue this bridging process and fully integrate our families into white collar prosperity, away from manual labour and the occasional spot of villainy that had been the only choice for 'our sort of people' for as far back as anyone could trace the family tree. I wanted to tell Dad some of the things that were going on in the way I knew Terry could confide in his family. But there was just no way.

As far as I knew, no-one in my family had a record - much less been to prison. In Farmer's family it was considered a touch suspicious if the young males hadn't served at least one stretch before the end of their teens. Frequent brushes with the law were actually considered an entertaining part of the game; something to joke about down the pub, and I envied that freedom.

Freedom, however, was heading my way in the form of a right nice little earner, for which Terry had me earmarked. He was late for our meeting down the 'Cod but lateness was, I fully appreciated, a prerogative always afforded a face of big Tel's distinction and reputation.

When he did breeze in it was like something out of a cheap western. The swing doors flapped open and the whole place went quiet. It took a few seconds for all the punters to realise that he wasn't there to beat anybody up, then everybody relaxed and started talking again. It was astonishing. Then people would jump out of the woodwork, practically begging him to let them buy him a drink. I watched as two blokes took their turn to approach slyly and palm him cash. It was all heady stuff, and the best part of it was he was there to meet me. My idiot, wannabe ego gorged on it.

"Right on Targett," he called, holding out his mighty mitt. "What's the scam, son?"

I grimaced through the pulverising handshake, knowing he was doing it deliberately for a chuckle.

"Hello, Tel. What can I get you?"

"Large v.a.t. please. I hear there's strippers on later. You sticking around?"

"As it goes, mate, I'm just nipping to the khazi. Uncle Charles is with me. Won't be a sec'." A new caper needed celebrating, I reasoned.

Back at the seat we settled down and I was ready for the pitch.

"Tell you what, Mick," he said before he started. "Give us that. I could do with a small one myself." Five minutes later he was back snuffling and snorting like a flu ridden hyena.

"Blimey, son. Bit less gluke in it next time, alright."

"A chap's gotta make a living," I protested with a grin.

So we were set, fuelled and ready.

"OK then. I've got a string of motors fixed. Ringers and

twinned up jobbies. What I need is a salesman and you, my boy, have worked your way into pole position for the job." He clamped a meaty hand down on my shoulder.

"You've impressed with the work you've been doing so far and I reckon it's time you took another step up the ladder and started earning some real dosh."

Manipulative flattery? Almost certainly. Incorrigible vanity? Without a doubt. Did he ever know how to play me.

"Sounds good to me, boss. What's the form? How does it work?"

"First off, do you know what a ringer is?"

I'd heard the word countless times but still didn't understand the mechanics. He sniffed and laughed and laughed and sniffed.

"You grammar school ponce. OK, what we do is we go to the scrapyard and buy the wreck of a motor, but make sure the log book comes with it. Then what we do is we send out one of our little car thief mates to nick a car of exactly the same make, model, colour and year. Then we get them back to the lock up and transfer all the identifying marks, tags and plates from the wreck onto the good car. Hey presto: our nicked car suddenly becomes totally legal. Everything tallies up. Then I get some blank service history books from a man I know, get some rubber stamps made up in the names of a few garages that may or may not exist, and then we have authentication in that way too."

In tandem with the plan, the coke begin to work. I felt so *alive*.

"Then we get you some ID and you go and rent a property. We put the ads in the paper, the punters phone up, come around and buy the cars and give you lots of money. Then you leg it out the back door and we all live happily ever after. The punters won't know any different because Swansea will just process the log book in the normal way, like they've bought a straight motor. Job done."

I swayed with the pleasure of a huge rush and grinned my appreciation at what he had told me. Superb.

"Okay I understand that. What's the coup with the twinned motors?"

He shuffled his bulk a little closer. "Right. Twinning cars is quicker and easier, but slightly dodgier. We get the boys to nick just about any car we want. Then we look around the streets and around the showrooms for an identical motor and simply use the registration number of that car for ours. Goddit?"

"Yeah."

"Then we get in a forged, blank log book and just type in the details, and off we go again."

"Why don't we just do that with all of them?"

"Risk minimisation, my son." He clamped a massive arm around me and hugged me to him. "We got to protect the salesman as much as possible. See, the forged log books don't have watermarks in, 'cos they're only printed on ordinary paper. Now although that's a factor there is practically zero chance it will cause a problem. Did you know there were watermarks in log books?"

"No."

"Exactly. And you are a relatively clued-up villain. In fact, only a car dealer would know to look for them, and we won't be meeting any because the cars won't be priced cheap enough to attract any. I buy and sell straight cars all the time and I never check the watermark because, like everyone, I never think anything bad is going to happen to me."

Grinning like a bastard, I felt the back of my throat go numb. "Like it, mate. Like it."

"But listen. I'll sort as many ringers as I can because it's the most professional way to do things and we'll make the rest up with twinners if there is no other choice. It takes more time and it's more expensive, but I don't want my main man going in anywhere unless it's as safe as it possibly can be. Doesn't matter what we get out of it, the front man keeps his liberty."

He swung his left arm around my shoulders once again and patted me on the cheek with his right. With the beer nestling in my gut and the coke weaving its magic in my head, it was never going to occur to me that I was being used. I felt more like a chosen one. I smiled, marvelling at how good it was to be a gangster.

We took our drinks to the bar where Terry introduced me to a couple of girls who turned out to be exotic dancers.

"Watch out for this one, girls," he warned, slamming me on the back. "This boy is a killer. They don't call him Muffin the Mule for nothing. Get his number. Pretty soon he'll be the ace face round here."

He edged away to talk to their minder and the older of the two went to the bog. As soon as she'd gone, the younger one hopped off her stool and stood so close to me she was wearing my clothes. She looked up at me with cute, appealing eyes, like she was going to ask me to help her with her homework or something. Then she uttered those magic words I was to hear so many times from then on. Those words that flatter vain, foolish men and make them think they're something they're not.

"Got any gear on you?"

The truth was, with all the stuff that was going up my nose I needed the car deal whether I wanted it or not. It was just so moreish.

I'd bought the Opel from Preston - Christ knows how long before, and opted to keep that for myself - but hadn't bothered getting my arse back up there to sort out anything else. The money selling the coke and the speed and working the plastic was good but erratic, and soon began to fall short of satisfactory levels. The deal with the cars sounded good because it would pull in bundles in one hit.

Terry's plan was to get four or five together, each of some seven or eight grand saleable value. After costs the scam would realise around thirty large to be split between me, Tel and Jimmy. It would take between three and four weeks before we were sitting on the cash. I celebrated my impending good fortune with customary verve and panache. I went on a week's bender down the 'Choke and the Yeoman. I actually went some forty odd hours without leaving the Yeoman, kipping down on the bench seats when I was tired, having meals sent over from the Suruchi Tandoori across the road when I was hungry and hitting a few lines when I needed a bit of livening up. It was magic.

Unsurprisingly, several blanks nebulise my memory but there was this one bit that was really weird. I though I was at home getting a shower. I was lying down in the bath enjoying the warm spray. Obviously I was pissed; of that much I'm sure. Funny thing, though - I had my clothes on. Actually, that's not the funniest thing. The funniest thing was when I did manage to get up and out of the bathroom, when I opened the door I was magically transported back to the Yeoman. Brilliant. Not only that, but everybody was there. All my mates. They were all there clapping and cheering and laughing. I grinned massively and hailed them a hearty greeting back, but as I tottered around they all began to back off, waving their hands in front of their noses in that timeless gesture that labels a chap a smelly bastard. Saucy gits.

They parted like the Red Sea as I weaved to the bar to get a round in. Then The Stomach elbowed his way through. "Don't get me one, you wanker. You used to be someone. What the fuck happened to you?"

Distressed at this unexpected slight, I returned immediately to the toilets to compose myself, and it instantly occurred to me how similar the bathroom at home was to the toilet of the Yeoman. Bizarre. I checked myself out in the mirror and thought I looked pretty good. What was he on about, the daft sod? I was only in there for a couple of minutes but when I hit the pub again they had all gone. I flapped my arms in mystification.

I lowered my ribcage onto the bar and scooped somebody's half-empty glass into my face. Then I was aware of somebody behind me. Close to me.

"Buy a girl a drink?" The voice dripped into my ear like it was honey. A woman? In the Yeoman?

"Micky Targett," I told her, extending a grubby hand.

"Cool name. Charlotte Smith." Her smile cracked and she wrinkled her nose and recoiled in disgust. "But Christ, you smell. You smell, and *baaaad*."

She took my hand nonetheless and like just about everybody else I seemed to be meeting around that time, mercilessly crunched the bones of it.

So what did we have here? I gazed into her face. Well now. She had eyes the colour of a bowling green on cup final day, and incredible black, tumbling hair, almost to her hips.

The strange little encounter, I am sure, contributed to my premature demise. There must have been so much blood rushing to my groin there was sod all left for my legs and head. I went dizzy up top and weak at the knees as I clung desperately to the driftwood of the bar for safety and solace.

That night I was punished. For every bad thing I had ever done or even thought of doing, I received an unholy visitation of dark and terrible retribution.

Another time, another world. Desolate, ravaged civilisations. A time of sin and savagery.

Out of the chaos emerged a few. The lucky ones? Battered and forged by fate's foulest plans, they roamed the earth once again. A savage, parasitical tribe, assuming authority, dispensing justice. Among their number strode a fearsome, emerald-eyed, ink-haired She-Devil who...

Enough already. I launched right out of my festering little pit and landed halfway across the room, ramming my guitar into the wall. There I crouched on the carpet in the harsh daylight, sweating, gibbering and shivering. I tugged the blind string and it shot up; the sun pelting in to bully and badger my sorry head.

I looked up at the God-like figures around me: the fearsome Mackay, a fistful of Bremner's shirt. The imperious Blackmore, hunched over the Strat' in a moment of unearthly creation. Sheene, not much more than a red and black blur, but still with the time to stick two fingers up at Roberts behind him.

Up onto my knees, I looked out of the window onto the back garden. My dad was out there bashing some innocent vegetable over the head with a big stick.

My old man was a wiry, tough, iron-fisted, granite-jawed, little geezer. You couldn't figure it out. I was lithe and artistic and he was squat and practical. If I had a problem I would use logic and charm. If he had one, somebody somewhere would be getting a fat lip.

But we did share one bond: We were both fucked without my mother. About a year after she died I broke down one day and bawled for hours in some kind of cathartic unburdening process, and since then had felt distinctly better. For the old guy, though, there was no such relief. He broke down and flooded tears every single day. For him, the agony never stopped.

Because of that, in part, and because of my apparent inability to mould myself into the image of what he thought a good son should be, he and I had a fairly tough time of things together. It was a prickly arrangement. We did not so much live together as co exist on the same premises.

I struggled into my rancid jeans and extracted the remnants and reminders of yet another night on the razz: a crumpled tenner, a wrap with some soggy, spoiled coke still inside, half a ton of change, an unused johnny and a scrap of paper that groggily declared an unknown phone number. I dumped the lot on the bedside table and went into the bathroom to spruce myself up. I must have been in there for twenty minutes, but came out looking and feeling more fucked than I did when I went in.

The kitchen clock depressed me. It was almost three. The old man was still hard at it so I made us both a mug of tea and walked them out into the sunshine. He took the tea but there was no word of thanks. He couldn't even be arsed to give me the usual stick about what was I doing with my life. In fact, he didn't say anything at all. We stood four feet and a million miles apart for five minutes, and neither of us could think of a single thing to say to each other.

He finished the tea, chucked the dregs on the roses and gave me back the mug. He returned to the garden. As I was walking away, dejected at the spurning of my little peace offering, he spoke. "That Terry called round while you were asleep. He says to be careful with the new car he's lending you."

I'd never driven a turbo-powered car before and was keen to give it some stick. Halfway down the street I noticed the stack of North London local papers, an Evening Standard and a note on the passenger seat. I pulled over.

'Get the gaff sorted pronto, my old son. I am ahead of skedyule and we are waiting on you. You might as well use this motor for the time being. It's safe.'

So I went house hunting and once again gained an insight into what an enterprising chap could get away with at the expense of an unsuspecting Joe Public. I zipped around telling everyone my name was Ian Paice, for a start. It was great.

However, as enterprising as I thought I was, people still kept asking me for ID and references, so at the end of an unsuccessful day I called Farmer for a meet. Outside the 'Cod the RS cooled its wheels. Inside Terry slipped a square of pink plastic across to me. It was a driving licence in its holder.

"Peter Williams," I read aloud. "One one nine, Horton Street, Leyton E10. Who's he?"

"He is now you. That's a forgery with a thirty year old's details on. Memorise them. Now you can prove you are who you say you are. That bloke's dead but it's all on the electoral roll - that's what counts. You'll also need that to open a bank account."

"Why do we need a bank account?"

"Asking for cash is OK for the cheaper cars but we're getting a Cosworth together and we can't expect someone to stump up twenty large in folding. Ask for cash for sure but it'll look iffy if we can't take a draft, and a draft is all we take. Strictly no cheques. By the time the punter susses something's up. we'll have the money and be long gone. Now what sort of places have you been trying for?"

"Single bedroom, self-contained flats."

"Hmmm. Have a look through the flat share lists. Get a room in a flat with someone, you're more likely to get away with no refs. You'll have to be on your guard but if the person is out at work then you'll have space and time. Apart from that it'll be cheaper, and we need to get a move on. Get stuck in again tomorrow."

What I liked about selling drugs was that I knew the person I was buying from and selling to. We were all mates and everyone was happy. Selling a stolen car would be different. I would meet my victims face to face. I would look into their eyes and I would shake their hands and then I would steal from them. The ringers might go unnoticed but the twinned cars would come on top sooner or later, and that meant I would be separating decent, honest people from large chunks of their hard-earned cash. It was as much a test of my conscience as it was of my bottle - and Terry and Jimmy's expertise in the workshop.

He was right about a room in a flat. The first place I saw was owned by an old kosher boy in Enfield. But it was so pokey and threadbare and depressing, and so dramatically overpriced that I was sorely tempted to take it just so that I could get the old git into trouble for being such a gross con artist. But even though, if all went well, I would be in the place for no more than a week, I was unable to commit myself to such an ordeal. Who could foresee the horrors lurking behind the fridge or under the duvet?

I was pleased with my decision. Jane White, advertising a single room in a smart, modern, ground floor flat with all amenities close to rail link in Mill Hill proved to be my kind of landlady. A genuine SWF. Solvent, professional, late twenties. Hello there.

"I'm specifically looking for a male lodger," she explained. "There have been some scares around the neighbourhood lately."

"Of course. Living on your own must be a worry sometimes."

"So what is it you do, Peter?"

"I'm a car dealer. I've just come out of a relationship down on the coast so I'm moving back to town to get things started again up here. I'm from the East End originally."

I gave her a few minutes of it and even I was staggered as to the fluency and believability of my bullshit. I rounded off the presentation with a closing line old Ali would have been proud of. "So how much money can I give you."

"Oh erm... Well it would be a month's deposit and a month up front. So..."

"Three twenty." I hauled a chunky wad from my back pocket and slapped down the notes. "When would it be OK to move in?"

She stood and crossed the tidy compact living room and I studied her progress with more than passing interest. She lifted an ornamental vase and turned to give me a Chubb key and a golden Yale. She smiled warmly. "As soon as you like, Peter."

Another meet with Terry. "Nice one, son. Now what you have

to do is get some letters sent to you."

"What for?"

"For when you open the account. They'll want to see some ID, which you have and which corresponds to your old place on the electoral roll. That's fine as far as it goes, but they'll want something with the new address on. A rent book from the old slapper would do it but don't bother her for that unless you have to. Get a load of correspondence sent to you and then hit the local TSB branch. They're the slackest of all the banks. You might have to pick out the dopiest looking cashier when you go in there and give her some bullshit, but you can handle that."

When it came to moving out of the old man's, I was suddenly stricken with guilt. So I just did it.

"I'm going."

"Don't make a noise when you come back."

"I'm not coming back."

He looked the way he did when he came back from the hospital that time. He looked lost, frightened and alone. The sight of him crucified me. Then I left.

That night, lying in someone else's bed in someone's else's house, the freedom was like oxygen. My imagination fed greedily on the prospects that stretched out before me like a yellow brick highway littered with ounce sachets of raw Charles and untouched six packs of chilled Holsten Export. I felt myself come of age that night. I felt myself grow and finally become a man, and with the dawn I finally found an elusive drowse and off I went into the sleep of the wicked and the unjust. And I can tell you, it is a much sounder version than the patchy, virtuous stuff most normal people get.

A couple of days in, my post began to arrive so I took some of that along with the driving license to the nearest TSB, which was in Tottenham. My guts were ripped by nerves to the point of nausea, but sure enough, ten minutes later I was walking out, having been told my chequebook would be with me in seven to ten days. I gave the cold, cyclopic eye of a security camera a perfect full-frontal but, Terry had told me not to worry as they recycle any 'non- event' film at the end of each day.

What I found more difficult to ignore was the police presence outside the bank. A uniformed WPC and a plain clothes officer got out of an unmarked Cavalier and walked purposefully towards me. Icy terror seized my spine and rooted me, helpless, to the spot. The only thing that stopped me from holding out my wrists was the fact that I couldn't move my arms.

But the real joke? A hoot, this one. The woman. The woman cozzer. It was the girl who had come onto me in the Yeoman that time. Her hair was piled up underneath her cap but there was no mistaking that one. I could tell just by those eyes.

How long would I get for this. Fraud? Deception with intent to obtain money under false pretences? I didn't know what they would call it. Prison would be what all my friends and family would call it. Poor Dad. What had I done?

I waited on shuddering legs and watched as they walked right up to me, the bloke easing around to my right and the woman to the left of me. Made sense. One arm each. I closed my eyes. When I opened them again I just had time to look around me to see the pair of them walk into the pub that was next to the bank.

I called an emergency meet down the 'Cod with a deeply concerned Farmer.

"Jesus, what did they say? Have they charged you with anything?" His chunky eyebrows head butted each other like pugnacious caterpillars.

"No. No they didn't charge me."

"Well, what did they do?"

"They didn't do anything."

"So what did they say?"

"Well, they didn't actually say anything either. They just walked past me and went into the pub."

It sounded really daft. Terry's features softened as he considered what I had told him. I hung on his judgement. We were like Fagin and the Artful Dodger.

"You sure they was Plod?"

"I know what a uniform looks like."

"Weird. Must be coincidence. If you were under obbo'..."

"If I was what?"

"Obbo'. Observation. No. If you were being watched they wouldn't have shown themselves so soon. They would have waited until the first car is sold and then throw the book at you. No. Must be coincidence."

"Some coincidence though. The bird speaks to me in the pub and the next time I see her is in uniform, outside a bank on the other side of London where I've just opened a moody account. Bit strong innit?"

"And you'd never seen her before that, no?"

"No but..."

"What?"

"Her phone number. The day after I met her in the pub I had a phone number written down. Had to be hers."

"Did you phone it?"

"No."

"But you've still got it, yeah?"

"I don't know. Could still be in my room at home. The old man cleans up like a hurricane though."

"Right, get out there and see if you can find it. But just give it to me. I know a man who can check it out."

I belted straight out to Upminster. Dad was home because I could see him moving around in the front room. So what did I do? I parked down the road and waited for him to go out for the evening. Why? Christ knows. Not that going there did me any good. There was no sign of the number. Or that soggy wrap of coke.

"Stay cool for a week," Farmer counselled. "I've got ag' with the last car. We'll run a few quid through the account to make it look like it's being used and to see if Plod show themselves. Hang loose. I'll be in touch."

Stay cool? Hang loose? That was easy for him to say. Doubt and suspicion ate their way into my consciousness like maggots into an apple. Every footstep, every car door that closed behind me, every time the doorbell rang. The ramifications of what I was involved in scorched their way along the burnt, frazzled wire of my nerves. But nothing actually happened.

It took Farmer a further five weeks to get everything sorted and the ads in the papers. The two of us and Jimmy shuttled them across from various sites all over the East End the evening before the papers hit the streets.

We had the Cosworth, the Escort RS Turbo I'd been using, a Fiesta, a Granada and a Sierra 2.8 Ghia. Luckily there was a lot of parking space near Jane's block.

I was in a buoyant mood all that day. At last things were moving, but when Terry and Jimmy left that evening the loneliness and the fear shackled me once again.

I went over all the paperwork. To the untrained eye it all looked perfect: log books, service histories, two sets of keys for each car. We even had a rubber stamp made up for PW SALES, which I would use to endorse the receipt I would insist all buyers took with them. There was nothing left to do.

That nights the few zeds I got were deeply troubled. Not by green-eyed Medusas. No. Much worse. My mum came to see me.

My dreams about my mother always took two forms. Sometimes it was the beautiful, idyllic summer's day sketch and I was the contented, short trouser-clad sproglet. Mum would be there, looking youthful and pretty and wearing this green, sleeveless dress that sticks in my mind from those days when the summers were always long and hot. Everyone smiled. It was a silent, cine film memory; an idealised snapshot of a better time and place far away.

The other version was not so rosy. Her darkened room at home. Her body ruined by cancer. Her wizened, agony-scarred face unrecognisable to me. Her mind addled and blurred alternately by unimaginable agony or stupefying pain killers.

That time it was the cosy, summer scene - not that the effect was any different. I awoke depressed and feeling seriously spun out by the freaky possibility that once again I had been crying in my sleep. I pulled back the curtains to see a powder blue dawn announcing itself all over London. Another sauna of a day when I didn't need one.

Jane, a City analyst, was up at six every morning. I listened with heightened senses to her every move: the buzz of her electric toothbrush, the ordered, numbered swish and zip of her dressing, the unscrewing of the coffee jar. I listened with overwhelming concentration as the front door clicked shut behind her. No more than ten minutes later, the phone was ringing. We were in business. Time to get my own back on the world.

It was clear Farmer had set the prices inordinately low on the Escort and the Granada. I got caught out a few times on technicalities; was the front screen heated? Were the rear windows electric? I muddled through. I also had a line for why they were so cheap. I was a car dealer and I needed to move that particular motor without delay for cash because I had an even better earner lined up that evening. Believable? We would see.

The first knock pulverised my already shot nerves, but I relaxed as soon as I opened the door and saw him. A retarded playboy, well into his forties; he had goofy teeth, a bent nose and thoroughly disunited eyes that swivelled independently of each other. His badly dyed, bouffant quiff was so muscly and powerful it seared all the way from his left eyebrow, across his swede and down to the nape of his neck. He sported a herring-bone suit. With flares. He wore a black, roll neck sweater and a gold medallion. I noticed two sovereign rings and a Bangkok special Rolex. In short, he looked like what he was: a mug.

Not only that, he was a mug on a mission because he was clutching a cheap yet very capacious brief case.

After a ten minute spin in the Escort we pulled up outside the flat where I let him knock me down fifty quid for a tiny dink in the bumper. We adjourned back inside to conclude the niceties.

He plonked the case on his knees and pinged opened the catches with that solid, meaty sound that always reminds me of... money, I suppose. I was expecting a sizeable wad, but the lame brain had brought it all in fives and tens. It took us the best part of twenty minutes to count out seven thousand one hundred pounds. Twenty seconds after he had driven off in his new and very illegal toy, there was a thunderous knocking at the door. My brain numbed with fear until I heard their voices. Terry and Jimmy had been parked across the street since early on.

"Well done, my son," praised Farmer, as he stowed

encyclopaedia-sized chunks of cash into his pockets." I may have to introduce you to some *real* chaps after this. What's next?"

"Nothing at all on the Sierra or the Fiesta but there are two blokes racing each other here for the Granada, and another says he is a cert' for the Cossie if it is as good as I say, but it needs to be a draft."

He squinted with suspicion. "So what's wrong with cash?"

"Says he's coming down from Suffolk and didn't want to bring that kind of loot with him."

Terry chewed on his lip for long, silent seconds, then pulled five hundred pounds from the wad I'd just given him. "If he's bringing a draft it will be made out to for the exact amount advertised. If he knocks you down on the price let him, and give him the difference with this. If he doesn't try to knock down the price don't sell him the car. Something's up."

I nodded my understanding.

"Is there a can of pledge and some rubber gloves in here?"

"Yeah, I think so."

"OK. Get started. Go over everything. Everywhere. Leave the place brand new. We have to be ready to get out of here at a moment's notice."

That made me very happy. They left to resume their vigil and I got to work with Jane's Marigolds and the spray. As far as I could recall into my murky past, the police had no record of my fingerprints and I intended it to stay that way.

Two pairs of time-wasters showed up to look at the Granada but then a bloke of around thirty arrived and gave it some serious stick around the block. He announced his intention to buy at seven two - down two hundred on the asking price and I agreed to that.

"Hold it for me, will you? I'll be back in an hour."

"Listen," I explained as diplomatically as I could. "I'm in business here. I have to take the first cash that comes along. You want the car, you'd better leave me something."

He leant sideways in the driver's seat, dragged notes from his back pocket and peeled two hundred off.

"I'll be back in an hour with a mate to go over the car

properly," he said, with a forcefulness that made my guts churn. "I'll have the cash with me."

The following hour aged me ten years, but what else could I do but stay, resigned to my fate? Fifty-six minutes later he was back with his friend who wore air cushioned shoes, a blue shirt and dark blue trousers. He could just as easily have scribbled PLOD on his forehead.

"Let's get this sorted without any fuss, son," they said, advancing on me like a human wall of justice and retribution.

They went carefully over the documents and nodded discreetly to each other. Then they went back outside and clambered all over the car. Then they marched me back inside and we all sat down and looked at each other. In my terror, I noticed my shirt sticking to me like a second skin. Then they pulled out vast amounts of money and gave it to me. I reckoned the cash had been signed over to them, because legally they had to physically hand it over in order to affect the arrest. All the time I was thinking about Dad. Poor Dad.

Then we all stood up. I've got skinny wrists so I figured the cuffs wouldn't be too tight. They offered to shake my hand and I sighed as I forwarded my arm. Then they both shook it. Then they left.

Close to tears, I waited for the uniformed boys to come piling through the door to make the arrest and to tear Jane's little flat to pieces.

"Fuck my old boots," Jimmy said as he actually grinned with genuine pleasure. "Didn't they look like coppers."

"You're telling me, mate," I concurred, slumping with relief onto the sofa. "Jesus Christ, I thought I was dead there."

"They may well have been," Commented Farmer, peering out between the curtains. "They can be good to sell to because the wankers think they know everything. Two down."

In apparent answer to his confidence, there came a knock on the door.

"Into the bedroom there," I told them. "Let yourselves out when I'm gone."

I opened the door to a truly massive man, very well dressed in dark blue pinstripes sporting wavy ginger hair and a huge ginger beard.

"I have come about your Cosworth motor car, young man," he boomed, with a faint, rustic burr.

I looked down and smiled. Another briefcase.

Apart from several near misses at blinding speed, the test drive went okay.

"What will you take for the car, young man?" Came the welcome probe.

We had it up for sixteen four fifty and for some reason I was suddenly feeling pretty cocky.

"Sixteen four fifty sounds about right."

His bone-rattling guffaws resonated throughout the motor. "Let's call it a flat sixteen, shall we? And I'll be out of your way in no time."

I was sorely tempted, but I knew I had to make it look good. "Sixteen three."

"You say sixteen three and I say sixteen. Do we deal halfway on sixteen one fifty?"

You fucking bet we do, pal. "Fair enough, my old mate. Now would you kindly slow down and get me home before you kill the pair of us."

But the case contained no cash - just the draft he spoke of over the phone. When he had left, Terry came in and studied it. It was made out to Mr. P. Williams as I had instructed, and was to the sum of sixteen thousand, four hundred and fifty pounds, as Terry had predicted. I had given him three hundred in cash.

I belted down to the bank to pay it in. Unfortunately, the Cosworth was one of the twinned up cars. The bloke had been happy with the log book when he left, but what would happen if Swansea got back to him telling him it was a forgery before the draft had cleared? Or what if he showed it to someone who really knew what they were looking at and they identified it as being moody? Plod could be on my case before the day was out. Even if I left the flat, I could just see myself turning up at the TSB to draw out the cash. It would be like marching into a gay club, dropping my strides and touching my toes; either way I knew what I was going to get.

Late that afternoon, somebody finally showed up for the Sierra. Paranoia was no doubt getting the better of me by that stage, but those two were clearly trying so hard not to look like coppers there was no way they could have been anything else.

One wore a purple shirt with big, round collars, a multi-coloured tank top, corduroy jeans and a pair of those old, black and white baseball boots, while the other cut a dash in an olive green velvet suit. They looked like *Play School* presenters.

They clambered all over the car and calmed me tremendously by finding the balls to knock the price down from five thousand three hundred to three thousand three. Surely no copper would have been so stupid. Verbally they slaughtered the car so much that I felt obliged to pose the obvious question: "Fellas, tell me. If the car is such a wreck, why are you buying it?"

"Because we are going to do it up."

Keen as I was to get the thing gone, I dug in on principal.

"Chaps. Really, listen. You can slag off the motor as much as you like but I know it's basically sound. Now if you are serious about buying the thing and you have pound notes then it's yours for four seven fifty, but that's only because I need the money quickly. Yeah? Now, thanks for coming over." Pretty cool I thought.

I related the story to Terry and Jimmy and they were in agreement. We were not about to let a couple of con artists hustle *us*.

When Laurel and Hardy pissed off we were all left with very little to do. There had been no other calls for the Sierra and none at all for the Fiesta. With things calmed down Terry and Jimmy headed off with the cash for the night and I sat next to the phone explaining to at least another dozen punters that the Escort and the Granada had been sold. Then Laurel called. His name was Peter too.

"Will you take four and a half?"

I huffed and puffed, trying to appear bored and disinterested all the while trying to stifle my utter delight. Me and the lads had agreed that as soon as the fourth car had gone or the draft cleared - whichever came first - we would call it a day. Not only was I going to appear with my liberty intact and my reputation enhanced, but my just rewards would be there too. What a business.

"Alright, Peter. You've got it. But that is the bottom line. Don't ask for anymore. And it needs to be cash, yeah? Don't spring any cheques or IOUs on me, OK?"

"No problem. All I need to do is have my mechanic to go over it. I'll have the money on me."

Bollocks. More agro. To facilitate things, I agreed to take the car to this bloke's garage the next morning. Then I took a stroll to a phone box and called Terry and gave him the address.

"OK, Mick. Nice one. I'll make sure Jimmy is there ten minutes before you get there. Back up. Just in case."

"In case of what?"

"Dunno, son. You never know."

This bloke Peter was standing on the corner of the Seven Sisters road and the side road he had directed me to. To my concern, he then waved me to the end garage of a narrow mews turning. I didn't spot Jimmy.

The mechanic heaved the car up onto a trolley jack and began his task of crawling all over it. Piece of cake. Not long now.

Not only did he pronounce the car in good shape, but actually told his mate he was getting a bargain. I smiled inwardly and prepared to do some counting. Then he rigged up a lead light and asked for the log book. It was the cheapest car and was causing the most grief. However it was a genuine ringer, so I handed over the docs. without flinching.

We were all down on our knees looking for the engine number on the side of the block when we all saw what we needed to see. Fresh scores gouged out of the side of the engine by some kind of revolving electrical tool. The mechanic instantly stood up.

"Peter," he said to his mate. "Can I have a word with you in the office?" Then he turned to me. "Won't take long."

"Sure. Whatever." I told them casually, feeling my legs turn to yogurt for the umpteenth time in twenty-four hours.

When they had climbed the stairs to the loft office, I crouched down again and double- checked. I didn't know too much about vehicle identification, but clearly someone had simply rammed a grinder onto the engine number to remove it without attempting to smooth down the rippling surface - much less re-stamp a new number in. It was so obvious, it was a joke. I had no intention of sticking around to find out what they were discussing.

The key to the car was still in the ignition, but it would do me no good because other people opening their garages after I had arrived were blocking my exit with their cars. I was out of there but the car would be staying.

I eased past it and began to walk normally towards the street. Then I saw Jimmy standing next to a parked car. Never before had I been so pleased to see a psychopath. I made a turning motion with my hand.

He squinted at me with confusion before mouthing the word; "What?"

I repeated the motion as my walk involuntarily turned into a jog. "Start the car." I mouthed. Then, without thinking, I was sprinting. I was at the end of the mews and then I was out in the street dodging the traffic. Suddenly I heard a voice scream, eerily noticing that it was mine only about a second later. "Start the car, you cunt. Start the car."

I guess Jimmy knew we had a problem and whilst I would normally have reservations about calling someone known as 'Cut Throat' a cunt, it had the desired effect. We hit the seats of his Capri, and then the key was in, the motor fired, in gear, clutch slipping and we were gone.

"What the fuck is going on?" he yelled, over the howl of the screaming engine.

He flicked a left and then a right, and then a couple of lefts as I crouched in the passenger seat, looking back over the headrest through the rear screen.

"It's on top. The engine number on that thing is a total mess. The bloke's mechanic sussed it right away. I think they were calling the Old Bill."

"If they weren't then they are now. We'd better get to a phone and let Terry know."

"Fuck that for now. We've got to get to the flat. Now. My stuff is still there. I've got to get it cleared. And the Fiesta is still outside."

"Risky. If that bloke back there is calling the cops now, they could be have a car over there waiting for us."

"Then put your boot down. The cheque book for the account is over there. The place is clear of prints. I just need to get in and get out."

Far from shatting myself - as I had been for days - the drama and the excitement pulled the best out of me. What a hit. Screaming through choked North London streets, driven by a maniacal nutter, on a mission to clean out a hot address with the police racing me there. I fucking loved it.

If Jimmy was as handy with a blade as he was with a car, then I said a prayer for his next victim. The Fiesta was parked up where I had left it and all was quiet.

"Alright, Jim. Watch my back, yeah? If anyone goes into the block hit the horn three times, right?"

"Right."

I'd anticipated leaving in a hurry, so everything that needed to go was packed in my big sports bag, apart from the clobber which I draped around my room to make it look to Jane, should she come a-snooping, that I was still in residence. I stood in the middle of the lounge trying to cover everything in my head. Had I wiped everything? Had I got everything? Were all traces of me erased?

I dropped the door keys onto the coffee table and pulled the door shut with my knuckles. No going back now.

Coming down the approach steps of the block I felt like I was in the final scene of *Butch Cassidy and the Sundance Kid*. But there was no volley of rifle fire to greet me. Not even a few coppers come to round me up. Just Jimmy. As soon as he saw me he gunned his Capri into life. I unlocked the Fiesta, chucked my bag onto the passenger seat and we got out of there.

Waiting. Oh yes, waiting. I waited the customary three working days and then called the bank to see if the draft had cleared. The clerk told me that while she was unable to give out personal details of clients' accounts over the phone, she would be happy to tell me, yes or no, whether a particular transaction had taken place, if I gave her the full details. I did and she gave me good news. I told her that I needed to make a substantial cash withdrawal immediately.

"It will be at least twenty four hours before we can arrange for sufficient funds to cover that, sir."

"OK. Please go ahead and do that then. I'll call you this time tomorrow with a view to collecting the money shortly thereafter."

"So it's cleared then?" Farmer asked.

"Yeah," I said putting down the phone. All three of us grinned.

Inwardly I was still livid over the shambles of the Sierra. They blamed it on the bloke they had got it from - some small time hood with a daft name - what was it now? Rimini? No - Romanov. According to them, this bloke had wiped off the number himself and was using the car on the streets for a while. When Farmer bought the wreck to match the car he called over the details to this Romanov, who said he would sort everything out and stamp in the new numbers. Obviously no one bothered to check this was done.

That was the first time I had any doubts about how solid big Terry really was. He let me go in there with a rope halfway around my neck. Aside from the risk factor, we had missed out on a cert' four and a half large between us. It was amateur night, and it wasn't over.

I called the bank again the following lunchtime and, at Farmer's insistence, tried to fix in my mind the fact that I was a legitimate customer. Think like a crook and I'd look like one. Think like a businessman withdrawing his own money and I would come across that way.

"When will you be in to pick up the money, Mr. Williams?"

Perfectly innocent question. Or was it? I tried to keep things vague, but what was the point? If the police were going to be there waiting for me then they would wait all day and for as long as it would take. I had no choice but to make my own particular walk to the gallows.

"Mick. If we're going to go, then let's go," Terry said. Where did all this 'we' bollocks come from?

"If it's on top then it's on top. Nothing we can do about it. If it's not on top and we leave it then it might come on top in the meantime, and then you'll be nicked because you hesitated."

He was right and that was that.

During the journey over, I fought to control the visceral chaos and psychological terror, and the way I did it was just by switching off. I stepped out of myself. Que sera. Don't think; just do. Just be.

The cheque was already written, so all I had to do was pull it from its perforation and slip it under the screen to the cashier. "Hi," I said smoothly. "I spoke to someone yesterday. This money should be ready for me."

The kid took the cheque, gave it one look and without a blink said, "Won't keep you a moment, Mr. Williams."

He stood up from his stool, turned and simply planted the cheque on the desk of his superior behind him. He nodded in my direction. Then he came back to me.

"Mr. Williams. Mr. Di Angelo will meet you at the far door." He pointed over my shoulder to the end of the bank.

"Why?"

"Because he will be dealing with your transaction."

I looked down towards the cul-de-sac of the far end of the bank. Switch off. Just keep switched off.

"Fine," I said without feeling. Without emotion.

Mr. Di Angelo opened the door from the inside and waited for me like an undertaker. I accepted my fate and walked past him into the airlock, and through into the rear office.

Waiting.

I am waiting. Sitting and waiting. But this was during the good times, before I began my scar collection. People were still nice to me then.

I am sitting in front of a big desk. The large man - the very large man - sits behind it. His partner, the smaller of the two (although he could still swat me like the low gnat he probably thinks I am) sits with his rear perched upon the desk, facing me. He speaks.

"Mick. Thanks for coming over again at such short notice. Den was impressed when I told him about our little chat this morning, and wanted to meet you as soon as possible to see if there was some kind of deal we can do about the business. Oh, and thanks once again for bringing that stuff over this morning from Terry. That's been a concern. It hasn't been possible for us to go to see him for obvious reasons, so cheers."

"No problem, Pete. Always pleased to help out old mates."

"I understand you and Tel go back a bit, Mick. Used to do a few bits and pieces together, yeah?" This was Masters. Dennis 'Demon Denny' Masters. Bigger, younger and harder than his partner. More extreme. My first meeting with him was proving to be as intimidating as I'd expected. I thought Chalmers had been heavy duty, but... Shit. They are pleased to see me and I'm still sweating buckets. Getting out of your depth again, Micky boy.

"Yeah, mate. Nothing much. A few cheques, few ringers. Bit of gear. You know."

Chalmers turns to face him and then looks directly back at me. For a minute I think it is one of those good cop bad cop things, but I soon see it is more than that. They are two men of the same mind. Communicating without talking. Freaky. Den speaks. "You got a dispatch business too?"

"Yeah. Been going about a year now. Five blokes on the road plus a part time girl in the office. I'm looking to get off the road though. Develop sales a bit. Expand properly."

"I see. Well we may be able to do something here. We've been looking at getting into bikes. We cover just about every other aspect of transport. If your company looks good and you're agreeable, then we may be in a position to make you an offer."

Yeeeeessss! Easy. Easy now, fool. Don't let them know you need it. If the offer's anywhere near sensible, I know I'll take it. I had to get off the road - my leg and my mortgage arrears told me that. The previous evening I had organised and filed my rudimentary books and daily job sheets and they seemed impressed, but Den expressed concern about under capacity.

"On average, your blokes are knocking out twelve, maybe thirteen jobs a day. You need to get more out of them than that. What plans have you got for expanding your client base?"

"I've got some genuine contacts in the companies we already have. Everybody that deals with us knows me personally, and they'd all like us to grow and succeed. Most of *them* say they know bundles of other people all over town who are crying out for reliable couriers. I just don't want to take them on until I know for sure we won't let any of them down. Got to do this slowly."

Then they do it again - that thing of looking at each other and without speaking, knowing what they need to say next. "Turkey time," Pete says. "What is it going to cost us to buy your goodwill? Because that is basically all you have to sell here. Apart from the radio system there's nothing tangible. It's just phone numbers."

Tricky one. I'd heard that a corporate buy-out norm was a price of one times annual turnover. That suited me.

"We've made thirty three thousand in the last twelve months. If we can agree on that, I'll throw in the radio system which cost me seventeen hundred."

There follows an horrendous silence, which I guess is a little more protracted and pregnant than the industry norm. It was Masters who broke it.

"Farmer never mentioned anything about you being a complete cunt."

There then follows a further interlude of incongruous calm during which I think perhaps that I have passed from one world to the next. Then Pete Chalmers laughs. A loud, fat, rich laugh. "What he means, Mick, is we respect you for trying it on, but don't take yourself too seriously. Buying goodwill don't work like that. Apart from anything else, there's nothing to stop you selling your accounts to us then calling up all your clients and starting over again. I'm sure a persuasive young man like yourself could pull off something like that." He holds up his flat palm to silence me as I open my mouth in protest.

"Now there are two ways we can do this. First, you give all your clients our phone number and tell them you are merging with the Road Rats. Then you come here to work for us and take all the phone calls so that your people hear your voice and are reassured it is a merger, and not a case of you using them to score yourself a few quid. You get off the road and get back to dressing, working and living like a human being again. Then, when the transition has been made, you get the wedding suit out and you chase up all those excellent leads you tell us you have, along with a few more we've got. For this we'll put you on a cash in hand basic of two fifty a week."

I am about to say yes when I realise there's more.

"Not only that but we'll front you moody travellers cheques, personal cheques, forged currency and plastic, as and when it comes up and as and when you want. That's just for openers. And of course we'll pay you for the business too. But not what you think it's worth. You can have either a deal through the books with payment of fifteen grand staggered over the next twelve months, or we'll trust you and your figures and give you a one off cash lump of ten large after the first month."

I soar up to that ethereal plane that is only accessible when a dream comes true. How long since I had felt like that?

So there I am with the big boys. Not only am I on the payroll but a nice bit of deserved wedge for the hard work I have put in up to that point. Yes, one of the chaps. On the way to being a proper face. I feel myself glow.

"What's the other option?" Spunky enough to go for anything.

"You walk out the door and we don't see you again."

Waiting.

He had the cheque between his fingers, easing it back and forth as if he could *feel* the crime.

"Frankly, Mr. Williams, I'm a little concerned over this withdrawal."

He ain't the only one. The pulse in my head was making me giddy. I'd been completely drunk and felt more in control.

"Me too, Mr. Di Angelo. I'm expected somewhere else and I'm already late. It's quite straightforward, is it not? I put money into my account and then I take it out."

"Well the way this has worked is a little irregular to say the least. The account was opened just six weeks ago. Since then there have been five or six credits of between one hundred and two hundred pounds cash with corresponding withdrawals. Then, last week, there was a single credit of nearly sixteen and a half thousand pounds and today you are presenting a cheque for practically its entire removal."

I remembered what Terry had said; think like a real customer. I've done nothing wrong.

"Indeed."

"Well..." He rummaged through a few papers on his desk which I saw included my initial account application form and a couple of balance readouts. "I see here you list your occupation as a car dealer."

"Yes, that's right."

"Do you have a car site?"

"No. I trade from home."

"Yes. Is that flat twelve, Oakland House, Palmer Road, N18?"

"Yes."

"I see. And are you on the telephone there?"

I relaxed a fraction of an iota because I could see the number there in front of him as well as he could. He just wanted to see if I had pulled a number from the directory. I told him.

"Is this your own property, Mr. Williams?"

"No. It's rented."

"Does anybody else live on the premises?"

"Yes. My landlady."

"I see. And her name is?"

"Mr. Di Angelo, I really don't think I need to be talking to you about my landlady. I appreciate the account is not regular but that is because my business is not regular. You must know we car traders don't run things the way other merchants do. Large sums go in and large sums go out. Often in cash."

"Just so, Mr. Williams. Just so. Erm, your landlady's work telephone number is...?"

"Mr. Di Angelo I have no idea what her work number is. I have no interest in my landlady's business or personal life and I fail to see why you should either. I don't mean to be rude, but really..."

"Mr. Williams why do you need so much cash today?"

"Because I want to buy a car."

"The vendor, will he not be content with a cheque or a bankers draft?"

"No. He insists upon cash. I don't like the idea anymore than you, but there you are."

He drummed on the desk with his fingers as he shuffled through the sheets in front of him. He knew something wasn't right but he didn't know what it was or how to find it.

"The draft I paid in was not stolen or forged and it has cleared with the full knowledge and blessing of its issuers. You know where I live, you have my telephone number. I am a legitimate businessman and..." I glanced opportunely at my Rotary. "... I have to tell you I am a very busy one. Perhaps we'll have a chance to discuss this further in a few days when I have sold the car I want to buy and need to deposit *that* money. If you feel unable to give me my money, would you kindly prepare a draft to the full balance of my account, shut the thing down and I'll walk over the road to Barclays and see how I get on over there."

Fairly poz, I thought

More finger drumming. Eventually he rose from his desk. Shit.

"Just one moment, Mr. Williams."

He must have known that leaving me alone in that cell was the worst thing he could have done. Naked, helpless and trapped. I closed my eyes and waited. Waited once again for something bad to happen to me.

I endured more than five minutes of silent agony before Mr. Di Angelo finally rejoined me. He was not alone. He had help. He needed it. He needed it to carry all the money. I sprang from the chair and whipped out the plastic Sainsbury's bag I had in my pocket.

Trumpets blared. A choir sang.

Out on the street after all the handshaking and apologising and the "We need to be so careful these days", the sun was shining. It was glory all the way. Made it. I had taken over sixteen thousand pounds that weren't mine out of a bank and nobody had got hurt. I pulled my nicked Raybans from my top pocket and slipped into my Essex swagger.

Out of the bank I turned left. Twenty yards down the first side street were Terry and Jimmy in Terry's fat X Pack Granada. As soon as they saw me the car blared into life. I hopped into the back and they took off like a dragster at Santa Pod. If the noise of the flaming tyres was not enough to alert everyone to the fact that three villains were making a getaway from a bank, then the billowing clouds of pungent blue smoke certainly were.

"'Old up. 'Old up," I shouted as I slammed onto the rear parcel shelf. We screamed down the road with me defying gravity until we met a junction. Farmer hit the anchors and I flew towards the front of the car, my head and shoulders jamming painfully between the two seats. Then, the second he saw it was clear to go, he stomped on the loud pedal and I was once again smearing my face all over the rear screen.

"Easy easy. Fuck's sake. What's going on?" I yelled.

"What happened? What happened? Where's Plod? Did they clock my plate? Shit, I knew we should have nicked a motor for this." I heard Farmer holler.

"The door. The fucking door." This was Jimmy. "His door ain't even shut."

To my horror I saw that he was right. I threw the bag under

his seat and leaned clean out of the car to heave it shut. We must have been doing seventy down a side street.

"Easy. Terry easy, Jesus. Slow down will you. What is the problem?"

"You tell me," he called over his shoulder as I tried to unstick myself from the ceiling. "The signal. You used the signal."

"Signal? What sig…?" Then I fell in.

We had agreed that if anything went wrong but I made it out of the bank I would give them a signal to let them know I was in trouble. The signal was me wearing sunglasses.

"Shit. Sorry, lads. My mistake," I tried to explain sheepishly. "It's okay, Terry. Really. Slow down. We're sweet." I grinned happily when I knew what it was.

"It was just sunny that was all. I forgot. Oops."

The car slowed. The mood changed from one of desperation to hope.

"Sunny?" Terry bellowed. "Sunny, you plank. So what happened?"

I reached down to the bag and pulled out one of the bundles and used it to playfully slap him around the chops.

"Sixteen and a half grand is what happened," I howled joyfully.

Back at Terry's warehouse, the coke was all over the place. I didn't really need it because the buzz I got from walking into the lion's den and then walking out with the necessary was enough to keep me flying for weeks. But I hogged loads anyway. More than I'd ever had in one go. When divvy up time came around, I was pleased I had.

I had paid out four hundred and eighty pounds to Jane in rent and this was paid straight back to me. Then Terry got to work listing his exes. Buying the wrecks, paying the thieves for the nicked motors, repairing the nicked ones with regard to new locks etc., buying the moody log books, service histories, tax discs and valeting the cars had cost him five thousand two hundred and fifty pounds. It sounded like a lot but I couldn't ask to see his receipts.

This left a net profit on the scam of twenty two thousand nine hundred and seventy pounds (I had left fifty in the account in some vain attempt to make things look more realistic. I wasn't going back for it). Split three ways we each came out with seven thousand six hundred and fifty quid plus some change. A fair enough chunk in itself and, bearing in mind we got away with it, you could say it was a just reward for a couple of months' play acting and about six days of concentrated terror. Then I thought of the debacle of the Sierra. That really pissed me off as, although it was someone else's mistake, there was only ever going to be one victim and that was me. No one even apologised.

I kept expecting someone to offer me some kind of bonus too. A tangible recognition of all I had been through on behalf of the chaps. That didn't happen either, and the resentment boiled.

Farmer had shelled out a ton of dough up front and had put the whole thing together so I could understand why an equal share for him was fair, but all Jimmy had done was work on the cars and help out now and then. He even let the Sierra slip through, and yet he copped for the same amount as me. Not only that, he had been working every day for the two months' duration of the scam, earned wages, slept in his own bed. Took zero risk.

To compound the insult I then found myself being asked to perform all manner of menial yet risky favours. Delivering packages, picking up money, dropping the occasional moody draft. It seemed like mine was the only face available to go up-front. Not just that though - it was crime wasn't it? And crime, well, it's just wrong. I don't mean against the law wrong, I mean the morality of it. People suffered and that screwed my head. That bloke who bought the Cosworth. He was really nice and I'd lifted a fortune from him, and I burned with the shame.

So, no more stealing. No more villainy. Unless, of course, there was an absolute *ton* of dough at the end of it.

I called up Preston Jack with a view to resurrecting my car dealing career. He answered the phone and it was great to hear his huge, syrupy voice, but there would be no car deals for a while.

"I'm back over to Santa Ponsa. Leaving on Thursday in fact. Are you up for it?"

OK, so I'd left under slightly tricky circumstances, but that was two and a half years before. Once again, Mallorca beckoned. Yes - too right I was up for it.

Before I left there were one or two things that needed sorting. Since I'd finished the scam I had been crashing in Nigel's spare room, but what with his little boy finding his way around that was only ever going to be temporary. I rented a one bedroomed flat close by in Bromley for ninety pounds a week.

I needed to pick up all my stuff that was still over at the old man's - something I wasn't exactly looking forward to. I'd called him a few times since I'd left, but I hadn't actually been over there since that night. I still felt deeply for him but didn't see how there was any way we were ever going to get along. I still had my keys so I just held my breath, walked in and started pulling stuff out of the wardrobes. He came into the bedroom and told me he was doing a nice cauliflower cheese for tea. That was it.

Over the meal I told him that I had taken on this nice little place down in Bromley so I could be near Nige because we were going to be working closely together. He was pleased. I asked him if it would be OK for me to crash the night and he told me there would always be a place for me. I was genuinely touched.

The other good news was that it was Friday night, so I thought I would hit the Yeoman to see if any of the boys were around. I got in there and things just kept getting better because it was Davey Watkin's birthday. I was in raptures. Top of the world, ma. A new home, a holiday planned and my stake money back in my pocket. To prove to the lads how well I was doing I made a concerted effort to spend the entire proceeds of the scam in one night. Everybody was pleased to have a drink and a laugh with me, except one of them.

The Stomach didn't move from his spot in the corner all night. I raised my eyebrows across the room at him. Know what he did? Bastard blanked me. What was that all about?

Not that I had time to worry about that because something was happening that was spoiling the ambience somewhat. For me anyway. The girl of my dreams walked in. Yeah, *that* girl of *that* dream. Weird thing was, even though she still had the plain clothes back-up, she was by then working as a nurse. But they didn't nick me and there was no need for any first aid either. What she did do, to uproarious acclaim, was walk up to Davey, take all her clothes off and shove her tits in his face.

It was all too much for me. I got out of there quick and for once, settled for a quiet night in.

CHAPTER TEN

Going back to Mallorca was unreal. It felt like I belonged.

By then it was around about the summer of eighty-seven, the sun was a killer (had I really *worked* in those conditions?), and in the airwaves there were the beginnings - the first stirrings of something coming. Something pivotal just around the corner, but no-one knew what. Remember Pump Up The Volume?

Some things, though, weren't quite so cool. Even though I had more money than I knew what to do with, effectively I was a punter once again. I had no bar in which to schmooze, no propping tickets to give out and no beach party to run. As well as that, the spectre of AIDS now loomed over the nocturnal proceedings. Everybody was just that little bit shyer than a few years before.

I was a Billy Bunter to be sure, in the queue with the rest of them. Well, not quite.

Preston's mum owned a small complex of three bedroomed, luxury villas that nestled nicely around their own private pool in an acre of wooded grounds. The whole spread, where I had crashed in my final days on the island last time around, was on the smart side of town, natch'. Jack had said that even though he and plenty of other relatives were over from Lancashire, he was sure he could squeeze me in somewhere.

I jumped a fast black from the airport and in the thirty

minutes it took to carry me to my destination, I was once again seduced. The island and all its life and beauty held me spellbound. From the first glimpses of its rocky, sparsely populated north, visible as the plane winged in from the Catalan coast, to the sectioned, windmilled smallholdings surrounding Palma International. From the packed, frenetic loopings of the Paseo Maritimo, overlooked inland by the cathedral and fringed on the seaboard side by the forest of yacht masts of the Club de Mar. From the first sightings of the packed tourist centres of Palma Nova and Magaluf, cosseted by breaths of orange and olive trees, carried on warm north easterlies across the island's agricultural interior, I travelled onwards and outwards towards the charm and the cosiness of my home. My Santa Ponsa.

All the way I was grinning like an idiot; all the way from the outskirts of town, past Las Rocas and Frank's place and out to Jack's mum's gaff. The cab fare was two thousand three hundred pesetas. I was feeling so good I flipped the driver a five.

I walked up the drive and heard a voice. "Mr. Targett, in person. The old town is honoured.

Back in the day, Captain Francis would spend as much time in Bugsy's as me - often more, as he was apt to crash over after eleven or twelve 'small' Bacardi and lemonades.

"What were you a Captain of when you were in the navy?" I had asked him, in all innocence, as we faced each other across the bar one night.

"A Destroyer. But please, I urge you, Mr. Targett. Security at all times. This is not a secure building."

The Captain had a marvellous, self-mocking tone that endeared him to everyone who met him. He was modest, generous, humorous and charming. He was a little short and was going bald, but as popular with the girls as he was with the blokes, because he was basically the nicest person any of us had ever met. We all knew his naval experience solely consisted of being a sixteen-year-old cabin boy on a rust bucket freighter in the merchant navy, and that his service lasted only as long as it took to get to Singapore, where he jumped ship on account of falling desperately in love with the first dockside hooker he met.

We all knew he had as much chance of Captaining a Destroyer as he had of stopping his gleaming dome from peeling in the sun every time he ventured out without the Chicago Cubs baseball cap, which he always remembered to put on at night but always managed to forget during the day. We all knew he was a bit mad, and we all knew he did far too much coke, but we all loved him dearly.

He explained that Preston Jack and Preston's mum were, at that precise moment, collecting more relatives from the airport and that things were in fact looking a little crowded chez Preston in the sun. Many apologies were to be passed on, but it wasn't a problem. Indeed it was *far* from being a problem. He grabbed my case and chucked it into the back of the open- topped, open-sided jeep he was renting. Off we popped.

"Fact is, Mr. Targett, after a period of some unrest in the oilfield, things seem to be picking up again. Six months ago, I got back with my old lot Amoco. I'm back in the North Sea doing three weeks on and three off. It's looking good for at least a couple of year's work, So I've taken on the lease of a nice little bolt hole up on the hill."

We trundled along merrily until he finally swung off the winding, hillside approach road, Calle Rey Fernando Aragon.

"Consider this your Spanish residence," he announced grandly, extending an arm out towards a small, white block of (obviously very exclusive) apartments, which stood guard over a dazzling azure pool.

"Not too bad, Captain. Not too shabby at all, my old mate."

It was a stunning place. Just eighteen months old, it was light, clean, airy and - perhaps most attractive of all - free. There were three large double bedrooms, a fully appointed kitchen, a bathroom, a shower room and a huge, luxuriously furnished living room: in one corner of which gleaming black boxes of hi-tech stereo, video, TV and satellite equipment were crammed. A terrace, three yards wide, ran the length of one side of the place and around along the front, overlooking the swimming pool, Santa Ponsa, the bay and out to sea.

That afternoon, as the sun slowly set, way out to sea like a huge, fat Spanish tomato, the good Captain and I took our leisure on easy chairs with feet propped up onto the terrace wall, and I was moved to think just how far I'd come. To facilitate these glowing thoughts and recollections I mixed us fearsome cocktails, as I had in times of yore, and Franny did what he always did and got the coke out. He slipped on The Joshua Tree.

I thought back to the time me and Andy were crammed into a filthy sweat box over in Magaluf; how we had to steal to give ourselves a chance. It was gratification delay of the rarest form, and the booze, coke and gorgeous surroundings combined to instil in me the greatest feeling of warmth and satisfaction I had ever known. A misty film of contentment gently stung my eyes and the slightest constriction, which I suppose could have been the Charles, gripped my throat. I sat in reverent silence and paid grateful homage to the weird beauty of my life.

However, I needed to be careful, because the brake pads were wearing thin, even then.

I met an Irish girl around midnight one night and I was well on the way. The period between two o'clock and ten the next morning, when I was awoken by her and her mate twanging elastic bands onto my naked, upturned rump, was a complete blank. It was the first time I couldn't remember if I'd shagged a girl or not.

"Have you checked the weapon?" asked the Captain when I reported back to HQ.

"No."

"I think you should. This could be a matter of historical record."

"What could?"

"The fact that you may or may not have shafted the ugliest female in the history of Santa Ponsa."

I actually thought it was quite funny that I couldn't remember.

A few evenings later, I was swimming in the pool. There seemed to be a lot of people running around, fussing and shouting and waving their arms in the air. I waved back and carried on with the ordered, measured rhythm of my stroke.

Franny explained to me later: swimming in the evenings was

frowned upon. In fact, because of the risk of accidents, swimming after dark was not allowed. However, that minor transgression of the by-laws was not the main cause of concern. The real problem was the way I had entered the pool.

"Shit. I wasn't naked, was I?"

Franny wasn't smiling so I knew I'd screwed up more than usual. He calmly told me that I was correctly dressed for the pool in my regulation Speedos. The major gripe was that I had entered the pool directly from the balcony of his apartment three stories above.

I listened, dumbstruck, as he told me the guy who lived below him was coming home at exactly that time, and looked up to see me, balanced on the edge of the terrace wall. To my credit, apparently it was a perfect swallow dive the young guns of Acapulco would have been proud of. I missed the edge of the pool by eighteen inches.

On that visit I was there for two weeks. For the second week we were joined by Franny's brother Bill. He had his mate Jim with him. Because of the arrangements there was nothing immediately suspicious about them crashing out in the same bed.

"Tell you what, lads," I offered. "We'll use my room as a shag pad. The first one back here with an old slapper can go in there. Anyone else home after that with anything has to negotiate. Fair?"

My logistical foresight seemed only to embarrass them, so I let it drop. I cracked on after a few days anyway.

Bill turned out to be an excellent bloke. He was more or less like Franny, except that he was gay, had more hair and less money. His appetite for drugs, however, certainly matched that of his brother.

Five o'clock was the time designated by the good Captain as 'cocktails on the poop deck' time. This meant that whatever we were doing - sleeping, swimming, diving, fornicating or whatever - all four of us had to report to Franny's terrace where we would drink cocktails and take drugs.

I had brought plenty of speed and coke out with me, which was concealed discreetly inside a zippered money belt I'd found in Romford market. Franny had a good coke connection on the island and Bill and Jim had brought out a couple of ounces of puff. Yeah - try moving that amount of drugs across borders now.

Franny's drinks cabinet was twice as well stocked as Bugsy's had ever been. I was head barman whilst Franny was chief lineman, and Bill rolled the joints. From five o'clock until the sun went down, or until we were once again capable of physical movement, we would sit in that wonderful, sun-drenched spot and get totally fucked up. It was decadent, it was idyllic, it was Santa Ponsa. It was my life, for two weeks anyway, and I couldn't have been happier.

Bill's bloke, Jim Titmus, was prone to babbling on about nothing, but he was a printer so I guess he had an excuse.

"I'm a partner in a firm in Redhill in Surrey. We have plate making facilities, a two colour press and we are soon to take delivery of a Heidelberg four colour. We have laminating facilities too. We do proofing, design, cutting, folding, typesetting, practically every printing process there is."

"Uh huh," I said.

"These new Heidelbergs are fantastic. The run through capability is phenomenal."

"That a fact?"

"Sure. It's costing an arm and a leg but it will be worth it. It opens up whole new avenues of possibility for us."

"I can see that it might."

"Yes. Blah blah, drone, zzzzzz... "

At the time, obviously, I had no idea that a few short years down the road Jim would effectively save my life. But I just got out of there and went for a walk. Having a stroll around the town was something I had been meaning to do for the previous ten days, but I couldn't seem to get around to it. Jim got me moving though. I grabbed a towel, pulled my cut downs on over my trunks and padded off to the beach.

It was bedlam down there. People were falling all over each other. New water skiing and windsurfing schools. A new disco had been built slap bang in the middle of town and there was a small army of proppers doing the rounds for that. In response, Caramba supremo Helmut had extra kids out too.

There were building sites everywhere, and cheap apartments and shops were spreading their white-walled tentacles all over the down-market side of the bay. Things were certainly changing in the old town and not for the better.

Something else that was different was Piet the Dutchman's shack of a beach bar. Different in that it wasn't there anymore. According to Franny, the local council in Calvia had passed a resolution banning the sale of drinks on beaches in Santa Ponsa. As Piet's bar was the only one on the beach it seemed that someone in power basically had it in for him, perhaps in the same way as people may have had it in for me.

There were changes in personnel too. Nothing lasts forever, but I was disappointed to hear so many had moved on. Ricardo was by then working in Lanzarote. Bouncing a disco door someone told me, being cool, taking no shit. Randy was working in the Far East and spending his off time in Bangkok. Pete the DJ was back in the UK, and of course Paul was never going to show his face back on the island. Frank and Simon? Gitta and Ingrid? Moved on. Grown up. Parents. Who knew?

Even though Piet's bar had gone, my memory told me enough about the layout of the beach to lead me to the spot where I knew I wanted to sit down. I spread my towel out, kicked off my trainers and my cut-downs, and laid out on the exact spot where I had met Vicky Patterson.

Me and Vicky had got it together during that first season but it didn't last long. It didn't last long because we both knew, somehow, that it was worth more than that. I can sum her up by recalling what she did the first night we got it on. I was getting my kit off.

"Wow," she murmured admiringly. "Not many people get better looking the more clothes they take off, but you do."

I was so touched, so moved by her affection I couldn't speak. Then this tiny light appeared in her eyes, a twitch of a muscle at the corner of her mouth. Confusion. Then her fabulous beaming smile, her eyes full of life, her head thrown back in pure joy.

"Hahahaha! Had you going there, you bastard, didn't I?"

How can you not love a person like that forever?

I laughed out loud sitting there on the beach on my own. Vicky Patterson. Wow. I'd spoken to her on the phone a couple of times. I wanted to go and see her, but it would be different, wouldn't it?

I crashed out with a huge grin on my face and when I woke up a couple of hours later, my skin buzzing from the sun, it was still there. I strode to the water's edge and flopped into the surf, swimming out for twenty strokes and then back. All I wanted was to wake myself up and prepare myself for what I had to do next. What I had been meaning to do since I'd arrived on the island.

I needed to make a pilgrimage. I needed to exorcise some ghost or other. I needed to visit the bar.

The very thought of Santa Ponsa niggled me. I was looking forward to the break and to renewing some old friendships, but I'd had no idea how I would truly feel. Spain had given me a hard time and had cost me. Not just in financial terms either. Meeting up with Franny and the chaps and thinking about Vicky and Piet and the others, though, had convinced me I had gained far more than I'd lost. So I felt confident about going to Bugsy's. I decided to do so during the day for two reasons. Firstly, there was less chance of it being open so I wouldn't need to go inside and see some berk running my lovely pub and, secondly, to get to the bar I had to go past the Monte Carlo topless place, which would definitely not be open. If I saw Martinez I had no idea what I'd be tempted to do, and I didn't need the ag' on holiday.

So it was up the hill, across the cul-de-sac and there I stood outside. Except that there was something ever so slightly amiss. I looked at Paco's on one side and then I looked at the Pepperpot on the other. I stood there looking for a good half a minute ,before I realised what was wrong with the pub. It wasn't there anymore either.

I gushed sweat in a fit of panic until I figured out what must have happened. Bernado had sold the freehold to Paco and he had knocked down the dividing wall to extend his restaurant. That was fine by me because if I couldn't have it then no one should, and it would be remembered the way it had been at the end: a place for fun, nutty people run by a fun, nutty bloke. That was a fitting testament. It would always be my bar.

I sniffed and checked my watch. Almost poop deck time. As I was walking back to the street I spotted a young kid sitting on the wall. I hadn't noticed him on the way in, but he looked settled. Had he been watching me. As I neared him and looked into his huge, brown eyes and handsome, adolescent features I could have sworn I'd seen him before. He had the courage to hold my gaze and I sensed he was feeling the same thing about me. I smiled at him but he didn't smile back. Then I left.

I grabbed a quick shower just as Bill was sticking on *Sign 'O' the Times* and settled down as Franny was hacking out four six-inch lines of Bolivia's finest. Feeling the need to excavate my blocked bugle, I blew my nose. Afterwards the bog roll looked like it had been dipped in raspberry jam. Eurgh. Right! I said firmly to myself. As of now, no more coke.

"There's a line here for you, Mr. Targett." Franny called.

"Nice one," I replied. I hoiked the burning flake painfully up my schnozz and recounted my experience. They listened attentively and then Franny began to speak.

"'You should be proud," he told me. "There are people all over Europe who know you. Blokes working in the North Sea, in the Far East, in Egypt. People in Scandinavia. Loads of people have great memories of their holiday out here and of the times they spent with you in that bar. You've made a lot of people happy. You're famous." He paused to dab a goodly fingerprint of wiz around his gums.

"On the rig the other day we had this new derrick man chopper over from Aberdeen. Never met him before, never even heard of him. But he'd heard of me and he'd heard of you too."

"Me? How come?"

"As soon as he'd got settled he asked for me by name. It was his first trip over to Europe and he'd been told to look me up, and when he found me he asked me about this place he'd heard of called Bugsy's in Santa Ponsa."

"No shit," I yelped in fascination. "Who was he? How did he know?"

"His name, believe it or not, was Rocky Calhoun. British Columbia. Randy Schnipper's cousin."

"Whoa." I gasped, lost for real words and suddenly struck by the enormity of ... well, of something.

"You're a lucky man. An influential man. People everywhere still talk about jumping your bones on the beach or about how they got fleeced in those dodgy drinking contests you used to run." Franny reached forward to pick up his Cubs cap which, true to form, he'd neglected to wear all day but was just about to don when he didn't need it. But he didn't put it on his head.

"In view of your services in the field of serving refreshments to the oil industry and to punters in general, I am going to promote you." He looked me squarely in the eye, and it was at times like those I had no idea if he was pissing around or not.

"No longer do you consider yourself a lowly Mister," he said, in all seriousness. "From this moment on, you are promoted to the rank of Commander. Your responsibilities will now be intelligence and reconnaissance. Keep the faith and remember, security at all times."

Bill and Jim looked on in mystification. I was cracking up.

"In recognition of your promotion you are now entitled to wear this fabled insignia. He tossed the baseball cap across to me. "Wear it with pride. All operatives in the field will now recognise you instantly."

I stuffed the cap on my head as I giggled uncontrollably at my mad, little friend. "You can rely on me, Captain," I told him.

"I feel certain I can. Now, your first duty." He picked up his glass and drained it. "Sort me another small one, will you, and rack us out another four lines. I'm off for a piss."

Later that evening, when Bill and Jim had gone out for a meal and some slow blues was drifting out to the balcony, I pushed back onto my head the symbol of my promotion and asked him a serious question.

"Listen, mate. This place here. A place like this. What's it cost?"

"Depends. By the week it's two hundred sterling, but if you have it over two years it comes down to about a oner. Couple of grand deposit."

I hawked back a mudslide of semi-liquid coke and ran over the mathematics. Money like that was nothing to Franny, but the reason it was nothing was because every three weeks for three weeks, seven days a week and twelve hours a day, he was working his guts out on a stinking oil rig in the middle of the turbulent wilderness known as the North Sea. If I could do that then I'd be out there like a shot. Problem was, I had no skills. The more I thought about it, the more of a problem it became - not being able to actually *do* anything. I was intelligent, I was capable and I wasn't lazy, but so what? So were millions of others who were better qualified, more skilled and a great deal younger.

I needed a stash. A hundred grand would probably do it. Maybe one fifty. I wasn't greedy. Just enough to live well on without having to work. Nice place in the sun and live off the interest.

Trouble was it had to be crime and the trouble with crime was that it was against the law. More than that, I was distinctly unhappy with the last scam. The drugs were a good earner though. Maybe that could be developed? As I said this was the summer of '87 and the timing is pivotal. I'd heard people talking about some new drug of choice. Still underground. 'Ecstasy' I think they called it. I didn't know anything about it, but just across the Balearic Sea something was going on in Ibiza. Men with names such as Rampling, Alfredo, Holloway and Oakenfold were creating the future, and before the end of the year they would ensure London would be the playground for a new generation of fun-lovers with money to burn.

Whatever was happening, my first port of call would have to be Farmer. Despite my recent promotion to officer status, he was my only intro.

I was desperately sad to leave Mallorca that time, but with the sadness came a determination. A determination to succeed and to return - and not before long. I had a goal. I didn't have much of a plan, but at least I had a goal.

CHAPTER ELEVEN

My hopes of an early route to that palm tree-lined retirement were effectively booted into touch as soon as I tracked down Farmer to the 'Cod.

"Young Micky boy. Bang on target. What's the scam? Hey, nice tan. Hope you haven't spent all your winnings."

I noticed that Terry had a small, black suitcase at his feet. Bizarrely, it started to make a noise - a ringing sound. Then he picked it up and answered it. Technology, eh? Terry seemed to be getting quite annoyed with the caller and ended the conversation by telling him, "Nothing doing until my man is out."

"Problem, mate?" I enquired.

"You could say that - Jimmy's been shot."

"What?"

"Last week in the Yaksak."

I tried to make the words come out of my mouth - form a sentence. "What do you mean he's been shot?"

"Pretty simple. Someone gets a gun, and you get in the way when they pull the trigger. That's it. Happens a lot in John Wayne films."

"Jesus." It was too strange, knowing someone that had been shot. "Why? How?"

"It's all to do with his old man getting offed. He saw one of the blokes involved the other day and gave it to him with the knife. *Badly*. So this little team of cunts get spooked and decide the best thing to do is to take the fight to Jim so they tracked him down, stuck the balaclavas on and let him have it halfway through his kebab."

"Fuck *me*! So what happened?"

"Well he dropped it and got chilli sauce all over his strides."

"No, I mean is he alright? Is he going to be alright?"

"He's not going to die, if that's what you mean. But he stopped a thirty-eight with his shoulder so he ain't taking up tennis anytime soon. He's in Whipps Cross with Plod all over him."

I felt sick. That was too close. The way I saw it, being a villain was about swiping loads of dosh, then getting clean away to live a life of unparalleled luxury and ease on a beach somewhere. It did not involve spending unusually long periods of time counting bricks at her Majesty's pleasure, and it most certainly did not involve waking up in a hospital bed to discover that one now had more than one's natural compliment of orifices. I may have been a little wild, but I wasn't up for any of *that* shit.

Farmer explained that he could still let me have a bit of gear, but as far as the kiting and the carding and any other scams went, there was nothing doing for the foreseeable. His primary concern was looking after Jimmy and making sure there was no further attempts on anyone's life - and then, perhaps when a truce had been called and peace declared, perhaps when everybody knew they could trust everybody else, then maybe he'd see about shooting a few of those fuckers.

I was at least grateful of the gear to sell, because - hundred grand retirement fund aside - I had commitments. By the time I had paid the deposit on the new flat, sorted out some engine agro with the Manta and deducted the outrageous cost of two weeks in Mallorca my stash was back down to around five or six large.

While I placed all the drugs I was selling over to my old chums in Essex, I'd got the Bromley flat to be near Nigel. The man was clearly making great strides, because all the frustration and anxiety I'd seen from him in recent months seemed to have disappeared. He was expanding the business at a rate of knots, and looked to be cruising down Easy Street in his brand new E reg. company Rover 827.

I suppose the reason I was hanging around was because I thought if I spent long enough in his company, a little of his magic dust might land on me. And if that failed, perhaps he would just give me some money.

Sometimes when I was feeling poor and raring to go, I'd hit the phone in his office and drum up a few life sales. Everyone seemed to be buying houses so there were endowment policies I arranged for friends, contents insurance, car insurance. Bits and pieces. They could get it all, plus a few grams of wiz under one roof - who could say fairer than that?

I didn't want wages or anything, although Nigel would flip me petrol money, get the beers in and spring for our regular midweek curry.

"How's the old man's dosh going?" I enquired as I ploughed through a mountain of prawn Madras.

"Good. Very good," he told me, calling for more brandies. "House prices are marching on right now, so I'll be over at the weekend to shift some from an overseas account into UK property. I'm in with this fund manager at Scandia Life. He reckons commercial and residential combined are going to put on thirty percent in the coming twelve months."

"Thirty percent? Jesus. Since when has all this been happening?"

"It's been happening all the time. You want to try spending a bit of time on *this* planet for a change. This is the late eighties. There's a boom going on. Don't you read the papers?"

It was a fair question. The answer was yes - I did. The sports pages of the Mirror were very incisive.

At around that time, I got a postcard from Mallorca. Just when I needed some good news on the money-making front I got precisely the opposite. Preston Jack had decided to stay in Santa Ponsa. The good news was that *he* was buying a bar in which I was welcome anytime. Terrific.

One night over at Nige and Nicolette's, it came to me. My sis-in-law was paying an invoice to Sidcup Streakers, the motorcycle courier company they used - and then I just knew what I had to do.

"We'll start our own firm." I looked at Nigel like I'd found the Holy Grail.

"Me and you. We'll go in together. You're paying these jokers, you might as well pay me. We'll start a courier company and clean up."

By the end of the evening Nigel had written himself a hit list of all the companies he felt he could ask to turn over their transport needs to us. I saw it as a match made in heaven. I would handle the riding side and organise the day to day, for which I would draw a salary. Nigel would set up the company, organise the bank, get to work on the clients and provide start up funds. He would be unpaid to begin with, but we would be fifty-fifty shareholders.

He told me to get whatever bike I wanted, so I zipped over to see my pal Steve at the Romford bike shop and he had just what we were looking for.

The year old BMW K100RS was 1,000cc of Teutonic power and efficiency. It was everything a despatch rider could want from a bike. By the time I had mounted a Motorola mobile phone on it and bought some new boots, gloves and wet weather gear, the bill had edged near to six grand. Nigel didn't flinch. "Don't fuck up," was all he said.

I knew that I wouldn't. I was just so pleased he was giving me a chance. My only worry was that he would lay on so much work I would start letting people down before we had taken on other riders to handle it.

Why hadn't I thought of this before? A couple of years hard graft, build up the old client base, expand into vans and trucks and then kick back and take it easy for the rest of my life. Poop deck time here we come, and nobody would be looking to shoot me or put me in prison for it. So what did I call us? What else? We were the High Street Heroes.

In the run up to the start of operations Nige was practically uncontactable. This I took to be a good sign, because he was obviously hassling all and sundry for their business. That was why, midway through our second week, I couldn't understand why only Nicolette was calling me up to make deliveries. All I did was sit on my arse all day at Waterloo station, where I parked up. It was ridiculous. Even without the initial outlay we were losing bundles from day one.

Nine days into the venture, having grossed the princely sum of seventy eight quid, I finally caught up with him.

"What's happening with all your tasty connections then?" I asked - not rudely, but with a degree of worry. What happened next chilled me to the core. Apoplectic with rage, he rounded on me.

"Oh I see. I get it. I haven't got enough to do around here as it is. I've got five companies to run without help from anyone and now I've got your arse to wipe too."

"What the fuck are you talking about? You *said* you were going to do this. Half of this is yours. If you hadn't said you could do this, I wouldn't have gone ahead. You're the one with the contacts." I was genuinely concerned for him. He looked out of control.

"Look what do you expect from me? Why the fuck do I always have to bail out all the losers?"

Yes, it was clear the ga ga express was pulling into the station ahead of schedule, and it scared me rigid.

"You and Nic got that list together, not me. This thing starts and ends with your so called 'contacts'. If they don't want to play, or they're just plain not there then it's over."

"Oh brilliant," he howled, throwing his arms in the air. "Fucking magic. I'm out six thousand and you're talking about it being over. Six grand and you're treating it like it's a plaything. Like some poxy hobby you want to pick up or drop as and when you want. This is the real world, dickbrain. You're not playing make-believe gangsters now."

As he ranted, a stapler smashed into the office wall. I was truly stunned.

"What is *wrong* with you?" I pleaded. "How can it be my fault?

All I'm saying is we decided to go along with this, because you said..."

"Me. Oh yeah, me. Had to be me didn't it. I'm only Joe Cunt putting up all the money."

I knew then that he had lost it. I knew then that I should have just given him the keys to the bike and walked. I should have told him to get some help too, but I didn't have the guts.

But I at least tried to see his point. He was taking on so much - looking after all of us, working so hard. So I did what seemed to be the only thing I could do: I left, rode home, made myself a cup of tea and cried my eyes out.

It was all going wrong and I could think of nothing to do that would make any of it go right. I was pushing thirty and I was doing something else that wasn't working. I was failing again. I just kept failing, like I owned the fucking franchise on it.

That relativity thing kept coming back to haunt me too. All the others (Nigel included) were established. People were buying their own houses, running Porsches, holidaying in the West Indies. Not me. Moreover, their careers were established, the hard part had been done and they were rolling their motors down leafy avenues, while I was riding someone else's motorbike into a dead end street.

More than that I had been guilty of what Farmer always described as "counting the money before you have it". Plan for it, strive for it - but never count it and never count *on* it. Never imagine it. I even thought of a name for it: the Dreams Failure Syndrome had me in its grasp.

I blew my nose and finished my tea. Then the phone rang.

Nigel apologised. He told me of the incredible pressure he was under, and how bad things would be if he couldn't make everything work.

"We're on the same side," I assured him, buoyed by warmth and empathy. "We work together, there ain't a lot we can't do. I wish I could be more involved with you. I feel shut out."

"Yeah, well. Don't get too close, old son. You don't want to get too close."

The problem, I knew, was that Nigel thought 'sales' was a

dirty word. He thought money had put him above it. His idea of a sales ploy was to spend a fortune on clients in pubs and restaurants, and then expect them to come across with the business. So I told him I would do all the sales work. All he needed was to let his people know that I would be calling.

I got the first batch of numbers, along with his assurances that he had made all the initial approaches. Not only had the first one I talked to not heard from Nigel, he hadn't even heard *of* him

"Mr. Wilshire, thanks for taking the call. The name here is Michael Targett. You won't know me, but I understand you deal with my brother, Nigel Targett."

"Sounds like the kind of call I used to make. What was the name again?"

"Nigel Targett. I understand he places some life business with you now and then."

"Er, no. I'm sure I would remember a name like that. Who is he with?"

A shiver ran through me.

"Well, he owns Kent Insurance Services - down in Sidcup."

"Hmmm. Well yes, I know of the company. They do have an agency with us but I think it's pretty much dormant. I don't think they do any business with us. I don't actually know a Mr. Targett."

Feverishly I checked the name against the number and the company. There was no mistake. Ten hours previously, Nige had assured me he did tons of business with the bloke. What the fuck was going *on*? He had lied to me again, and each lie was like a knife through the heart.

"What can I do for you anyway?"

What hope was there? I was on my own. Everything had gone. I had no one. I had nothing and I *was* nothing.

"Hello there?"

"Uh?"

"What was the call about?"

What was the point? "Motorbike couriers."

"Oh yes?"

"Yes."

"Well I don't believe we use them."

"Right."

I was at Waterloo Station again. As I was walking towards the chemist I thought about all my carefully nurtured dreams, and saw that apart from a few precious nights in Bugsy's, and those evenings spent with a head full of sunsets on Franny's terrace, none of them had come true. I'd never won a race on a motorbike and I'd never nailed the solo in Stairway To Heaven. I would never be as dynamic as Mackay, as brilliant as Blackmore or as brave as Sheene. I'd never had a job I'd really liked, I'd never had a decent car and I'd never had any real money. I'd never been in love. None of my dreams had come true, and now none of them would - and if that was the case, then what was the point of anything?

My legs moved but I didn't move them. The words were mine but I did not form them.

"Box of paracetamol, please."

"Which size, sir?"

"What is there?"

"Packs of ten, twenty or the family pack of one hundred."

"Yeah, that should do it. I'll take the hundred."

I rode straight home stopping only once at my local off license to buy a bottle of Courvoisier. Back at mine, I placed the bottle and the pills on the mantelpiece, sat down and looked for a reason not to do it.

Everything I wanted was just so far out of reach. I had no job, no house of my own, no family I was close to, no friends, no energy, no enthusiasm, no vitality, no interests, no prospects and no hope. I had placed so much faith in Nigel and he had let me down so badly. The bike business really did seem like my last chance.

I wanted to be... If only I could be... *ordinary*. I wanted a brother who wasn't mad. I wanted my mother back; she would have known what to do.

Nothing. Suddenly everything was nothing. I wanted to be on the Night Flight to Shoebury again. I wanted to sit down in the warmth and the comfort and slowly drift away, not caring where, when or even if I woke up. I wanted to be somewhere else; to be some*one* else.

All day and all evening I sat in silence, staring at the brandy and pills. How had it come to this? Why was I so vulnerable?

At eleven in the evening the phone rang.

"Evening. How goes it, old son?" He sounded drunk. I was so tired and so frail, I couldn't defend myself.

"Alright," I sniffed.

"How'dit go today? Plenty of biz?"

"Well you know. Not too bad seeing as the first bloke I spoke to hadn't even heard of you."

"What? What are you talking about?"

I wanted to laugh at him but I was too tired. "Never mind."

"Who? What?"

"Peter Wilshire at M&G."

"Peter fucking who? I never said talk to him. Simon Marlow I said." Suddenly he was screaming again.

"You said Wilshire or Marlow, and neither of them have heard of you. They've heard of the company because it is the only agency on their books that places zero business with them. Nigel, what's going on?"

It went quiet. Eventually he said, "What about the others?"

"Leave me alone," I managed to say, before putting the phone down.

Five minutes later the phone rang.

"Don't ever put the phone down on me again, you cunt."

I put the phone down.

Three hours later it rang again. I hadn't moved. I wedged the handset between my ear and shoulder and waited.

"You there?"

I breathed to let him know I was.

"Look, this isn't easy for me. I'm under a lot of pressure."

"Sure it's easy. Just don't lie."

"There are lots of things you don't understand. I'm trying to create things. I've taken courses of action that are very serious. Things *must* work out for me. I have no choices left."

"I don't want to hear."

"None of this is easy. The pressure..."

"You bring it on yourself, you moron. You've got to stop lying to people."

"I don't lie, people just don't understand me."

"You're doing it now."

"What are you doing tomorrow?"

"Fuck knows." There was a plan formulating in my head that I might be having a chat with my mother.

"Keep trying."

"You what?"

"Keep trying. You're a good salesman." I think that was the first time in his life he had ever told me I was good at anything.

"What's the point?"

He fell silent, and then after a minute he said, "Yeah, what's the point?" As he put the phone down, I wondered if he had a box and a bottle on the mantelpiece too.

I got a couple of hours ropey sleep and then - considering the alternative was to end my life - I dressed and went for a ride on the bike. On auto-pilot, I drifted in to Waterloo station because I knew I was at least sure of a decent cup of tea there. I sat in the corner of the café, wondering what Nigel was into that was sending him so far off the rails. Maybe he had over- borrowed. Maybe it was something to do with Farmer. Anyway, if he thought he had problems, maybe he would care to check out the inside of *my* head.

With a massive effort I pulled out the list again and called Lucy Parker. She was the wife of a bloke Nigel played cricket with and I knew them both because I made up the numbers when they were short. I needed a friendly face. She was manager of a branch of Pickfords travel. She rattled a biro between her teeth as she perused our rate card.

"Yeah. Compares favourably. We do about fifteen trips a day. Let's hope you can ride better than you can bat."

As I was swinging the leg over the BM downstairs I heard the soft warbling of the Motorola.

"High Street Heroes."

"Hi, it's me."

"Me who?"

"Lucy."

"Lucy? Lucy who? Shit. Sorry, Luce. You threw me there."

"Something's just landed on my desk. Can you come back up?"

It was the first real job we did but there was a proviso. "For the time being it's just me. I can handle your fifteen jobs a day in my sleep but if three or four come in together there'll be a bit of a backlog."

She was fine with that. Also on the list was Nigel's accountant. I knew him to be tough, no- nonsense bloke who was about to do nobody any favours at all. When he asked me how many riders we had on the firm, I did what any self-respecting company director would do.

"Seven," I told him.

I was riding like a lunatic, but after a fortnight the two accounts were ticking over. I took on our first rider.

I kept the pills and the brandy but shoved them under the sink.

I froze my nuts off riding that thing over the winter and through into the spring and summer of eighty-eight, but whilst we were always busy, we never seemed to get in front. Not proper in front. Wages, petrol, phone bills, repairs. It was never ending. I felt like the horse in Animal Farm.

Nearly a year into operating, I had built us up to five riders when it happened.

Some dope. Some muppet in a hurry or some arsehole not even looking, and there I was: lying in the crash position in Goodge Street with an army of well-wishers around me. That's how easy it happens; how tough life is on two wheels.

The scar on my chin where my bottom teeth had pierced my lower lip would heal to look quite mean, so that was OK. The two small bones I broke in my right wrist would, in theory, not impinge upon my nocturnal self-pleasuring. Problem was my knee.

"Laxity in the posterior cruciate ligament," I was smartly informed by the young consultant who patched me up in UCH.

"I'll secure it temporarily in a half slab cast, but you must get to your local hospital in the morning. I'll write a brief report for you to give them."

Posterior schmosterior, I thought. If it wasn't broken how bad could it be? I found out when I stood up and tried to walk. My leg simply refused to do what I told it.

I got a call through to Nicolette and told her to put Jez, my number one rider, in charge. Then I cabbed it out to the old man's. He rushed around with cups of tea and plates of food and told me how dangerous motorcycles were. I needed that, didn't I?

By the early evening my leg was completely numb between thigh and shin. My right wrist throbbed with the menace of distant thunder and I was unable to feel my face from top lip to the point of my chin. The phone rang.

"Ah, old son. How goes it. Spot of bad luck today I hear."

"You could say that."

"What's the damage?"

"I've split me face open, fucked me knee and broke me wrist in two places."

I sensed his fury gathering momentum.

"You're joking naturally."

"I don't believe I am."

And then, suddenly, the maddened maniac slipped into gear again. "Well that's just great. That's just fine and dandy innit? Looks like another nice few grand I've spunked because of you."

I immediately thought of the pills and the brandy.

"What the fuck is it with you? Can't you do anything right?"

"It was an accident, you idiot," I countered weakly, my head reeling. "It was not deliberate. It was accidental, that's why they call them accidents, do you see?"

"Oh, very fucking smart. Always got a smart reason for blowing so much of my money. How long will you be off?"

"I don't know. It all depends on what they say about my knee in the morning but it's going to be at least four weeks with the arm anyway. Just get the claim forms in the post tonight will you?"

"What claim forms?"

"For the insurance, the BUPA and the income replacement. There'll be no problem. Lots of witnesses. I'll be able to string this out for ages and hopefully make a few quid."

"I need to check to make sure that's alright."

"You can check all you fucking like. I pay into these schemes and I'm smashed to bits here. I don't want any problems and I'm not hanging around any NHS corridors. OK?"

After a sleepless night Dad ran me over to the Nuffield in Brentwood. I quoted our group insurance policy number and fell limp with relief when the receptionist verified its existence on her screen. At least he'd got that right. The prognosis, though, was worrying. The face would scar but heal. The arm would be fine after three or four weeks.

"The problem is this cruciate," explained my new and incredibly expensive orthopaedic consultant as he eased my massively swollen knee one way or the other. "Not good. Lot of stress here. Trauma. We need to get this properly immobilised. We'll know more in eight weeks. The nurse will show you to the plaster room."

Eight weeks? Shit. Eight weeks and *then* rehabilitation. My first reaction was how annoyed Nigel would be. In fact when I called him he was as nice as pie, which I took to mean he had indeed fucked up my income replacement policy. He suggested I crash at his place while I recovered so that I could be nearer to the business - maybe even get into the office and hit the sales hotline. He picked me up in - now wait a minute - the new Rover had gone, making way for a brand Mercedes 230. Of course things were going to be alright.

On the way back he told me how the riders, marshalled by this bloke Jez, were rallying round, holding things together. It looked like I could keep things going. Staying rent-free at Nige and Nicolette's helped as I was able to give up my flat and save a few quid.

Eight weeks down the line, when the plaster came off, I was shocked at the wasting of my muscles. Then it was massage then gentle, loosening exercises. After a fortnight I hit the pool three nights a week grinding out length after boring length. Two weeks of that saw me toughened up enough to get down the gym and after three weeks there it kind of looked like I had two legs again. My physio discharged me soon after.

My pal Steve at the bike shop had fixed up the stricken BM while I was still in plaster. He actually paid one of the showroom's mechanics to work privately on it to keep the cost down, but still conjured up a bill on company paper to rival the national debt. This we slapped into the insurers, who forked out with no questions asked and we had a little share out. The company had stood still for well over three months but we were still operational.

I had to swing my skinny leg over the bike sooner or later, so one day I just held my breath and did it. It was no big deal. I should have sat in the office and taken it easy for a further six months, but you can't tell my sort anything.

I bought a house shortly after, because I knew it all.

I was hanging out with Nigel one weekend and noticed him hunched greedily over his calculator.

"Mm mmmm. Praise be to the goddess Maggie," he whistled.

"How so, mate?"

"This property boom is going to run and run. Do you know the average house in the South East is putting on seventy two pounds a day? And it don't take time off, you know? So between my two places, my tasty little nest egg is packing on something like six hundred notes a week - and all I have to do for that is sit around on my fat arse, running down the batteries in the calculator trying to keep pace with it all. What a system."

There was something I'd been meaning to talk to him about. "Can you get me a mortgage?"

"Don't."

"Don't what? Can you do it?"

"I can get anyone a mortgage."

"So what would the repayments be on say, a sixty grand loan?"

"Forget it."

"Why?"

"Because it's a mistake."

"Why is it?"

"Because you're in the wrong business and you're too irresponsible."

"What's wrong with my job? I'm a company director. No one needs to know I ride a bike. What do they do, then? Come around to check on you?"

"What happens if you have another accident and you can't make the payments?"

He walked right into that one.

"I'll have insurance, won't I?"

He shied away from my searching gaze and worked on some figures.

"On sixty thou' with an endowment... about four twenty, maybe four fifty a month."

"No trouble. Not much more than the rent I was paying and things are on the up. I can feel it."

So after a year in business, funded by a shaky company held together by little more than exploited friendships, with an erratic, below-average income, working in the world's most dangerous profession behind bungee cord testers and with a leg one accident away from being entirely non-functional, I took my first steps into the property market. Everybody else had a house; I wanted one too. Everybody else was making money from property, so could I. Bricks and mortar, what could be safer?

Nige did his bit and scored me the mortgage, although that achievement, at that time and in that place, was effectively on a par with taking the proverbial candy from the proverbial baby. This was the second half of nineteen eighty eight and the very zenith of that stratospheric arc of the Thatcherite boom. Bank and building society managers had their lending targets to meet, and you got the impression that if they didn't make them, they would have their clerks on the street outside branches all over the country with barrow-loads of cash, just chucking the stuff away.

It was real gold-rush time and I dived into the biggest seam of all. Well, not quite. Docklands was just up the road but I bought a two bedroom, end of terrace rabbit hutch on the A13 in a place called Beckton. It cost seventy three grand and I didn't bat an eyelid because even though it took every penny I had, I knew the value would be going through the roof forever, acting like a second salary; there for me to collect when retirement beckoned in a few short years. I relaxed and thought about Franny's poop deck.

But work was slow. I endeavoured to lay on new business but I just couldn't drag us up those last few notches. I struggled by as best I could, but after four months in the house, I was already in arrears with the mortgage. And my leg never got back to normal.

Then something brilliant happened. Terry Farmer got nicked.

Because of work and the accident I hadn't seen him for ages and had consequently been off the gear for some time - and I had to admit that I felt, well, pretty ordinary actually. I had a couple of old nicked bits of his sitting around the house like a stereo and some imitation designer clobber, which I ditched as soon as Nigel called me with news.

Soon after, I got a call from Kerry Farmer, the big fella's wife. She told me he wanted to see me. The Scrubs.

Terry was there on remand while the CPS decided exactly what they were going to hit him with; the bulk of the charges revolving around the stolen goods found in his warehouse which, according to the DC who was on the case, made the place look like "A veritable Aladdin's cave".

At his committal hearing at Wanstead Magistrates Court, I had listened from the public seats as the copper (this DC Black) listed the goodies, they had found. I felt quite sad when he mentioned the moody Ralph Lauren polo shirts because they had been quite a good seller. I felt even sadder when I glanced casually down and noticed I actually had one of them on. I cut out of there like a greyhound out of its trap.

Kerry explained to me that Terry needed some puff taken in for him and showed me how it was done.

Now, some girls visiting their loved ones preferred the old trick of hiding the gear under their tongues, and going into a full mouth-to-mouth snog as soon as they walk in, transferring the stuff over - which is immediately swallowed, to be retrieved safely at a later date. This clearly was not an option open to me and Terry, because his reputation as one of the toughest faces to come out of the East End in recent years would plainly suffer, should he be spotted snogging some bloke in the visiting room of the Scrubs. And I've never really gone for geezers with beards.

The 'bottling method' - i.e. shoving stuff up one's ring, wasn't favoured by the man either since a rather nasty trick was played on him down in Swaleside where he was seeing out eighteen months for ABH a few years before. Denny Masters, known (among other things) for an iffy sense of humour, handed over to Terry a lump of puff wrapped in Bacofoil. Nothing wrong with that, except that it was a whole ounce - and Denny had gone to deliberate lengths to fashion as many sharp edges to the thing as possible. He sat there grinning as he watched Terry try to work out what he was going to do with it. According to Terry, it had looked like one of those World War II sea mines with the prongs sticking out of it. I asked what it had been like, and he suggested that perhaps I shove a conker in its shell up my arse and find out for myself.

No, Kerry was very specific in her instructions. A couple of quarters rolled into spheres and wrapped tightly in cling film sitting inside the lid of a pack of fags. Cigarettes were permitted in the visiting room but the fags and the lighter had to be kept on the visitor's side of the table, meaning the prisoner had to reach across, supposedly in full view of the screws, to pick up and light each cigarette. Thus, for even the most dextrously challenged old lag, it was simple. You got a fag and palmed the gear one ball at a time, swallowing it as you lit up a snout. Piece of piss.

Not that swallowing balls of hashish with nothing to drink is easy. To compound matters, Terry was a staunch non-smoker, so by the time he had coughed, gagged and spluttered his way through the two lumps of gear and a few Bensons he had wheezed himself into a crimson-faced seizure. I'd been in the place ten minutes and we'd still only said hello.

"One day, Tel, you'll thank me for that." I couldn't help grinning.

"I know, son. You're too good to me. I don't deserve it."

I looked around and wondered what had happened to the glamour of crime. Where were the laughing, swaggering, moneyed villains I had all but deified whilst learning my hood's trade at Terry's knee? Sad, bitter little men gazed forlornly at their sad, tatty, resentful women while dirty, disinterested kids hung around, sullen and bored. Fuck all that. Jesus, the number of times I had put my liberty on the line. Running a courier company was tough but at least nobody wanted to bang me up for it. Yeah I thought, as Terry hunched forward to talk - fuck all that.

"Need you to do something for me, Mick."

Oh, I see. Didn't think it was a social call.

"I don't know how this is shaping up but it's pretty clear I ain't gonna get bail, and I need to get something delivered. What I want you to do is go see Kerry and ask her for the key to the little lock-up."

"The little lock-up?"

"Right. She'll give you directions. Now this place ain't in my name so don't worry about it being watched. Right? Plenty of stuff in there, you know? The usual. Don't touch a thing, don't even *notice* anything. What you want is in the far right corner as you walk through the door. You'll see a large, brown packing case. Wedged behind that is a black briefcase and between the two of them is what you're after. It's a brown paper package, about two feet by eighteen inches. It's pretty heavy. Then what you do is call the number that Kerry'll give you, and take the package to the man who answers the phone."

"Anyone I know?"

"No. There'll be two blokes. Get the number of both of them from Kerry. Try Pete Chalmers first. If he's not around then it'll have to be Denny Masters."

If, ten years before, someone had told me I would be riding a bike in the same race as Sheene, I wouldn't have been any more awestruck. Chalmers and Masters were names to be used in hushed tones of reverence, or with malice to frighten or threaten an opponent. The thought of it all scared me shitless but that old crime buzz was there for me again. I'd sure missed it.

"What's in it?"

He shook his head. "Can't tell you, mate - and do yourself a favour and don't open it. It belongs to those two and Denny has a way of looking through you. He'll know if you're lying."

We shot the shit for a while. We spoke of the bike company. "Doing OK but it's a bit like hard work." We spoke of Nigel. "I just don't know if I can trust him anymore, Mick. He told me he'd bribed DC Black to the tune of two grand to get him to lose the file - know anything about that?"

No, I most certainly did not. Nor did I want to.

Soon enough, a burly warden stepped behind Terry and pressed firmly on his shoulder. "Finish up now." And that was it.

That evening I made a point of parking the bike a couple of streets away from his house when I called on Kerry. She was running around panicking trying to get the kids in bed, and organise a baby-sitter before she went out to work in a Leyton pub.

To hear that she needed to work at some grotty boozer in order to pay the bills while Terry was away disheartened me intensely. He was supposed to be a proper face, stealing from the rich to give to Swiss banking institutions for them to look after for eventualities just like getting nicked and banged up. Surely they weren't skint. Surely crime *did* pay.

She had everything ready. A thin Yale and a larger key for a padlock, the address and directions to the lock-up and two numbers.

"The first number is Denny and Pete's office. Try there first. If you need to speak to someone outside of office hours try Pete at home. He won't like it but he'll definitely be the less annoyed of the two."

She saw me blanch. "Don't worry, they're really alright. You know what you're doing."

I was pleased *she* thought so. But it was too late to go there that night. Darkness had fallen and Kerry said it would look bad to go there before the morning.

Up early on the next day, a Saturday, I belted over to the address in Bethnal Green. Cautious as ever, I parked up a few streets away and readied the keys as I neared the garage. First the padlock that secured the door itself to the frame of the garage, and then the Yale in the twist handle. Then it was turn, pull the door towards me, then up and over. As part of the same movement I stepped quickly into the gloom and pulled the door back down behind me.

I was in and safe. I could see sod all, but at least I was in. Then, slowly my senses acclimatised. Boxes. Lots of boxes of different colours and sizes, some stacked right up above my head to the ceiling.

As I calmed I grew more confident and more curious. Brand names everywhere. Hitachi, Grundig, Phillips, Beefeater. Forget it. I told myself. Get the right one and get out of here.

From a call box I dialled the first number - the office, but all I got was a recorded message. I dialled the second number.

A woman answered. She spoke with a deep, almost husky but quite well-mannered tone.

"Hi. Is Pete there?"

"Who is this?"

"My name is Mick. I'm a friend of Terry Farmer. He asked me to get in touch with Pete about something."

"Pete doesn't do this at weekends."

"Yeah, well. Normally I don't either. It's kind of important. I just need to give him something and I'd rather it was sooner than later. He there?"

I counted the silence out in seconds. I reached five.

"Terry who, did you say?"

"Farmer. It's pretty important."

"Hold on."

I heard her walking away, heels clacking on the polished parquet. A rough diamond who'd polished up her accent? Or was she genuine posh, attracted to her polar opposite? Late thirties, dyed blonde? You could list the clichés all day long. Sauna, sun-bed, aerobics? The health club? Peugeot 205 in the drive? No. Different class. Mercedes sport. Pool in the back garden.

Apartment in Marbella. Just being involved in that silly little caper stirred up a hornet's nest of old feelings and wild dreams that had been lying dormant for ages. The dreams weren't dead after all. They were just resting. Just giving me a rest.

Then I heard him walking towards the phone across the same stretch of floor. I knew it was him before I heard him speak. The purposeful walk. The heavy tread. Then the voice, rich and dark.

"Who is this?"

"Hello, is that Pete?"

"Yeah. Who's that?"

"Pete you don't know me. My name is Mick. I'm a friend of Terry. He's..."

"Terry who?"

"Terry Farmer."

"And?"

"Yeah. Thing is, I know you'd prefer not to be disturbed at home, Pete, but I've got something to give you from Terry and I'm anxious to let you have it as soon as possible."

"Do you know what's in it?"

"No, but Terry said..."

"OK here's what you do. Hang onto it and call my office at ten on Monday morning and someone will tell you what to do. The number is..."

"Actually, Pete, I've got that. It's just..."

"Well why are you calling me here?"

"It's because I'm keen to get this thing to you. I'm just doing someone a favour is all."

"Best you make sure you do it right then, son."

"Yeah but..."

"Ten o'clock Monday morning. Don't let me down now. And don't phone here again." Then he hung.

I stashed the thing in my loft and didn't sleep a wink all weekend. To double the inconvenience factor I had to organise all the riders around my absence on Monday morning. I looked up the phone number prefix and saw that it was in South East London so I sprinted through the Rotherhithe Tunnel and was in a phone box by nine thirty.

"Hello, Road Rats."

"Hello, is Pete there?"

"You Farmer's mate?"

"Yeah."

"OK. Come round. Know where we are?"

No more than ten minutes later I was swinging into a yard close to Limehouse Reach. As I pulled in I had to brake and swerve to avoid the enormous, fire-breathing Volvo unit that was manoeuvring a trailer into position against the far fence. In front of me was a newish, brick- built warehouse some thirty metres square, with a gaping hole of a mouth that was exposed by a raised roller shutter. Backed into the doorway was a brand new Mercedes van and behind that, clicking and whirring as it loaded pallets, I could see a small, electrical-powered fork-lift truck. As I parked up next to a gleaming, silver Daimler, I noticed the sign writing on the doors of the Volvo and the van. The logo featured a lorry cab, and behind the wheel was a grinning, leering, rat with slick backed hair, gleaming teeth and sunglasses. Underneath the artwork was the legend 'Road Rats'.

I killed the engine and was removing my lid, when the driver of the Volvo dropped athletically from the cab and sauntered over to me.

"I'll see if I can get you properly on the way out." His wild, green eyes danced with mischief. "Whatchagot?"

"Got this for Pete," I told him, unclipping the package from the back seat.

"OK, I'll take it."

I flipped it under my arm. One half of me just wanted to unload the thing, but the other made me want to stick around. This was Masters and Chalmers after all. I felt that I should meet them at least. I stared at the fella facing me. All rude, vital manliness, he wore a golden skull earring that dangled from halfway up his ear, and I noticed that he wore it there because the lobe in its entirety was missing.

"Did you just phone up?"

"Yeah."

"You shoulda said, mate. Here comes Pete now."

I wasn't sure what I'd been expecting. Pete Chalmers was as known for the acuity of his brain as much as the speed of his fists. Farmer was a criminal but Chalmers was a gangster. As it happened he was solid and tough-looking, was about five-nine and looked pretty much like any other bloke in his mid-forties. Confident, friendly face, greying slightly at the temples. All the same, he still crunched my hand in the mangle of his fist.

"You must be Mick. Thanks for coming over, son. Come up to the office. We'll have a chat."

Up darkened stairs to a small landing, and then through another unmarked door. I half expected the obligatory hand-cranked generator with the crocodile clip terminals, junk food containers, beer bottles and blood stains up the wall, plus the customary snarling Rottweiler. What I saw was a tidy, organised office featuring a fax machine-photocopier in the one corner, a Compaq computer terminal on each of the two large wooden desks, and ranks of steel filing cabinets down the length of one wall. Along the fourth wall was a sink unit and counter tops upon which sat a kettle and a microwave.

"Cup of tea, son?" I was offered by one of London's top faces.

"Yeah, lovely, Pete. Cheers."

He spoke as he filled the kettle.

"Sorry I wasn't able to see you at the weekend but I have a spectacular amount of grief with the old woman at the moment. Know what I mean? Sugar?"

"No ta."

The package was still under my arm. "No worries, mate. I'm pleased to be able to help out Terry and any friends of his."

"Good boy. How is he getting on? Have you seen him lately?"

"Yeah, I was over there on Friday. He..."

"Where have they got him at the moment?"

"He's in the Scrubs. He seems to be OK. He's not too optimistic about his chances of getting away with anything though. It all seems to be fairly cut and dried. He's getting his head down and just getting used to the idea that he probably ain't going to be around for a while."

"Any idea what he might be looking at?"

"Not really. Could be eighteen months, could be four years. All depends on the judge."

He placed a mug of tea on his desk and then took the other around it and sat down. He motioned for me to pull a spare chair forward to sit across from him. Then, for the first time, he acknowledged the package. "Here, let me take that from you." He placed it on his desk and, to my huge disappointment, didn't even look at it.

"Yeah shame that," he said thoughtfully, sipping his drink. "Only carelessness that got him caught. As usual. Too many toerags around him. Probably got grassed. He's a bit wild but he's a good operator most of the time. How do you know him?"

"Me and him play for the same rugby club. I met him a couple of years ago and we got on from the start. Teamed up for a while. Made a few quid. It was good. As you say, it's a shame, especially if it was avoidable. Good bloke."

He watched me with his shiny hawk's eyes.

"You weren't involved with him when he got nicked, were you?"

"No, no. I was well clear. I think it was just him and his cousin."

"Oh yeah. That nutty little bastard that stabs people. How is he?" I was surprised to see him cradle his mug to draw warmth from it. The way a woman would.

"Cut Throat Jim? Don't know. Ain't seen him at all."

He scoffed. "That what they're calling him these days, is it?"

"Among other things. Yeah, bit unstable. Know him too, do you?"

He nodded.

"Talking of unstable..." He flicked his eyes to the door as we heard boots clomping up the stairs. "Here comes another one."

There was a courteous knock and in walked the driver of the lorry.

"Ready to go," he announced. "Got the paperwork?"

"On the clip. Who's doing that one, Paul?"

The bloke pulled a wad of green papers from a clip by the door. "Benny."

190

"Make sure he's got street maps for everywhere he's going, yeah? I don't want to be sending someone out to go and rescue him when he gets lost again."

He grinned, nodded and was gone.

"So what is it you do here, Pete?"

"Bit of everything. Local, same day and long haul. Overnights. We're starting to do a little bit of cab work but that's only an overspill from the firm across the street, but we're thinking of buying them out. We've got three limos which we put out for wedding hire. Bit of storage because, apart from this, we own garages and lock ups. Paul there is a shit hot mechanic so we do servicing and repairs, stuff like that. Motors and transport is what I know. Grown up with it. I still enjoy it, which is why I still get up early and come in myself."

He stopped to take a drink and reflect upon something for a few seconds.

"The eighties have been good because there has been so much money around but I get the feeling it's going to take a downturn soon. And yourself? How long you been despatching?"

"Bit more than a year this time around, although I've been riding bikes for about ten years in all."

"Uh huh. And which outfit are you with?"

Never one to miss out on an opportunity, I handed him a business card.

"High Street Heroes? You're having a laugh, son. What maniac thought of that?"

"You're looking at him. Me and my brother are partners but all he really did was help set it up. I could do with getting off the road so that I can get the whole thing built up into a reasonable sized company, but my hands are pretty tied. You'd think it wouldn't be that difficult, but..." I shook my head with a light-hearted but rueful dejection, searching for the empathy that would endear us to be some form of kindred spirits.

I didn't think I had overdone it. I was trying to sell myself. Get on with the man. Then he put his mug down on the package that I had sweated over all weekend, and stared at me across steepled fingertips.

"You won't want me to detain you any longer then."

To say the rest of the day passed slowly is an understatement, and I was pleased when it was six o'clock and I was drifting slowly back out along the Commercial Road to my little place in Beckton.

Doubts as to my ability to run my own company haunted me constantly. I was riding like a lunatic for eight, nine hours then working half the evening typing invoices and sales shots. Any spare time I did get was taken up with interviewing riders, chasing new customers or placating existing ones whenever we let them down. I was doing it all for one hundred and fifty pounds a week. Interest rates were screaming through the roof and I wasn't even covering the mortgage anymore.

Somehow I'd really got my hopes up with Pete Chalmers. Later I would be able to identify that little episode as a mild dose of Dreams Failure Syndrome (DFS). Chatting with him, I had envisaged the scenario of being bought out, having a right wedge of dosh thrust into my pocket, paying off my mortgage arrears and being taken into the business to learn the ropes of full time, sophisticated criminality. It wasn't quite Courvoisier and paracetomol depressed but I felt those icy fingers reaching out to clutch me once again.

A headache developed that produced a ringing in my ears that took me ten seconds to realise was the bike phone. I swung the BM into a garage forecourt, killed the engine, pulled off my helmet, jumped off, knelt down by the side of the machine, shoved my greasy gloved finger in my right ear and the phone in my left. I prayed it wasn't a late job. Prayed it wasn't Nigel calling me up to give me more bullshit.

It was Pete Chalmers. He told me he wanted to buy me out, put a right wedge of dosh in my pocket so that I could pay off my arrears, and take me into the business to learn the ropes of full-time, sophisticated criminality. He didn't say that in so many words but that was how it added up, and the first thing I had to do was get my arse back over to his warehouse to talk some turkey with Demon Denny Masters.

CHAPTER TWELVE

So I went to work for a couple of gangsters called Denny
Masters and Pete Chalmers and all my dreams came true. That's
how it happens, I suppose - these odd little twists of fate and
fortune. The swings in my life would have unbalanced a trapeze
artist, but with that one move I felt I would be on an upward arc
right off the edge of the graph for the rest of my life, gliding that
shiny Aston down Easy Street.

The influx of ten thousand untraceable pounds into my
grubby little mitts made all the difference in the world. I got the
Alliance & Leicester off my back for starters.

Looking for a quick sale of the BM I called my old mate Steve
over at the showroom in Romford. Considering the abuse the
thing had taken I thought the three six he offered me was pretty
reasonable. I put five hundred to it to make it back up to his
outlay on the thing and handed the cash over to Nigel, plus a few
hundred more for the extra bits and bobs he'd bought. It was the
first he knew of the whole deal. I thought he might be pleased,
but on the doolally scale he went from nought to sixty in about
point three of a second.

"What have you done? You fucking idiot, what have you
done?"

It was all there again. The sweating, the slavering, the purple
face and the bulging eyes. I was afraid of him but only in the

sense that true, medical madness is a very frightening thing to behold and, for sure, old Nige was certifiable. It felt like I was leaving him behind in some way; moving on up, and I was glad of it.

"Sounds like the best deal all round," I told him calmly. "I get a regular income and can pay my mortgage without risking my life every day. Jez and the boys stay employed and will earn more dosh than they would have. The bank gets its overdraft paid off. Lucy and all the other customers will get better service because their couriers are now five times the size they were. You get your money back."

"I put in more than that," he screamed.

"The phone is all dismantled. You always said Nicolette needs one for her car. I'll bring it over."

"The business. The business, you fucking moron. I should get money from the business. It was half mine." He spat the words out with massive effort, like they were great gobs of sticky hate.

I thought about what he had put me through. I felt so strong. I felt reborn. "Just as ye sow ye shall reap."

Whatever *that* meant, Nigel didn't take it well and as I left him he was reduced to gasping, spluttering impotence. He really looked a danger to himself.

"Oh yeah," I said, turning around one last time. "I'm starting to get nasty letters from the bloke at the hospital who put my leg together. I've paid my private health premiums. Get that sorted, will you?"

The transition from Heroes to Rats was smooth. I needed it to be. I kept myself together, bought a couple of new suits and hit the gym and the pool. Divorced from all stress, I paid the leg some real attention and felt fitter than I had in years. In addition, I embraced the ordinariness that had gently enveloped my world. I was a fully paid up member of life's middle stream. I wasn't a star but I had no problems. I wasn't loaded but I had no worries. It was just what I needed after so much doubt and struggle. Then...

One Friday afternoon I was in the downstairs radio room, seeing the week's business through to it's conclusion. With me was Irish Pat who Pete had hired to kick off their new minicab venture. Released from the road I was soon my old buzzing, ticking, selling-machine self. Cold calls, referrals, bugging people I knew. I was laying on good business just as I had promised Pete I would.

Apart from the fact that Nigel and I weren't speaking and I had to shell out six hundred and fifty quid in medical fees because the claim didn't get paid, I was perfectly content. I kept a certain bottle of Brandy and a certain box of pills at the Beckton house. A keepsake of days long past. A token to remind me of how far I had come, and an incentive to keep on going.

I had a nice little pad in which I could afford to live, I had a few grand to spare in the bank and a Ford Escort in the street. Which *wasn't* stolen. I enjoyed the job that I could virtually do in my sleep. All was well. The problem, for a chronic under-achiever like me, is that when things are hunky-dory, things need to be just that little bit better. When life is 'OK' it's only a matter of time before life needs to be absolutely splendid. I got bored with hunky-dory. I needed more.

Pete Chalmers stuck his head around the radio room door. "Alright, Mick? How's it going?"

"Yeah cool, Pete. In fact I think that might even be it for the week. Jez is parked up for any late stuff just in case."

"Pat can handle that if it comes in, can't he? Pop upstairs, son."

I grabbed my jacket and followed him.

In the office already were Denny and Romanov - the crazy bastard who had nearly skittled me the day I had arrived to deliver Farmer's package all those weeks ago. And how about that for a coincidence? Romanov. That name was too unusual for it to be anyone else. Romanov the car thief. It was that dozy fucker who had nicked the Sierra Farmer had bought for me to sell that time. When I found out I called him every bastard under the sun for making such a mess of the engine number. We laughed about it in the end, and me and him became mates. He sprang from his seat as soon as I walked into the office. "Hey, Mick. My main man. What's the scam? Got any decent Sierras for sale?" He pumped my hand with exaggerated gusto, even though he'd seen me ten times that day already. "You know me and you are going to have to start hanging around together. Got an idea I can learn stuff from you."

"Let me know and I'll be there, bruv."

"OK, girls, calm down," said Masters from behind his desk.

Then I was looking down at him. Masters. *Demon* Denny Masters. The Lord of Leyton. The King of Wrong. The massive hams of his shoulders. The chunky, scarred cubes of his fists. The cropped hair and the eyes. Vile, humourless eyes; leaking spite. His face like a bowlful of last week's potato salad. I knew I'd never get used to being around him.

"Mick. Need to talk to you about something." Behind me I heard Chalmers lock the door.

My first thought was they were going to shoot me. The figures for the Heroes income I had given them hadn't matched up and that was what you got for lying to gangsters. Denny reached down into his desk drawer. What he came up with was no nine millimetre, though. He was holding a black plastic bag in his left hand and then, with a paper tissue between his right hand fingers, he delved into the bag to pull something out. I was aware of Romanov grinning at me like he couldn't wait to see my reaction. They were all clued up on something and the joke was like a succulent peach they were all sharing on a hot, summer's day - but made a point of not passing to me.

Then it was like the movies because Denny Masters, having already cleared a space on the gleaming mahogany of his desk-top, pulled a white roof slate from the bag and carefully laid it down. As he did so, I noticed a small lump and a light haze fall from it. It took me ages to fall in. I heard their kiddish giggles and then the sun burst through the clouds. It was like a choir of angels. It was... enlightenment.

"No!" I heard myself say. "No no no *nooooo*!"

Pete padded to the fridge and pulled out four cans of Stella which he handed around. So transfixed was I by what I had seen, he had to fold my fingers around the can for me.

"Christ, Den. How much is there?"

"Just a kee," he said, like it was a gram of the trodden-on wiz I used to sell to my mates down the Epping Forest Country Club a few years before. I approached with caution and with awe, like it was some kind of religious icon. There actually seemed to be a light shining from it.

"Holy shit. How much does it cost? I mean how much is it worth?"

"What it costs don't concern you. What it's worth is whatever it can be sold for. Which is why you've been asked here to discuss it. Bolivia's finest. Comes to us courtesy of our connection in Spain. We usually get one every two or three weeks but we are looking to step that up. We thought that as you have some experience in the field you might care to lend your efforts to the cause. Make a few quid for yourself and for us too."

"What's it cost me?"

"Nine hundred on the oz."

"On tick?"

"Sure, we can front it. We know you ain't going nowhere."

"Yeah, no worries. Tell me though, is it raw? I mean pure? What sort of cutting will it wear?"

Chalmers arrived at my shoulder proffering the tools of the trade; a bank card and a straw. "Be our guest," he said with an enticing leer. "And rack out one for each of us while you're there."

I heard Romanov giggle. "Alright working 'ere, innit?"

That weekend is now sketchy. I recall still being in the office on Saturday morning, but the first thing that comes back clearly is waking up at my place on Sunday afternoon. Curiously, I was in the single bed in the small bedroom. Even more curiously, I wasn't alone. I had no idea who she was and was pleased to be able to haul myself out of the bed without disturbing her. I hit the bathroom and scrubbed the inside of my tacky, rancid gob for a full five minutes. As I was having a slash I heard noises coming from my bedroom.

I eased open the door. Romanov I recognised, it was his three lady friends I couldn't quite place. The weird thing was, it was alright. So what if there was an orgy, to which I was uninvited, going on in my house? Didn't faze me.

My hangover stirred and my nose was badly blocked. Coffee. I sneaked back into the small room and pulled on a pair of boxers, which proved to be a fortuitous move because downstairs on the sofa, chairs and floor, there were six slumbering people. I didn't know any of them.

"Getting the kettle on, lad?"

I whizzed around. "Jesus, you made me jump then. Yeah, right, coming up."

I stepped over a couple of bodies and through to the open-plan kitchen, where I filled the kettle. The girl who spoke had slept in her jeans and T-shirt, and I watched her as she stood, a little unsteadily, and took a seat at the breakfast table near to me. She carefully touched her closed eyes.

"Shite."

"What's up?"

"Left me contacts in again."

She proceeded to scoop out the offending lenses and plop them in the appropriate bottles she fished from her bag. Then she put on a pair of glasses. Not ordinary glasses, though. These had big, square, tortoise-shell rims holding the proverbial bottle-bottom thick lenses which magnified her eyeballs to twice their natural size. I wanted to tell her that she must have very good eyesight to see through those.

"Black, three sugars please. Hurry up - I'm gasping."

"Your accent," I said as the kettle gurgled. "You a scouser?"

"Fazakerley."

"What's your name?"

"Julie. Who are you?"

"I'm Mick. This is my house."

"Oh yeah. I remember."

"You remember what?"

"I met you last night."

The Fear. I couldn't remember *anything*. I joined her at the table with the drinks. I looked at her and grinned.

"What?" she said.

"Those glasses. Excuse me."

"You're not going to tell me I must have good eyesight to see through them are you?"

"Wouldn't dream of it."

"Good. I'm not so much short-sighted as three parts blind. I normally wear contacts, but they do me head in when I leave them in all night."

"You look..."

She sipped her coffee. "I look what?"

"You look..."

"Yes?"

"You look lovely."

She looked down sharply into her coffee, sipped again.

"So listen. This may seem daft but I think I may have had a few last night. Where did I actually meet you all? I'm assuming you lot are all together, no?" I waved my arm in the general direction of the lounge.

"Yeah This is my lot. So don't you remember any of it, or just parts?"

"To be honest it starts to get a bit hazy around eight on Friday."

She thought I was joking.

"We were at the comedy club in Leicester Square. Don't you remember that?"

I gulped coffee and shook my head.

She turned in her seat and pointed to a girl curled up in the corner. "That's Sandy. It was her birthday yesterday so we all went up there for the evening. Are you telling me you don't remember your friend getting up on stage?"

"What friend?"

"I think he's your friend. He came back here with us last night I think. Bit Italian looking."

"Yeah, yeah. He got on stage?"

"Yeah."

"He got on stage in the Comedy Club in Leicester Square?"

"Yeah."

"What for?"

"To tell some jokes. He was dead good too."

The beast of nausea stirred in my gut...

"Listen. This lot here. Is this everyone?"

She surveyed the human wreckage. "That's all of us. Why, got some spare bodies unaccounted for?"

"You could say that."

I looked her over. She was tall, maybe five seven or eight. Dark bob, blue eyes, pale skin and a lovely honest, open face. You could tell just by looking at her that she would never lie to anyone about anything, because she had no conception of how to do such a thing.

"You're staring," she said.

"I'm sorry."

"I bet there's fuck all in your fridge."

"How do you know that?"

"You're single, living on your own. Any shops around here? I'm starving."

We went for a stroll to clear our heads, grab the Sunday papers and score bread, bacon, sausages and eggs. Romanov and the four girls from upstairs all looked pretty edgy and all buggered off after the first coffee. The little one I had been with clashed eyes with me and then looked quickly away. I didn't know her name, I had no idea who she was, where we had met or what we had done.

My other new-found friends all began to drift away during the early evening. It turned out they were all from Essex, Brentwood and Upminster mainly, although I had never met any of them before.

Finally there were three of us: me, Julie and a gorgeous little American Indian girl called Jade. She was on her own because her bloke, another American, was back in the States trying desperately to organise a work visa or something, so that he could get over here quick before his little darling got corrupted by some crazed, drug-fuelled maniac.

Julie wasn't attached at all, and actually lived quite close to me in Forest Gate. By the time I ran them back to her place, I knew I would be seeing both of them again before long.

There are two problems with cocaine. One becomes evident straight away, and the other after you've been on it for a while. The long-term realisation is that, well, quite frankly, it's not very good. For the price you pay you would expect it to be a lot better than it is. That's why people have to keep doing more. Cocaine always makes you think that the next line will be the one to hit the spot, and guess what? It never is. Addiction by deceit I call it. The immediate problem, though; the prima facie drawback with old uncle Charles is that it makes you want to have a drink. That's definitely the trouble with cocaine: the drink. You have one line and you need a beer. You have a beer and what do you know? Time to hit a few more lines.

The thing about the stuff the chaps started laying on was that it really was a top notch bit of gear, which is the way we like our problems. I mean you couldn't sell it raw - you just couldn't.

"Don't spoil your customers from the off," Chalmers had wisely counselled me. "You give them the good stuff, it'll take them ages to get through it and they'll always want it that good."

Too right. So on the Monday following that mad, inaugural weekend, I clearly needed to do some shopping. I went out and bought a mortar and pestle from Debenhams, a half kilo box of white glucose powder from Boots, a roll of freezer bags from Woolworth's, a set of Stanley knife blades from B&Q, the latest issue of Cosmopolitan magazine and a set of very expensive and incredibly accurate electronic scales. Who the hell said drug dealers don't have to work hard for their money?

Few people on the right side of the law can have any notion of how fiddly and complicated the mother business can be. If *News at Ten* and *Miami* bloody *Vice* were anything to go by, you'd think that all you have to do is go around wearing a silly suit, grow your hair into a ponytail and call people "motherfucker" before you shoot them. Give me a break.

Denny and Pete suggested the stuff was good enough to wear a fifty-fifty bash. That is to say, for every gram of coke on the table I could add another gram of filler material and be left with two grams of gear of an acceptable standard. Thus the average punter, the consumer at the end of the line who is buying a gram (or perhaps a twenty pound wrap) in a pub or club, can only realistically expect his stuff to be of a certain standard and no better. All dealers cut their gear for the street sales. If they didn't, they wouldn't be making enough money.

I opted for a more generous cut of around two thirds-one third. What I did first was divide the ounce I'd got from the chaps into two. One half I set aside and the other half, (fourteen grams) I tipped into the mortar along with five grams of glucose. Then I ground away for a good ten minutes. Yeah, who said it was easy money.

Then I emptied the entire nineteen grams out onto the spotlessly clean glass top of my little breakfast table and went at it for another ten minutes with one of the blades. I dabbed a little onto the end of my tongue, lashed it around my gums. The instant freeze pleased me so much I weighed out another couple of grams of glucose and crunched that into the brew as well. Having arrived at a happy formula, I decided that my toil and ingenuity merited a reward, so I hacked myself out a generous eight incher and scoffed the lot in one hit. Ah yes, what a business. Sweet sister coke. Where would we be without you? Then the searing exhilaration as it scorched through to my brain, bridging those synapses, badgering those neurons, flooding those neuro transmitters and generally pushing all those naughty little buttons we all have but so rarely use. Wired? I was plugged into the national fucking grid.

Then, of course, I decided I needed a drink. I put a tape on the stereo. Then something weird happened; I looked at the clock and it was morning and nearly time to go to work. Better get a move on.

I got the Cosmo and ripped the front and back pages into approximately two inch squares. Always use a magazine, never ordinary paper because sweat goes through that. I folded the squares into loads of little wraps. Origami for druggies. Then I weighed the stuff out into point nines. Soon enough I had a neat little pile of wraps. Problem was, I was two grams light. Surely I hadn't done *that* much? Oh well, plenty more where that came from.

The other half an ounce was to be for a potential bulk sale, so I only cut in two and a half grams of glucose which I shovelled into one of the freezer bags giving me sixteen and a half grams in total. I then wrapped that bag tightly inside two more bags for safety. Already I was looking forward to that evening because I had a special treat planned. I was going to see Vicky Patterson.

Upon my return from the last Mallorca trip when I'd stayed with the Captain, I had called her up to say hello and she'd urged me to get down to Margate to see her. Two years later I got around to it. But I wasn't the only unexpected arrival. Seven pounds three ounces of Gina Louise had beaten me to it, and not by any conventional means either. Once the young one was asleep Vicky started telling me what is was like when dreams don't come true.

"He told me he was firing blanks," she said as she gave me coffee.

"What? Who?"

"Gina's father. It wasn't a trick, he thought he was. Then, to get us a few quid, he held up the Halifax in the High Street and got nicked. He's got a record as long as your arm so we won't be seeing him for a while. He told me to get on with my life and forget about him."

I watched her in silence as her eyes glossed over.

"Things haven't gone the way I wanted. This really wasn't part of the plan. Don't get me wrong, I love Gina and I wouldn't be without her. She's my life now, but it's hard. It feels like I'm starting all over. I have joy but there's no fun. It looks like the old ways are finished for me, Bugsy. Feels like I haven't been out in a decade."

I listened quietly as she hoisted her legs up and folded them underneath her, both sadness and worry clouding her usually shimmering blue eyes.

"It's a mistake. That's what it feels like. This feels like someone else's life but I'm living it.. I shouldn't be here now. I should be scorching on some beach somewhere during the day and then going out dancing and ripping it up at nights. That is what I'm all about. That's what I *do*."

I wanted to tell her that I knew. Vicky was showing symptoms of the Dreams Failure Syndrome in all its savage destructiveness. Whatever that was.

"Well I don't know where that Paki bastard is," she said, lightening the mood. "He was supposed to be here half an hour ago."

"Who is this geezer then? Safe is he?"

"Ishy? Yeah, good as gold. He's been good to me. Lets me have Rocky or Soap bar on tick. Same as the wiz. He's cool. Good bloke. Bit over the top sometimes, but he's so warm-hearted. Been seeing him for a couple of months."

"Well that's good."

"Yeah, he's okay. He says he's from Lebanon but someone told me he's from Southall."

At that moment we both looked up as a pair of legs stopped on the pavement above, and then swivelled around to begin their descent down the steps to Vicky's basement flat.

"Talk of the devil."

Ishmael Zamaan, as he called himself, was everybody's idea of a drug dealer. He looked like an extra from that Pacino film Scarface. He had jet black hair pulled back into a tight, sleek ponytail, dark skin, a gold tooth and white shoes. *White*! He should have just stuck a sign over his head saying 'Dodgy geezer'. It would have had the same effect, but he would have looked less of a prat. But for all that, Vicky proved to be a fair judge of a man's character, because Ishy was indeed as good as the gold in his tooth.

He windmilled into her place, full of bounce and buzz and good feeling, keen as mustard to be a friend of a friend - especially if that friend was holding quality powder. It was the first time since Spain anyone had called me "Man". He offered me his hand but instead of the normal handshake he scooped my thumb into his palm and we shook like that.

"Mick, my man. How's it going? What's happening up in the big smoke? Hey, you ever get over Kensington way?"

"Nah, mate. Not my area. I'm from the other side: East London and Essex."

"Pity. I could introduce you to a right few faces there. Anyway, how's tricks? Vic tells me you're holding decent bugle."

Straight to the point. I liked that.

"Yeah, mate." I pulled the gear from my pocket and grabbed a Thompson Twins album from a rack beside the sofa. I'd actually removed the surplus two and a half grams from the bag for personal, so I had a precise half ounce for sale.

"Hold on," Ishy said, leaping to his feet and grabbing a mirror from the wall. "Might as well do this properly."

I pulled my AA card from my wallet and lifted out enough for three lines. As I was doing so, Ishy plucked some from the bag on the end of the longest fingernail I have ever seen on a bloke and dabbed it onto his lips and tongue. As he smacked and sucked, he pulled a crisp fifty from his bulging wallet. I didn't know if he'd cleared his savings account to make a favourable impression, but it didn't much matter. Just so long as he didn't come out with the normal bollocks about it being too cut, he could do what he liked. He hit his line.

"Thing is, Ishy," I began to tell him, "my people are interested in getting good reliable contacts. Not just one-offs. I need to be doing decent amounts every week, especially if I'm coming all the way down here. And it'll be twenty-eight and a half grams to the ounce, guaranteed."

"How much?" Was all he said.

"Thousand fifty on the oz. I can go cheaper, but if I do you know exactly what I'm going to do to it."

I caught his huge, brown eye just as Vicky dipped down for her line; she dragged so hard and long she nearly lifted the mirror clean off the coffee table.

"So don't knock me down, mate. It's black label and it's well cheap and I ain't taking no vote on that. You know I'm right."

He grinned and showed me his gleaming tooth.

"My man, I like your style. Vic, where you been keeping this boy? He's a class act. Tell you something, class," he assured me, holding out his spread, pale palm towards me. "You give me two minutes and I'll give you your answer, and I'll be as straight with you as you were with me."

205

"I'll drink to that," I said, and pulled the bag away from Vicky before the whole stash disappeared.

Ishmael Zamaan (or whatever he was called) was nobody's fool, which is why he became a customer. He knew I was going to be his supplier as soon as he'd hit that first line. In fact, I reckoned that very few people in the entire country, at that level, could get it as cheap and as good as I could. I began to appreciate the position of privilege in which I'd found myself. It was great being a gangster. I got rich because of my place in the outfit and Ishy got rich because he knew me.

Of course, he wasn't my only outlet. I resumed contact with my old mates out in Essex and soon realised that I had unearthed good, solvent customers in the form of Julie and her circle of friends. Ishy was good for bulk turnover but the bits and pieces to the others was where the proper mark up was at. The sums were just beautiful.

I would buy an ounce of speed from the chaps at eighty quid. I spooned in a glucose and flour mix and bloated that ounce out to forty grams, which I would knock out at around a tenner a pop; bringing in close on four hundred notes. That would usually take a fortnight. The coke was even cuter. The ounce cost me nine hundred and I ended up hitting it just as hard as the speed; I would sell those forty grams at sixty quid each grossing a very respectable two thousand four hundred notes which would normally take me around three weeks to pull in.

There would be discounts for larger amounts, of course, but including puff sales I was clearing over a monkey a week. Add to that the stash I was running down to Ishy most weekends, and the net income was getting on for the grand mark. On top of that I had the two fifty a week from the job. Alright, that might not sound like a fortune now, but back then - eighty nine I think it was - that was five times the national average. And it had happened from nothing within a couple of months. It was just too easy. And it was only the beginning.

The problem was, it was nowhere near enough. The first casualty was the car. Well, how the hell was I expected to run around dropping off top-grade gear in an Escort?

My mate Steve at the bike shop steered me to a pal of his who owned a site on the strip in Seven Kings and I scored a stunning Jaguar XJ12 It took care of just about all my savings, but with an income like mine, who cared? Midnight blue, it had the skirts, the spoilers, a Jaguar figurine on the bonnet and a hundred watt Kenwood stereo.

Masters hit the roof, demanding to know what I thought I was: "A fucking idiot, wide open, empty-headed, drug dealing spade, or what?"

Julie thought it was outrageous, and we began to see quite a bit of each other. Restaurants, the cinema. I even let her drag me to the theatre once, I think.

When the weather broke into the summer, I popped around to see Steve again. It was just a social call really, but I ended up coming away with a nice, new Suzuki eleven 1100 EF. The leg felt up to it, so it was daft not to treat myself.

Friday nights were just the best. Cocktails on the poop deck, London style. The good thing about it was that the four of us joined in and enjoyed it - even the bristling, growling bear that was Demon Denny Masters. We'd work hard all week and then, at the stroke of six o'clock on Friday afternoon, we would shut up shop, rendezvous without fail in the upstairs office and kick-start the weekend. Paul's orders and mine, which had come through during the week, would be bundled up and prepared for us.

The chaps had two safes; one behind a print of Constable's Haywain in the office, which was the decoy one, easy to find in the event of a raid. The other, where the gear was kept, was under a false concrete slab in the floor of the warehouse that no one would ever suss.

The problem was the stuff normally had to go straight back into the safe, because within the hour, all four of us were too out of it to risk taking it away. We invariably got through a case of Stella between us, along with five or six grams – all before the normal world was sitting down for its fish and chips. I went through thirteen consecutive Fridays having to leave the Jag at the yard because I was too wrecked to drive.

For all his glowering menace Den was an outrageous raconteur, albeit with a malicious edge. Always the stories about how some bloke's wife was actually that bloke's sister, or how some face was chasing boys down Patpong Road when they were meant to be on holiday on the Costa with the wife and kids. Dirty stuff, like how he'd seen a film of some rival's missus with the Labrador. Nasty playground shit but strangely compelling when you're into your second gram.

After we had put ourselves into orbit in the office, the normal modus operandi would be to head over to the West End with Romanov. He had a flat in Bermondsey and we would cab it over there to catch our breath before heading on. Then we'd get changed (I kept fresh clothes at his place for just that purpose) load up with more coke and sod off for the rest of the night.

We were a chart-topping double act. He seemed to know everyone in London and there was nowhere we couldn't afford to go. We had screaming nights throwing the Charlie around every time we went out. We loved everybody and everybody loved us. All that love didn't come cheap, but I was earning money so fast everything was a bargain. *Life* was a fucking bargain.

Then suddenly, in the space of a fortnight, everything got thrown into overdrive. Suddenly it was like I was living in a film. I wasn't just watching it, I was in it and the entire virtual, celluloid extravaganza was sound-tracked by the rolling thunder of a stomping bass beat. I hated going to bed, and when I did I couldn't wait to get up. Even when I was just walking around it felt like I was driving a fast car, and when I really was driving a fast car, it felt like I was at the controls of a Harrier Jump Jet. I was starring in my own personal video game.

This could actually be dated because I remember, at the time, hearing about a bomb on a plane in Colombia. Avianca flight 203 left Bogota on the short trip to Cali. It was only in the air five minutes when an explosive charge ripped through the fuselage, bringing it down the quick way. With a hundred and seven innocent people on board. Investigations revealed that a man in a suit brought the device onto the aircraft in a suitcase, but everyone knew whose bomb it was. It would be the beginning of the end for Pablo Escobar.

But back then I wasn't even aware there *were* victims of the cocaine trade, or any other drug trade for that matter. A time would come when I'd feel it would have been an upgrade to have been on that plane myself, but in those days I was eating sunshine and shitting rainbows. And it kept getting better.

The quantum leap really began, strangely enough, with the four of us getting blasted in the upstairs office one Friday afternoon. Ripped. Wired. Buzzing. Proper chaps. At around ten me and Romanov cut out and headed over to his. I was fishing out a suit or a pair of trousers or something when he stopped me. He was hacking out a couple of tramlines of coke so big, a table place mat would have been more appropriate than the credit card he was using.

"No. Don't bother with the Showaddywaddy outfit tonight. We're doing something else. Put some really shitty clothes on."

"Why?"

"Because we're going somewhere really shitty."

"We go somewhere really shitty every week. Those overpriced, West End tourist traps you take me to are a joke."

"I know, but tonight I can promise you something especially degrading. Ever been to an acid house party?"

He dropped to his knees before the altar of his snow-covered coffee table and whacked a chunky ten incher of uncut up one nostril, like he was delicately sampling the bouquet of a prize-winning rose. He dropped the rolled twenty down for me without a word.

"Behave," I told him. "How old are you?"

"Now you should know that don't mean diddly squat. Well? Have you?"

"No. But I know I wouldn't like it."

"How do you know?"

"Because the music is shit."

"Oh - and this from the man who was dancing his tits off to Gary Glitter last weekend."

"That was different. That was a seventies night."

"Yeah and you were too old for it the first time around. Ever had an E?"

This was a good point. I was supposed to be a drug dealer and there was a drug craze, a drug *culture* sweeping the country - and I knew nothing about it.

"No," I told him honestly waiting for him to take the piss. Which he didn't. "You?"

"Sure," He shrugged. "I've done everything. And I've been raving."

"What's it all about, then? The E thing?"

"Fucking untrue, mate. Better than coke."

"Yeah?"

"Too right."

"What is it though? It's just a pill, innit?"

"Yeah. Or a capsule. Munch one of those and you're straight through the happy door."

"What's in it then? I heard there was smack in there, mixed with coke or something."

"Christ knows, mate, but whatever it is, it's the biz. And the tarts love it. Gets 'em going. Know what I mean?"

Forward through new frontiers then. "Alright. I'm game for a laugh. Where is it?"

"That's the thing. It's a secret."

"What do you mean it's a secret?"

"No-one knows where it is."

"Well, how does any bastard get there then?"

"Of course the *organisers* know where it is. Word is out that we have to be parked outside the Dun Cow pub in the Old Kent Road at midnight, then some nut in a white Sierra rips past and we, along with anyone else who is meeting there, chase after the fucker and he leads us to the place. It's a right laugh."

"Are you for real?"

He howled piratically at my naivety. "That's what you gotta do. It's illegal innit? No licences, no council permission, no fire certificates. It ain't a disco you know. Just a bit of a light show and a DJ in a barn somewhere, and up to ten thousand bouncing space heads. You'll love it. So put on those old ripped jeans, some trainers and a T-shirt. We're going to make it so, bitch. Jenny and her mate will be here in a minute."

"Who are Jenny and her mate when they're at home?"

"You don't remember Jenny?"

"Should I?"

"Not if you don't remember the women you go to bed with, I suppose."

"Whoa. Back up. How's that?"

"You remember. Ages ago. Last winter not long after you started working for us. We all went back to your place to crash out. You were with little Jenny."

"Oh yeah. Right. That was Jenny, was it? I was wondering."

"Sure is, and she keeps asking after you."

"Yeah? What does she say?"

"She says you were so fucking useless she wants to have another go, see if it was true."

He was always winding me up like that.

So we dressed down. I even managed to dig out my old 'I choked Linda Lovelace' T-shirt. Then we sat around waiting for the girls to show. We hit a few more lines. I told Romanov to get the brandy out but he refused, insisting that if we were going to do this thing we were going to do it right. "No alcohol."

"None?" I whimpered.

"None."

"What about the five or six pints we've just had?"

He belched horribly. "That don't count. Take my word for it, booze is a killer, especially when you get on the pills. They cancel each other out." He made little circles with his fingers up beside his temples. "Fucks with your enzymes and all that. Take my advice, boy, stick to class As."

Who was I to argue with that? So then Jenny and her mate Andrea showed up, and for twenty quid she sold me a little white pill with the shape of a bird stamped into it. A Dove she called it. We swallowed one each and, once again, my life changed irrevocably.

Come the witching hour, all four of us were sat in Andrea's car. For over one hundred and fifty yards down the Old Kent

Road stretched a line of knackered out motors full of weird-looking, long-haired, stick thin kids with eyes like golf balls, wearing baggy jeans, flowery T- shirts and silly hats. Tangy swirls of marijuana breath hung sweet and heavy in the air. I didn't think too much at all of the magical powers of Ecstasy, but I had to admit the atmosphere was electric.

True to the plan, at one minute past midnight, a white Ford Sierra came blasting out of nowhere, sounded its horn three times and belted off towards Lewisham. There were whoops and hollers all around, everyone jumped into their motors and away we went in hot pursuit. It was hilarious.

"This your first ware'ouse then?" Jenny asked, drifting a skinny hand onto my thigh.

I relaxed and breathed deep. "Yeah. Yeah it is. So what happens, Jen? Have you been to many? That right it goes on all night?"

She looked up at me and, as the lamp posts flashed by, I copped her eyes in stroboscopic effect and saw that they were all pupils. She had no irises.

"Yeah. You'll be amazed at the energy you'll have."

I wondered if that was some kind of slur upon the performance (or lack of) that I'd turned in that last time. Then I felt myself fascinated by how deliberate her speech, and indeed all of her movements were. She didn't move like a drunk, not helplessly. She was fully aware and capable, just doing everything calmly and slowly. I got a hard-on just watching her.

All the while, the relentless monotony of the music in the car was beginning to give me a headache. So much so that I even asked Andrea, to a reply of raucous laughter all round, if she had any Zep or Springsteen. Romanov's response was to turn up the volume. And then... Then... As we continued driving, the thump of the drum and the mad synthesisers began to make some kind of sense. It was just the strangest thing. I felt myself being drawn into the relentless loop of the music and would have been quite happy to stay there in the car, just driving around for the rest of the night. Jenny mentioned some bloke called Gerald. Maybe she knew him. And when each track (seven or eight minutes long as they all were) drew to a close, I suddenly thought it was the end of the world. I actually started to panic, terrified I would never have the chance to hear anything quite so wonderful ever again. But, luckily enough, there was always more. Each new tune sounded fresh and inventive and dazzlingly different. I never thought I could like that shit, but for some reason it was really growing on me.

I regained some of my youth that night as I was magically catapulted out of reality and into a world in which I instinctively knew I wanted to live. It was the greatest social event to befall me since my fourteenth birthday, when I'd got served down the 'Choke for the first time. Maybe even greater because I had been born to rave.

The E kicked in for real just as we were parking up outside a huge, grey, nameless warehouse on a secluded industrial estate near Catford. I was pleased Romanov had denied me the brandy, because I didn't want anything to interfere with the high I was getting from that solitary little pill. Something truly ethereal was going on. Light, airy giddiness to begin with; a slight fluttering in the stomach and then rush after rush of staggering joy.

I cast wary glances all around but was relieved to see I wasn't alone. You could tell that *everyone* looked exactly how I felt. You just knew. Everywhere you looked there was a huge, blissed out grin. I was so overwhelmed with a wonderful feeling of goodwill and humanity that I started shaking hands with people. Up and down the line, like Prince Michael Targett. Everyone loved me too.

As we patiently shuffled towards the door massive bass vibrations and the rat tat tat of the drum were calling us onwards and ever closer. Sacrificial lambs to some psychedelic slaughter. By the minute I felt the drug flow more and more to my groin. I still didn't know what kind of relationship I had with Jenny, but when that first wave of sexual delight swept me away, I really didn't give a toss. We were nudged up together as it was but then I stepped directly behind her, ground my tackle into her arse and wrapped my arms around her. With my left arm I grabbed her waist and pulled her in closer and tighter to me. As I did so my right arm reached around and found her left breast which I kneaded and squeezed for all to see. A knee in the bollocks and a smack in the mouth could and should have been her reply, but, no. It was alright. It was alright because Ecstasy made it alright. Jenny did nothing. Nothing other than loll her head back onto my shoulder, moan softly and let me do whatever I wanted.

I would have been more than happy standing in the queue all night just groping her. If that had constituted the rave scene in its entirety I would have been sold on it for life. But there was more of course. Oh, was there ever more.

Another twenty quid (raving not being at all cheap in those pioneering days) and we were in; closer towards the inner dungeon of depravity. Roll up, roll up. Welcome to Catatonia. Leave your psychoactive capabilities at the door and step inside! As we opened the big swing doors to the main room, someone hit me with a brick. That's what it felt like when the noise, the heat, the lights and the smell pulverised my senses. "Fucking hell," I bellowed, barely able to hear my own voice. "This is un*real.*"

I couldn't hear her, but I could at least see Jenny laughing. Then her lips were on my ear. "Knew you'd like it," She yelled. "Knew you were better than all that coke and booze. Let's get a drink. It's boiling in here already."

By the time we picked our way through the crowd to the makeshift bar, I was soaked in sweat. I scored us a couple of cans of lukewarm coke at a quid a pop. Then she was tugging my arm again.

"There's money here. This is what it's going to be like from now on. No more poxy discos. And look at this lot. Everyone's on it. What a captive market, eh?"

I was so wrong-footed by what was happening to me, I wasn't the least surprised to hear this odd, little girl use a phrase like 'captive market'. It seemed as sensible as anything else. But I did as she suggested and took a look around at my new, madly-flailing chums. The absolute chaos; the complete integration and the instant, tactile friendships that were being born at the rate of a hundred a minute all around lead me to perceive a startling aura of... innocent sin. There was the charged, lascivious atmosphere of a Roman orgy, but everybody knew what they were doing, and everybody was delighted with the choices they were making. People were kissing and holding and embracing, and they couldn't have been happier. This was no corruption of the young and vulnerable. Everybody knew the score and they were having the time of their lives. I certainly was. And Jenny was yelling again.

"You've been standing here for half an hour now. Why don't we go outside?"

Half an hour? Come on. Two or three minutes maybe. It was true, I did feel pretty rooted to the spot, but my feet were tapping away at a rare old pace. Decision time. I tried to swig back the last of my coke but discovered that I was holding just a hot, empty can. I suddenly felt very confused and more than a little worried, but I knew I'd be OK. I knew I'd be OK because I knew exactly what to do next. I bent down to talk to Jenny and my head dipped and twitched like a bladder on a stick in marvellous, thick-skulled delirium.

"Listen," I bawled. "I'm going over there to stand next to that weird-looking bastard with the mad hair, OK? That's where I'll be."

Before she could reply I was off, and I was off in more ways than one, because what I had to do was dance - and once I'd begun, there was no end in sight. See, I'd always liked dancing, I'd just never been any good at it. I always worried that I looked a bit of a prat. But in there, in that place it didn't matter. It didn't matter because in there *everybody* looked like a prat. Black, white, girl and boy. Every single one of us was a whirling pill-head; a fully paid up, plugged in spaz jockey and we were 'AVIN' IT!

Not that those other weirdos remained weirdos for long. Of the six or seven hundred people wedged into that sauna I think I must have spoken to at least all of them, and they were all fab. How about that? There wasn't one wally amongst the lot of them. If I wasn't dancing, I was gabbing away to the person next to me. It was absolutely brilliant.

At one point I was slumped against a wall, watching intently as drops of human rain fell from the ceiling to land between my feet – 'chilling out' I think someone called it. I was struggling to read the back of a bloke's T-shirt nearby. It was something like; 'I DO have a drink problem – but at least I haven't got …'

I was trying to make out the rest when Jenny bounded over and sat beside me. She was smiling and looking radiantly gorgeous.

"Enjoying yourself, Mick?"

I bobbed my head in time to the crack of the snare . Boom boo ba DA. Boom boo ba DA. I smiled gormlessly.

"Listen," she said. "I've got to talk to you about something. It's important."

"Uh?"

"It's the pills. I've got to talk to you about the pills."

"Gop."

"I know what you and Paul do. I know you are in with some proper suppliers. OK? Now I've asked him before and he's said he can't do anything at the moment. I think he might have a bit of agro with his boss, but we're wasting time. Is there anything you can do? He doesn't know I'm talking to you about it."

"Fnnnff."

"Mick are you alright? Do you want to get some air?"

No. Air was not what I needed. Dance was what I needed and without a word I was off and running again. I stood directly in front of pulverising strobes and closed my eyes. I listened to the wonderful yet disturbing sounds and moved my body, slower this time, and felt myself carried away on some wild, glorious journey. Soon I was magically transported. It was scary at first, but I somehow knew that I was in no danger, and then I was amongst jungles and waterfalls and lakes and deserts. I could feel the heat of the sun and the spray of the water. I could hear the crash of waves and the hissing of foaming surf. I could see all the animals and all the people being friendly and kind to each other. Everybody in the world really did love one another and it was all going to be alright. The whole world was going to be alright. I could see the music and I could hear the colours. There really were dreams that came true and if only everybody could just...

Then the music stopped and someone heaved up a roller shutter and reality along with stinging daylight flooded back. It seemed like half an hour at most since we'd gone in there.

Like ugly, bedraggled, wretched refugees, we traipsed outside back into the real world. I spied Romanov talking to some woman and dragged him away. I was sodden and covered with dirt and sticky drink, but I was definitely in the mood for romance.

"Where are the girls?" I demanded.

"Gone. Ages ago. What happened to you?"

"Nothing. I've just been dancing."

"No, I mean how come you didn't want to screw Jenny? She was dying for it. That's two out of two now. I'm starting to get worried about you."

"She was? Oh shit. I don't even remember seeing her."

He laughed his deep, confident laugh. "You must have been so wrecked. Those Doves are good ain't they? In the end I had to do it for you."

"Do what?"

"The girls. The pair of them. Over there by the fence."

"Ah, you bastard. I really wanted to go with her."

"Too slow, mate. The Wayne Sleep act is fine but it don't get you laid, does it? I didn't mind filling in for you. Looks like you owe me one though."

He meant it too.

I needed to pick up my stuff from the warehouse in order to get down to Ishy that afternoon so he could get started on his Saturday night sales. I also needed to get back to Essex in time to start my rounds too. There was obviously something else I needed to talk to Ishy about. I needed in on the pills. And right then and right there I started to grow my hair.

Me and Romanov cabbed it back to the yard. On the way I noticed that my knee was twice the size it had been the previous evening yet I hadn't felt a twinge all night.

It was a bright, clear, Saturday morning. The south London mean streets were practically deserted apart from bargain hunters on their way to markets, dog walkers, amateur footballers and fucked up nut jobs like us two.

I eased back in the minicab seat, rested my head and closed my eyes. All manner of mysterious, other-worldly patterns formed behind my liquid lids. Gorgeous, swirling images. Images of kindness, of beauty and of love.

As professional as ever, Pete Chalmers was at the yard to organise the weekend deliveries and to organise me and Romanov. He roared with laughter when he saw us.

"Well well. The dynamic duo. Mick, you look like you've just gone ten rounds with Mike Tyson. What you been doing?"

"Dancing."

"Who with? Nellie the Elephant?"

"We went to a warehouse party," Paul told him. "Tell you what, Pete. Could do a lot worse than get into that. Twenty notes a ticket and all you do is open the doors. Bit of a light show, couple of DJs who know what they are doing, few chaps on the door and cram them in."

"Let's go inside."

We followed him into the main warehouse. I pulled down the shutter and secured it as Romanov snapped on the lights. Guided by his own radar, Pete walked to the spot some twelve yards in from the door and four in from the left side wall (by my reckoning) where the safe was located. He and Denny were the only ones who could find it without taking all day. A surreptitious miracle of engineering, it was comprised of a false concrete lid which laid over the safe, perfectly flush with the warehouse floor. I watched as he dropped to a squatting position and pulled out his Swiss army knife. You needed a specially designed key to dig down, turn and lift up the heavy concrete flap. There were two such keys in the entire world and Pete and Denny had them built *into* their own Swiss Army penknives. Only two people on the planet knew the combination to the safe: Pete and Denny, and it was never written down anywhere. Romanov was still talking. "I reckon we could squeeze in close on two thousand in here," he said splaying out his hands in the direction of the vast, echoing space. "Tins of Lucozade and bottles of spring water at a quid a go, and then..." He turned to face us and he was wearing his cheeky grin. "Then there's the gear. Fifteen quid minimum for those little pills. Lot of folding for one night's work."

"Yeah I know," replied Pete, pulling two boxes from the safe. "Me and Den have been talking about it. Wouldn't do it here though. Too close to home. Got a couple of places in mind. Thing is, if we are going to do it we want to do it all - and as daft as it might sound, we haven't got a proper Ecstasy source sorted yet. Either of you two know a dependable wholesaler?"

"I can get bits and pieces, but no real numbers," Paul told him.

"I'm seeing a proper bloke down on the coast this afternoon. He might know something," I said.

"OK. See what you can see. Paul, here's your stuff." He handed one box to Romanov. "I need to talk to Mick about a few things. If there's nothing else I'll see you Monday, son, yeah?"

"You got it, boss man." He stuffed his gear into the rucksack he always carried for that purpose and hauled it onto his shoulders. "I'll get a cab from across the street. Laters."

"Yeah, and be careful," Pete called.

As he stepped through the door in the roller shutter I shouted, "Oi, Paul. Tell that Jenny to give me a call will you?"

He just laughed, closed the door and was gone.

Up in the office, Pete was making coffee when he surprised me.

"Did you hear big Terry got transferred?"

The mere mention of the name got my heart beating uncomfortably faster - like Terry Farmer was a ghost from the past I would rather not see again. Or even think about.

"No. Where is he?"

"Wayland."

"Where's that?"

"Norfolk. C cat. Holiday camp."

"How long's he got left?"

"I'm not sure, at least a couple I think. Shame. Be good to see the old bastard again. You been to see him? Or Kerry?"

I shook my head and looked away.

"Whatever. Listen, what I want to talk to you about involves getting at it with the plastic. Now you say you've done this before, yeah?"

"'Sright."

"OK. Now what we want to do is move a bit up market." He reached down into his lower drawer and pulled out a plastic bag which he tossed across the desk at me. It contained cheque books, guarantee cards and credit cards. A couple of gold ones shimmered amongst them.

"As you know, we've been moving into cabs to the opera, coach trips to the races - shit like that. Moving away from Sharon and Wayne going to Southend for the evening, know what I mean? Good thing is, Rupert and Annabel get just as pissed, and when they lose stuff on the coaches it's fortunately worth a lot more to us. Amazing the things people leave stuffed down the back of the seats."

"So I see." I sipped my coffee and prepared for what was coming. I wasn't happy.

"So," he said. "Wanna go to work?"

I didn't really. I had things sweet enough with selling the gear, but I was loathe to disappoint - or rather, scared to. I'm sure Pete would've been philosophical had I declined the offer, but frankly, Denny frightened me. Just something in the way he looked at me sometimes. Dare I say no? I made a quick mental note to start saving money.

"Love to," I heard myself say. "But what about work?"

"Don't worry about the radio work from now on. Pat's doing good and we are going to get him an assistant, and we're also going to give Jez a rise and put him charge of the blokes. What we want you to do is compress your sales work into three days and get at it with the plastic in the other two. You'll still be on the same dosh."

Now that was a bit more like it.

"Thing is," Pete continued, "a lot of the cards and books we are turning up are for couples and women. It would help our earning capabilities if we had a tart on the firm - you know, like a husband and wife act? Know anyone?"

A beautiful warm glow lit me from inside. She'd moved around the time of Terry's arrest but I'd managed to get her new number. "Yeah. Yeah I do. Leave that to me."

"Great. Give her a shout and see if she wants to go to work."

"Roger, Roger."

I really liked Pete. He truly was a model professional criminal. Always in control, never got angry, never looked like getting violent. OK, so he had Denny to do all that for him, but at times he verged on the poetic with his philosophies and analyses of life and of crime. I once heard him giving Romanov a lecture about selling gear to some scumbag who had a reputation for being a grass.

"Paul," he advised, with ecclesiastical patience, "how many times have I told you? You won't get nicked for a mistake *you* make, you'll get nicked for a mistake someone *else* makes."

I thought back to the Sierra and the engine number. Different world. Different class.

"It's your liberty at stake boys, but it's our way of life. You want to break the law, you got to *know* the law. You don't take precautions then you lose, and if you lose it means they've won."

"Who are they?"

"They? They are anybody who ain't us."

He'd play little tricks too. We were drinking coffee and talking about the plastic when he said something right out of the blue.

"Wanna line?"

"Yeah. Love to."

"Wrong!" he sang. "It's nine o'clock on Saturday morning, you're off your nut and there's about five grand's worth of drugs that you're going to drive all the way to the coast in the pimpmobile. And you look like you've just crawled out of your own grave. Jesus Christ, Mick. Maybe you ought to get off it for a while."

"I'm just a bit knackered, Pete. Thought it might liven me up."

"I'll make us another drink, then we better go." He took our mugs to the sink, washed them meticulously and made fresh coffee.

"Now, back to business. What I was thinking would be a good

thing would be to go abroad to work some of this plastic and the books. Less risk. Know what I mean?"

"Really?"

"Yeah. It's so common over here these days. Every toerag is at it and that nauses things up for the rest of us. I think we'll get over to the Med, and get at it there."

How fucking cool was that?

"What we want to do is combine that with some other stuff we are getting into - namely forgery. We have access to a fairly good supply of moody Sterling and travellers cheques, which are obviously best changed up abroad. There's some proper dosh to be had here and we want you to be in charge of it. Hopefully there'll be you, your lady friend and Paul along for back-up and general help. All being well, there's more to be had from this than there is banging out the gear. A lot less bird too, should it all go wonky, which it won't. Then you come home, chuck all the dodgy ID away, get some more and off we go again."

Bingo. Was this rolling or what? Drug dealer and international villain. A proper face.

"How's your Spanish?"

"Not all that hot I'm afraid."

"That's OK. You'll be posing as a tourist anyway. You had your place in Santa Ponsa right?"

"Yeah."

"You'll know Costa De La Calma then?"

"Sure. Just up the coast from where I was."

"Did you know I usually go there once a year?"

"No." I was genuinely taken aback.

He nodded and smiled. "About ten years now."

I was agog. "So you were out there when I was there?"

"I guess so."

"Jesus, that's amazing."

"What did you call your place?"

"Bugsy's. Edificio Princessa."

"Oh yeah," he said, like he was remembering a mildly amusing joke.

An electrifying tingle shot up my spine. I felt like he was going to tell me something that would shake me clean off my seat. He didn't disappoint.

"Don't tell me you've heard of it?" I asked cautiously.

"Better than that. I went in there a few times."

I burst out laughing. "No. No way. You're kidding me."

"Between Paco's and the Pepperpot, yeah? The owners of The Pepperpot, Doreen and Stewart, I know quite well. I used to eat there."

I slapped the side of my own face to make sure I wasn't dreaming. The world was indeed a strange and beautiful place.

"Hold up. Hold up," I said. "You're not going to tell me we've met before, are you?"

He smiled indulgently, knowing he held all the aces. "Couple of times. Not my thing obviously. Full of pissed up kids. Thing was, I couldn't believe a bar could be run by people who were so wrecked all the time, so I had to go back to see if it was just a one-off, but nope; every time I went in there you were all slaughtered."

I fell into rapturous hysterics as he grinned smugly. "Shit, that's too much," I told him drying my eyes and shaking my head. "I couldn't keep a secret like that."

"Well you know. Bit of discretion. A man should never show his hand too soon."

If I thought that was mad, what he said next blew me away entirely.

"I was actually looking for the geezer that ran the place before."

Suddenly, shit got real. "You know John Durridge?"

He shook his head. "No. Never heard of him. I was after Luis Martinez."

I felt very tired, very quickly. I'd been having a nice time until then.

"You know Luis Martinez?"

"Yeah. A while ago I heard you telling Paul about some spic keeping you out of your bar. I'm presuming that was him."

"Small world," I conceded. "Yeah, that was him. If I added up the dosh that bastard cost me, it would fund all our habits for a year."

"Must have been difficult for you. Foreign country. Young bloke not really knowing what you were doing. I have a lot of respect for that. Strikes me we might be able to do ourselves a lot of good with this foreign business thing and settle a debt at the same time."

"How so?"

"Apart from being a sleazy, no good pimp, Luis is one of the best fences I've ever met, and I know a few. He pays a flat thirty percent, which is better than UK rates."

"So you figure whatever we nick on the plastic we can run straight round to him?"

"Right. And not only in Mallorca. He knows people all over Spain. This could be a regular little cottage industry we've stumbled onto. Safe too. Luis has contacts in the police. Bribable ones. He'd love a deal like this. In fact, he'd love it so much I reckon he'd be persuaded to part with thirty-five percent for our stuff, with the difference going to you towards settlement of what he owes you."

I couldn't speak. I couldn't speak because of the grin that wouldn't leave my face. Eventually I calmed down to tell him that I thought it was the most wonderful plan in the history of the world. I wanted to stay there all day to discuss the fine details, but Pete said that we both ought to be getting off.

"See if you can get up to see Terry. He'd like that I'm sure."

"Yeah. Yeah you're right. I will." I looked into my box and counted all the neat little bundles. "Even though the dodgy bastard used to overcharge me for his gear."

Pete smiled again. Another little secret. "It's only contacts, son. He was just further down the food chain. Who do you think he was getting it from?"

I smiled. There was so much I didn't know. I heaved my body out of the chair and was shocked to sense no feeling in my knee whatsoever.

"Actually," I told him sheepishly, "I think I'll give it a miss down in Margate today. Maybe go tomorrow when I'm in better shape."

"Won't your man be needing his stuff for tonight?"

"Yeah, but I'm just too knackered. I'll give him a call. He'll understand."

"Wrong! Don't you listen to anything I tell you? A man is only as effective as his attention to detail, and only as strong as his last delivery. You let him down and he lets his people down and you're yesterday's news and before you know it they've gone to someone else. We ain't the only dopers on the block you know. Go home and crash out for a couple of hours. I'll call you at..." He looked at his silver Rolex. "...one thirty. Ten minutes in a cold shower, then you have *one line* - and then you get your arse down there. And don't turn up the stereo on that thing so that everybody within five miles knows there's a drug dealer coming."

And that was exactly what we did, except that the shower was warm, I had five lines and I cranked the amp up full blast.

Down at Vicky's everything was double cool. Ishy was turning out to be a pleasure to deal with. He didn't bother checking and weighing the coke and I didn't bother counting the money. It was all too sweet. Anyway, he didn't need to check because Vicky had her nose in the bag doing just that, even before I had dropped it onto the table.

And who said crime didn't pay and drugs were no good for people? Ishy had ditched the clown's outfit and was a lesson in smart casual. Vicky looked as pretty as a picture too. New clothes, proper hair-do, expensive make up, hired help with Gina. She looked as gorgeous as she had done that first day I'd seen her on the beach.

We got the niceties out of the way by having a line each, and then I stood and clapped my hands together.

"Ishy, my boy. Talk to me."

"For you, class, anything. What can I tell you?"

"Es."

He flashed the tooth. "You come to the right place, ace. What do you want to know?"

"Well, what the hell is it for a start?"

"What do you mean?"

"Well I hear all sorts of lurid stories about it being a mix of smack, coke, speed and Christ knows what else."

"MDMA," I heard Vicky call from the kitchen.

"That's it," Ishy confirmed.

"That's what?"

"That's what Ecstasy is. MDMA. That's what it's made of."

"Yeah, but what is that? Is it some kind of plant or something? Does it grow?"

He stood up too and called out to Vicky. "Hey, Vic. Get this man. He's class. Gets me every time. We can't ever lose touch with this boy. No, Mick. MDMA is a chemical. It's man-made. That is the abbreviation for the real word which, when you write it down, goes all the way across the page." He held his hands a yard apart.

"Some mad, debauched crazoid in a lab somewhere cooks it up, bless his little cotton socks."

"Right. So you got any connections? Can we get something going?"

"Funny you should say that. I can lay my hands on good pills but I've got a mate out in Holland who knows one of the chemists who is actually brewing the shit up. This is coincidental, because I was going to mention this to you anyway. I should be able to get a good supply going and get you an ounce for...twelve hundred quid."

"Hmmm. Do you know how that might break down?"

"OK now check this out. A while back one of the underground magazines on the acid scene did a survey of the different types of pills that were doing the rounds. Imagine that eh? What job do you do? Oh I sample illegal class A drugs for a living. Anyway, the best out there is known as a Rhubarb and Custard, so named because they come in mauve and yellow or red and yellow capsules. The Rhubarbs were analysed in a lab and they found out that each one contained around a hundred milligrams of raw MDMA."

He'd secured my interest. "These the best on the market, yeah?"

"About as good as they get. Blow your head off."

"Vic," I called. "Have you got pen, paper and a calculator?"

After a few seconds rummaging she came back with what I needed.

"So let me get this right here," I said. "You can lay me on an ounce of the stuff for twelve hundred quid, which is twenty-eight grams, which is twenty-eight thousand milligrams. Right?"

"Right."

"OK now if we put a hundred milligrams of the gear in a capsule we'll have a very saleable product, yeah?"

"You got it."

"OK, so at a hundred milligrams a pop, we squeeze obviously... two hundred and eighty units out of each ounce. Current market value on the one is still fifteen quid so an ounce will gross... " I did the calculator walk. "Four thousand two hundred quid."

"A swift three large from each ounce. How long would it take you to unload two hundred and eighty top grade Es, Class?"

"I've got absolutely no idea, mate, but the sums certainly appeal."

"And don't forget, you don't have to make them that good. This is a real business now. Forget the summer of love. The hippies have moved out and the businessmen have moved in. Already the rave culture is letting people down. Getting pills made out of MDMA is harder and harder. There's MDA and MDEA - inferior replacements. You put out a product with say... fifty milligrams of the real gear in and that will be an acceptable hit - and you'll have five hundred and sixty to the oz."

I greedily hit the calculator but Ishy was in front of me.

"At fifteen quid a throw that's eight thousand four hundred quid gross. Seven thousand two hundred notes profit on the ounce."

"Holy shit," I declared. "So does a cap or a pill make any difference?"

"Not really. Some producers have access to those machines that compress the powder into pills, that's all. More professional. Also, if you use capsules there is always the chance that some freeloader further down the line will open them up, cut something in there and sell on for a profit and impinge upon the good name of your product." He shrugged. "Risk you take."

"No chance of getting hold of one of those machines?"

"I asked around a while ago but you have to be so careful. I mean, what are you going to be wanting one of those for, right?"

"Good point."

"But I'm pleased you're keen, Class. It's the thing of the future."

"You ain't the only one who says that."

"It's a fact. The rave scene is exploding out of sight and it's affecting everyone, not only clubbers. Before long, everybody in the country who is out on a Saturday night - be it at a rave, disco, club, pub or just down the chip shop is going to be on the pills. It's the drug of the future. It's got Charlie beat all ends up. None of this diving out to the bog every half an hour to powder your nose. No snorting and sneezing your way through the evening and, most importantly, no forty, fifty or sixty quid to get yourself a decent buzz. Fifteen notes gets you up there all night."

"I see what you mean but I can't see it taking the place of coke. It's not that expensive."

"That's easy for you to say, but to the wally on the dole or to the average geek in the office struggling to pay the bills... There are loads of people who will take an E that would never dream of going near coke. Got to be ready to serve them up. If you don't then someone else will."

"Nah. I can't see people not being able to afford their gear."

"Mick, we're not talking about junkies here - just recreational users. That's *our* market. If people can't afford to get smashed on drugs of a weekend then they'll either cut down or stop. Not everyone goes out housebreaking just to get a fix you know."

"Mate, we've made tons of dough and we'll make tons more. As long as it stays illegal we got the best product in the whole world."

"It will continue, yeah, but I sell to the end user. My punters don't *need* drugs, they just like them when they've got the money, which, fortunately, has been most of the time lately. But don't get out of touch, Mick. Don't you read the papers? There's a cold wind starting to blow. Word is a recession is on the way. Make sure you're ready for it."

If Pete Chalmers had surprised me about being in Bugsy's then I surprised him just as much by tracking down Dixie and taking her round to the warehouse on the Monday morning.

We hadn't seen each other for over two years and she wasn't up to much so, yes - she was interested in talking to my new employers about getting at it again. Especially when I mentioned the foreign travel.

I marched her up the stairs into the office like I was leading a prize heifer by a ring through her nose. I was pretty pleased with myself for being able to help out the chaps in such an effective and pleasant fashion. I knocked and went straight in.

"Pete, Den. Got someone here to meet you. The best lady kiter in the business and a good friend of mine. This is Juliette: Juliette Dixon. But everybody calls her..."

"Dixie. Dear oh dear. As I live and breathe." This was Pete.

Masters was silent. His face would not have looked out of place on Mount Rushmore. It was difficult to know who was the more surprised - me or the pair of them. Certainly not Dixie.

"Hello Pete. Hello Denny. Nice to see you both again," she oozed, She could have told me she knew them.

Pete was grinning, and plainly he had the inside track information on what had gone down in the past. Denny, on the other hand, wasn't smiling. Denny wasn't smiling at all.

"Tell me, Mick," he asked, regaining his composure and forcing the thinnest, most miserly inference of humanity from his lips. "Did you know that we know Dixie from some time ago?"

"No, Den. I had no idea. But I mentioned your names to her, so I guess she thinks it's all alright."

"Well then. If she thinks it's alright, I suppose it must be. Nice to see you again, Dixie my dear. Been a while. How are you?"

"Certainly has, Den. And yes, I'm fine, thank you."

The mind boggled at the history those three might have had.

figured I'd get told about it - as and when someone decided it might be alright for me to know.

CHAPTER THIRTEEN

Until the raw gear came in from Ishy's alleged Dutch connection, I had him lay me on a hundred ordinary Es at eight quid a time. I trusted him on the price because I knew Vicky would make his life an eternal misery if he tried to stitch me. They were the same type as the first one I had bought from little Jen - the Doves.

I hassled Romanov for Jenny's phone number on the pretence of wanting to get into her pants and ran them round to her. I told her she could have them on tick at ten quid a shout, and she was delighted. Presumably to express her delight, she dragged me into her bedroom and screwed my brains out there and then. Now, ordinarily I would think very carefully about following Romanov into the same *building*, let alone the same woman, but with a business opportunity like that one in the offing, I was prepared to make an exception. She insisted we did one each, and the difference between sex on E and doing it straight took my breath away. It was a slow, relaxed and splendidly languid session that lasted for hours, only slightly blighted by the fact there was no blow job on offer, on account of her jaw seizing up. But even that was a bonus as it stopped her from talking. Her parents were downstairs watching Crossroads. She was nineteen.

That Sunday evening she phoned to let me know she had nine hundred and eighty quid for me and were there anymore Es, please? I didn't ask what she'd sold them for because it was none of my business. All I cared about was that we were rolling with two-way traffic. As any courier worth his salt will tell you, an empty ride back from a delivery is an expensive way to operate. Coke from London down to Ishy; pills from Ishy back up to London. How sweet do you want it?

I thanked Jenny heartily, told her I'd be in touch and asked her not to tell Paul about anything we had done. Technically I was stepping on his toes selling to her.

"Who was that?" asked Julie.

"Just a bit of biz. I can sort it next week."

It was inevitable really that she and I would become lovers. Why? We were just so well- suited. I was worried that getting it together would spoil our friendship, but, well, you can't stand on the beach and not dip your toe in, can you? Sure, it was bad form getting together with little Jen at the same time, but as with selling the gear, it didn't feel like I was doing anything *seriously* wrong. It wasn't as if any of us were committed.

I introduced Julie to drugs too, which was as thrilling a piece of corruption as I could remember. She smoked a bit of dope and got pissed occasionally, but I showed her how she should have been living. She snorted two lines the size of eyelashes and then sneezed for five minutes, non-stop.

"No problem," she explained almost apologetically. "I think I was getting a cold anyway."

She calmed down and I made her do a couple more. The words 'water' and 'duck' sprang to mind.

So as that incredible decade was drawing to a close, there I was: around thirty years of age and things could not have been cuter. I had a legit job working three days a week; I was making a bomb selling drugs, I had a Jag XJ, a top of the range Suzuki, my own house, an unreal social life, loads of friends and a couple of lovers. My employers had plans to send me overseas to make me even richer. Chris Rea may have been stuck on the highway to hell but I was heading in the opposite direction.

And I was raving like it was all going to end tomorrow. Shoom was great, until they got up themselves on the door. Nicky

Holloway's The Trip. Spectrum in Heaven. And in September 1989 Britain's first legal all night rave took place. Raindance, and if I needed any proof that I was a chosen one of the age, they held it in Jenkins Lane, Beckton, a short, pilled-up stagger from my house.

At that time it became clear that - to some of my friends at least - a baby was the thing to have. Once one of them got one they all wanted one. A gurgling, farting sprog seemed to be the latest fashion accessory, like it was a Technics stack system or an Audi Quattro.

My sunshine sister Vicky Patterson had one, and I was even related to one - although I hadn't seen much of my nephew since his father and I had had 'words' some seven or eight months previously. There were babies everywhere, but I still had not seen the one who apparently owed his life to me.

When I was rooting through my old suitcase looking for traces of Vicky, I'd come across the beer mat upon which Patsy Chetkins had written his number, all those years before. My heart was pounding as I reached for the phone. I closed my eyes and instantly I could see her bright, pretty, freckled face grinning at the thought of the wild holiday season to come. Pulling her leather jacket closer around her to ward off the nip of the pre-summer night air, and gaily bawling out Dicey Riley Robbie when he was slow to bring us another round.

I biked it out to North Grays to a house that was pure Essex excess. Parked ostentatiously around the horseshoe of the gravel drive was a Mercedes 300, a Range Rover and a Golf GTi. The house was mock Tudor, and amongst many other well appointed delights, it boasted six bedrooms, four bathrooms, a games room (a full sized snooker table was parked in the corner) and a back garden at the end of which, visible to the naked eye on a clear day, was stabling for Lauren's two younger sisters' horses and a medium sized show jumping course.

All this was pointed out to me by Lauren's mother Barbara, who was as bonny and charming as I'd found her daughter to be, all that time before. I'd been looking forward to meeting Patsy again because he was clearly a powerful and influential bloke, and we'd spent a pleasant hour or so in the bar that evening before he had to go. Unfortunately he was away on business in South Africa.

Lauren was out working but would be back before long and Mrs. Chetkins bade me wait in the cavernous living room while she made the tea.

"Someone in the lounge wants to meet you, Mick," she called from the kitchen.

He was sitting in the corner surrounded by toys, quietly playing. When I walked in he looked up and smiled shyly. I took off my leather and placed it on a chair and squatted down in front of him, transfixed.

If ever there was a child who looked nothing like its mother then it was Lauren's little boy. He had huge, brown eyes, long, jet-black ringlets and dark skin the texture of satin, and when he looked at me I felt myself grinning and crying at the same time. I was probably as responsible for his being in the world as his father was and it broke me up. It was one of the few things I'd ever done for reasons other than greed and selfishness. Shame I was so rat-arsed at the time. Through my emotion I heard Barbara calling.

"No sugar for me, thanks," I called back, wiping my face with my sleeve.

She brought the tea through and sat down and the three of us played together for a while.

"This is uncle Mick," she explained. "He's a friend of Mummy's."

The boy responded by cracking me on my duff knee with a Teenage Mutant Ninja Turtle.

"What did Lauren call him?" I asked hoping it wasn't Juan, or Pedro, and certainly not Mick. That would have finished me.

"James," she said. Then she immediately placed a hand on my wrist.

"Mick, we've been waiting years for you to get in touch. Lauren still doesn't like talking about it, but she'd love to see you. She was in such a state that night, bleeding very badly. She was in real danger herself; let alone the lad. None of us had a clue she was pregnant - not even her, so you can imagine how shocking it all was. Her father and I barely left her side until he was born; then Patsy went over and called in to see you. We both came over that Christmas, mainly because I wanted to meet you - but you weren't there. I was so disappointed."

She swallowed more tea and I prayed to whoever might be listening that she didn't start crying, because that would surely have started me off again.

"Got to use your loo, Mrs C."

If I had trouble composing myself then things were only going to get worse. I heard Lauren coming through the front door.

"Who's motorbike is that, Mum? You're not knocking off Hell's Angels while Dad's away, are you?"

"Not exactly," I said walking out of the toilet bang on cue.

When I saw the initial mystification on her face I thought it had been a mistake to track her down. Then, when she recognised me, she shut her eyes. Two seconds later, when she opened them, she was crying. She walked towards me, slipped her arms around my waist and rested her head on my chest.

"Good to see you, Mick," she snuffled. "Where've you been all this time? Where've you *been*?"

I stroked her hair and felt myself choking up again. It was just too weird. I'd met her once before in my life - and then just for a few brief hours - and there I was, like some conquering hero, home from the wars.

I stayed for tea. Lauren's two sisters came home from school, and so then there were four chattering Chetkins women. The boy had it made; no wonder he kept his eye on me.

The two sisters ate and cleared off and Lauren, Barbara and me talked about Mallorca and the bar.

"But you did alright out of it, yeah?" asked Barbara.

"I came home with more experience than money, but I have no regrets."

"Neither do we," she said, and reached across to pat the back of my hand. "Tell you what. You two have probably got years of catching up to do. Go through to the lounge and make yourselves comfortable. I'll get James up and bathed and to bed."

"Oh, would you Mum? Cheers. I'll be up to tuck him in," said Lauren.

And that's how it happened.

I worried about it. I had sensitivity. Jenny was by far the youngest, but I always thought she was the toughest. Julie was strong and independent so I thought that she would be OK. Lauren, though. Somehow it felt precarious. Like walking on eggshells. She had a father who was more than just a shrewd businessman and she had a son who owed his life to me. The whole thing scared me, like it was too close. I know it wasn't my smartest move - me and her becoming lovers, but it seemed like I had no control over it all; events were sweeping me away. A succession of mad things were happening and I just carried on letting them.

Soon enough Jenny was getting through a regular two hundred plus pills a week. Bolstered by that confidence, I wanted to push the idea of getting Den and Pete to lay on the rave they had been considering, or just move a few more of Ishy's Es along through them. Strike while the iron's hot and all that.

It was the Friday night routine.

"So how about it, boys?" I asked as I drew the sharp Bolivian up and over the raw, tenderised steak of my nostrils. "I can get good Doves for… nine quid a pop on the hundred, less, of course, for the big numbers. They're still going for at least fifteen in the barn. The figures speak for themselves. Are we going to organise a party, or what?"

Pete and Denny looked across at each other. Pete spoke.

"The jury is actually out on this one at the moment. We've shelved the idea for a bit and it's looking more and more likely that we ain't going to get involved."

"Why not?"

"Don't you read the papers, boy?" This was Masters. "Watch the news? This is not only illegal, it is highly visible. Warehouse parties, field raves - whatever you want to call them - are getting busted every weekend. There is a public outcry. You have one in the middle of Dartmoor you might get away with it; anywhere else and the drug squad's all over the place in minutes. Which brings me to the point. You can't have a rave without Es and there are some very disturbing things coming out about this shit."

"Like what?" I asked.

"Like it kills people."

"Do what?"

Masters sighed heavily and turned to his partner. "Will you explain things to Tweedle Dee and Tweedle Dum arsehole here?"

"You didn't hear about that girl who died at her eighteenth birthday party? Essex. Overheated or something. Her old man's a copper. Her family made her deathbed pictures public."

"Ahh Jeeezus."

"Don't tell me you're hooked on this shit as well, are you?" Masters sneered a little too nastily for my liking.

"I'm not hooked on anything," I told him, but feeling that was about as bold as I ought to get.

"Eighteen," he continued, shaking his head. "Same as my Carly. Bad publicity, that's what it is. People are taking notice. Bringing drug-taking into the public eye - which is bad news for all of us. Parents, action groups, social workers, Plod. It's giving dealers a bad name, making us look like criminals. So raves are off the agenda and we're not going to get into the Ecstasy business either. If the law is chasing E dealers, they won't have so much time to go after us Charlie boys."

"But it's the new thing, lads. Coke has had it's day. All this attention will blow over, it always does."

"No," Masters boomed and slammed his hand onto his desk, sending up a vast cloud of cocaine powder. "You do as you're told and shut up. Now, neither of you two cowboys are dealing this shit, are you?"

Romanov looked at me and I looked at him. We both shook our heads. I knew he was telling the truth because if he was dealing, he would undoubtedly be selling to Jenny and I would know about it.

"Good. Now you keep it that way. We're doing well as we are. Regular, reliable, safe. Not even a hint of trouble with customers, other firms or the Old Bill. Nice and easy. Subject closed."

Pete fished out four more cans and handed them around. He eventually broke the heavy silence.

"Besides, you two are going to be a bit busy for the coming week or two."

"Oh yeah? What's happening?" I asked.

"Holidays." He said, with a smile.

Me and Romanov grinned at each other like a couple of kids. "Good working 'ere, innit?" I said.

As usual the following morning I turned up at the yard to meet Denny and to collect my drugs for the weekend's deliveries and to pick up the Jag.

I'd got all the way back home when I realised I'd left a jacket over there that I'd wanted to wear at the weekend. Curiously, Denny's BMW was still parked outside the warehouse. Not fancying anymore lectures I thought I'd grab the jacket from the radio room, then try to sneak off without being noticed. I opened the door and they parted with a violent jolt.

"Your mum never tell you to knock before you go into a room?" Dixie said, the least unfazed of the three of us.

"Something you want, son?" Masters said, practically breathing fire.

"Left my jacket," was all I said. I reached around to the hook behind the door. "See you Monday."

On Sunday afternoon I got the call I'd been expecting.

"Need to see you, boy," rumbled the voice like a thundercloud. "Anyone there?"

"No, but there might be soon."

"If they turn up before me, get rid of them. Thirty minutes."

The time dragged on me like quicksand. I didn't know whether to run, call the police, call Pete, hide or what. The door bell rang. He had to turn sideways to get through my front door, and that was the first time I truly appreciated how big the man was. The whole room seemed to go cold when he walked in.

"Den, before you say anything - I didn't see anything and I know even less."

"You'll see what I tell you to see and you'll know what I want you to know." He took two steps towards me and I knew better than to back off. I had to take what was coming. He gave me both barrels of the *look* and I knew, as I gawped back into the dead, grey eyes of that godless cunt, that I would never have an answer to him, and that was because he was mad, and there just isn't an answer to it. You can't fight it because it's stronger than you and you can't run from it because it will always find you.

"And if you ain't happy with that then I'll slice you open as slowly as I can and leave you for the flies and the rats. You've been told."

Going back to Mallorca with what seemed like an army behind me was a thrill I'd have waited for all my life.

Me and Dixie flew out together on a joint yearly passport as Mr. and Mrs. Carson and Pete and Romanov were at the airport to collect us in a nice open-top Rover. The weather was glorious and I felt like royalty. We cruised into Santa Ponsa and Pete dropped me and Dixie off at the Verdemar apartments to dump our bags and change into fresh clothes. Then we bundled back into the car and drove the two or three kilometres along the coast to this cool villa Pete had access to. Not long, I thought, before I'd have one of my own.

We plotted our moves and decided to get a clean start the following Monday. The gorgeous weather and being back in the old town were chewing lumps out of my hide; I was desperate to get out on the razz, but I managed to slow myself down and appreciate that I was there on business. Soldier like a good pro, and my hundred grand or so and happy retirement were well within my grasp. I rarely got out of bed at that time without the aid of a few chunky lines, but I forced myself to leave all supplies behind, which was a far from easy thing to do.

However, as the sun dipped down on that memorable Saturday evening, there were other things occupying my mind. All Pete would say was that we'd get things sorted, and his reputation was not earned by making false statements. Apart from those he made to the police anyway.

It was maybe nine thirty when the four us cruised back towards town.

"Dinner at the Pepperpot, I think," Pete announced airily.

"I'd recommend the Stroganoff," I said.

"I'm impressed you can remember what it was like."

"Look, I wasn't out of it all the time. There was one June the ninth I think."

We parked up and ambled across the cul-de-sac, where Pete was greeted by the owners of the restaurant Doreen and Stewart. Clearly agitated to see me, they were placated when Pete explained it was a holiday, and I was not considering opening anymore bars. We got a nice table on the terrace where we could see the street, and - most importantly - the Monte Carlo topless Bar.

We ate, we drank, and whilst I fought to control the butterflies in my stomach, we were merry too.

Sitting there, I mused about whether I would have changed anything in my life. There was Dad. Lying helped a lot there. I told him I was a partner in my own firm and we were doing really well, and that pleased him. And of course he was knocked out over Nigel's success, and chuffed to bits about his grandson. Short of bringing Mum, back he was as well off as he was going to be.

I hadn't seen much of Nigel since I had sold the Heroes and discovered that he had effectively stolen my premium for the Private Patients Plan. He blamed it all on someone else, but there were too many cock-ups; too many holes appearing. No one was *that* cursed by staff incompetence. I thought about the way he had pissed me around when I was trying to get the Heroes off the ground. All the lies and unfulfilled promises. I shuddered and shooed it all away to the back of my mind.

I worried about the girls a little but I carried on screwing around simply because I thought that was what successful villains were supposed to do.

Then there was the fearsome spectre of Denny Masters. Despite what I was worth to him, he would have undoubtedly slit me from groin to throat if I let slip one breath of what I had seen at the yard that Saturday morning. And he would enjoy doing it too. But I didn't even know his wife and even if …

"There he is."

"Who?" I was miles away.

"Recognise anyone, Mick?"

My mind zeroed in, my senses co-ordinated and my vision sharpened. White Renault. Three women and one man. It was him. Even after all those years, there was no mistaking the fat, sleazy shitbag.

"We're on," I said.

"Listen, Dixie," Pete said. "Me and the chaps are going to take a stroll and have a word with someone. Sorry to leave you on your own. Order whatever you want."

"You boys take your time. I brought me knitting."

I wasn't pissed. I was just right. Besides, it was business and it was Pete's call. Even though he was carved from solid rock I had often wondered how Pete was with the rough stuff. Having a Rottweiler like Masters as a partner, it could have been a nice guy-tough guy relationship. I needn't have worried.

"Lock it, Mick," he ordered calmly as we slipped into the bar. Martinez, all five foot four of him hardly visible, was behind the beer pumps. He heard the steel bolt slide shut on the door.

"Hey, we not open yet..." He looked up and saw the three of us and knew it was trouble. I suppose after a lifetime of deceit he knew the signs. There may have been a back door but he was a long way from it, and sensing he might have gone for it, Romanov eased his loose, powerful frame down to the far end to block any escape route.

"Luis," called Pete as he ambled casually to the bar. "Long time no see."

The Spaniard squinted through the dimness. Then with the recognition came enormous relief. "Oh God. Peter! It's Peter." He clasped a stumpy hand to his chest. "Peter, you and your boys look like bad men. You should not play jokes. I was so pleased to get your call. How you been?"

Pete ambled to the bar and offered over his hand, which

Martinez greedily and gratefully accepted.

"I've been meaning to get around for a while. How are things?" Pete said.

"No bad. Can't complain. How things in London?"

"Yeah, so so. When you over next?"

"I don't know, man. Money is tight. The wife, she complain about everything. Is no easy. Hey, you and your boys want a drink?"

"No thanks, Luis. We can't stay."

Then, attracted by the conversation perhaps, two of the girls appeared from the back. One wore a purple teddy and huge, white shoes. The other a yellow bikini without the top. It was like some kind or red flag to Pete.

"Get those fucking whores out of here when I am talking to you!" he screamed.

They may not have spoken any English, but they knew without being told that it wasn't time to go to work just yet. They scuttled off out of sight.

Up until then I had been hanging back. Would he recognised me? The mullet, along with the tan, had gone.

"Someone here to meet you, Luis," said Pete, beckoning me forward to his side like a favoured son. Five years.

He scanned me for clues.

"Across the street. Bugsy's Bar," I told him. You remember the boys you kept out. You remember John Durridge. You remember the trouble you caused?"

Five years. Had Pete Chalmers not given me that moment I would have paid well for it. I would have paid handsomely just to look into that greedy bastard's face at his moment of dark realisation. Andy Thompson had forfeited his right when he ducked out early, and perhaps this was my true reward for being brave enough to see things through. Yes, this was my reward, and I savoured it as I saw the fear in his eye when he cracked on that I had come back to haunt him.

"Of course," he blurted, giving it his best shot. "It is young Mick. I remember now. Mick, how you been?"

If Pete gave Romanov a signal to move then I didn't see it.

Next thing he was behind the bar too and I'll die before I forget what he did. A casual glance at the rack of booze on the shelves and then the slow, deliberate selection. He was no yob; he knew exactly what he was doing.

Jack Daniels. Had to be. He held the bottle by the base and with slow, controlled force brought the neck crashing down onto the bar in an explosion of noise, glass, booze and violence. Then, holding Martinez's eye with a shocking stare, he stuck the jagged end into his own mouth and toked long and hard on the Bourbon. When he pulled the bottle away we could all see that he was bleeding from the top lip. The maniac scared the shit out of me - and I was on his side.

Martinez didn't know whether to cry, beg or just die on the spot. I almost felt sorry for him. Almost. A sheen of sweat coated his twitching face as he struggled for air. Pete let him suffer for long seconds, then moved in to read him his rights. He reached forward and grabbed him by his stupid, leather, boot lace tie and hauled him bodily across the bar so that he was flat out on his chest. At the same time, Romanov placed the bottle on his back between his shoulders and left it there free standing.

"If you move," he said, droplets of blood spattering down onto the Spaniard's right ear, "if you move and spill my drink, I'll cut your fucking face off."

I heard the faintest 'snick' and I saw that Pete had a flick-knife in his hand and held the long blade gently against the baggy pouch under Martinez's left eye.

"We are going to be bringing a lot of stuff to you. Same rules; all receipts and cash up front - but now the price has gone up. Thirty five percent."

The Spaniard was making rapid, petrified, steam train noises.

"And no complaints. You owe this man a lot of money and this is the way you are going to repay it. You're quite lucky really."

"Please." The words came in hot, frightened chuffs from his twisted face. "I can't breathe. I can't ..."

I was in heaven. I leant forward, elbows on the bar. I looked for the perfect line - and for my sins, I found it.

"Is no my problem," I said.

"You," Pete said, tapping the flat of the blade on his cheek, "are now working for him. OK? You are responsible to him. If you complain, upset anyone or come up short with the money... Then Demon Denny will come to see you. Understand?"

"Si si si. Yes I understand. Why you need to be so tough, Peter. I am working with you now."

"That's good. That's good. Now this is out of the way, we are one big, happy family. Everybody is happy."

There was another metallic click, and magically the knife was gone. "We'll be back in a few days. You'll need a few million to begin with. Entiendes?"

"Yes yes."

Romanov left the bottle balanced where it was, effectively pinning him to the bar. So we left him like that. Outside I was all but overcome.

"Listen chaps, I know you didn't have to do it like that. Thanks. I have brothers around me." Then we walked over the road to rejoin Dixie.

As the song went, the future was so bright I had to wear shades. Ray-Ban Aviators at that. We were so expert and so professional, no-one stood a chance against us. The standard of our product was such that we changed up fake travellers cheques and Sterling at will. Not that the opposition was up to much. Most of the people working in the exchange places didn't care what they were given. I swear you could have scrawled the words 'fifty pounds' in the corner of a KitKat wrapper and they would have handed the pesetas over. While we were out doing that we hit the better shops for all manner of superior goods with racks of gold, platinum and plutonium credit cards. We got up early in the morning, worked at it all day and went to bed early and sober. Shopping for a living.

Our second Sunday was another rest day and I elected to just plod around on my own. I crashed out on the beach for a few hours, and then, suitably refreshed, I repaired to The Rising Sun, which was now owned by my dear old friend Preston Jack. We had a chat and talked over old times, and I was pleased to learn that things were going well for him. He told me that drinks were on the house, and once again I was moved to reflect upon how kind the world could be when you had friends with some degree of influence.

I settled down in a comfy terrace chair with a San Miguel and drifted in and out of a calming sleep like an old, full-bellied farm dog in the sun.

Whilst fraud and deception is certainly not physical work, it is demanding in terms of concentration and the constant strain upon the nerves took its toll. Dixie was born for it, but I found it immensely wearing and had been looking forward to my day off all week. I snoozed and drank and drifted and grinned.

"Commander Targett. This is not the time nor the place." I heard a voice say.

"Your presence is required, sir. Are you aware of the time?"

That voice. I sprang bolt upright in my chair and a massive surge of blood to the head disorientated me.

"Commander Targett. Ten to five. The poop deck awaits."

"Captain Francis. You jolly old jack tar you. How the devil are you?"

"Very well, Commander. Very well indeed." He pumped my outstretched hand and sat beside me. "Didn't know you were over here."

"Mid-way through a fortnight's trip. I've been up to the bridge a couple of times looking for you but there was no answer. When did you get in?"

"Yesterday evening. I've just come to say hello to Jack and then I'm off to meet a man I know downtown. Do you know Pascal the Frog?"

"Don't believe I do."

"Best you come along then. Useful contact, but hurry. You know the rules. We have to be on deck by five."

We scored four grams from Pascal and headed for the hills. I mixed the cocktails and he cut the lines. It was just like old times. I was even wearing the old Cubs cap he had given me. It was bit ragged, but at least I still had it.

I was supposed to meet the others for dinner at ten for a team meeting kind of thing, to plan the following week and just to thrash out any queries. I kept saying to Franny, "This'll have to be the last one. This'll have to be the last one."

I awoke at close on midday feeling like shit - and then I felt ten times worse when I realised what I'd done. I left Franny snoring and sprinted around the bay to The Verdemar. There was a note on my bed.

'Down by the pool, dickhead - Dixie.'

The three of them were there. All fresh, all relaxed, all sober.

"Shit. Sorry, everyone. I know this is pretty bad of me. Very amateurish. I met an old mate I haven't seen in years and... "

"And you got off your face and couldn't get out of bed," Pete clarified. "We have a warning system on the firm, Mick. Three fuck-ups and you are out. Doesn't matter who you are. This is number one."

I sighed deeply. What could I say. "Fair cop, Pete. Bollocking accepted. I hold up my hand."

"You look like shit. And you stink. Where the fuck have you been?"

"It's true. I've got a mate who lives on the far side of town. I haven't seen him for ages. We had a few drinks. You know how it is."

"Yeah. I know how it is and it ain't got a lot to do with a few drinks. You're mushing your own brains, Mick. You're a good worker and you've got talent. We're a team here and we've lost a day because of you. There's no way you can go out now in that condition. You're supposed to be a wealthy gold card holder but you just look like what you are; a fucked up little coke head."

That hurt, but what could I do? But then, the comforting arm around the shoulder part.

"Sit down here a minute, will you. Paul, would you get some coffees in please?"

I pulled a chair up under their parasol and sat with Pete and Dixie.

"There's work and there is play, yeah Mick? Next time I won't be around and you're supposed to be running things. Paul's just getting his wages and a bonus, but you are getting your five percent extra on the fenced stuff for a reason - and that is because you are supposed to be leading the line here."

"You're right, Pete. I know what I've done. I'm sorry, and it won't happen again."

The verbal gale was subsiding. "Look. Get a few coffees down you, get some sun, get some kip. We'll start again in the morning and work to make it up during next week."

Franny knew pretty much what I was into when I explained he would have sole command of the poop deck. But it was worth staying straight. We stole almost thirteen thousand pounds worth of goods on the plastic. In addition we changed up twelve thousand in moody fifties and twenties, and close on nineteen grand in forged travellers cheques.

Luis was moaning already about how tough some of the items were to place, but that was bullshit and we discovered the sweet network of contacts he really had. Me and Dixie nicked this fantastic necklace and earrings set from a jewellers around on the far side of the bay. Luis weighed us out for it, but playing a hunch, Pete strolled around there the following day - and there the stuff was, back in the window. So how about that for a neat circle of criminal intrigue? We stole the stuff and got paid by Luis. Luis sold it *back* to the shopkeeper who then put the same goods straight back in his window for resale, whilst getting weighed out by the credit card company. Everyone's a winner - except the credit card company, and we all know what they do to maintain their profits.

We learnt that Luis knew shopkeepers he was able to deal with on that level all over the island and beyond, and we made it his business to steer us towards those stores, thus guaranteeing a safe grab for ourselves and a quick turnaround for all. Then we'd go back the next day and nick the same goods, but with a different credit card. It was too much.

On the last visit to see Luis that first trip I was met with a surprise. Luis was not there but the door was opened by a young man. Good looking little bastard he was too. He helped me in with all the bags and poured me a beer. I climbed onto a bar stool and called him over.

"I know you," I told him.

"And I know you too, my friend," he replied confidently.

"When?"

"A couple of summers ago, across the street. I saw you looking at the restaurant. I think you were looking at the place where your bar used to be."

"That's right. I also remember another time as well."

"Yes. Many years ago. I was a boy. At Bugsy's one night. In the winter."

The chill of weird, inexplicable coincidence snatched at my spine. I took a long slug of San Mig.

"What's your name?"

"Rafael."

"I asked you that question once before and you did not give me that answer then."

His handsome, young face flushed with deep embarrassment.

"I know," he admitted. "I was afraid."

I smiled with the confidence my years and experience had given me. "Rafael, listen. You don't have to be afraid of anyone. And never deny who you are."

Luis' nephew nodded his understanding, and softly thanked me. Then, as calmly as you might ask directions of someone, he requested to know if I could get him any acid.

Ten minutes later, Luis showed up and shelled out for that last batch of stuff. He seemed to think it was some mandatory exercise to wince and haggle and try to knock us down, but it was all too simple. We showed him the goods and their corresponding receipts, and he gave us thirty-five percent.

In total, that fortnight he shelled out four thousand five hundred pounds. Of that, two hundred and twenty five pounds constituted the first instalment of money he had deprived me of by keeping me out of the bar. Of all the dosh I made on that trip, that was the most satisfying.

We all put our trust in our boss, and at the end of each day handed over all the money and goods we had changed up or stolen. Bringing all that money back through UK customs was obviously a no no. Pete had accounts in Spain and would move the cash back home through the banking system.

Like a good soldier I was in at nine on the following Monday morning. At noon Pete called me up to the office. I was hoping he hadn't told Denny about the cock-up over there. I got the impression Denny was looking for reasons to get shot of me.

"How's business this morning? Much happening?" he asked.

"Er, yeah, good. Got that laminators from Chingford on line. First job this morning. They do up to a dozen a day - bikes and vans."

"Good. I've been to the bank already this morning. It's as per last Friday's exchange rate. I've itemised it all on this sheet anyway. Well done."

He dropped a purple paper brick on the table. For a fortnight's work out in Mallorca I had earned eight thousand one hundred and twenty pounds. That was the way it was.

Following the unqualified success of that first trip, Pete and Denny decided it was worth throwing all our energies into that line of work. This was fine by me for two reasons. Firstly, of course, it was a ridiculously easy and relatively risk free way of earning a ton of dosh, and secondly, it presented me with the chance of making even more with a sideline that none of the others knew anything about.

As soon as we'd got back I had belted down to the coast to talk to Ishy. I talked to him about lysergic acid diethylamide. LSD. Acid. He told me all I needed to know and said he could sell me all I wanted to buy.

Back over there on the second trip, I was already having trouble with Dixie. The problem was I was supposed to be in charge but I was still the junior. When Pete or Den weren't around was Dixie really going to listen to what I said? Was Romanov? I mean I'd done a lot with my life, but compared to them I was still wearing shorts and sucking my thumb.

Romanov, for instance (and I got the info from Pete so it had to be true) had done four years inside and had got through twenty-one legitimate jobs before the age of twenty five - including being a bullfighter. He'd managed that one by going on the organised bullfight trip when he'd holidayed in Benidorm with his mates. During the afternoon what they used to do was bring a baby bull into the ring and call for pissed up volunteers to fight it. Romanov jumped in there and felled the thing with a flying karate kick to the shoulder. The promoters had been so impressed they offered him a job on the spot. Having nothing to go back to the UK for, apart from visits to his probation officer, he agreed to stay on.

He had been a footballer - semi pro with Dagenham - a farmer and a fireman. He had also worked for the settlements department of a merchant bank but had felt the need to swiftly tender his resignation when he was caught attempting to divert nine million Dutch Guilders from a foreign exchange deal he was settling into his own Abbey National savings account.

And my erstwhile partner Dixie? Now while it would be easy to call her the archetypal gangster's moll, Dixie was different because when she needed or chose to be, she was entirely self-sufficient. Word has it even - although it was Romanov who told me and you can't believe everything that bastard says - that when she split with mad Butch Barker, and strictly to help with little Wesley's upbringing, she was obliged to turn a few tricks to get by. Personally I don't buy that, because Dixie did not have to sell the family jewels. She was too much of an artiste. All she had to do was put them on display and she could drag out the promise of Utopia indefinitely, coaxing the most ardent of suitors to spring for the best of everything in the meantime.

However, although she had been around the track more times than Steve Cram - word was she had screwed half the villains in London, and would have undoubtedly got around to the other half had they not been banged up at the time - she was very limited in her knowledge of all things foreign: blokes, customs, food, whatever. Thus when we were away on the runs, her parochial instincts resulted in an insecurity that restricted her pretty much to British men. And British men who had enough money to impress our Dixie, were few and far between in places like Arenal, Magaluf and Lloret. But find them she did, and the reason she did was because she was good at her job - and the reason she was good at her job was because she had to be.

No one seemed to know her true age but I figured she was on the down slope of thirty five, and appreciating that her income was pretty much related to her looks, she knew that she really wouldn't be getting a better chance than the one I plopped in her lap. For the most part she worked professionally. However she just could not resist a bloke with money, and it was only on that second run out to Mallorca that I saw a problem coming right around the corner.

He was a wildly successful pig farmer from Bolton and he had a yacht moored in the Club de Mar that he could have leased out as a cruise liner. He had invited Dixie aboard for dinner the following evening. I didn't like it. "Dixie, look. Don't go," I pleaded. "We are behind schedule. There's lots of work to do."

"Yeah? So? I'll see you back here after I've been to the boat. What's the problem? Just don't tell Paul, Pete and *especially* Den."

"Look, you set one foot on that gangplank I know there's going to be trouble. Does he have a wife?"

"Yeah, but she ain't here."

"What a surprise. Dixie, please. If anything happens to you how am I going to feel? We don't know who this geezer is, what he's like. What if...?"

"Oh, listen to him. He's all protective. Mummy's little soldier!"

She threw her arms around me and kissed me until I was wearing half a lipstick's worth of purple woad on my face. What could I do? Later that night I met up with young Rafael. He comforted me by racking me out a line of coke the size of a porn star's dick.

"Man I tell you, I think you are the only one who takes me seriously," I told him mournfully. "Any suggestions?"

He thought and nodded slowly. "I see what I can do."

That night - the night before Dixie's date - the yacht slipped its moorings and drifted out into the Bahia de Palma, where it was rammed amidships by the incoming Barcelona ferry. The thing didn't sink, but apparently the salvage fees cost the bloke a drug baron's ransom. Needless to say, dinner was off.

Dixie blamed fate, but I looked at Rafael with new admiration. He was still just a kid.

"The most important thing in life," he counselled me the next day as he chopped out a couple more, "...is that a man can have a friend he can trust above all others. Above family, above his woman. Even above money." He despatched his line and handed me the straw.

"Now, talk to me about acid."

It fascinated me. It really did. You could see everything. I peeked over the operator's shoulder and it was all there in stark X-ray: the camera, spare roll of film, after shave, sun tan lotion, pack of johnnies - the lot. However, as efficient as it was, Ishy had assured me that no X-ray machine in the world could detect a flat packed sheet of acid. This was at Gatwick too so I knew Palma airport would be a breeze. It was the third of our runs to Spain.

We caught a fast black to the Honolulu hotel in Palm Nova where we were staying and jumped the rumbling Otis to the fifth floor. Funny old way to make a living.

Rafael was supposed to meet us at the airport so I was anxious to locate him as quickly as possible, to get the acid away from me as much as anything else. Dixie said she was keen to get some kip, having been out the previous evening (if not with Denny then with some Billy the Axe or Freddie the Fist or other) and wanted to look her best, should she bump into the bloke from Bolton again. I looked down at my holdall. Was she that close to Masters that she would spy on me? There was a lot at stake. A lot more than a few grand's worth of class As.

"I'll get moving," I told her. "Pete sent all our stuff over to Luis' bar this time. Quite a bit of Sterling, a few cheques but not a lot of plastic. Looks like an easy one. We'll forget about tomorrow and get a clean start on Monday."

"Right, cheers."

For the millionth time I took in the iridescent starburst of her beautiful hazel eyes, the Cupid's bow of her mouth, thought about the deep, throaty sexiness of her laugh. As I was leaving, I caught a peachy view of her silhouette as the late afternoon sun poured in through the open window, making a nonsense of her blouse. Romanov (not with us on that trip as Denny needed him on a tricky debt collecting job) had once grubbily told me about all the aerobics and jogging and netball she put herself through in order to maintain her exemplary figure. "Little white, pleated skirts. *Pleated*. Know what I mean?"

But the same, prying sun that showed off her body could tell a different story when she turned her face towards it. Too many nights out with Fingers Whatsisname. Too many wild weekends with Slugger O' Thingmejig. Too much coke, booze, fags. The pain of the abortions; being up all night seeing to the kid. The let downs, the betrayals, the arrests.

I tried to imagine her fifteen years ago. Christ, fifteen *minutes* ago would have done me. Apparently there were blokes - top faces - cutting each other to pieces on her account. Pete told me that she had been responsible for the outbreak of two gang wars to his knowledge alone. And what was Masters doing risking the family life I knew he treasured?

I tried to picture her in her early twenties, and then tried not to. I was too close. Forget it. All I knew for sure was that she would never let me down. When Rafael spoke of the importance of real friends, I knew Dixie would always be one of mine. I took another look at my bag, slid out of the door and clattered down the stairs, alarmed that the lump in my throat was at least equal to the one in my groin.

"Oh, Mr Woods," called the receptionist as I was preparing to make the step from the relative coolness of the lobby into the rioting furnace of the midsummer Mallorcan street.

"That's Wood. John Wood."

"Yes, sir. Your car is here. I was just about to call you."

Up until that day I had never been in a stretch limo. Certainly not with two bikini-clad babes, one of whom was intent on feeding my nose with as much cocaine as it could handle, while the other was happy to feed her face with as much of my dick as she could take. Which was basically all of it.

One of them, whose bobbing head was framed by my splayed thighs, I recognised from Martinez' bar. The other - little sister coke wriggling around on the seat next to me - was sensationally new. She was too good-looking and too bright-eyed to have been in the business for long. She had one of those dispenser jobs - like an inhaler but full of Charlie, which I knew took around two grams. She tapped some out onto her fingertips and then smeared the magic crystals all over my lips and tongue, before quickly lashing them off with her own. She had obviously not read the good hooker's handbook and the bit about never kissing a trick on the mouth.

It had all been quite a shock, but the sudden slowing of the car reminded me that not only we were moving along a public street, but that we were slap bang in the middle of Magaluf. And by then we were all ridiculously naked. I glanced to my right, and the physical exertion brought with it a foaming wave of pleasure. I smiled and an angel stroked my cheeks with a garland of lime blossom. I blinked and butterflies danced across my eyelids. I heard a moan and took long seconds to realise it was my own. That was some *good* shit.

Through it all I worried that people looking in would start complaining about the girls, the nudity and all that coke flying around. Wouldn't you? It sure must have looked like I had cracked it big time. Then I realised and I began to laugh. So *that* was why everybody was looking at me. It was because they couldn't see me. It was the glass.

"It's the glass," I heard myself say. I became aware of a slight easing of the excruciating pleasure emanating from my groin.

"Que pasa, guapo?"

Two gross, bright red lips grinned up at me. Jesus. Those lips, so wet and juicy and muscular. Did she train them in step class or what?

"The glass," I explained. A dozen heavenly lips kissed my hand as I placed it upon the externally mirrored barrier that kept the money and the power on the inside, away from all the grubby, grabbing hands on the outside. It looked hot and sweaty out on the street - out there on the cluttered old avenida. On the inside, though, with the air con working overtime and the girls working even harder, there was no problem at all. I was on the inside alright, and with no plans ever to leave.

Meanwhile expert number one got back to work, making me yelp with shocking pleasure as her tongue took a few unexpected laps around my scrotum, before returning to the mundane drudgery of the best blow job I'd ever had. And the buzz wasn't just the physicality. Part of the thrill was knowing this was happening because of who I was. Sure anyone could *pay* for this kind of number, but who has ever had it laid on them because of who they are? Masters? Chalmers? Farmer? Big Patsy in his younger days even?

The muchacha next to me had just given me another couple of valves of the coke and then magically produced a crystal flute of chilled champagne from somewhere. Bit of class or what? The bubbly went down well, as I was becoming a touch dry, and it was especially refreshing when I sloshed it around the anaesthetised walls of my mouth and throat. I handed her back the empty glass, and she... Well Christ knows what she did with it.

Then she spoke to her mate so softly, it had to be a century's old secret they were sharing. Moved by what she heard, the girl on her knees released my dick from the savage wetness of her mouth. I took the opportunity to check out the old chap and was pleased with what I saw. Once or twice recently, I had been having trouble getting the old boy upright. I put it down to stress of business. That time though, it was clear there would be no visit from Mr. Floppy. Defiantly tumescent, even through that little snowfall. What? Oh yeah, I got it. Tiny flakes of coke rained silently down on the shiny, gleaming dome. They had a trick or two up their sleeves. Looked like it was going to be a long ride.

Then a little shuffling and rearranging was called for, not least because *we were out of fucking cocaine!* The dumb bitches had dumped the last of it all over my knob. But wait! Phew, close one. The blow job queen was into the fridge and I relaxed again when I saw her pulling out a bag of gear that must have gone at least two ounces. Not that I needed anymore, with the front of my face already completely numb. It's just nice to have a bit of spare. You know, just in case.

Unscrewing the nozzle, she dipped into the bag and refilled the dispenser. Six hits later, she handed it back up to her mate and then sank two whole glasses of champagne in succession. Suitably refuelled she joined her pal on her knees and we were nearly ready for the off again. Team effort, I thought. Good to see. But this time around we had a minor alteration that would call for all my tungsten-coated resolve.

Little sis grabbed my right ankle and hoiked my leg over her head, and my foot eventually came to rest on the elbow shelf of the far door, thus leaving room for the two of them between my sprawled knees. Immediately they embarked upon a joint offensive (pincer movement). This time little sis gave my dick an almighty lashing with those cute, pink lips while the blow job queen raised my entire scrotum on her scarlet, razored fingertips and drew dazzling, teasing patterns all over and around my nuts with the rippling whip of her tongue.

Yeah, well. I had just died and gone to heaven. How the fuck had an Essex oik like me pulled this one off? I did my best to lie back and relax, but that wasn't easy. Situations like that call for the utmost self-control. I had great fun trying to figure out what was the more satisfying: resting my head back with my eyes closed watching the pretty patterns formulate, or looking down fondly at my two new friends as they lapped away at me like two playful puppies.

How long did it go on for? Didn't matter. Ecstasy is timeless, isn't it? An hour long glimpse of heaven is probably the same as a minute.

Little sis kept at it while queenie diversified. That tongue of hers. I bet she could do press ups with it. Eyelids, neck, ears, nipples. She had me covered. Then, with practised skill, they manoeuvred me around so that I knelt my right knee on the seat (weirdly it gave me no trouble at all) and stretched my left leg out to give me balance. Queenie had wriggled beneath me and in an instant had resumed the never ending task of fellatio. I thought little sis was getting the drinks in again until I felt her soft hands behind me bending me over. Then with a careful palm on each cheek she was gently easing me apart and moved in with that laser guided tongue of hers. The pleasure seared through me, so much that I didn't worry about not having showered for a couple of days.

There followed more drinks, more coke and then someone was ripping open a familiar square of plastic and then they were both kneeling on the seat looking out of the rear window with me rubbered up and ready to go. Heads together, they chatted happily as they passed the dispenser back and forth. Not wishing to be left out of the narcotic party, I grabbed the bag from the fridge, and with all the indulgence due a VIP (very important pig) sprinkled a good two grams onto queenie at the delta of her back and buttocks and then reached across and endowed little sis in the same way. Grabbing a straw, I knelt on the edge of the seat, slammed into little sis and I was off, shagging like a Gypsy's whippet. After bashing away for a while, I leaned over, dipped the straw into the miniature Eiger on her mate's back and whacked a massive hit up my nose. Did Jim Morrison ever have it so good? Snorting like a hay fever stricken boar, I pulled out of little sis and piled into queenie and off we went again, reaching across to do more Charles at the appropriate moment.

Eventually something comfortingly familiar permeated the surrealism. I wasn't sure where the rumbling started - somewhere down in the transmission of the car probably. I slipped effortlessly into overdrive. I engaged turbo boost. It was so good, I felt like I was letting one of them down by not being able to share it with both. The flat slap of my stomach on her arse was so fast we all but broke into a round of applause, and then...

If there was anyone within earshot they would have called an ambulance for sure. My head spun in stupefying ecstasy as I pounded into her with piston powered convulsions. I came and came and came but with the orgasm I felt my dick, strength, spirit and entire being seep and sag and flee from me like smoke into the air. I fell out of her and crashed helplessly to the floor of the motor.

Like true professionals, they scooped the excess coke from each other's back, returning it neatly to the bag, before flopping onto the rear seat to gawp down at the conquered prey. As I peeled off the sodden condom and held its awesome contents up for all to see, like a cup final trophy, they shrieked and howled with laughter. What could I do but join them in convulsive fits of hysteria, marvelling at the sheer romance of it all.

Then I woke up. No worries, though. It wasn't a dream. You couldn't dream anything like that. The girls were gone, but Rafael, that good-looking, teenaged spic bastard was there. In spite of all the coke, or perhaps because of it, I had slept and slept well. I was still in the limo, parked somewhere, but it was dark.

A perfunctory inspection of myself told me that if I wasn't in control of all my limbs and faculties then at least they were still in my possession. I was alive and clothed and apart from my groin feeling like it had been through a mincer, I felt pretty good.

"Hey, hombre. You have a little fun today no?"

I sighed, my mind still a pink cloud. I knew I was smiling and I knew I couldn't stop.

"Rafa, I love you. Where are we?"

"Cala Fornells. Near the casino. You wanna play?"

"I've done enough playing for one day thank you. Jesus. How many times did we go around the island?"

"How many times around the planet you mean. Man, you been in here so long I thought you were going to move in the bed and the sink of the kitchen too."

"How long have I been asleep?"

"Nearly two hours. I figure you deserve it after all the effort you put in."

I sniffed and felt the brick wall of the coke still wedged up my nose, and realised I was still way high. I reached down to the little fridge and grabbed a can of coke – 'the real thing' as they used to say. I drank slowly and drew in revivifying lungfuls of pristine Mallorcan air. We sat in blissed out silence for long, peaceful minutes.

"I got something for you," I eventually told him.

"Good. Good man. I knew you were the one for this."

"Let's get back to my place to sort things out." I remembered Dixie.

"Sure thing. Hey, you wanna drive?"

"I don't think so somehow. Is your man not here?"

"What man?"

"Your driver. The bloke who was making this thing go all day."

"That was me. A friend of mine lend me the car."

Suddenly my smile was gone. "OK. OK, how much of that did you see?"

Then it was his turn to do the grinning. "Put it like this, Meeky boooy, when the video come out we gonna be rich."

I stared at him with bulging, bloodshot eyes until he howled with his high, girlish laugh.

"No, hombre. I'm only joking. Your secret is safe with me."

I heard him chortling to himself as he walked the length of the car. He climbed in and the mighty V8 purred into life.

"Hold on, mate," I called to him. "I'm coming up there too."

As I leant forward to get up, the pain got me in the back first. Then the knees. Then everywhere else. I made it woozily out of the car, only to find my vertical hold temporarily maladjusted and I nosedived the spiky flora at the side of the road. Another three or four minutes saw my sorry carcass in the passenger seat, next to the guffawing Spaniard.

On the short journey back to Palma Nova, my young accomplice told me everything. He told me of the future. He told me of his dreams and of his plans and of the power and the glory of money. He had it all mapped out and I was very impressed. So impressed that by the time we drew sedately up outside the hotel, I had forgotten everything he said. I finished the cola, belched and threw the can out of the window. "OK," I said enthusiastically, suddenly full of beans. "What's the plan?"

"What you mean?"

"What are we going to do?" I clapped my hands together. "The stuff?"

"Stuff?"

"The stuff you brought. You gonna get it?"

Through the fog came some degree of rational thought. "Oh yeah. Right." I opened the door and placed a trembling foot on the tarmac.

"Where's the key?" I asked.

"Reception maybe?"

The clever bastard was right, but for an eternity I fucked around going up and down in the lift, finding the right floor and fumbling with the key, until I finally managed to get into the room. I didn't have a clue what time it was, but fortunately Dixie wasn't around. I grabbed my bag and piled back out into the street. The limo was attracting a lot of attention so as soon as I was in the front seat again I told Rafael to haul that thing out of there.

"Is no problem, my friend. The windows are black and the doors..." He reached to the dash, flicked a switch and filled the car with a chunky, solid 'onk', "...are all locked."

It was then that I saw it. I knew. I realised what he had done. It was a trap and I was the suckered rabbit twitching in the snare: charmed, softened and delivered on a plate. I looked at him murderously. I saw the courtesy screen still up and knew the Guardia Civil cops were now locked inside the car *with* me. Scheming bastard.

"Drop the screen," I spat venomously.

"What you say?"

"The screen, you fucker." I thumped the divide with an unfeeling fist. "Lose it. Show me what you are."

"Hey. What you think? You think I try something? How long I know you? What you think?"

I saw him reach for his gun ... Then I heard the screen buzzing back down.

"Anytime you say, man. Anytime. You free to go. You don' like me or the way I do things then you let me know and we say goodbye. Fok, man."

I scanned the rear of the car and could not believe what my eyes were showing me. Nothing. I leapt out, clutching my bag to my chest. At least a dozen bystanders were stopped in their tracks by the sight of the sweating, puffing maniac, but they weren't police.

"Get in the car, man. Come on. We got to go."

I climbed weakly back in and looked at Rafael. Then I started crying.

He drove us out to the deserted point between El Toro and Santa Ponsa.

"Easy, man. I know how it can be. The coca, she take me like this sometimes. Well, maybe not so bad, but I understand what is paranoia. I open the window."

"I'm sorry, Rafa," I whimpered. "I'm really, really sorry."

We pulled off at the side of the road and I blew my nose and wiped away my tears. Rafa got me a beer from the fridge and as I breathed deeply I began to feel better. I listened with committed intensity to the hypnotic, orchestrated chirrup of the crickets.

I emptied the contents of my bag all over the floor of the car. With trembling fingertips I freed the plastic pins which secured the base of the bag and then pulled out the polythene covered cardboard which I unwrapped and held up proudly by the edges.

I gazed lovingly at the massed ranks. Three thousand double-dipped purple oms for which I had paid eighty-five pence a pop. I sold them to Rafa for the equivalent of two pounds twenty five pence. He counted out the pesetas there and then. Bunce up front, no quibble. No cut to Masters and Chalmers, no split with Dixie or Romanov. Just pure profit for yours truly.

I had been on the island for less than eight hours. I had been drugged out of my head and I had been screwed out of this world and I was already close on four and a half grand up. Yeah, it was good to be a gangster.

CHAPTER FOURTEEN

Every other Sunday, with my head still ringing from the drugs, I would struggle around to Dad's for the afternoon lunch that was intended to hold the family together. Seeing as my family basically consisted of Dad, Nigel, Nicolette and their boy, who were round there attending to all of Dad's mail and assorted paperwork, it was inevitable that me and my irksome brother would patch things up. I was doing great without him but the distasteful fact was that I needed his help with something.

"I need to extend my mortgage," I told him casually. "I'm buying a new place."

"Don't be a dick. I can't be arsed with you and your idiot schemes."

"What's the matter with you? I'm trying to put business your way."

The roly-poly, little fat knobhead went through the whole tiresome sighing routine, rolled his eyes and called me all the mad twats under the sun.

"What are those two blokes paying you now?"

"The same. Two and a half a week."

"Well how do you expect to extend your mortgage then?"

"The same way we got the first one. By lying on the application form. What's the problem?"

He looked me over in that way I had always detested, like I

was the little jumped up prick and he knew everything. Soon, though, we'd see who was jumped up and who knew what. Not only was I homing in on my hundred grand, I'd found this fantastic place. A life of ease and luxury was a year away. I was still only thirty. I think.

"You can't carry on shysting forever. Look at Terry. Don't you read the papers? There's a recession on the way."

True, there was a lot of doom an gloom in the dailies and on the news. This was eighty-nine. The bubble old Maggie had huffed and puffed so hard to inflate had burst. Stock markets were all over the place. Interest rates had been hiked yet again, this time to a stratospheric fifteen percent. But it didn't bother me. I was bullet proof.

"Not as far as I'm concerned there ain't. Things have never been better and it's only going one way."

"Up to you, but don't come whining to me when it all goes tits up. The only thing is you'll need to get proof of some pretty sizeable earnings from your... employers."

"Why?"

"How much do you want to borrow?"

"I need to bump it up from sixty-six grand by about another hundred."

"Well that's why, you berk. The lenders ain't going to chuck another hundred big ones at you just because we ask them nicely, especially as you pissed them around and got behind with the first few payments of the existing loan."

"Yeah, but whose fault was that?"

"Don't look at me. If you can't handle your finances it's not my fault." A blue rope throbbed on his temple.

I didn't want to go to Pete and Denny and ask them to lie on official forms about what I was or wasn't earning.

"Look, how about the Heroes? The building society don't know it's no longer trading. It's still on the register of companies, isn't it?"

"Yeah."

"Well then. Can't we just get some moody accounts together or some sort of verification of my mega salary?"

And that was precisely what we did because, back then, that was precisely what you could do. A little creative bookkeeping and the building society had another hundred grand's worth of business, Nigel copped commission on the loan and another endowment policy and I moved into a magnificently appointed, incredibly overpriced converted warehouse loft with terrific river views in Metropolitan Wharf in Wapping. Dad was well chuffed. He came round, looked out over the Thames and pointed out all manner of local points of interest, entertaining me with tales of days gone by - mainly concerning all the fights he had been in down the Prospect of Whitby and the pitched battles that had raged all over Wapping and Shadwell with the fearsome Cable Streeters. It fair brought a tear to his eye.

"We've done well without your mum," he said nodding his appreciation. "You and Nigel have done really well. I'm proud of you and your mum would have been too."

Confusingly, the agent who sold me the new place seemed to be talking about an entirely different market to the Beckton house one. It was as though Beckton was built on a nuclear waste dump and Wapping High Street was Fifth Avenue in New York. Not only that, it depended on who you were talking to if you wanted to believe the South East property market still had a way to go to its peak, or that it was poised to bomb totally. I dumped eight grand on the old place, but so what? I needed to be quick lest some other shrewd sod beat me to the loft.

I added another huge lump of money to the mortgage, effectively clearing me out of cash again, but it didn't matter and even though the repayments were pretty horrific, my income had to be seen to be believed as well. I figured I could run the flat and salt away about a hundred grand over the coming twelve months. Then I'd maybe rent out the place, tuck my stash in some high interest account - and then I'd be gone. No more crime, agro or risk. Just poop deck time for the rest of my life.

To complete the master criminal set-up, I found a fantastic, old, leather dentist chair down Petticoat Lane and planted it right in front of the windows looking out over the river, and from the comfort and safety of my lair I plotted and weaved and tricked and schemed.

Of the three girls I was seeing, I was spending more and more time with Julie, who was consistently amazed and amused by what I got up to. It was a base ego trip. She knew I sold drugs because she got through quite a lot of them herself, but she didn't really know the scale of things.

"Christ, Mick," she blabbed on seeing the Docklands place for the first time. "Just what *do* you do for a job?"

"I'm in transport."

"Transporting what? And to where? And does the owner know about it?"

By the time I had moved in I had accumulated something of a wide fan base. This was due to two factors. Firstly, there has always been that attraction towards somebody who is so patently a villain. People just like being around crooks. Successful, generous ones anyway. As I had been enthralled by Farmer and then Pete and Den, so others were dazzled by me and my lifestyle. Secondly, about half of Essex and East London knew they could score from me.

The wholesale business was very safe and pretty much ran itself. Ishy was by far and away the largest buyer of the coke that I got from Pete and Denny, and Jenny moved most of the Es I was picking up from Ishy. Also, Rafael was beginning to call across some large numbers of trips that I also got from Ishy, and there was a friend of Julie's out in Brentwood who took a fair bit of puff that was also supplied by Pete and Den.

But I carried on street dealing - not because I needed the money, although it was obviously the highest mark up, but because I simply enjoyed doing it. I loved being the man, which was a pretty stupid situation to allow to develop, but I was a happy little apprentice villain with excess beer vouchers on the hip.

Jade was a Cherokee Indian who had dual nationality. Her boyfriend had never made it out of the States and it was looking like he never would. Immigration were giving him all kinds of problems over his visa. She was sure she wanted to make a career and a life in the UK, so was understandably torn. She went back to visit him as often as she could, but obviously that was not cheap. To console herself she would spend extended periods of time with me and Julie turning our heads into porridge. A situation, beginning with a call from Ishy, was bound to develop.

It's here, class. The eagle has landed, with the accent on E, know what I'm saying?"

"Not exactly, Ishy. I've got a bit of a headache. What are you on about, old son?"

"I'll give you a clue; this stuff is MDMAzing."

I got down there fast and there he was: grinning, flashing the gold tooth and generally behaving like some dodgy drug dealer.

"Really? This is the raw shit, yeah?"

"Raw ain't the word for it, my man. This gear is fucking brutal. You know how hard it is to get this stuff in this form in this country? I'm only doing this because it's you, you know."

"Ishy, tell me one thing for truth."

He froze. "Anything, class. You my brother."

"Where you from?"

He looked at me and then Vicky and then back to me, clearly wondering what kind of backhand googly I was trying to bowl him.

"Beirut. What about yourself?"

I offered him my hand and the biggest grin I possessed.

"Ishy. I love you, mate. Don't ever change a thing."

Whenever there were any drugs on the table between me and Ishy, Vicky would be drawn into the equation. We trusted each other like blood. So, when there was an ounce of what looked like Demerara sugar for sale at more than the price of top quality cocaine, I instinctively turned to her for corroboration.

"Mick," she began in earnest. "You know me. I've done it all. Get yourself some. You don't know."

Then there was Ishy, looking like an Afghan rebel in an Armani jacket. Urging, coaxing.

Then I thought about what Mick and Den had said about the dangers of this drug and the bad publicity. Not to rock our cosy, little boat. Ranting about how Plod were running themselves ragged chasing E dealers whilst coke, puff and wiz boys were having things relatively cushy. You only get three chances.

"How much on the oz, again?"

"Twelve hundred. Check it out, my man. You got to check it out."

Then I thought about Jenny and the way she was screaming at me for Es; always more Es. Ishy was only able to get the Doves in by the hundred and they were still costing me eight quid a unit, but Jen said they were sometimes slow in being shifted because by that time there were inferior imitations on the streets. If I could get my *own* brand going in London then my hundred large would come rolling in all the sooner. Then why stop at a hundred? I felt immortality beckon.

The inspirational deciding vote came from an unexpected source. I pictured Jade's waist-length black hair and her proud features, like unblemished Rosewood.

I can feel an angel sliding up to me

"Better sort me two ounces," I told Ishy.

I suggested to Julie that Jade might like to join us for the weekend. "Walk by the river, get down the Prospect, hit the West End for a show, do an E, visit the Tower of London... "

"Excuse me?"

"Well I've never been to the Tower of London before."

"Not that, you muppet. Are you saying you want to do an E with Jade?"

"Did I say that?"

She looked at me and into me, the way only she could. Reading me. She smiled and nodded.

"Jade likes you actually."

I smiled. "Everybody likes me."

"Yeah," she said. "Everybody does, but tell me, Mick, how did it get to this stage? How did it all get to be like this?" She swept an enquiring arm before her, indicating the river, the flat, the lifestyle, the drugs. Me.

I didn't know if it was a compliment or a commiseration. Maybe a bit of both, but there was a tint of sadness in her voice and a trace of regret and worry that the whole, crazy roadshow was ultimately doomed; that I was living - albeit living very well - on borrowed time.

I shrugged. "Dunno. It all just happened. Life just happened and all I did was get in the way. When you think about it, the whole crime and drugs bit is what life leaves over for us weirdies when it has taken all the best bits. What I do is just an alternative, left-handed way of doing what everyone else does."

In the meantime this miracle elixir had to be tried and tested, so we got at it there and then. I weighed out a hundred milligrams on my electronic scales and we had that each. Eighteen minutes after we took it Julie flipped into orbit. I took three minutes longer. Everything Ishy and Vicky had said was true.

Not that we let it rule our lives. No - we achieved a very satisfying mix by doing acid half the time as well. Once we got our levels of tolerance established and I could be sure she wasn't out to murder me, we had a series of fascinating evenings. We'd sit up all night like a couple of old hippies, watching the plants dance and the shadows sway while we listened to every form of music from my old Pink Floyd albums to her latest Indie CDs by the Mondays and the Roses, The House of Love and Primal Scream.

Not that I was letting business slip. After an intense week of testing, I'd got the mix just right and had set Jen on her way. It was beautiful.

From a couple of weightlifting wholesalers I bought black capsules and yellow capsules of a dietary supplement, which I emptied down the bog. In the black ones, I shoved roughly a hundred milligrams of MDMA with the ballast made up of flour. These were to be known as Midnights: the approximate equal of anything on the street, and would retail at the usual fifteen quid a hit. I let Jenny have those for the customary tenner. Then I combined the black and yellow caps and put in around two hundred milligrams of raw gear. These were to be sold as Stingers, and would be billed as the ultimate psychedelic love experience. I let Jen have those for eighteens and she moved them onto her connoisseur clients at around twenty-fives.

It was all a bit gimmicky but it worked. Soon I was moving an ounce a week through Jen. Along with personal sales I was netting close on two grand. Sales of other drugs bumped that up to about three. That alone equated to a yearly net income of a hundred and fifty thousand, at a time when the average gross was less than twenty. Then she needed two ounces a week.

For all I knew Jenny could have been making more than that, but it wasn't my place to ask. She was a shrewd kid with loads of contacts, and she knew the rave scene inside out. My biggest worry, I thought, was keeping news of this gold mine from Romanov, and therefore from Pete and Den.

I was also concerned about her personal safety, but she invariably took out her brother Ricky with her when she was selling. He was only twenty-two but he was a lump and a half, and curiously he was staunch anti-drugs, so he served as an adequate and clear-headed deterrent to any yob who fancied his chances, although how he would shape up to some of the organised gangs who had the London clubs sewn up remained to be seen. The bigger field raves where there were always lots of freelance pushers were fine, but as the government introduced new legislation to outlaw those kinds of gatherings, everyone was forced indoors to smaller, legal clubs. Those places were usually sorted for drugs by collaborations of the promoters and the security blokes.

More than that, should the worst happen, how would she stand up to police interrogation? She had no record, no job and was on the dole. All her money was safely hidden. If she got caught she would just say she met a bloke in a pub who fronted her the stuff. Wouldn't she?

It was a genuine worry because Jenny was becoming something of a celebrity. The Midnights were flying away and the Stingers were the talk of the London club scene. Sure, people were buying from her and then cutting the product down and recapping. That was bad enough, but the unforeseen by-product of that only added to the notoriety, because soon everybody knew that if you wanted a genuine Midnight or Stinger then a skinny little kid from Bermondsey called Jennifer Baddows was the go-to source. She revelled in it but it scared the shit out of me. And obviously she had people out working for her as well. If they got caught and talked?

I shoved it to the back of my mind because I had other things on the go. One Saturday evening, with the summer sun a juicy, dripping orange, hanging directly over the Thames right outside my window, the intercom buzzed. My two friends had come to play. There was an air of 'I dare you' about the whole thing and we all popped a Stinger each. I rammed six discs into the Akai and hit random, got plenty of drink out of the fridge, dragged the dentist's chair out of the way and spread the king-size quilt out onto the polished oak.

We started out slowly. Touching, holding hands, gentle massages. Then, as the temperature rose and the waves of paralysing pleasure started to wash over us, we were suddenly down to our underwear. As much as I wanted to get into something like that, I was a little concerned as to how we would handle it all, but any embarrassment was quickly dispelled by the magic of Ishy's MDMA. And being a good old Essex boy who was raised on an adolescent diet of heterosexual porn of the most rudimentary nature I was especially intrigued to see the girls begin to kiss, cuddle and caress each other. Then Julie spoke. It seemed like the first time anyone had said anything for hours.

"Mick. You take care of Jade from the waist down and I'll handle the top half."

In the second of hesitation before I got down to things, I heard the boy's voice in my head. It was like he was in the room. "Go on, class. Go on. You got to check it out, my man. Check. It. *Out* ."

And, of course, he was right.

The sun went down and came up again before we finally crashed out, exhausted but sated by sheer hedonistic indulgence. Not only that, when we woke on the Sunday afternoon we were all able to look each other in the eye and talk it through, like we were discussing a film or reviewing a book.

"Promise me one thing," Julie said the next time I saw her on her own.

"Sure."

"Never tell anyone about the other night."

"OK."

"Never!"

"Jesus, relax. I don't want anyone to know," I said, imagining Romanov wincing with jealousy when I hit him with the details.

"Something else too."

"What?"

She looked into me - through me with an intensity I hadn't known she possessed.

"If you ever go with Jade on her own I'll never talk to you again."

"Shit," Jade said as I shoved a Stinger into her mouth, to shut her up as much as to turn her on. "If Julie ever finds out about this she'll never talk to me again."

"Danger is exciting," I told her. "Has all my training fallen on deaf ears?"

Jade's problem was that she very rarely got to see her bloke. Her other problem was that she loved sex and hated going for months without getting any. Would it be OK if no-one ever found out?

"Not many people get better looking the more clothes they take off…" I told her, "…but you do."

I put my hands on the sinewy satin of her body and she melted onto me. It could have been the words or it could have been the drug, either way I didn't care.

Meanwhile, our own particular brand of peripatetic villainy was in such demand, we quickly had to expand from Mallorca to the Costas, a couple of times to Madrid and, when summer faded and the late season began, down to the Canaries. Wherever we went, Martinez would be there to meet us with his thief's grin and his peseta crammed wallet. Once me and Rafael had arrived at our understanding he would invariably be there too with my extra, undeclared bonus, in exchange for a sheet or so of Ishy's OMs.

Along with the money we scored for the moody Sterling and

travellers cheques, we would take Martinez's cash and bank it in Pete's special account at the Bank of Bilbao, return home triumphant and empty-handed and then Pete would lay the dosh on us. Luis and Rafa would load up several large suitcases full of stolen goods and fly back to Mallorca to flog it. Perfect.

I even found myself forgiving Luis halfway through the repayment of his debt. For the sake of inter-firm goodwill, I released him from the obligation Pete and Romanov had so dramatically enforced. Romanov said I was nuts but our point had been made.

Although my income was obscenely high, I was finally forced to take notice of the recession everyone had been bleating about for so long. My mortgage repayments and the service charges on the Wapping flat were beyond ridiculous. Nothing I could not handle, of course, but sufficient enough to make me appreciate that we were now definitely in a new decade. The difference between the early nineties and the eighties was as abrupt and unpalatable as walking out of the front door of a warm, comfortable house into a freezing storm. I got away with it but a great many didn't. So many had been screaming along the eighties motorway, only to slam into the nineties brick wall. Weren't gonna happen to me. I looked firstly at margins.

As things were established so nicely and as my customers were mostly good friends too, I was reluctant to cut into the quality of the coke I was selling or the MDMA I was moving to Jen. Consequently, my income more or less governed by external factors, it was upon my outgoings that the axe had to fall.

On average, I was finding my way through about seven or eight grams of coke a week, unless there were any parties on and it was likely to be more. In addition I was popping nine or ten Es, unless I was out raving and again the total would increase. If I was having grief with my schnozz, as I often did, I'd also dab one or two grams of wiz, and once I'd found my levels, I explored the murky interior of my own head to the tune of half a dozen or so trips.

I therefore figured my expense on the drug front was pretty much trimmed to the bone already, so I looked elsewhere for budgetary regulation.

At that time, normally upon Julie's instigation, I was doing a lot of eating out and the places I frequented were not cheap either. Normally flash, designer, West End restaurants or up-market Essex eateries; evenings that might feature the occasional walk-on part for TV micro- celebs, back-bench MPs or second division footballers. I was loathe to rule out this pleasure because even though it was a drain on resources, I took my healthy appetite to be a sign that I did not have a drug problem.

There was only one thing for it. Into the winter the bike had to go, and the Jag just felt too expensive and clumsy in traffic.

I called up Steve and ran the Suzuki back round to him. I was staggered by the level of depreciation to which those newer models were clearly subject.

Bizarrely, Chris over on the strip in Seven Kings said much the same thing about the Jag he had sold me less than a year before. I had no idea those things were such an unsound investment. Luckily he had something on his forecourt that was ideal for me. Smaller, yes. Nippier, yes. Cheaper to run? I'd have to see. A real eye catcher too. OK, I had to put twenty-five grand to the XJ to buy the thing and I had to borrow a load from Pete to do that, but the Ferrari 308 was a highly desirable model.

Nigel said I was mad but I knew he was only jealous. Although he did smile when my insurance premium was due.

That car brought back the whole relativity angle though, and I don't think it did me any favours. I was reaching some kind of perverted apotheosis that, I believe, robbed me of some of my motivation. I stopped trying. It was like everything was cool because I had achieved what I had set out to achieve. Growing up in seventies and eighties Essex and London was just that: a public exercise in achievement. What good you did in the world, or indeed how happy you were counted for nothing. People did not buy houses to live in; they bought them so they could boast to their friends of their capital appreciation. The one who ended up owning the most, won.

Nobody I knew (not anyone my age anyway) had done what I had done, and it was unlikely anyone would do it better. And I knew this because when I was cruising the street in that thing and slammed down hard on the go-juice pedal, that engine would scream and *every*one would be looking. And that was what it was about.

I got the sack just after I got the car. A few times, for whatever reason, I had been unable to make it into work on time. It wasn't a problem.

"Don't worry about coming in anymore," Pete told me. "It don't affect the gear or the carding and kiting or the away trips. You're looking a bit knackered lately. Why don't you get off the shit? We're going to be getting a full-time salesman in to take your place. You won't miss the wages, will you?"

I was a little shocked but he had a point. Why should I knock myself out for what was essentially loose change?

If that was a turning point, then a remarkable high water mark occurred that same week which appeared to capture the entire zeitgeist; to crystallise the whole sentiment of what was happening in my life. I was due to see Jenny on the Wednesday. She had money for me and I had caps for her. She must have had an amazing life, but you would never have known it. I hadn't seen her smile in months. She wasn't looking too clever either. With pale skin and those blue circles under her eyes, she looked like she had missed out on her youth. She looked thirty instead of twenty. A genuine product of the rave generation and the E-culture, who spent her waking hours in a soporific, nocturnal shuffle between one surreal, stroboscopic cave and the next. In with the night people. In with the vampires. She looked like she hadn't seen the sun in years. I thought a nice meal would do her good.

The thing about owning a Ferrari is that when you pop out somewhere - beer, food, anywhere - the temptation is just to keep on popping. With that in mind I suggested a jaunt out to a terrific restaurant Pete had taken me to ages before in an Essex village called Finchingfield. The Mill was the kind of gaff where you would be likely to find dishes such as chestnut and otter soup, followed by signet pie garnished with dock leaves. The 308 whisked us there in no time. Jenny only picked at her food and I wasn't that hungry either, but the maitre d' was a nice, friendly Italian bloke who made us feel really at home. He told me he knew a lot about cars and as much about women, and he wished to commend me on my taste in both. We popped a couple of Stingers each over coffee and as we drove away I saw her relax for the first time that evening.

On the way back the steering wheel began to feel distinctly spongy, and there seemed to be lots more bends going home than I recalled there being on the way out. It got so bad that as we were screaming along the A127 near the Upminster turn-off, I felt obliged to pull into the Hilton National to get a room for the night. By then it was all I could do to get my wallet out, so the following romantic entanglements proved to be less than passionate or even noticeable. Jen just laid on her back with her legs open, quite possibly unaware there was even anyone else in the room much less inside of her. I did my best and bashed away for a while, but crawled off when it became apparent that it was all going nowhere anyway.

We woke up when the chambermaid came in at noon.

I drove Jen home in complete silence and then headed back to mine for the much needed shutting of the eyes. Sometime during the afternoon the phone rang.

"Hi, sexy," trilled Lauren. "How's it going?"

"Hello, darling," I croaked. "How are you?"

"Fine. 'Ere, you're not still in bed, are you?"

"No. I just got back from my daily five mile run actually."

"Daily run? Yeah right. The only running you do is when you are on the bog."

Always there with a delicate, sympathetic word, our Lauren.

"Anyway. Bit of news I thought you'd want to hear. Dad is back from South Africa and wants to see you."

This was indeed news. I still had no idea why I was held so much in the thrall of this man who I had still only met once. I felt I needed to be briefed as much as possible.

"What you doing tonight?" I asked.

Gianluca, as by then I knew him, was pleased to see me. He immediately cracked on and handled it like the old pro he was. "I know a lot about cars and as much about women," he told me smoothly as he handed out the leather volumes that were the menus. "And may I compliment you on you taste in both, sir."

"You're very kind."

Not having eaten since the previous evening, I was quite peckish and as we tucked into half a cow and a field of King Edwards each, I got to grilling Lauren.

"Look, Mick, I don't know what this is with you. Just be yourself."

"Yeah but, Lauren. I'm a villain. I sell drugs and con multi-nationals out of lots of money for a living. Do you want me to tell him that? Is he still at it? Has he ever been at it?"

"Mick. One of the reasons Dad is so successful is because he never tells anyone who doesn't need to know what it is he is up to. But I will say he knows a lot of the chaps from South and East London, and by that I mean a lot of the *real* chaps. There's nothing you can say that would shock him."

"Fine," I said brightening.

"Except drugs."

"How's that?"

"He cannot abide drugs. He's sold them for sure, not a problem there, but he doesn't take them himself and will not tolerate people who do. He doesn't know I do them, so turn up nice and clear-headed, and look smart."

"Blimey. OK, but what about me and you?"

"What about me and you?"

"Does he know?"

"Does he know what?"

"Lauren. I've been to bed with his little girl."

She chewed thoughtfully. "Well, I haven't told him, but then again he often seems to know things without being told. Does it matter?"

"It might."

"Why? It's not as if we're engaged or anything is it? We're not even going out as such, are we?"

I didn't know if she was pleased or otherwise about that and I didn't have the guts to ask.

"Yeah but... some blokes get touchy about who their daughters are messing around with."

"Mick, I'm a big girl now and he trusts me so stop worrying and just relax and be yourself."

I stopped worrying.

Nice restaurants, good wine and a convivial atmosphere always made Lauren randy, so fortunately there was a different desk clerk on duty at the Hilton National. The Ferrari's engine was running a lot better than mine, but with the added tonic of half a gram of wiz, I was still up to the job. Just.

"Wow, there ain't many women who get better looking the more clothes they take off, but you do."

"Jesus Christ, you wally. You gave me that bullshit the first time and I didn't buy it then. Tell it to someone who'll believe it."

Once again the maid woke me around lunchtime. Beside the bed I found a note from Lauren saying she had cabbed it to work and that she would call me when Patsy wanted to meet up.

A stunning thrash into the East End in the Italian chariot saw me feeling quite perky. So much so that I decided to go for a jog. I actually made it all the way down to the street before I pulled up, gagging and gasping for breath. I took the quick way straight back up and as I opened the door the phone rang. It was Jade.

She told me how she had just got off the phone to her boyfriend in America and had been left, once again, feeling sad, lonely and out of luck. Did I want some company? I suggested dinner.

The 308 was getting more mileage than I had planned and I was beginning to know the menu at the Mill like I had written it myself. Gianluca was bowled over to see me. Twice could have been a fluke, but three times on the spin? And by then the waiters were all in on the gag too.

"Your usual sauce, sir?"

"Remy Martin is it not, sir?"

Jade was too wrapped up with thoughts of her bloke to notice. In fact she was so preoccupied I don't even think she saw me heave the car off the A127 into the carpark of the hotel. She was so sweet and she was so lonely. Who was taking advantage of whom? One Midnight each later and we gave up pondering all the ramifications.

Julie had been away on business during the week and called me on Saturday afternoon.

"Fancy a meal tonight?" she ventured.

Hard by at The Mill, things were getting out of hand. Gianluca was by that stage running a book on the variables: would it be a different girl? What colour hair would she have? How tall? Stuff like that.

We had a lovely dinner with a tremendous claret Gianluca had recommended and a great chat, but it was me who was subdued that night. I had a strange feeling which I would identify later as the first question marks I ever placed against my lifestyle. At first I just thought it was indigestion, but I soon realised it was more than that. I didn't know what was coming next but was somehow sure that whatever it was, it wouldn't be as good as what had passed before. It was like it had simply got to be too much for me, and that the conclusion of that phase of my life was shrouded in grim inevitability. It was so good it just wasn't good anymore and, sooner or later, the levelling hand of reason and fair play would come around and deal a few aces back to my old adversary: life.

Gianluca and the chaps just thought I was a bit knackered because of all the action I was getting, but it truly was the heavy burden of resignation bowing my shoulders.

So enraptured was he that, at the conclusion of the meal, he brought me his own personal decanter of VSOP Cognac and, if I had let him, would probably have OK'd me a night with his missus too. It was orgiastic self-congratulation at its grossest. When we were leaving the waiters and the bar staff lined up at the door to shake hands and see us on our way. Julie thought it was some kind of wind-up.

"Probably my guv'nor," I told her. "He comes here a lot. Must have told them to look after me."

I opened the car door to let her in but then I stopped, gripped by a sudden melancholy.

"Hold on," I said. "I think I've forgotten something."

I walked quickly back and pulled Gianluca to one side.

"Listen. I don't know when I'm coming back. Maybe never. But I wanted to thank you for not just doing your job very well, but for being a part of this. This is kind of like my dream and it wouldn't have happened so well if you hadn't been in it."

It had been a long time since someone had looked at me like I really did come from Mars. As smooth as he was, he was lost for words. I reached for my wallet.

"Look, you've got to take this," I told him, unplugging the not inconsiderable contents, which at a guess, must have topped a grand. "Share it out between you all. I don't know how much there is, which is good because it would be wrong to put a price on a dream."

I saw the concern in his face.

"Mick, something is not right. You seem sad. What is it?"

I shrugged and said, "It's over."

PART THREE

CHAPTER FIFTEEN

The call came. Lauren said that Patsy would like to take me, Lauren and Barbara out for a meal. For one heart-stopping moment I thought he might have been a patron of the Mill, but I was pleased and tremendously impressed to hear that Patsy owned his own pub-cum-restaurant. Something else no-one had bothered telling me. I'd even heard of it. The Vicious Cock, near Orsett, Essex was known for its peaceful surroundings, elegant, country furnishings and trouble-free reputation. I had never been there.

By the time the wheels of the 308 were crunching the gravel in the drive, I had gone something like thirty-four and a half hours without taking drugs of any kind. I felt diabolically unwell.

Lauren was hanging around in the bar to meet me, and she steered me through to the smaller and more exclusive of the two restaurants. There, along with Barbara, was big Patsy Chetkins. Any doubts I had entertained regarding his villainous credentials were dispelled in the time it took his handshake to turn my hand into a bruised pulp. Anyone with a shake like that had to be bang at it.

"Young Mick," he said, placing his mighty paws on my shoulders. "It's been too long, son. First you didn't get in touch for years, and then I'm off the scene. Good to see you. How've you been?"

I looked into the intelligent grey of his eyes and was warmed by his obvious and genuine affection for me. He was an odd-looking bloke. The receding rust of his hair, the unfeasible youth of his freckle-dashed face. The fat, pink lips. I felt I had a friend for life.

"Pretty good, Patsy. Keeping in front and getting away with it, can't ask for more than that. And yourself? Things looking OK over there?"

"Yeah yeah. So so. Be a while before anything comes of it, but when they let Mandela out and hand things over to the blacks, as they surely will, well then the economy is going to collapse, and the Rand with it. Then's the time to be over there standing by with some Sterling to snap up a few bargains. Be some very cheap companies for sale."

"Pat, don't start talking business now. Mick doesn't want to hear about all that, do you, Mick? How are you, love?" Barbara stepped forward and kissed me on the cheek.

"All the better for seeing you, Barbara. How are you, darling?"

"Very well, thank you. Well, this is lovely. About five years overdue but we're all here together. Shall we sit down and order? I'm starving."

"Yes. Let's do that. Get you something to drink, Mick?" said Patsy, summoning a hovering lackey with nothing more than a vague glance in his direction.

"Lovely, Pat. Gin and tonic, please. Nice place you have here."

"Thank you. It ticks over and never a hint of any trouble. Last bloke who caused any agro in here was Dick Turpin, and he was way off his manor."

We settled at a corner table. I noticed that Patsy placed himself with his back to the wall; a position that afforded him full vision of the entire room and everybody who entered and left. Throughout the course of the evening a veritable procession of men (no women) filed past our table to pay homage to him like he was the Pope. It was like it had been with Farmer in the old days, except it was about a hundred rungs further up the ladder. There was no stolen plastic changing hands here. There was no dashing out to the carpark to empty a boot full of nicked televisions and stereos. These were refined men: intelligent, elegant men - criminals so far advanced in their profession they were no longer recognisable as criminals. They were not so much interested in buying video machines as the companies that made them, and when they moved together their decisions influenced the fiscal well-being of entire communities. I thought back to Farmer holding court over housebreakers and scumbags.

That said, by the time the evening was drawing to a close, I was no nearer to discovering just what it was that made Patsy Chetkins tick. We talked of baby James, and Barbara told stories about Lauren as a child to make us laugh. We talked holidays, football, food and what we were watching on television. All very nice, but I thought that when the coffee came and went, big Pat would pack the womenfolk off to some parlour somewhere and we would pass the Port the correct way around the table and talk some turkey. Not a bit of it. Patsy made his apologies, declared himself quite tired, grabbed his missus and buggered off. I did get a moment as he was shrugging on the Crombie.

"Good to see you again, son. Now you stay and have a few drinks with Lauren. Anything you want, just stick on the bill. Move your car around to the rear get it in the morning. The boys in blue are pretty hot on that kind of thing round here. Sorry I've got to run, lots to do over the next few days, starting in the morning. Make sure Lauren gets in a cab too, will you?"

Of course I did not want to be accepted into the family business at director level, but I could not help looking upon it as some kind of snub. A cold shoulder.

"No trouble, Patsy. Thanks once again for the meal, it was lovely. Barbara was right it was nice for all four of us to get together."

"We will again, young Mick. We will again." He offered me his hand and I knew I had to take it.

"Don't forget, son," he told me, suddenly quite serious,

"anything you need, anytime you need help, you know where I am. Here's our cab. See you."

And that was it. Not only that, but it was pretty clear he was expecting Lauren home - thus effectively outlawing any dabbling around. All in all, I couldn't help but be disappointed.

Even though the cab fares cost me an arm and the leg that I didn't get over Lauren, he was right about leaving the 308 at the Cock. It gave me the chance to return the next day to do some serious sucking up.

I had met Ron, the restaurant manager, over dinner and collared him as he was getting the lunch tables laid out.

"Is Patsy around, Ron? Could do with a chat if he's available."

"No, Mick. He left the country this morning."

"'Scuse me?"

"Yeah. I don't know how he keeps up with it all. Mallorca this time. Maybe only a week."

Two days later I got a call from Pete Chalmers. He had some work on. Bit cloak and dagger. He got Romanov to take me to a car hire firm in Mile End where I rented a Transit van in a false name and drove to a specific paper merchants in Stratford. There, I paid cash for thirty thousand sheets of a particular brand and weight of A3 paper. I then transported it a mere two or three miles across the East End to a printers that backed onto the River Lea in Hackney, leaving the consignment with a bloke who looked like something out of a Dickens novel, called Arthur Coltraine. He was expecting me. I drove the van back to the hire company and called base camp from a phone box nearby. Romanov was there within minutes to pick me up and take me back to the warehouse.

In the upstairs office Pete was waiting to fill me in. "Recognise that?" he asked, pointing to a package on his desk as he handed me a coffee.

Surprised as I was, I looked upon it fondly. The package Farmer had asked me to pick up and deliver to the chaps a year and a half ago had been my passport into the life.

"Never thought I would see that again."

"Do you know what's in it?"

"I got asked that question before. The answer's still the same."
"Take a look."

It was open at one end. There were about eight thin sheets of metal, each separated by a sheet of card. Each featured a design in a different colour: blue, red, yellow and black. I didn't recognise them individually. Then I picked out some lettering on one of them and then I knew. I had never seen them before, legal or otherwise. They were the stuff of legend and detective movies. I gasped in awe as the marvellous truth dawned on me.

"Jesus, Pete. Printers plates. You're printing... You're going to print your own American Express travellers cheques."

"Been a long time coming. We had everything sorted to make the initial print run a year ago, but the bloke we had lined up to do it for us got nicked doing something else, the stupid bastard. Two bob job it was as well. Luckily the plates weren't on the premises at the time. It's taken us this long to arrange for another printer. We've been using Arthur to print off loads of MOT certificates and log books. That has gone well and he is sound as the pound he prints."

"So how does it all work?"

"Any printing of this type starts off with scanning. What you do is get an example of what you are going to print and you shove it under a scanner, which is basically a camera that costs half a million quid. This is why forgery of this type is rare. The logic being that if you can afford to buy one of these things then why bother breaking the law with it? Once you've got one you can charge the earth for legal work. Anyway, we managed to get into a bloke who was getting skinned by his missus in the divorce court and he was up for it. Terry knew him too and did all the communication which was why he had the things at the time he went down. We had the bloke scan a fifty and a hundred pound Amex. travellers cheque."

"What did that cost?"

"Too much. Sufficed to say the bloke can now make his alimony payments without worrying. But that is only half the job. What the scanner does is split the design up into the four colours that constitute all printing and these are then transposed onto film. From the film you get the four differently coloured plates that you see. That is the easy part. Then you take the plates to a sufficiently corrupt printer and you get your product."

He rose from his desk to look out of the window over the yard as Romanov mashed the gears of a sixteen-tonner he was trying to back into the warehouse.

"The equipment that is needed to print the things is about as expensive as the scanner, so there are all the same attendant problems as before, but thanks to the recession nailing small businesses to the wall, Arthur needs money. Problem is cheques and banknotes aren't like running off any other sheet of paper. There are all the usual safety devices you have to negotiate. Embossing equipment and technique. Obviously you need a numerator for the numbers. Then there is the water mark, which comes down solely to the skill of the printer. As well as that there is the ultra violet. You seen these ultra violet detectors they have in the pubs and the clubs these days?"

"Yeah. All over the place."

"You wouldn't know, but if you stick an Amex cheque under one of those things it lights up like a Christmas tree. Problem is only certain parts of it are treated. All of a banknote absorbs UV light so that would be easier, but it's harder with a cheque because it's only certain bits. Again Arthur reckons he knows what to do. All very fiddly and time consuming but we have to get it right."

"How many are you going to knock out?"

He retook his seat behind his desk and took a sip of coffee.

"Twenty million quid's worth."

It was the scam to end them all, for the chaps as well as me. Hallelujah.

The plan was Dixie, me and Romanov would take some quarter of a million quid's worth away to the continent by road. We would drive to Paris and hit every bank and outlet there before sprinting to Marseilles. Then it would be over the border and straight to Madrid. Laying waste to that great city, it would then be Barcelona and the coast, to work our way down until there was the first sign of trouble. Pete seemed to think we would have at least a fortnight before word got out to all those little exchange bureaux and the shit was really hitting the fan. We would have plenty of spare passports, and of course all the cheques would be differently numbered so we would never be passing the same one twice.

"On the runs we've done so far we know how easy it is. You've not had a hint of trouble and our cheques will be better than those."

He added that me and Dixie and Paul would have a head start of at least two weeks before he released any of the other cheques onto the market. It would be our reward as faithful employees. Our pioneering groundwork over in Spain had convinced him and Den they were onto a winner. The bulk of the other cheques had already been ordered by various gangland contacts, one firm in particular taking a flat ten million. These were going for between fifteen and twenty five percent of face value.

"I quite like getting up in the mornings," Pete told me. "But I do find myself getting tired these days. What we'll probably do is pull this off and flog off the Rats and all the other little companies. Spend a bit more time abroad. Relax and smell the roses, you know? You stashing plenty away for retirement, Mick?"

That really was a good question, the answer to which was simple. With a mega scam like this one on the way, I didn't fucking need to.

The only fly in the ointment was we had to wait. Old Arthur needed time to perfect things anyway, but we would need to blend in with a million other sun-loving tourists who were all changing their money up too. Only a few weeks into the new year and we had around six months to go, but it was all set. Poop deck here we come. I thought a little celebration was in order.

I don't know if it was the promise of more money than even I could spend, or if it was the drugs causing a treacherously dangerous chemical imbalance, but I think I started to fall in love with Julie. There was no thunderbolt; there was no divine intervention. Nothing happened that I did not understand. That was how I knew it was real.

I was sprawled naked on the quilt beneath the river view windows. Julie padded on legs of jelly back from the kitchen with another bottle of Evian. There was clearly something on her mind. "I spoke to Jade yesterday. We had a real good heart-to-heart."

As stoned as I was that cut right the way through to the nerve.

"It's Travis, her bloke back in the States."

I flopped back down onto the quilt in relief. "Oh yeah? How is Geronimo?"

"Don't call him that, you pleb. There was half a chance he was going to come over for a visit but he's got some work on so he can't just yet."

"Very commendable." I rolled over and hoovered up another line from the awaiting ranks. My coffee table looked like a plan of the Battle of Waterloo.

"She's so disappointed though. She was counting on seeing him this time."

"Can't she go to see him?"

"She's trying to work something out but she is even more skint than him. She is struggling to pay the mortgage as it is. If she rents her flat out it won't get anything like her repayments so she can't even do that."

"Can't she just sell the place?"

"Same problem. She's in negative equity. Even if she can sell it she won't get half of what she paid for it. Haven't you heard? There's a recession on."

"Actually I did hear some penniless former company chairman whining on about it on the news last night."

"Alright for you drug dealers."

"Entrepreneur, my dear. International trader."

"Oh yeah? New York, Paris, Wapping?"

"Very good. So what's the answer then?"

"Well it's all about money, isn't it? If she enough she would be able to quit her job, leave enough in the bank to cover the mortgage, get on a plane and stay long enough with him to work out where they're at. Life just isn't fair."

"Look, you'll be doing me a favour. I know that sounds like a bunch of crap but it's true. I need to purge myself."

"What are you talking about, you maniac?" She sobbed, unable to take her eyes off the ten grand bundle on the table.

"Me and you. I should never have let it go so far. If Julie ever finds out she is going to be so upset."

"Don't you ever tell her." Her tear-spattered face suddenly turned to stone. "If you ever tell her I'll cut your liver out and nail it above your front door."

"Pardon?"

"Don't you ever tell her."

"Of course I won't. Jesus what are you, fucking nuts? Look, I'm in a position to be able to do something really important for someone that I truly care for and I'm going to do it. It's a dream come true. The Milky Bars are on me."

I took her beautiful face in my hands and stared into the perfect, brown almonds of her eyes. The weird thing was I meant it too.

"Just imagine how lucky I am, that I can do this thing. Do you have any idea how good and how special that makes me feel? I can help you change the course of your life. Take the money. I don't want to hear anything else about it."

She grinned and said the only thing a nice girl could say after she's been given ten thousand pounds in cash. "Did I ever tell you you're dynamite in the sack?"

Suddenly I was broke again but with the big one to come in the summer who cared?

A couple of days later I was hanging around at mine doing a bit of hoovering when the Motorla rang.

"Mick?"

"Yeah. Who's this?"

"Mick, my boy. Good to hear your voice again. Surely you remember your old partner?"

I felt like I'd just been told a close relative had died. Nothing could have prepared me for that shock. There was no reason for me to feel it was a bad thing, I just knew that it was. It was very bad indeed.

"Big Tel, you old pirate, you. How are ya? Where you calling from?"

"Oh don't worry, son. I am well and truly on the out. You obviously didn't hear about my appeal."

"Appeal? No, mate. No bastard tells me anything."

"If you'd been in touch with Kerry she would have told you."

"Ah yeah, well. Sorry about that, mate. I've er... I've been a bit busy."

"So I hear. Busy and successful. Done very well out of my contacts and my advice."

"Yeah well. Not too bad. Can't complain."

"Good. Good. I'd like to see you."

"What for?"

"For a chat."

"Er... When?"

"As soon as possible."

"Can't see you tonight, mate. I've got someone coming round. In fact..."

"I don't mean tonight. I mean now."

"Where are you?"

"In the phone box across the street."

I sighed. There was no way out.

Three minutes later he was pacing the flat, overdosing with the irony. "How do you do it, mate? How do you get by? This is too much for any reasonable person to have to put up with. Have you spoken to the DSS about getting rehoused? And that motor. Don't you get embarrassed? You turn up down the pub to see your pals, bet they take the piss."

"I'm pleased to see you," I told him and in one sense I was.

"You had the chance to see me a lot more throughout the last five hundred and twelve days."

"I know. I know, mate. I've been lazy. It's been really poor of me. I apologise. How's Kerry?" I winced as soon as I said it.

"She's OK. Cheered up a bit now that I've told her she isn't going to be cleaning up the puke and the crap in that shithole of a pub seven days a week."

I shut my eyes to make it all go away. My heart was pounding, my soaked shirt clung to my back.

"So, what's your plan, my man," I sang gamely. "Had time to get anything on the go yet?"

He flopped onto the Chesterfield next to me.

"Well I've had a chat with Dixie to see if she wants to get back to work but she said no. Apparently she already has a job, thanks to you. My old pals and suppliers Denny and Pete tell me they aren't prepared to front me any gear on account of being happy and secure in their sales as it is, thanks to you. But I don't need no plan. I've got money in the bank. I'm looking at it."

I knew what he meant and I knew he wasn't on, but my indignation was drowned out by the fear. I had known fear in the past. I had known terror and horror with a headful of acid, and the heebie-jeebies and the snakes and the spiders closing in. But this was no hallucinogenic nightmare. This was something infinitely more frightening. This was real life. This was getting shoved into a corner by some wild, psychotic animal whose relationship with logic and reality was a stormy one at the best of times. And this was certainly *not* the best of times.

"You've made a lot of money out of me, son. A *lot* of money. You owe me."

"Tel, what I've got I got myself. If I'd known you wanted paying for favours I wouldn't have come to the Scrubs that time to do *you* one."

"Shut the fuck *up*. Always so very smart, you poncy Essex cunt." His eyes blazed and his lips were coated with bubbling spittle. In the same league? I wasn't even in the same species. He leaned across yet closer to me.

"I'm going to bleed you. You'll still be able to carry on. I'm not greedy. I need you active and healthy and working. All I want is a share. *My* share. It's three hundred a week."

I looked back at him through my timid, glassy eyes. Just to make sure I understood, he drummed it home.

"You will give me three hundred pounds every week. If you don't, I'll give Jimmy a call. I'll tell him to use a rusty blade. He'll slice you to pieces and feed you to his cats. You were right all that time ago, he never did like you."

I looked at the floor beneath my feet and saw that his foot was on mine.

"Seeing as I need to get a cab back to my humble, little slum we'd better start now."

I took in his awesome bulk. Weren't people supposed to *lose* weight in prison? To demonstrate his mastery he simply clicked his fingers, and to demonstrate my subjugation I raised myself solemnly and on leaden legs trudged to the bedroom, where I kept my weekly float. I returned and held out six fifties, which he snatched and crammed into his empty wallet.

"You got all the spine of a fucking wine gum." He said. Then he hit me.

He was gone when I came to. The entire left side of my face was in flames and I was lying a fair way from where I'd been standing. I shuddered at the thought of the damage I would have suffered had he caught me square on. The last thing I needed was a visitor, but the intercom buzzed. It was Jade.

I left the door open and started packing ice onto my cheek, pondering my induction into what, I surmised, was probably not a particularly exclusive club: those sorry individuals who had been knocked out by Terry Farmer with one punch.

"Hi," said Jade closing the door. "I wanted to call in on my way home from work. I got my ticket sorted out today so... Jesus. What happened?

"Nothing really. Just had a chat with an old friend and he has an odd way of making a point. What were you saying?"

"Mick you ought to get someone to look at that. Who did it?"
"Just a bloke."

"Why did he hit you? What did he hit you *with*?"

"Leave it, Jade. It's not that bad. I'm not a tough guy. I'm just a worker"

"You've got bits of carpet in it. Sit down."

She set about me like a pioneer woman patching up a cowboy. It was quite horny. I should have got belted more often. I let her chirrup on. Her flat was in the capable hands of a letting agency who had already found suitable tenants. Her employers, aware of her romantic complications, told her they would keep a place for her at the firm for as long as it took her to sort it all out. She had an open-ended return ticket to Phoenix. She was set. Ready to fly off in pursuit of her dream.

Strange, though. She was on her way to see the man she loved deeply, the man who loved her as much in return. I knew all about that and cared for her immeasurably, but it seemed the most natural thing in the world to ask her to stay over and the most natural thing in the world for her to say yes.

During the night, as pounding headaches kept me from sleep, little Jen called me from the police station, but as soon as Jade had left I got busy and called Pete. I was so perturbed about the Farmer situation that I felt I had to deal with that first.

The headaches were so bad I thought I must have had concussion so I asked Pete if he could pop over to see me. I asked him to bring Denny along if he was around and available.

"Don't tell me," Den said with a leering grin. "You've had a visit."

"How did you guess? I didn't realise this was his normal calling card."

"Not his normal one," Den said as he spread his bulk onto the sofa. "He must still like you a bit. In the old days you used to get a T carved into your cheek."

"I was hoping he had hit me with something. I'm not happy that this is *without* using a weapon. Hang on a minute."

I plodded to the kitchen sink and underneath, in the cupboard where I had left them, was a box of paracetomol tablets and a bottle of brandy. I never thought I would be seeing them so soon. I pulled them both out, grabbed four tablets and carried them and the brandy back through to the lounge. I uncorked the Courvoisier and washed down the pills.

"This boy," grinned Pete. "Proper breakfast. Dontcha just love him?"

"You don't look too bad," commented Den. "Probably his left hand."

"Question is, why did he hit you at all?" Pete commented logically.

"That's what I want to know. He tells me he went to see you two first."

"Yup."

"What did he say?"

"To be honest, Mick, I think he was a bit pricked off with the fact that you hadn't been to see him or Kerry, especially as you've been doing double well for a while now. She's been struggling all this time. Another thing is Dixie."

I flashed a look at Den who returned it with a stony, unswerving stare.

"What about Dixie?"

"Terry not only used her for his little shopping trips - he was also knocking her off, so word has it. Now, not only doesn't she want to work for him, she probably doesn't want to get across him either. Maybe someone else is giving her a portion. I don't know. Whatever the situation is, he's well pissed off about all that too."

My eyes flicked to Den's and then just as quickly away again.

"But she works for you blokes."

"And that's her choice, but it was you who put her up to it."

"You asked me to. I thought I was doing you a favour."

"You did, Mick, but this has nothing to do with us."

"What about the gear? He says you've cut him off."

"That's right." It was Pete doing all the talking, with Den boring his eyes into me.

"Why?"

"Are you kidding? The man is straight out of the boob. On probation. Not only that, but he scored some fluky appeal. Plod are bound to be massively pissed off with that and are more than likely following him around, especially with that stupid feud of theirs still going on. No way can we deal with someone in that position. Apart from that you are moving a lot more than Terry ever did. We ain't rocking our own boat."

I flapped my arms in exasperation. "But you're making me a victim of my own success. I've worked hard, we've all made a few quid. Things are going nicely, but I'm the berk being made to pay for it."

"What do you mean, *pay*?" Den spat. "So he's got out, come round, given you a clump and got it out of his system. You've got a shiner but believe me, it could have been worse. So stay in for a week and take it easy. If you're after some revenge kick, forget it. It ain't that bad and even if it was I wouldn't harm Terry. I've known him for fifteen years. He ain't got a lot of style but he's alright. A few more brain cells and a bit of luck and he could have been where you are. So count your blessings, forget about the rough stuff and swallow it."

"If it were that easy, Den. If it was only a question of taking a whack, I wouldn't have bothered you two but this ain't the end of it." I pointed to the alien growing out of my cheek. "This is just to let me know that he is serious. The maniac is putting the squeeze on me. Hey, you geezers want a line?"

They looked at each other. Two men, one mind.

"Mick, it's not ten o'clock yet," Pete said.

"I need some anaesthetic. I'm not feeling too good and those pills ain't working. Small one?"

"Of course not," said Pete. Den just looked away.

I had a little sectioned off box made at the back of the sink cupboard in the kitchen where I kept my personal. My heart sank when I saw I was down to my last gram. Of anything. If I needed more I would have to wait until the end of the week to see Den and Pete or zip down to see Ishy. I had to load up anyway because... Shit! Jen. Must get onto the solicitor. I hacked up the gram and got rid of half of it.

"I'll bell you tomorrow for what I need at the weekend," I told them as I walked back into the lounge, sniffing for England.

"What do you mean he is putting the squeeze on you?" Den asked.

"He wants money. Demanding money with menaces."

"Do what?"

"He threatened me. He wants a weekly tribute. Three hundred a week."

"For how long?"

"I don't know. Maybe indefinitely. Maybe until he can score a drug connection. Who knows?" They didn't seem to notice that little dig.

"Have you paid him anything?" Pete asked. "Fuck off, Mick.

Tell me you haven't paid him anything."

Den was smiling.

"How do you think I got this? My voice was suddenly a shrill yell. "The bloke's a fucking gorilla. What was I supposed to do?"

"Stand up for yourself," Den sneered.

"I did. Look what happened." I noticed that my face wasn't hurting anymore. "Be serious. You know I wouldn't stand a chance against him. He's an animal."

"Alright, alright. Calm down. You'll seize your jaw up," Pete said, always the voice of reason. "What did he threaten you with? Just a kicking every now and then if you don't cough up?"

"Worse than that. He said he's going to let Jimmy Mulroney loose on me. A beating I can handle, but Jimmy is *disturbed*. Hang on a minute."

I ducked out to the kitchen again and zipped through the last of the gram. I soaked the wrap and shoved it down the waste disposal. Back in the lounge the chaps were on their feet.

"Well, Mick, it sounds like there is really only one thing you can do," Den told me having clearly established a course of action while I was in the kitchen.

I clapped my hands together perking up considerably. "Alright, I knew I had brothers."

"Pay the fucker," he snarled.

If I was gobsmacked by that, what happened next completely poleaxed me. Suddenly there were three men I didn't know standing in my lounge. Crazed victim of one of our scams? Jimmy Mulroney keen to get started sculpting my face? How the fuck…? Then I saw that two of them were in uniforms.

"Pay who?" said the suited one. "Who's he got to pay, Denny boy?"

Den? He knew Den? Masters himself was as shocked and speechless as me.

"You must be Mr Targett. Michael Targett," said the bloke, turning to face me.

"Who the fuck are you?" I said.

"You are Michael Targett are you? This is your flat?"

Den and Pete were edging past the coffee table in such perfect unison, they looked like two players on a table football team.

"Listen, Blacky, we'll be running along now," Pete said. But, no. They weren't going to be running along anywhere. The two uniforms stepped across.

"No, Pete. Stick around. You don't have to leave. Once we rip this place apart I'm sure there'll be enough to take the three of you down the station. Long time since we had the pleasure of your company. I heard the Road Rats were going well. Didn't know you two would be backing a nasty little E pusher. I mean how low can you go?"

Then everybody looked at me. How could they know? The way Den and Pete were looking at me meant Cut Throat Jimmy would have a job recognising me after they had finished. Little Jen. Shit. She'd talked.

"Nice to see you again, Mr Black," said Den. "Still a DC or has that long overdue promotion finally come through?"

"Always the joker, Denny boy," replied the smartly dressed Poirot in his late thirties. "Yes, what was it you said the last time I put you away? 'Don't give me too much porridge, Judge, I've had more than the three bears put together already.'"

"Yeah yeah yeah. Anyway, listen, that is Mr. Targett wearing the cricket ball on the side of his face. He used to work for me and Pete at the Rats, but he doesn't anymore. We heard he had an accident and we came here to see how he is. Now we've done that we're leaving. Nice to see you chaps and all but..."

The man was holding up a hand. "Ordinarily I'd say yeah, OK Den. But this Ecstasy shit. This is a bit more of a problem. Been causing a lot of grief. All over the tabloids and the early news. I'm getting several kinds of earache from upstairs about it."

"So what exactly does this have to do with us, or him?" Pete wanted to know. I shared his curiosity.

Just as I allowed myself an iota of relaxation, thinking how lucky it was I had dumped the only evidence of drugs that were in the flat up my nose, the good DC laid it on me. How Jen had been brought in well and truly nicked, but how, during her time in the cell, she had called for help, claiming to feel hot, confused and sick. I watched him and saw the words fall from his mouth like stones.

"A doctor was called. He examined her and found her hallucinating and delirious. Her temperature was a hundred and eight - the highest the doctor had ever encountered in a human being. Jennifer Baddows died at six nineteen a.m. this morning."

My hands gripped the back of the armchair I was leaning against as the copper fixed me with his iciest stare.

"She made one call between the time of her arrest and her death. It was to you, Mr. Targett. Now we'd like to know all about it. Put the kettle on, son, and Den, Pete, sit down. No-one's going nowhere."

CHAPTER SIXTEEN

I needed help with the Farmer situation and it was painfully clear it would not be forthcoming from Masters and Chalmers. It was time to call in a favour.

Patsy Chetkins was back from Mallorca and I wasted no time in getting out to Essex to see him. When he was in the UK he worked out of the Vicious Cock, and I caned the 308 down there at warp speed. The radio told me some hardcore ragheads were bringing a shitstorm down on Salman Rushdie's head because of a book he'd written. I would have gladly swapped places.

The cops had a search warrant but nothing to arrest me for, so as a posse of uniformed Plod swarmed all over the house, DC Black, me, Den and Pete sat around having 'a little chat'. The longer the chat continued, the more confident I felt, because basically they had nothing. They found nothing and they had nothing.

I explained that Jen was someone I had met about a year before and saw socially from time to time. I had no idea she took drugs, much less sold them. She had called me the previous evening to tell me about her arrest and ask for help. I told her to keep calm, to be as co-operative as possible with the police and to ask to see a solicitor before giving a statement.

The copper sat there and looked at me.

"You lying little cunt. She got them from you. She told us that much."

My heart leapt into my throat, but wait. If she had said that, I'd be down in the cells myself already. Bluffing. I shrugged. "If she said that, I don't know why. I'm not a drug dealer," I told him, hawking back a run of coke for all I was worth. "I don't take drugs and I don't know anything about them. If that's what she said then I suppose I'd better call a solicitor."

"Maybe you should."

I shrugged again.

We went around in circles a couple of times as he prodded and probed for a weakness, but he was running out of steam. Eventually, when the troops sadly announced that the only drugs on the premises were ninety-six paracetomol tablets, they called it a day.

As DC Black was leaving I once again assured him of my full co-operation, whenever he felt it might be needed. Before slamming the door he once again called me a lying little cunt.

Then things started to get *really* heavy.

"You lying little cunt," screamed Den. "What the fuck have we always told you about dealing Ecstasy?"

I bluffed it out with the coppers and I had no choice but to do the same to them.

"What are you talking about?"

"We didn't just fall off a Christmas tree, you wanker," shouted Pete, usually happy to be the tolerant one. "It's a bit too fucking much. A bird gets nicked with tons of the stuff, down her pants *and* in her bloodstream, and the first person she wants to speak to is you. Do me a favour."

"Well, she's not likely to phone her mum, is she? She got scared, she knows I've got contacts... I think it's a perfectly natural thing to do. She could just as easily have phoned Paul, except she knows he ain't got a brain so she phoned me. Yeah, that's an idea. Talk to Romanov. He knows Jenny better than I do. If I was selling her drugs he'd know about it. Ask him."

It was a hell of a bluff, but I felt confident Jen would have kept schtum about our set up. They looked at each other in silence. Another discussion through the airwaves.

"You fucking slippery, little… If you're lying… "

"Easy, Den," said Pete, raising a calming hand. "Maybe he is, maybe not. One thing is for sure, though. We can't carry on dealing drugs with him."

"Oh *what*?" I shouted.

"Same situation as Terry. You got Plod all over you." He pointed to the door via the pride of London had recently left. "He fancies you for this and that bastard has no off-switch. That means you may well be watched. Followed. We can't afford that. You can still do the trips abroad and you are still in line for the cheques in the summer. We want you, we'll call. You need to speak to us, use a phone box." Then they got up to leave.

As they were walking out the door, Pete stopped.

"This may have been down to you, Mick, it may not. Fact is, we're in the spotlight exactly when we don't need it." He held two fingers in front of my face. "Second fuck-up."

Short of asking Patsy if he had a supply of decent cocaine, I was looking at being deprived of my main source of revenue. Sure I could still get the MDMA from Ishy, but now that Jen was... Shit. Little Jen. It was a mark of how screwed up I was that she was my very last consideration. Someone was dead. My lover had died of drugs. We were only supposed to have a good time and to make a few quid.

If Masters and Chalmers couldn't help me with Farmer, then I knew a man who could. I sprayed gravel all over the manicured lawns of the Cock in my rush to get to him.

"Nasty one, son. How did you do that?" He asked, crushing my hand as he inspected my cheek.

"It's actually part of what I wanted to talk to you about, Patsy. Can we go somewhere quiet?"

"Say no more."

I followed his powerful bulk as he trod the deep pile up the stairs, along a subtly lit corridor and through a thick, oak door. He ushered me into his lair and urged me to pull a chair up to the desk. With his back to me he opened the doors of a walnut cabinet, its interior illuminating automatically. Soft chimes played Land of Hope and Glory.

"What can I get you, son?" he asked over his shoulder.

"Er, anything, mate. Gin and tonic."

"Ice and lemon?"

"Please."

He poured one for each of us and parked himself behind the desk. Then he sat looking at me.

"I'm all ears," he said.

I didn't know what to say and what not to say. What to leave in and what to omit. I just had to wing it and hope he would be sympathetic. The surprises weren't long in coming.

"There's this bloke. Heavy duty. His name is Farmer, Terry Farmer, and... "

"Oh, young Tel. How is he these days?"

I felt faint. "You *know* him?"

"Sure. Haven't seen him for a while. Nice bloke though."

I gulped half of the tumbler down in a couple of swallows. What if they were friends? His comment gave me heart, though. If he thought a psychotic like Terry was a nice bloke, then what did that make him? And if he knew Terry then he knew Terry was a criminal, and if he thought a criminal was a nice bloke... Yeah, I was getting the hang of it.

"I used to think he was a nice bloke too, Pat. We did a few bits together, dealt in a few cars, bit of buying and selling..." I watched him nod in knowing approval.

"We had a casual relationship which kind of faded, with no-one owing anything, a couple of years ago. I built up my motorbike firm and, well, he got nicked."

"What for this time?"

"Receiving and possession of puff, I think. There may have been some other charges. I'm not sure. Anyway, he got me to make a delivery to a couple of mates of his. One thing leads to another and they ended up buying my company. Not only that, but the blokes employed me to develop the sales, not just of my side of the business, but theirs as well. Everything went well and the fact is we have all done OK. Now Terry is out and he seems to think he can walk right back into my life and demand a slice."

"A slice of what?"

"My income. He is putting the squeeze on me. He battered me and told me that if I didn't come across with three hundred quid a week, maybe more, he is going to have someone carve me up."

"Have you given him anything?"

The shame shivered through me once again. I reddened and looked at my feet.

"No disgrace, son. I know you're not a hitter. That was why I was so impressed when you stood up for my Lauren all that time ago. As well as that, I know what a handful Terry can be. He's a powerful lad."

"You're telling me. I caught him with a peach of a right-cross and he didn't even blink. It only took him six or seven punches to get me down. He's quick for a big bastard."

"No disgrace."

"Fact is, even if I could afford the money, it's not fair, is it? The recession is hitting us all. I've got a lot of outgoings and not too much coming in at the moment."

"Tell me something, Mick. When Terry was away did you take care of his wife?"

Kerrriste! This fucking thing with Kerry.

"No, Patsy, I didn't - but only because I didn't realise there was an obligation. I'm not very old-school. He got nicked after we'd gone our own ways, and the only profit I made from his lead was what I carved out for myself. If I'd *known* I was expected to drop her a few quid, then of course I would have done it."

I drained my glass and he refilled it all the while keeping a contemplative silence.

"Yes, I can see your point, son," he said eventually. "Thoughtlessness was what it was, am I right?"

I wanted to reach across and kiss his hand. "Exactly. Less than that. Like I say, I just didn't know. I thought Terry was a big face and I assumed he would have left some kind of fund for his missus. I obviously overestimated him."

"I see. Yes, I understand. So what do you want me to do? Is this why you have come to see me?"

I wondered why we had been sitting there all that time.

"Well, yeah. I guess it might help that you know him. If you could just have a word and maybe explain that what he is doing just isn't fair. And the worst of it is, all this started with a favour *I* was doing for *him*."

"I don't think I know him well enough to just ask him nicely to stop what he is doing."

"Oh."

"Which leads me to my next question: do you care what happens to him?"

"How do you mean?"

"It's quite simple. If I can't ask him nicely then I'm going to have to use another way. Do you care what it is?"

I fingered the swelling on my face. "Well, I wouldn't really want to see him harmed. I've got no real grudge. I just want him to leave me alone."

He nodded encouragingly, like I had got the answer to that one right.

"OK. Now you say that you sold your motorbike company to the two blokes Terry had you deliver this package to?"

"That's right." Suddenly he was looking at me intensely; a light kindled in his eyes.

"So they were in transport themselves presumably?"

"Yeah."

"Masters and Chalmers. Christ almighty, you're with Pete and Denny!" he blurted, as if he was naming that tune in one.

"Patsy, this is all too much." I put my hands up against my temples and massaged gently.

He leant quickly forward across the desk as the urgency of the moment seized him. It was the most animated I had ever seen him.

"Think, son. Think as long and as hard as you like. Have you ever mentioned my name or Lauren's name to them? Do they know that you know me? And have they talked to you about me? Think, son."

It occurred to me that me, Romanov, Pete, Den and Dixie never talked about personal stuff. Birthdays, wives' names. None of us bothered with that. Perhaps it was some kind of subconscious defence mechanism - not to let your partners in crime know too much.

"No," I told him.

"Think, Mick. You have to be sure."

I did, and I was.

"Fine. And you *never* must. Be aware of how important this is. Never give my name to these people. Now I'm going to do a magic trick for you. The package that Terry had you take to Pete and Denny, do you know what was in it?"

My nerves were on fire. This was all getting a bit close. "Patsy, if they knew I was even talking about this..."

"This is too important. Answer the question. Do you know what was in it?"

He was just too much. I couldn't resist. I was too tired. I needed a line.

"Yes. Yes I know what was in there."

He did it again. "American Express traveller's cheque printers' plates."

He looked at me and grinned. Not just the grin of someone who was ahead of the game but the grin of a man who profited handsomely *from* being ahead of the game. But as he looked at me and I gazed in wonder back at him, something came to me. A conversation; a wisp of a memory tapped urgently on my consciousness. Something Pete had mentioned not long before. Goddit! Then I had the opportunity to pull one out of the hat for the great Patsy Chetkins.

"You're the main buyer," I told him with a smile. "You're their chief punter. You are going to buy ten million pounds of cheques from them as and when they come off the press."

"But Pete hasn't mentioned me to you at all has he? Not by name."

"No."

"You're a clever boy, Mick."

"Thank you, Pat."

"Drink your drink, son. We are going to have a nice, long chat. Forget about Terry and tell me a few more surprises."

We huddled together and I felt like I had found some kind of kindred spirit. I'll tell you a secret if you tell me one back. I had no idea of the stakes for which we were playing.

I wanted, no - needed to impress Patsy. My income had taken a massive hit. This was survival. Cover your arse. Choose your corner. I felt the ground shifting beneath my feet once again and I reached out for the only helping hand I saw available to me. I sat down on that warm seat, jumped the Night Flight To Shoebury and told Patsy everything he wanted to know.

Patsy exuded such monolithic solidity, it came as no surprise that I never heard from Terry again. I didn't know what happened to him and I didn't care, just so long as he was out of my life.

What did come as surprise was who turned up at my flat next.

"Alright, Micky boy? What's the scam?" With a bag of coke to match the size of her black eye was none other than the kite queen herself: Juliette Dixon, and boy, did I ever need a hit.

But that wasn't all she'd brought with her. As I was cutting a couple of lines on the sideboard she pulled out a smaller plastic bag containing what looked like a tiny lump of coke and a home-made bong. Where the gauze would normally be, a diaphragm of tin foil was stretched , held in place by an elastic band and pierced by a dozen or so pin pricks.

We did the lines and then I watched Dixie ease herself down onto the smooth leather of the Chesterfield before crossing her classic limbs. She lit a cigarette.

"Who hit you?" I asked.

"Den. You?" I fingered the bruise, which was still determined to impolitely hang around. It was getting on for a week.

"Terry. You seen him lately?"

"Terry? No, not for a while." She dabbed the ash of her cigarette onto the tin foil.

"So why did Den do that?"

"Well. I suppose it's my fault really. I was pushing him to divorce his missus. He's always said he'd never do that but I kept on yakking and pushing, giving him earache about me needing security. I should've known really."

"Don't give him the right to do that, does it?"

She shrugged in resignation, her beautiful, sad eyes far away. "'S'pose not."

"Mind you. You can bang on a bit, can't you?" I said with a grin.

"Don't you start." The beauty of her smile all but broke my heart. That was one of the things I liked about Dixie, she had this lovely self-deprecating manner; a charming ability to laugh at herself. I knew she was tough but I could see how vulnerable she was too. It was so good to see her.

"Listen. I've got something here for you," she said as she dabbed the last of her ash onto the foil, grinding the cigarette butt out into the ashtray. "Got anything to drink?"

"Yeah. What do you want?"

"Malibu and lime?"

"Try again."

"What is there?"

"Beer, gin and brandy."

"GT please."

"There's no tonic."

"Mick. How do you live like this?"

I laughed. "Bachelor flat, innit?"

"Get us a beer then."

I came back from the fridge with two cans of Stella. She took hers and ground the edge of it hard onto the rock of coke through the bag, reducing it to powder.

"We're not going to get very far on that, are we mate?" I observed with the eye of an expert.

In silence she patted down the ash on the bong to cover up the pinpricks. Then, with a stylish fingernail, she scooped a smidgen of the ground coke onto the ash.

"What are you doing, Dixie?" I asked as I sat next to her on the sofa. "What is this?"

"This," she said as she offered me the makeshift pipe with one hand whilst holding her flaming lighter over the prepared powder with the other, "... is crack."

Ladies and gentlemen, please take your seats. The Night Flight to Shoebury is ready to depart.

Something was happening with the women. The women in my life. With all the aggravation I'd hardly noticed, but something was definitely going on. Jade was in the scorched desert of Arizona looking for rainbows and yellow brick roads. Looking for dreams. Lauren seemed to be around less and less. Not available for dates and sometimes not even returning my calls. Patsy warning her off? Keeping her clear of the trouble I clearly represented?

Jennifer Baddows. Little Jen. Romanov had been in touch to let me know the details of the funeral. How could I go to that? I only dealt with her, but how could I be sure what she had and had not said to people? Did Romanov know the drug that killed her came from me? And what about her brother? Big, clean-living Ricky? Would he be pleased to see me? I didn't go to the funeral but I did mourn her. I mourned her and I missed her and whilst I couldn't allow myself to be blamed for her death, the thought of not seeing her again brought me to my knees. I finished with the clubbing scene. I took all the music tapes that reminded me of her and binned them.

And Julie, my lovely Julie. She was away on business half the time but was always there for me when she was in London. But we didn't seem to laugh as much as we used to. We didn't seem to do anything as much as we used to. It was the drugs or the lack of them, and with the pressure I was under I became irritable and short-tempered and she caught some flak. I was wrong but I couldn't help it.

In spite of my behaviour she was still angelically good to me. If she wasn't the only one who knew I was in freefall, then she was the only one who cared.

"It's OK," she told me one time. "You don't have to worry. "I'll always be there to catch you."

"Catch me doing what?" I queried defensively.

"Not catch you out. I don't mean it like that. I meI've got you." She reached out and gently took my hand.

"Whatever happens, I'll be there. I love you and if you ever fall I'll catch you. I'm strong enough for both of us."

She was just too lovely. I thought about how good she was to me and how horrible and thoughtless towards her I had become. It was wrong. The world was all wrong. I hung my head and let the sobs take me away.

"Mick. You've got to get off drugs," I heard her say. "Nobody, however tragic, cries this much." Julie had given up doing gear but she was always prepared to sit and look after me while I carried on.

"It's just a phase, I think."

Then... Then one night Dixie came round and brought me crack cocaine.

"Crack? But smoke make me cough."

"This won't. The smoke is cool. Trust me."

She was right. It was smooth and cool and I felt, as I had all those years ago when Randy had given me my first ever line in Caramba disco in Mallorca, like I was at the dentist. That taste. That smell. It wasn't all that nice. Then I exhaled.

I wasn't sure how long I had been sitting there with my eyes closed. There was a voice, I knew that. Through the comforting, cosy, loving blanket I was suddenly wearing all around me, I could hear a voice.

"Mick. You alright? Darling? Good innit?"

Dixie.

"Let go of the pipe, Mick. Mick. Mick? Give me the pipe, it's my turn. Oi, relax your fingers."

The message took a minute or so to get from my brain to my fingers and all I could do was sit there, lolling my head, stupefied with pleasure.

The hit was so instant and so intense, but so fucking *short*. By the time Dixie had chopped up a little dose for herself and done that, I was coming down. It was outrageous. As she laid her head gently back against the firm, polished leather I knew what I had to do.

"Gimme that," I told her, grabbing the pipe. She murmured something. A protest? No. I watched her beautiful face soften into the pleasure shape.

"Not cheap, Mick. Need some money, darlin'."

"No worries, Dix. Don't you worry about the money. In fact, don't you worry about anything," I told her as I lifted a dose out of her plastic bag with the edge of a credit card.

"I think me and you are going to do just fine."

When and only when it was all finished, we went to bed. I tried to get her to go out to get some more but she seemed more intent on seducing me. I didn't argue. The sex, though... Maybe it was the drugs. Maybe we were just too relaxed.

It was like going to bed with someone famous who didn't live up to the expectation. Perhaps the promise was too much. There were no tricks. The blow job was sparingly used and, I sensed, begrudgingly given. There were no gymnastics on the dentist's chair. But that wasn't the point. Dixie didn't have to put on a good show. It was like going to a Beatles concert; it didn't matter if it was crap, just so long as you could say you had been there.

She could talk though. Even after we had finished she would not shut up, and what did she want to talk about? Business. Could I get hold of any drugs? Did I have an E connection? Had I paid Terry any more money? Had I heard from Terry? Did I have any scams on the go? So much for romance. Still, we've all got to make a living I suppose. I told her to lay me on some more crack. She was still talking when I crashed out.

CHAPTER SEVENTEEN

I got summoned. Fortunately it was five in the morning, so I was up.

"Need to see you." Masters was never very good at disguising the fact that he was extremely pissed off.

"Sure, mate. What's up?" The Amex cheques, I thought. Were we ready to go early?

"Not over the phone. Come to the yard."

"When?"

"Couple of hours."

As I put down the phone I wondered if Dixie had told him about me and her. Fuck. He didn't like me at the best of times and now I was knocking off his girl. What was I *doing*?

When me and Romanov first began kicking around together he told me a story, one that doubled as a warning. I already knew, even before I'd met him, that Den was capable of visiting upon his victims a violence of a quite cataclysmic intensity. Then Romanov took me to one side.

"Just do yourself a favour, don't ever let *that* motherfucker get radical on your arse."

"Don't worry about me. I'm a diplomat. I'm one of the good guys."

"I mean it, bruv. He be all *kinds* of wrong. He ain't like ordinary people."

"Jesus, Paul. What do you think I'm going to do that might annoy him so much?"

"You could probably think of something. Anyway, word goes that years ago, like when he was a youngster he got his girlfriend pregnant. Back then he was a wild one obviously but he was all up for doing the decent thing, you know, getting married and saving up for a little slum somewhere. Anyway, he found out that she'd been two-timing him. All the time she'd been seeing him she was doing some other geezer, and so there was a question mark over who really was the father of the kid."

I knew already I didn't want to hear what he was going to tell me.

"Know what he did?"

"No I don't, and I don't think I want to either. What? The bloke ended up wearing his own bollocks for earrings, right?"

"Far from it. He didn't do anything to the bloke, which is probably the worst thing he could do because even now, after all these years, the bloke is still waiting for it to happen, still can't go out without thinking the person walking along behind him is going to finally do for him. No. It was the girl. It was his own girlfriend. Know what he did?"

I wished he'd just hurry up and tell me.

"Do you know what Thalidomide is?"

I felt the bile rising. I couldn't believe the man's *imagination*.

"Yeah, right. Can you believe that? He managed to get hold of some. Fuck knows from where. Dosed her. A few months later the kid comes out looking like a fucking cabbage patch doll. Fifty-fifty chance it was his own. Can you believe that?"

Well, frankly, yes I could.

"Worse still…" Romanov was talking again. Romanov wouldn't shut up.

"In the run up to the birth he started telling everyone he was worried there might be something wrong with the kid, how concerned he was. Sure enough the kid arrives with four little flippers. So everyone *knew* what he'd done. Man be a human land mine – don't tread on him."

As I sat watching the clock, Paul Romanov's words rattled

around my brain like stones in a biscuit tin. I hit another couple of lines of the atrociously cut down coke Dixie had sold me, and decided that if he knew about me and her then I'd be dead already. He would come round personally and wake me up to kill me rather than risk me taking off. I resolved never to shag Dixie again. Unless she gave me lots of crack cocaine and asked nicely.

As the 308 growled out of its subterranean lair I felt a creeping sense of dread. What was so important at that time of the day? I blasted across an ice-heavy Tower Bridge into the austere depths of pre gentrified south east London.

I parked and hoofed it up the stairs to the main office, where I sensed the air of a war council. Den was seated behind his desk, Pete was leaning on his elbow against a filing cabinet drinking coffee, and Romanov was sitting on the front of Pete's desk. It was seven fifty a.m.

"Hello, son," Romanov said.

I had deliberately steered clear of Paul since Jenny had died. I didn't know what he knew, but I always felt that he knew something.

"Hello, mate. Alright?"

"Hello, Mick." This was Pete. "Kettle's just boiled."

I passed the sandpaper of my tongue over unclean teeth. "Any beer in the fridge, mate?"

Pete and Den looked at each other and I heard Romanov speak.

"This man. I love him," he said. "Bruv, I've missed you. We ain't been seeing enough of each other lately. Let's get together again soon."

"Help yourself," Pete said with a sigh.

I did. As I popped the can of Stella I got straight to it. "So what's up?"

It was Den's show. He had taken charge.

"Remember Arthur Coltraine?" He asked.

"Arthur. Arthur. Er..."

"Old Arthur, over at The Wick. Arthur the printer."

"Oh yeah, right. Old Arthur. How's he getting on? Nah, don't tell me. He ain't been nicked?"

"No," said Den, with exemplary restraint. "He hasn't been nicked. But right now I'm sure he wishes he had. I'm sure that he would readily swap a few years lay down, in exchange for what happened to him last night." He drew calmly on his coffee.

"The old lad is, after all, sixty two. Having three big strong boys kick the door of his place in and batter the crap out of him at half three this morning was never going to do much for the state of his health."

"Jesus. But the job," I asked. "The job. It's still alright isn't it? I mean, he'll be OK to finish the job, won't he?" A prickly heat swarmed all over me.

"He's actually not so well, Mick," Den answered, looking too relaxed for my liking. "He'll survive, put it like that, and even though they tortured him he would be able to complete the job…"

I closed my eyes and the room swam. What was I doing there? How had I ever become involved? I had A levels in French and Geography for Christ's sake. Den was still talking.

"He *would* be able to complete the job, if the job was still there to complete. Which, of course, it ain't. Because that is why they were there. The bastards knew, you see. They knew exactly what they were looking for and they knew where to go to get it. They didn't want anything else. They had *information*." He had to force the word through his clenched teeth, as if he was saying the name of a man who would murder his son.

"The poor old sod stood up to them but they cracked him around and then they got to work on him with the metal snips. He lost two fingers before he gave up our plates, our films, and the paper we were going to use. Then they slammed him over the head to keep him quiet and then they left."

I got to a seat quickly. I felt sick for a couple of reasons.

I *needed* the dosh from the Amex job. Things had got way out of control sometime before, and with the loss of my drug revenue, I was in over my head. I remembered again Farmer's advice: never spend your money until you've got it in your hands. I had the income from the runs abroad, but these were sporadic because it was winter, and I had income from Rafael selling

Ishy's trips when we did go. I owned a second hand Ferrari and a loft apartment which were both bleeding me dry. That was it.

Then I felt sick about poor old Arthur. He was such a harmless, innocent soul. Then the realisation came to me. I tried to deny it to myself but it wouldn't go away. Reality. Some tough motherfucker. There you are in a tight little circle at the bar with all your mates feeling pretty invincible and what does reality do? It elbows its way through, scatters everyone all over the place and walks right on up, grabs you by the lapels and nuts you square between the eyes.

"Someone knew." I heard Den talking, like a mantra.

"You know security has been our strong point, Mick," chipped in Pete. "You know we are always safe. So what happens? The biggest score of our lives, retirement time. Then for the first time ever, we get rolled. Nothing we can do about it either. A friend and reliable contact bashed up and our plans in ruins."

They were all looking directly at me. Directly into me.

"Mick. Have you mentioned anything to anyone?"

I looked at the floor between my feet and solemnly shook my head.

"Answer him!" shouted Den.

"Of course not," I blurted. "Jesus, I need this deal. This is my fucking meal ticket as well as yours. Without putting too fine a point on it, I am rapidly going skint. Do me a favour."

"Someone might pay a lot of money for that information," Den was saying, his voice low and heavy. "One particular man I am thinking of right now."

My heart perceptibly stopped beating. Getting close now. One question and they could have had me. Did I know Patsy Chetkins? If they asked me that what would I say? Maybe they had followed me down to the Cock. Maybe they knew I knew Lauren. I felt the coke working against me. I was shocked, frightened and confused. It was so difficult remembering what I had said to whom.

"It's OK, Mick," Pete's voice was saying to me. "Anyone got tissues?"

I was so fucked up I hadn't realised I was crying.

"Don't fucking cry, Mick. Jesus. We just had to find out what you knew, that was all. It's OK. Mick. Paul, you got any coke on you? Give him a line or something for fuck's sake."

Sobbing uncontrollably in front of hardened gangsters had never been part of the plan, but what could I do? My grief was genuine.

Den's grief was genuine too. It went further than the money with him. He took it personally, or rather he made it into something personal. Living up to his reputation as one of the hardest faces in London, he felt he had no choice to make his intentions plain.

"Someone knows. Someone has mentioned something, someone has found out. There ain't that many people could handle a job like this. We'll need to make some visits."

His glare focused primarily on me as he delivered his speech, for that was ultimately what it was. How many times had he practised it? How long had he waited to say those words?

"We're going out onto the streets, lads, because someone... somewhere... knows. And you..." He pointed his pudgy forefinger at me like the barrel of a gun. "...You're coming with us."

I thought I would just be along to do the driving, or as a lookout, but no. Den took some kind of perverse glee in bloodying my hands.

He had told me to go home, to be ready and wait for the call. I'd secured plenty of drugs from Ishy and Dixie. How else was I going to get through it?

From the outset it was clear Denny was having a ball. He was born for a situation like that. The Amex plates were just the excuse he needed and if he had an atom of decency in him, he kept it to himself. And each time before we went out on our vendettas, to eliminate my consciousness from the proceedings as much as I could, I would smoke at least one rock of crack and do loads of MDMA. It was the only way I could cope. It took the edge off the screams. But nothing will ever take the edge off Jonesy.

We were out in Edmonton somewhere. Fortunately Romanov

was driving, because I was blitzed. We hung around in the car park of the place until there was only one car left. The doors were open so we strolled in. Through the reception area and out the back into the main print room. I was so smashed I was walking on a trampoline. I giggled lightly and Den must have thought I was looking forward to the evening's work because he slipped me the wink.

It was deathly quiet, which was not what we wanted, so Den approached one of the two huge machines that practically filled the room and started it. Close up, the clattering was overpowering but within a couple of turns the machine and me fell into an agreeable rhythm. It sounded really good. Alerted, our target soon made himself known.

In my bombed-out state it was still clear the bloke knew nothing. How did I suss that? Simple. He wasn't phased at all by what he saw when he emerged from his office. Eight in the evening, confronted by the awesome sight of Demon Denny Masters, immaculately dressed in his shin length Crombie, backed by two six foot yobs wearing black leather and gloves. What were we there for? To get a quote for printing some leaflets?

"Den?" he said, advancing without hesitation, without fear. "What you doing here?" He offered his hand. It would the last thing he did voluntarily for some time.

Den was there with the clichés again. I felt like telling him to get a new script.

"Hello, Jonesy," he said, seizing the man's hand with absolutely no intention of letting it go. "Now there's two ways we can do this; one is the nice way... and the other ain't."

I watched the man's eyes. Mystification; one, two, three seconds and then - when he knew it was no practical joke - the fear. The kind of fear born out of a reputation for insanity. No quarter. No compromise. He knew what Demon Denny could do and within three seconds he knew he was going to do it to him. Colour drained from his face as he spluttered for his words. Denny raised an eyebrow in Romanov's direction and the cosh slammed into the tuck behind the man's left ear.

I legged it back to lock the front door. While I was there I pulled out the pipe, shaved some powder from a rock I'd scored from Dixie and hit up as much as I could. A semblance of control. Got to keep it together. By the time I got back the man was still lying on the floor next to his grinding machine, but was bound at the ankles and wrists. He was coming to.

"Time to go to work," Den said to me. I breathed deeply and held it in, trying to recapture whatever might be left of the crack high. Den tapped my elbow. Then he did it again. I looked down and saw that he was holding something for me. I made my eyes focus and then realised. Garden secateurs. I took them. Then Den looked around, found a chair and pulled it up next to the prostrate form of the man, of Jonesy, so that he would get a good view.

"Start with his courting finger. Right hand," Den instructed with the attention to detail of an expert. "Always a bit of a ladies man, our Jonesy. Oi, Jonesy. You remember how you came onto my missus when we all went to the fights that time?" I looked down and saw that he was crying.

"Denny, please. Stop. Don't hurt me. What can I give you?"

It was clear Den didn't care about the Amex job. He was just using the whole exercise as an excuse to settle old scores. He knew those plates were gone for good, but who was going to rein in the leash? Even Pete was keeping out of the way.

I knelt down beside the man and for some inexplicable reason found myself worrying about my knee. Don't hurt yourself, a voice in my brain said. I made a grab for his fingers but all I found was two white knuckled fists. Was he going to let me do it, just like that? Then I felt Romanov next to me. He was kneeling on the Jonesy's throat, and at the same time, ramming the point of his knife into the back of his hands. Jonesy relaxed, not because of the pain of the knife but because he was falling into unconsciousness. He had passed out again.

"Get the snips on his finger," Den barked. Then, in order to wake the man up again, Den decided to splash fluid on his face. He did this by urinating in his mouth.

Eventually, through a series of desperately weak gasps and

splutters, the man came back to life, such as it was. He seemed spent. Too weak to move. I still had the secateurs clamped around the second knuckle of his right index finger. My right hand was around the two handles and was reinforced by my left.

"Do it," my master said.

There wasn't much blood and I knew when I was through to the bone because of the increased resistance and the grinding. Jonesy was howling and when that happened Den started laughing. Then I hammered down as hard as I could, my whole body shaking with the effort and finally the resistance broke. I was through. The top two joints of his finger swung loose, although still joined by a shred of ripped skin.

"Good boy," I heard Den say. "How do you like that, Jonesy?"

Jonesy was making hurried, chuffing noises. Hyperventilating. Trying to fight the pain.

"What do you say, Jonesy?" Den called above the row of the machinery. "We got all night. You gonna tell me where my plates are?"

Then something unbelievable happened. Jonesy seemed to relax. His body eased, went limp, like he had just recalled something of vital importance. There was almost the hint of a smile. Later I would appreciate it as being the final idea of a man who knew he was going to die. If he was lucky.

"Got something to say, mate?" Den shouted.

Jonesy nodded his head. He no longer appeared to be in any pain for which I was grateful.

"Go on then."

He hesitated, as if looking for the right words. Then it became clear that he had found them.

"Everybody, I mean everybody, has fucked your wife up the arse."

I should have run right then. Just got out and bolted. I looked at Romanov, his handsome face already crumpled with dread. Then I looked at Den and saw that he was already away. So far gone he wouldn't be coming back for days. Not even angry. He was as controlled as only true psychotics can be. Then his foot came back and smashed into Jonsey's temple and he was unconscious again.

Without a word he walked to the thrashing machine and grabbed a cloth hanging from its frame. Then he crouched down and, with a vile gentleness, wiped all the piss away from Jonesy's face. Then, kneeling beside him, he took hold of his head, one hand on his crown and the other under his chin, looking like he was about to administer the kiss of life. Then I realised.

Remember Midnight Express? In the prison the American kid loses it in one scene and bites the bloke's tongue off. But, no. Demon Denny wasn't going to do that. He was no cheap, pale imitator. No way. He settled his fat lips all around Jonesy's left eye socket. Then, grotesquely straining all the muscles in his mouth, cheeks and throat he heaved and sucked and scrabbled with his tongue and his teeth until he had what he wanted. What he wanted was Jonesy's eyeball in his mouth. I watched him do this. He clamped his teeth around it and wrenched it away. Then he plucked it out of his mouth, spitting something clear as he did so. He squeezed Jonesy's cheeks, opening his mouth and rested the eyeball gently on his tongue, leaving it for him or whoever else might see it. Like a warning, or a calling card.

"Nothing for us, boys," he said standing up. "Nothing for us here." Then we left.

The next day I got in touch with Dixie and handed over all the available cash I had in exchange for crack cocaine, and spent the following seventy hours in bed smoking it. Then I called Patsy, who invited me down to the Cock. I thought that at least I should give him the opportunity of clearing his name.

"Yes, son. Nice one. Thanks for the heads-up."

I waited to hear the spice of his hidden agenda. What it was all about. I would have waited some time.

"Excuse me?"

"Son?"

"Patsy, I'm having trouble holding on here." I necked half of the gin and tonic he had just given me. "Are you saying it *was* you?"

He looked at me like I was on drugs or something. "Yes." It was as though I had given him a good tip for the Derby.

"Pat, do you understand what you've done? Do you understand what *I've* done?"

"Thing is, Mick, you don't appreciate what is going on here."

"No, Patsy. Forgive me for being so forward, but I don't think *you* appreciate what is going on here. I gave you that information during the passage of an innocent conversation. I had no idea you were going to do what you did. I was involved in that deal. There's money coming out of it. He's going around mutilating half the printers in London, and I am implicated in that. And that poor old sod, Arthur. It all started with your blokes going round and bashing him to bits. Jesus, did they have to do that?"

"Let's have a few home truths here, Mick. First you'd still be shelling out to Terry Farmer if it wasn't for me. Second, I only use pros. If Arthur Coltraine got damaged it was the minimum damage possible. Third, don't ever think Denny and Pete were doing you any favours. Pete comes on as Mr Nice Guy but he's just a user. They have the bulk of those cheques sold. Do you really think you were going to see any of them? And if you were do you think they were going to give you a head start? Get real. And the gear. The coke and the wiz and the puff. Do you think they were doing you a favour, letting you have it at the prices they were charging?"

He knew so much. Everybody knew so much and I knew so little. I looked at him with a tired, soggy head, like one of those stupid little nodding dogs people used to park on the back shelf of their cars.

"Seriously. Don't tell me you didn't know. Who do you think they get it from?"

It was all too much. I had to get out of the business. Out of the country. Just out.

"Don't worry about the Amex cheques. They're mine now, or rather they will be when I can find a printer. Shame old Arthur isn't as dextrous as he once was. I could've got him to do them. You'll get your chance to go to work with them."

That news lifted me greatly. In spite of everything crumbling around me, there was still light at the end of the tunnel.

"Hey. I don't suppose you know where Denny and Pete got

the scanning done do you? I could do with knowing that. Got an order for something coming up myself."

I didn't know, and Patsy always seemed to know if I was telling him the truth, so he only asked me once.

"Pity," He said. Then he surprised me again.

"How's your dad?"

"He's OK, thank you. Getting by."

"He misses your mother I bet."

"Very much so. We all do, but him more than anyone. She was all he knew. Sometimes I wonder how the grief doesn't kill him. Mark of his strength I suppose."

"He sounds like a fine man."

I smiled. "He is. I never got on with him too well before Mum died, but it seems to have brought us closer together. It took a tragedy for us to become friends, and that's what we are I think."

"It often works like that. Have you told him you love him?"

It didn't seem like an odd question as I had dwelt upon the point myself.

"No. I haven't."

"You must, son. You must. Don't wait until he is dying. Tell him now."

"Is your father still alive?" I asked.

"No. He died a long time ago. He was... I..."

Well, what was this? A weakness?

"My father was a worthless man, Mick. He caused me and the rest of my family great hardship. A father-son relationship is the most precious there is. Get closer to each other, while you can."

"I will."

"Good. Something else. I want you to be on your best guard. Keep a look out to see if you're being followed."

"Who's going to follow me?"

"Den and Pete of course. You say Den still might suspect you had something to do with Arthur Coltraine getting rolled. Maybe he'll have you followed to see where you go. Maybe he followed you here. If he puts me and you on the same side ... First thing he'll do is kill you and the second thing is he'll seriously consider going to war with me. We don't want any of that, do we?"

I closed my eyes.

"What is it?" he asked.

"A few days ago. There was this car. I kept seeing it behind me. I couldn't see who was in it. Probably nothing."

"Sure?"

"No I'm not. I was down the coast anyway, seeing friends down there."

"If he had followed you here, I'm sure Den would have been talking to you about it by now, or quite possibly stabbing you and then talking to you about it. So be careful. If you need to come here take a roundabout route. Get on a train, take cabs."

I nodded my understanding.

"One last thing before you go. I caught my Lauren with a wrap of coke the other day. It was second class crap so I don't suppose it came down our little line. There is something awful about the idea that, indirectly, I may be selling lethal drugs to my own daughter, but I'm sure it didn't happen like that. She's seeing some dick-brained car dealer at the moment. Probably came from him. He won't be around for much longer, but if I find out you're supplying her with anything stronger than vodka, we're finished. OK? Now, you are doing too many drugs yourself. Get off the shit. You used to be a good-looking kid."

Far from getting off the shit, I made a concerted effort to get on it more than ever. In this endeavour I was ably assisted by my new druggy partner, Dixie. The next time she came around she had a real surprise for me. She pulled a wrap out of her purse, along with some silver foil which she spread out flatly on the coffee table. With her pocket knife she lifted a small amount of the brown powder from the wrap onto the foil. Then she gave me a cut off drinking straw, and readied her cheap, plastic lighter.

"What's this all about?" I asked in all innocence.

"This," she replied as she held her lighter flame under the foil, "…is heroin."

Then I was back on the train. Friday afternoon. Couple of beers and that warm, comfortable seat. Hassled and tired and sick of everything, and just needing to be free; free of it all, just for a moment. Who cared where you woke up? Who cared *if* you woke up? Take a chance. Catch the Night Flight.

And that's what I thought of when Dixie lit the flame under the foil.

"There it goes, see? Chase it. Quick. It's going to waste. That's it. Keep it in your lungs. Hooold it!"

"Hang on." And ... exhale.

"Jesus. You alright? You look a bit pale. Don't worry it happens a lot the first time. Just be ready to..."

I put down the straw and waited. Thirty seconds later I had my head down the khazi being violently sick. It felt strangely pleasing.

"That's normal," Dixie assured me. "Don't worry about it."

I rinsed out my mouth, and having staggered across the ploughed field of my living room floor, rejoined her on the sofa. Then I heard a noise. It was a little bit like distant thunder, or perhaps surf crashing on rocks. I looked around me, checked the TV and the stereo which, were both off. I soon realised that the noise, growing louder by the second, was in my own head. I actually heard the hit coming. Then it was on me.

Dixie had obviously done smack too because she smiled and knew what I wanted to do. She settled back as I rested my head on her lap. I didn't want to move, I didn't want to go anywhere. I didn't want to change anything. I just wanted to lie there and close my eyes. Everything I needed was inside my own head and body. In that moment, all my dreams came true.

Dixie sat and held me and talked. Jesus did she talk. Everything about everything. Something about those Amex plates. How was I managing to make ends meet? She was so sweet and kind. I told her not to worry; everything would be cushty, I had plans. I told her about the acid runs to Rafa, but assured her I had it all sussed and she was in no danger. Of course she promised not to tell the chaps. What a doll. If she was going to tell them anything she would have to tell Denny about me and her being lovers, so I knew I could trust her.

Heroin was exactly what I needed because it took away the pain, the fear and the uncertainty. Denny would never hurt me and Patsy would soon be making me rich, but I still had the savvy to appreciate that times were hard, financially speaking. The mortgage wasn't going away. Money was tight. Brother, can you spare a grand?

The life I had fallen into had become the norm. I no longer noticed how good I'd had it. When I'd gingerly edged the Ferrari away from the dealer's the day I bought it, I had felt like I was under the most wonderful spell in the world from which I would mercifully never be free. Only months later I was caning the thing to within an inch of its perfectly engineered life, bumping up and down kerbs, leaving it outside pubs all day and all night. But that uncaring familiarity did nothing to ease my pain when the day came to sell it.

"What has this been into?" cried Chris, gripping the sides of his face with his hands. "Of all the cars I've ever sold, this was my favourite. What have you done to it?"

"It's been garaged, serviced, pampered, the lot," I told him stiffly.

"So has my missus, but even *she* looks better than this. Have you been racing it or what?"

"Do me a favour, mate, don't give me this old number again. Do I look like a tourist? Just tell me what it's worth, and please don't ask me if I know there's a recession on."

I'd had that thing for less than a year and dumped over eighteen grand on it. I banked some cash and bought a right nice Granada from a sleazy looking bloke over in Croydon, having phoned up the ad in the Exchange and Mart. I called Nige with the details and left them on his answer machine so that he could swap over the insurance.

I hadn't spoken to him for a while. Not only was he still doing great, but he was actually expanding. He spent most of his time down on the coast in Hastings and Eastbourne where he had the temerity to buy not one, but two estate agencies.

"This recession is just a glitch," he had told me confidently. "A blip. House prices are going to dip for about a year, but then there'll be so many bargains everyone will come out of it with renewed guts and confidence, and despite Queen Maggie stepping down, we are going to be into the biggest boom in history. I'll clean up."

Thatcher gone. Christ, wasn't it that bitch who started all this shit? Anyway, I did some investing of my own with Ishy.

Me and Dixie were doing occasional trips to the Canaries through the winter and into early spring but not on the scale of the summer runs. Rafa was still moving acid and the added income was welcome, but I was kicking myself for not banking dosh when it was rolling in. I didn't want to think about what I had earned during the previous two years. I didn't want to think about it because there was nothing left.

I spent quite a bit of time with Ishy and Vicky during that little stage. He was still getting the MDMA from his man in Holland, so we always had that but what we did most was get mangled on acid.

"You should come down and do it with us," I recall Vicky prompting a while before. "You're into mind-bending experiences, aren't you?"

"Yeah right. I have to look at my mortgage statement every month, that's pretty fucking mind bending."

Ishy would cram all his selling into Saturday afternoon so we had the decks cleared for Saturday night and all day Sunday, and we would sit around burning holes in our brains. I learned, with their tutelage, how to really *enjoy* the terror.

I can feel the devil walking next to me.

I was aware that things had gone way, way beyond the stage of doing drugs for a laugh. The motivation had shifted. By that time I was doing drugs because I couldn't imagine being straight. I didn't like my life and I felt an urgent need to get as far away from it as I possibly could. In short, I had become what I always said I wouldn't: a drug addict. And what did I do, once this mortifying admission had been made? I got onto my suppliers and ordered up copious amounts of incredibly dangerous and addictive class A gear. Well what else would a drug addict do?

Bearing in mind he had been cost a major part of his income, what with Jenny so inconsiderately dying on us, Ishy was consistently cheerful and always pleased to see me. So he gave me a couple of trips, rolled a dozen spliffs while he was still able to do so, sorted out enough tapes and CDs to get us through the next eighteen hours, and we waited. I half expected him to batten down the hatches too, because with acid there was always that unnerving hiatus between hearing the storm warning and the hurricane finally hitting.

So I was down there and the customary quilt had been spread out on the living room floor. There was some weird, spooky kind of music going. Then someone said, "I live just for today, don't care about tomorrow - what I've got in my head you can't buy, steal or borrow."

I glanced over at Ishy in admiration. His eyes looked like two plates of jellied eels.

"That's great, man," I told him with a hippy's sincerity. "That really sums it all up."

Then a crucifying wave of acid broke over me and I was washed away in the rip tide. Time was suspended. Real life was put on hold. Icy fear gripped me. Fingers of death tickled my spine. Still Ishy was talking, no - chanting.

"My brightest stars, my inner light; let it guide me - experience and innocence bleed inside me."

Man was a Goddam poet, that's what he was.

"Close the curtains would you, Mick?"

Where that fitted into his mystic insights I did not know, but after a few seconds, or perhaps an hour, I saw what it was he wanted me to do. I hauled myself onto my feet and tottered over to the window. I don't know how long I was there, could have been ages. I made the mistake of looking up out of the window, up to street level. My entire being gripped by a throttling synaesthesia, I got into a sort of loop and couldn't get out. Then the weirdest thing happened: I saw a ghost. Or maybe a skeleton. He was so thin. I had trouble making it out. My fear was that it was little Jen come back from the dead to haunt me, but then I saw that it wasn't her. I only saw it for a second before it vanished, but I did recognise it. It was the ghost of Paul Romanov.

I closed the curtains and flopped down again. Ishy was still going on, except that... Saucy bastard. It wasn't Ishy at all.

I drift in inner space, free of time
I find a higher state of grace in my mind

I stretched out and rested my head against the sofa. I looked up and there was Vicky standing over me, grinning, all lips and gums and sexy pinkness. Christ, she was gorgeous. Then her tongue... Her tongue! Flexed and muscular and forked, it lashed the air, checking, tasting, forewarning. Oh shit, I wished she wouldn't do that. Then she took her skin off. She stood there and ripped her skin off from the waist down. Her skin was heavy and black and looked like it needed renewing for sure; but to just stand there and do it, in front of me and that other fellow... Tasteless. Then she just chucked the shed skin into a heap in the corner. I kept an eye on it to make sure it didn't try to reform.

"The music, Mick. Listen to the music," she said.

Music? What music?

I believe in live and let live
I believe you get what you give

Did I hear that or did I just think I heard it? Then a horrible thought occurred to me; we were all taking drugs. What if Vicky's little girl walked in?

"She's over at my sister's," Vicky said, able, it seemed, to read my thoughts.

I looked up at this marvellous woman, my longest standing female friend, as she twisted slowly and mesmerically in time to the music.

She was close to me. Too close and I became compelled to stare straight into her crotch. My god she wasn't wearing any trousers! What the fuck? Her tight, cotton pants left nothing to the imagination. I tried not to look but I had no choice. As she swayed to the music her movement pulled the cloth fractionally to one side. Tiny hairs showed themselves momentarily then, as she moved back with the beat, were obscured by the rich glory of her thigh. Then with a jolting horror I saw. The tightness of her knickers, the protruding hairs. I had been mistaken. There was something in there that wasn't just her. I knew, of course, what they were before the first one scampered out. Childhood fears, classic nightmares. You never get over them.

The first spider scrabbled it's way free and scuttled down the inside of her leg. Then a second and then a third. Then her pants split and there were *thousands* of them, flying through the air, filling the room, crawling all over me. I screamed but there was no sound. I shut my eyes and prayed.

"I always get my sister to look after her. Wouldn't want her to walk in on any of this, would we?"

Didn't we have that conversation hours ago? Years before even? I opened my eyes and...

"Thank fuck for that."

Ishy lit up another spliff and sucked in so hard and so deep I thought he was going to take in all the air in the room and leave none for Vicky and me. I actually felt short of breath.

"For what?" I heard him say. At least I thought it was him.

"What?" I said.

He exhaled. He exhaled so much that a cloud of blue smoke floated to the ceiling, multiplied in size and density and slowly began to fill the room from the top downwards.

"You said thank fuck for that. For what?"

What was that lunatic on about? I looked to Vicky for help.

Untie my hands, you're the best that I have

"Excuse me?" I said.

"Mick," this was Vicky. "What are you going on about?"

I started to feel hot. Hot and confused. I didn't know what was going on. But suddenly I was so hot. I reached over my head and ripped off my shirt. Then Ishy panicked me momentarily by moving across and kneeling right beside me. He was on me. He was practically in me. He held something close to my face, under my nose. It smelt as weird as I felt. I quite liked it.

"Drugs," he said simply. "Drugs are life. Everything else –
sleep, sex, work … everything else is just waiting. Sniff and I'll
see you in a minute."

I looked into the wilderness of his eyes and then down as he
lifted his thumb from the top of the tiny bottle and rammed a
spare finger into the side of my nose, blocking off a nostril. How
many hands did he have?

The metallic familiarity comforted me. Real Amyl. Proper jet
fuel. Eight seconds later, as my body burned and my head
exploded I rocketed into orbit.

Dive through the circle describe what you hold

Oh gaaaad. The room spun crazily as I shot upwards off the
floor to land with a smack against the ceiling. Total seratonin
drought. I looked around and then down, and there were Ishy
and Vicky, way, way below. So far away I was petrified I would
never get near them again. Vicky - eyes closed in ecstasy, drifting
in space and time on the ebb and flow of the music. Ishy - gone,
shot, blasted. Gnome-like, squatting on a fat, four foot high
toadstool, nodding and grinning like the thief of Baghdad.
Timeless. How did they manage to attach themselves to the floor
like that? Then they were at the end of a long, dark tunnel and
then they were right with me, and then a dozen, no - a thousand
shadows were up and dancing with us. All holding hands. Ring a
ring a roses, a pocketful of acid …

Ghouls and spectres swirled into my brain and whisked off
again, leaving flashing comet tails of fear, loveliness and devilry.
In all of it I just had time to catch a glimpse of myself: splattered
against the ceiling in a foul, psychotic drug frenzy, ripped
through with dark fear and crucifying paranoia. It was fucking
brilliant.

Drink and dissolve through the lines in your hands

My head melted in the heat of re-entry and lolled helplessly
around on my shoulders like a basketball supported by a blade of

grass. I flapped my wings and flew with gentle swoops and dives, stroking Vicky's hair, slapping old Ishy on the back as I passed. Christ, what a pair. What a couple. They were so talented. They knew what to do and Ishy had been right; everything else was just waiting.

So I got into a routine of spending the weekends down at the coast with those two and a few evenings a week with Dixie round at my place. I really enjoyed heroin. Not so much because of the pleasure, although here was plenty of that. No, it gave me security. It made me feel safe. It made me feel protected from a harsh world, even though I knew that world would be coming around to collect the massive debt I had run up soon enough.

That scene with Jonesy at the printers, for example. That had embedded itself deep within my psyche and would pop out to mortify me. The smack, though, took care of it for me. Chased away the demons.

It also helped me forget about how close I was to screwing up things completely. The trips out to Spain and the extra dosh from Rafa for the acid just about covered the mortgage. I had a second hand Granada and very little money. I was relying on Patsy Chetkins, a man I hardly knew, to do the right thing and deal me in on the Amex scam as and when it happened. *If* it happened. I had royally screwed up, but smack made it OK. I knew it was only a temporary respite, but that was good enough.

CHAPTER EIGHTEEN

As the spring broke in the foul year of our Lord 1991, and that muppet pretty kid was still banging on about being the one and only, I was relieved to get word from Pete Chalmers that there was another run about to happen. Lanzarote. They were making all the preparations and I got on with a few of my own.

I called Rafa, took his order and got straight onto Ishy and placed mine. A good trip (pardon the pun) would see me with enough cash to keep all the plates spinning for a few months. And I needed to keep the flat, because the market was crashing so fast it would have taken a miracle to find someone to give it away to. But that was OK because I was sure Patsy would be able to turn up a printer for the Amex job soon. Then I'd be home free.

Keeping it together, though, appeared to be a task I found increasingly difficult to manage as my connection with reality became ever more tenuous.

Something had happened. Something titanically pivotal. The problem was, I couldn't remember what. I was sure it involved travel. Yes, that was it. I was on my way somewhere to see Randy Schnipper. But then I thought, that couldn't possibly be it. I hadn't heard from or seen Randy since I'd left Spain the first time around. It had to be work. Maybe I had just overdone it on something, and the chaps had shoved me on the plane out to

Lanzarote. Yes, that was more like it. Martinez or Rafa would be out there waiting for me, and they would straighten me out in time to go to work.

I got my head down and got in line. Passport control was no problem, but then as I walked through the arrivals concourse I was staggered by how cold it was. Too cold for ... Hang on. Maybe I was up north visiting Randy after all. Aberdeen? I listened to the voices. No Spanish accents but no Scottish ones either. My entire being pulsed with an unholy suspicion. The eerie chill of panic cramponed its way up the frayed rope ladder of my spine. The Fear. Faces everywhere. Ants and bugs squabbled and rushed and worked all around me in treacherous swarms. Threats everywhere. *Jesus! Shit! Don't touch me!*

"Get away." I heard someone shout. I whirled around and suddenly gagged as the head of a writhing snake appeared in my throat. Yet still I felt the irresistible shift of travel. Had I gooned around on some extra-terrestrial parabola? Flirted once again with lunar possibilities?

"I think I've got off at the wrong stop," I whimpered to a blur passing by. "Where am I?"

The person was a shape-changer, Reptilian in manner, bull-like in appearance. Kraggenknaffers, Vicky called them. He ignored me anyway and I was quite glad of that.

Then, an angel.

"Hi, Mick. How was your trip? You don't have much of a tan." I looked around for clues.

"Mick. Over here. Shit, have you been drinking your duty free again? Oh, Christ, Mick. Your eyes. Your arm. What have you had? Jesus, what have you *done*?"

And so the reality - not for the first time and I knew not for the last - proved to be much more horrific than the nightmare. Julie was there for me as she had so many times, but this time it wasn't enough. As I swayed and staggered and dodged around in front of her for a full five minutes, she pleaded and cajoled and swore and even resorted to hitting me a couple of times. She told me where I was and where I had been, and as my grizzling tears started she was finally able to make me trust her. She bundled me, face upwards, into the back of her car, whereupon I immediately vomited with shuddering force. I felt the weighty wetness land back down onto my face, and then the lights went out.

Sleep - bad shit. I try to do without it as much as possible, that's why I've been getting Dixie to bring me round a bit of wiz lately too. The thing is, how the hell are you supposed to know what's going on when you are asleep? They could be doing anything to you.

I remember being awake long enough to see the silver snake. I warned Julie.

"Mick, it's only the river. It won't hurt you anyway. It's on the outside. I won't let it hurt you."

Julie later told me that the twenty-four hours following my arrival at Gatwick were her idea of a living nightmare, the worst of all conceivable horrors. Mad screeching, violent accusations. I foamed at the mouth, threw up black tar and leaked blood from the mysterious, tiny holes in my left arm. She said she had never been that close to insanity before. She took two days off work to help me through it and then had to take off another three to get over that.

I woke up alone and I was pleased about that. I knew I had been into something beyond normality, such as I could remember normality being, so I took my time with everything. I had been in much less harmful motorcycle crashes.

I had no quarrel with the outside world and even less interest in it. Nor any notion or concern of time. It did not matter if it was night or day. I could have turned on the TV. I could have picked up the phone, contacted my fellow man. I could have rejoined the outside world, if there was one still there, but I felt a dark and dreadful foreboding, like something terrible was about to happen. This horrible fear grew in intensity, until it mutated into a realisation: nothing bad was about to happen. That was because it already had.

I needed a drink and was gratified to see that there was tons of beer in the fridge. I could not remember putting it there, but that was no indication of anything because it had taken me the best part of an hour to remember my name. So I drank.

I felt the earth moving again. Tilting. I was losing my footing, scrambling and clutching for grip. I was hanging on by my fingernails, walking the cusp between recuperative sleep and brutal wakefulness.

The trips to the toilet were tough to take as I had the whole bathroom, all four walls, decked out with mirrors. It was impossible to get away from me. I looked like... I looked like something I would not want to meet in a dark alley - and I don't care who I meet in dark alleys. So I kept drinking.

Every so often I would throw up and, as I hadn't eaten for days, I was starting to feel a tad peckish. The last thing I needed was to have some lunatic delivery boy buzzing around. Handle currency? Deal with people? No way.

So I did something I had not done in a while when I was hungry. I looked in the fridge. Bingo! I didn't fancy playing around with fires, working the oven and stuff, but luckily there was enough produce in there that even I could prepare. When preparation involves no more than ripping off a cellophane wrapper, I'm as good a cook as the next man. There were some dead animals in there that were cold and did not need to be warm again. There was some green stuff too. I ate them and that made me feel okay.

Then I fell asleep.

When I woke up I felt like I was better. The reason I felt like I was better was because I felt so bad. The feeling was an OK kind of bad. It had a distant, nostalgic kind of familiarity to it, this badness, and reminded me of old things like flared trousers, Deep Purple albums and my little bedroom back at the bungalow in Upminster. Nostalgia and gratification and relief fought for control of my senses. I was quite emotional. I had a hangover. I felt like I had another chance at normality.

I got out of bed, had a slash and padded out into the lounge. There were cans and bottles and a few food wrappers strewn all over the place. I was about to cap off another beer when something caught my eye. It was on the worktop above the fridge. I couldn't for the life of me remember where it had come from, or if I had ever used it, but it seemed like the right time to give it a try. It was a kettle. In a box in one of the cupboards were some tea bags. I felt like I was making real progress. Milk from the fridge completed the effort.

Buoyed by these achievements, I thought it time to communicate my survival to another member of the human race. I picked up the phone and was greeted with a signal from the dead zone. No-one in. I followed the flex to the wall and saw that it had been pulled from the socket. Naked and on my knees, and with visual capabilities on a par with those of a pensionable bat, I faffed around for an age before managing to replace the lead.

Then I couldn't remember anyone's number. I concentrated hard and it seemed to work because the phone rang. I placed the handset against my ear and listened.

"Hello?" said a tiny, female voice.

I said nothing.

"Hello, Mick."

I thought I knew the voice and I was reasonably sure I was called Mick.

"'Oozat?"

"Mick? Mick, is that you?"

"Who is this?"

"Mick, it's Vicky. Is that you? Christ, you sound terrible. You haven't been attacked, have you?"

"Vicky! Blimey, it's me old mate the Vickster. How are you my dear? What do you mean, have I been attacked? What's that supposed to mean?"

"Oh, Mick. I'm so glad I've found you. I've been ringing for days. It's all gone wrong." She collapsed into howling fits of dread and worry.

"Ah, Vic, don't cry, darling. I'm here. What's up? Stop crying now or you'll start me off. Please, Vic. You're starting to freak me out."

"I'm afraid, Mick. I'm so afraid. We got busted. Me and Ishy got carted off a couple of days ago. They let me go because Ishy stuck his hand up and said all the stuff was his but they're denying bail. The first time we had a load of stuff in the flat for ages and the old bill crashed in. Ishy says it's too coincidental. Mick, he thinks you grassed him."

Tripping, gouching, stoned, drunk, or just plain sober, the word 'grass' always had a galvanising effect on me. I was suddenly as straight as I could remember being for years.

"What the fuck do you mean?" I bellowed. "Why should I do that? What the fuck did he say? Has he mentioned my name to the police?"

In her fragile state it was possibly a little over the top. She was quiet but I detected the rhythmic heave of her sobs.

"Vic, look I'm sorry. I didn't mean to shout. I just get a bit touchy when I hear something like that. Why does Ishy think I had something to do with it?"

"It was what you said last time you came down. Remember?"

"Vicky, be serious. Most of the time I can't remember who we are when I come to see you, much less what was said. What?"

"You were talking about your friend dying and that maybe there was something wrong with the MDMA."

"I was?" This was certainly news to me.

"Yeah."

"Vic, I don't remember that but if you say it's true then it is and I accept that. But I didn't mean it as any criticism of Ishy. I know he knows exactly what he's doing. He's my friend and he's your bloke."

"That's what I said."

"Good girl. Now do you know if he has mentioned my name to the police?"

"Well, he said your name in front of them and I think one of the cops heard that. Just your first name though."

"When was this?"

"Two days ago."

"OK. Well they would have been here by now, I suppose. Listen. Does he need a brief? I can get the best."

"No, it's alright. He's got the duty bloke and he knows him from before. I spoke with him as well and he don't give a lot for Ishy's chances."

"Really? What did he say? How does he see it?"

"Fifteen hundred trips and an ounce of raw MDMA. How would you see it? Ain't personal use, is it? Not even for us."

"Jesus Christ. And he thinks I put them up to it. I can't believe that."

"He says you're going to pay, Mick."

"What?"

"That's what he said. I'm only warning you. He knows some really heavy blokes."

"You're not serious." He said that? I've got violence coming?"

"He didn't say that, but I think that's what he meant. He's got friends all over down here."

"You're kidding. Does he think that me and my lot up here are going to be worried about a few pikeys and fairground workers?"

"He's got a lot of respect down here. People depend on him. Not just for their gear but for their livelihoods."

"I don't believe I'm hearing this. That Paki dirtbag was peddling wraps of wiz in penny arcades until he met me."

"Don't shout at me. I'm frightened. Aiding and abetting or something. I might go to prison. They might take my baby away from me."

"Hey, hey. Don't talk like that. That ain't going to happen. I'll do everything I can to help you and Ishy."

"Will you?"

"Of course. You're my sunshine sister. Me and you go back too far for it to be any other way."

"Great. I knew I could rely on you."

"'Course you can. Now with any luck Ishy will be thinking straight, but I need you to get to see him and tell him that I had nothing to do with this."

She sniffed loudly and I felt the tension ease.

"Yes. Yes I'll go to see him in the morning."

"Good girl. Keep it together now."

"Right."

"Right."

"OK. I'll go now. I just wanted to fill you in."

"Alright. I appreciate it. Let me know how it's all going."

"I will. Mick?"

"Yeah?"

"Can I ask a favour?"

"Anything."

"Could you let me have a thousand?"

What could I do?

It was a sour twist. They were good together but I didn't need any of that bollocks about grassing Ishyp. Shit, what a mess. I was safe from the police but whatever he was thinking it was another source of revenue lost.

I was still pondering when the phone rang again. It was turning out to be a busy day.

"Hello."

"Hello, is that young Michael?"

"Yeah. Who's that?"

"Michael, it's Mrs. Rogers here."

"Mrs. Rogers. Hmm. No, you've got me there. Can you give me a clue?"

"Mrs. Rogers, Michael. My husband Peter and I live next door to your father."

"Mrs. Rogers! Yeah, right. Gotcha. How you doing? Hey, he hasn't locked himself out of the house again has he?"

"No. It's not quite like that. He's here with us now. I'll put him on."

Then the old guy was on the line. But it didn't sound much like him. There was a frailty about him. He sounded scared.

"Mike, something's wrong. There is something happening. I don't know what's going on."

I waited.

"Well, yeah. You better tell me what it is then."

"This morning Nicolette phoned up to say that Nigel was in some kind of trouble and there were some blokes coming to see him at the bungalow here. She said that he owed them some money. She said that he has the money obviously, and that he is going to send them a cheque in a few days but they are really pushy."

"Why are they looking for him at the bungalow?"

"She said it's because he does a lot of his business from here. He gets mail here, you know that. Anyway she suggested I get away for the day because I would have probably lost my rag with these blokes. So I went out."

I listened to my heart thumping ever louder. I could *hear* my pulse. This was going to be bad. I just knew it. Of all the bad things that were happening, this was going to be, by far, the worst.

"So I've been out. I had a game of golf with my mate Stan. You know Stanley, he's got that nice car. Anyway he invited me back to his place. I had a few drinks there with him and his wife June..."

"Dad, get on with it." As I gripped the handset tighter and tighter the lubricant of my sweat nearly caused it to pop from my grasp like a bar of soap.

"Well I came back and I couldn't get in. My key didn't fit the door anymore. Then Dorothy, who lives next door, came rushing out and told me that some men had been to the bungalow during the day. She saw them crawling all over the place and asked them what they were doing. They said they were bailiffs from the court and that they had come to repossess the place. They told her that they would have to break their way in because they needed to change the locks. They said the mortgage hadn't been paid."

"That's bullshit, Dad. The mortgage was paid off when Mum died. The insurance took care of all that."

"That's what I thought, son. Anyway, Dorothy got really scared and so she let them in with the spare key that I leave with her. They might have damaged the place so she was right I tried to get hold of Nigel to see what it's all about, but he has that stupid answerphone on. I can't get through. Can you help, son? I'm worried. I don't understand."

It had to be a mistake. Mum's life was covered by insurance that had nothing to do with Nigel. He couldn't have screwed that up because he hadn't been involved.

I told dad to sit tight. Evidently it was about eight in the evening and he assured me that he was okay for a bed for the night where he was. I needed to get some smack to calm me down, but nowhere near as much as I needed to get hold of Nige.

The answering machine was still on at his place so I left a message, urging him rather forcefully to get back to me without delay. I had a nasty feeling it was going to be a long night so I dressed and kicked my heels for ten minutes. Then I called him again. The machine.

It was not uncommon for him and Nicolette to sit there listening and select which calls they felt like answering. I had seen them do it. Was that how to behave? Whatever it was it provided them with a superb lifestyle. Although Nigel was based down on the coast a lot of the time, they had moved from Bromley and bought a mega place in Otford, further out in the Kent green belt. Six bedrooms, two bathrooms, three huge reception rooms and massive grounds overlooking farmland. This for Nicolette and the boy, and Nigel at weekends. They were practically recluses, very rarely venturing over to see Dad on Sundays even.

I called a third time, waited for the tone and opened up.

"Listen to me, you pair of cowardly cunts. I want to know what is going on and I want to know now. I know at least one of you dirty, snot-gobbling wankers is sitting there listening to this, so just pick up the phone and talk to me and we'll get it straightened out."

I waited for long seconds.

"You pair of cowardly, cocksucking *CUNTS!* What the fuck have you *done?* You greedy, ignorant, moronic, jealous, shit headed, cunting, fucking..."

"Stop. Stop it. Don't you dare talk to me like that."

"Where is he?"

"He's not here."

"Where is he? Out in the kiddy's sandpit burying his head? *You* tell me. What the fuck is going on?"

"Can't you stop swearing?"

"Funnily enough, Nicolette, I don't think I can. My dad has just phoned me up close to tears and telling me he has been locked out of his own house by some bailiffs - and you tell me to stop swearing."

"You'll have to speak to Nigel."

"It could be weeks before I can find that jackal and don't tell me you don't know what's going on. You phoned the old man this morning and told him to get out of the way. Why?"

"Because you know what he's like." I was gratified to hear her voice crack.

"What, you mean he might not have let them just waltz in and take possession of his house for no good reason. Funny how he's like that, isn't it?"

"There is a good reason, though."

"Like *what*?"

She hesitated and I knew that she had decided there was no easy way to tell me. So she just told me. "The mortgage hasn't been paid."

"Mortgage? What mortgage?"

"The mortgage that Nigel took out on the bungalow."

The words rattled around the cavernous wasteland of my brain like a pinball.

"But the bungalow is half mine. How could he have taken out a mortgage. The building society would want my consent."

She chuckled a horrible, sneering laugh. "You're pathetic. If you had spent half your time on this planet you might have known what was going on. You never owned half the bungalow. Nigel owns all of it and he always has."

Through my stupefaction I sensed that she was enjoying telling me.

"What are you talking about? The old man said that the place should go to me and Nige jointly."

"So?"

"What do you mean, so? What the fuck are you saying?"

"Nigel got your stupid father to sign the house over to him solely. It was easy. If we had put his own death warrant in front of him he'd have signed it. He never reads anything."

"Well, of course he never read anything. It's his own son! Do you mean that...? Is it...?"

For the first time in my life, I was speechless. I had no answer to this. It was beyond my comprehension.

"Cat got your tongue? At least you've stopped swearing."

"What sort of person are you?"

"I told you, it's not me. Speak to Nigel."

"But you knew. You knew all about it."

"What did you expect me to do?"

"Do you have any idea what the old man is going through? He is scared shitless. His house, his home. That was where he and Mum were going to retire. It was their dream."

"What do you want me to do?" she yelled.

"Phone him up. An apology, an explanation and a solution, in that order. That'll do. I've got a phone number here. Fortunately he's not going to have to sleep on the street tonight, he's at a neighbour's house. Got a pen?"

"I'm not talking to him."

"You stinking, cowardly *RAT!*"

"That's it."

"Just one thing before you fuck off back into the hole you crawled out of - why?"

"Why what?"

"Why what? Are you joking? The house. Why did he mortgage the house? He doesn't need it. He doesn't need the money."

"You sad moron."

"You what?"

"Talk to Nigel."

"I intend to. Where is he?"

"I don't know. I really don't. He's not here."

"You make me sick." I slammed down the phone.

I thrashed the Granada out to Essex. Dorothy and Peter were fussing around with cups of tea and slices of Victoria sponge. There was no way to make it easy so I just said it.

"Nigel has ripped you off."

He was a decent, hard-working, straight up bloke, and what did he get for it? How must he have been feeling? To have his soul ripped out. By his own son. This was not right. This was the most not right thing I could ever have imagined.

The only fair thing about it was that I was there to witness it, to be a part of it. Yeah, there was some kind of poetic justice at work. After all the frauds and scams I had perpetrated, this seemed like a payback of sorts. A little out of proportion maybe but I had few grounds for complaint. But dad? I looked into his eyes when I told him. He had been betrayed by the one person in the world he believed in and of whom he was proud, and now he was left with nothing. If Nigel had been so devious as to mortgage the house, what chance was there of any cash left?

I explained to him what had happened as I saw, it but he wasn't really listening. He didn't care to understand. My mother had handled things when she had been alive and my brother had well and truly taken care of them after she died. He didn't know much about mortgages and surrender clauses and he didn't care.

"If he was in trouble I would have helped. I would have sold the bungalow if necessary. But he worked it all out and he stole from me. Why, Mike? Why?"

I had to get out of there. He was OK at the Rogers' place for the night and I left with the eviction notice the bailiffs had left. I made my excuses and bolted for it, glancing once at the dark, empty, tomb-like shell of someone's shattered dream.

I told them I would call them first thing in the morning. I had half an idea what to do.

I arrived back in Wapping totally exhausted. It was getting on for midnight.

I parked the Granada downstairs and let myself into the flat. A couple of stiff gins, maybe try to find Nigel one last time and then bed. I needed to be on the ball in the morning.

"Hello, Mick."

I'm not sure if my feet actually left the ground, but the whinnying yelp I let out reverberated around the flat for long seconds. Someone had broken into my flat. Worse, they were still there.

On the Chesterfield were Denny Masters and Pete Chalmers. Hovering behind them was Romanov. I was relieved I had not disturbed a burglar, but my relief evaporated in seconds when I saw the looks on their faces.

"How did you get in here?" I asked.

All I got for an answer was Denny's heavy sigh.

"You made it back then?" Pete said. "You're powers of survival, Mick, are amazing. Some auto."

"Anyone want a drink?" I asked, pouring out half a tumbler of gin and scenting it with a couple of bubbles of tonic. They were not even bothering to answer. Pete got up and walked over to the windows to look out over the silvery, snaking, shimmering river.

"We think we know pretty much what happened, Mick. We just need to hear it from you."

That's it, I thought. *He's talking about Patsy. They know I told him about the plates and now it's payback time.* I looked down at my fingers and wondered if it would be the last time I saw them all together in the same place. Bluff it. Had to keep bluffing it.

"What happened? How do you mean? What happened when?"

Instead of answering me, Pete looked down at the area of the lounge in front of him by the kitchen door, and then out into the kitchen itself. It was strewn with beer cans, two empty bottles of gin, a half finished tube of Pringles, various chocolate bar wrappers and lots of food containers and cellophane.

"Do you actually live like this, Mick?" he asked with undisguised contempt. "Is this what life is like for you?"

"Had a few friends over and it got a bit lively," I shrugged. "I've been over to see my dad and haven't had a chance to clean up yet, that's all."

"Ask the scumbag where he's been for the last week," Masters barked from over on the couch.

"Yeah. Good one. Mick, where you been recently?" Pete said.

I drew the cold tumbler back and forth across my forehead. Couldn't they have asked me an easier one? Bluff it.

"Don't mess around, boys. You know where I've been."

"Sure. We know where you've been. We just want to know if you do."

I breathed in and out slowly and noisily. "Lanzarote," I said.

"Good doggie," Denny said. "Pete, ask the scumbag what he did over there."

"What did you do over there, Mick?"

This was obviously going to be a drawn out affair, so I sat

down on one of the armchairs. I took another gulp of gin figuring that I was going to need it. "The usual."

Romanov, who was looking unusually thin, snickered and moved around the sofa to sit next to Den. I saw that he was wearing his gloves.

"Oh, that's your idea of usual, is it?" Of the three of them, I always thought Pete was the one who cared for me the most and he looked like he wanted to break my legs. Then he bowled me an unplayable bouncer.

"What happened to your arm, Mick?"

I looked down and saw the bandage Julie had wrapped on me that was visible below the upturned sleeve of my shirt, and suddenly I felt sick: a psychological, association kind of sick. Very Pavlovian. He mentioned my arm and I felt ill. I pressed the glass to my forehead once more, but it did me no good. I was suddenly boiling and itchy and sweating.

"Well?" demanded Den. "Don't you remember? It was only a week ago."

The claustrophobia was overwhelming. I couldn't get away from them and their stupid questions and the heat and the fear and the sickness and Ishy wanted to kill me and Jenny was dead and Nigel had stolen Dad's house and I had no money and Patsy had stolen the plates and Jonesy had no finger and his eyeball was in his mouth and then and then and...

My body jack-knifed violently at the hips and I vomited half a pint of gin right across the coffee table and down the other side to land on Masters' immaculate brogues. The tumbler spun out of my hand and shattered on the pine flooring. I coughed up a meaty plug of phlegm and spat into the pot-pourri. Well, I thought with a doomed and curiously untroubled finality, that ought to speed things along. And so it did. Pete cut to the chase.

"How long you been selling acid to Rafael?" The words echoed around the room and then circled my head like vultures.

"That's bollocks. He told you that because he wanted me to do it, but I told him no and he was pissed off."

Pete strolled to my shoulder and fished inside his jacket. Onto my sticky coffee table he dropped a sheet of purple OMs. Do not pass go, do not collect two hundred pounds. The only question that remained was whether this was all they knew or whether they knew about Patsy taking the plates too. Then I noticed something. The sheet of trips wasn't complete. A portion had been torn off - not along the perforations, but roughly as if in a hurry.

"We beat it out of him," Den said seizing the edge of the rug to wipe his shoes. "Little fucker ain't so pretty any more, but we know."

I sighed in dejected weariness. "You got me. I was just greedy, that's all. I saw a chance to make a few quid and I took it. I'm sorry. But I was always careful. Nobody got nicked, nobody got in trouble."

"You do many of these yourself, Mick?" Pete asked.

"The odd one, now and then."

"The odd one, eh?" He picked up the sheet and looked at the torn end.

"What would you say would be a safe number? How many could you take in one go before you lost it totally?"

I closed my eyes, and like a cinema screen, my itchy lids showed me huge splodges of broiling purple.

"Depends. Two or three maybe. Depends."

I remember hoping they weren't going to kill me or beat me up too badly, because if they did I wouldn't be able to help my dad in the morning.

"There seems to be about sixteen or so ripped off of here. An experienced druggy such as yourself, Mick. What would happen if you did sixteen of these things?"

I looked up at him and for the first time since I had met him, I saw a glimmer in his eye that told me he was at least as mad and depraved as Masters. I suddenly felt very scared.

"Amazing what the human body can put up with."

There was so much I didn't understand

"You risked everything. More than that, you risked Dixie and Paul too. That's unforgivable. You're a mess, boy. You're a liability."

He didn't say much more. He didn't have to. I couldn't figure out how they knew about the acid. Maybe Rafa had been caught selling them and had spilled the beans when the heavy stuff started. Whatever had happened, Pete only had one more thing to say to me. He had some very important information regarding my career. He told me it was over.

"Fuck up number three, Mick. You're out. You were one of the best I've seen, son. Con man, dealer, salesman. You had it all, but you just couldn't keep off the gear, could you? Well, now it's all gone. No kites and cards, no more trips away. Finished. You're out."

Then they all got up to leave. I made the mistake of following them.

"Lads, look. Let's talk it out. We can still do some stuff together. I can still work. You can still make money out of me. I got good connections."

Denny whirled around. "Those connections have been severed. In the UK and abroad. You've got nothing." Then he calmed himself and I saw the vacant sign come on in his eyes. Lunacy on tap. "I never did like you," he hissed and then there was the flash of the sleeve. He was faster than Terry, but not quite so devastating, which was a shame because I stayed conscious and had to bear the pain, and there I was, once more assuming the supine.

The bathroom mirror told me the outside of my lip was swelling by the second, whilst the inside was pouring blood. I ran my tongue around the inside of my mouth and one tooth on my upper west side was loose, so I reached in and plucked it out. I didn't think it would be too noticeable, just so long as I never smiled again and that seemed a fairly safe bet.

Whatever drugs I guessed they had spiked me with during the previous week or so were pretty much out of my system so the vision that confronted me was not distorted. There was no pulsing of the eyeballs, no stretching of the nose, no blazing of the hair. Which was a shame because what I was looking at was the truth, and I could really have done without that. That sick bastard reality was there again, just when I didn't need it. I looked exactly like what I was: a knackered out, fucked up loser.

Then the buzzer rang.

"Seen you looking better, handsome." It was turning out to be quite a night. "Who was it this time? Den?"

"Uh huh."

"Thought so. I came round here to see you, to warn you, but when I got outside I saw Den's car. I hid around the corner until they left."

"Best thing, Dixie. Wouldn't want to have annoyed them." I said as I towelled off my aching face. "Want a drink?"

"Yeah, ta."

I walked past her and, side-stepping the debris, fixed us a couple of gin and tonics.

"Well it's official. I am totally unemployed."

"What? You make as much money for them as I do. Why you? You haven't done anything wrong."

She took the glass from me.

"When I say *they* sacked me, really I mean Den. It was that business of me and him, you know? It was never going to work and in the end he just got pissed off. Then when they were talking about giving you the bullet, they figured that as I was only a part of a team, I might as well go too."

"Ah Christ, Dixie, I'm sorry." We sat down on the Chesterfield.

"So you're definitely out too, are you?" She asked, placing a caring hand on my thigh.

"Yup. Most people get a gold watch. I got a tooth knocked out."

"You got off light. When they found out you were selling gear to Rafa, Den wanted to kill you."

An eerie blast of horror shuddered through me. "How did they find out about that?"

"Martinez heard Rafa take a call from you and sussed what was going on. Then he got to the postman who was delivering the mail and checked it first. It was only a matter of time before an envelope came through from the UK. He called Pete straight away, and him and Den flew out and were there before me and you."

"They told you about all this then?"

"Mick, you were so fucked up I'm not surprised you don't remember. I was *there* and after what those animals did to you, I wouldn't want to work for them again anyway."

The missing days. The missing week. I was getting close to the truth and the closer I got the less I wanted to hear it. I took a long slug and prepared myself.

"So what did they do?"

"You and Romanov got back to the hotel fairly drunk and Den and Pete were there. They said there was a change of plan, a problem with the hotel room or something, and that you would be staying out at some remote house further along the coast. So they took you there. Don't you remember any of this?"

I shook my head in sorry silence.

"There was a cellar in this place. They said it would be best if they did it all down there because no one would hear."

I coughed harshly and reached forward to place my glass on the coffee table. Neither me nor Dixie were perturbed by the fact that there was a lake of puke on it.

"Like I say, Den wanted to kill you and he would have done it, *and* got away with it. Pete was in two minds. Romanov does as he's told, like always."

Out. Out. Had to get out. Forget Patsy, forget Ishy, forget drugs, forget ambitions, forget... dreams. Leave, run, go, get out. I wanted my life back.

"So how comes I'm still alive?"

She looked down and stared into her drink.

"You've told me this much, Dixie. You might as well let me have it all."

She sniffed and I saw the tip of her perfect nose redden. "It was me."

"What do you mean it was you?"

"I did it. I stopped them. I suppose I saved your life."

I picked up my drink again.

"I screamed at them and told them I'd get the Old Bill and if they stopped me from leaving they would have to kill me too, and I meant it. I wasn't going to let them kill you, Mick. You're a dick sometimes and I'm out of work because of you, but I like you. We're good together. What was I going to do? You'd have done the same for me."

What was I supposed to say to that? I just kept quiet.

"So I guess they figured that if they couldn't get away with killing you, they would teach you a lesson you'd understand."

"Which was what? Jesus, I don't understand why I can't remember."

She took my arm and rolled the sleeve up fully. "This is a nice job, Mick. This bandage. Who put this on you? Couldn't have been you."

"A friend. She took care of me. Tell me now."

"First they got some hosepipe and shoved it down your throat. Then they got one of those funnel things and poured a pint of cheap scotch into you. Den was wanting to give you kicks and whacks, but Pete said that if you did die the police would think it was because you were some idiot pissed punter, and if there were any marks on you that would start an investigation. Den didn't like that but he saw the sense. So there's you, rolling around on the cellar floor heaving your guts up everywhere." She sipped her gin slowly.

"Sooner or later though you were bound to crash out. Den didn't like this because he and the other two were wired and up for fun and games on account of all the coke they were doing. Then Romanov had an idea."

"Paul was in on all this too?"

"He's a pleb, isn't he?. He just does what he's told. Anyway, his bright idea was the sickest fucking thing ever. They had the trips that you sent ahead to Rafa. So they ripped a load, dozens it could have been, off the sheet, rolled them up into a little ball and shoved them down your throat. To make sure you swallowed them, they poured another half a bottle of booze in your mouth and clamped your jaws shut."

I was too stunned to comment,. too shocked to move. I could not even blink, couldn't even cry. All I could do was listen. The lost week? It was a lost life. I had to stop her, but I had to know.

"I wanted to stay with you, but... I stuck around for about an hour. You were nodding off most of that time while the others just sat around waiting. Doing more and more coke and getting pissed and waiting. Then... then you started moving. Twitching. Slowly at first but faster and faster as the acid kicked in. Soon enough, you were the screaming mess they'd hoped you would be. That's when I couldn't take it any longer. You were crouched in the corner petrified, and they were all jumping out at you, shouting, scaring you. By then it was five in the morning. I went upstairs to get some rest. I woke up and went back down again at ten and it was still going on. Well, kind of. Pete had gone to bed and Romanov was crashed out in the corner, but Den was still at it. Still doing coke, still scaring the life out of you. But by then you looked like you were just shot away. You were still crouched in the same corner, still hiding, but your eyes were just staring. It looked like you were blind. Like you'd seen too much. Oh, Mick..."

She started to cry and I pulled her to me and held her and hugged her. What had we become? Bonnie and Clyde. What a joke. What a total fuck-up I truly was, and I had dragged lovely Dixie down with me. I felt self-loathing on me like a ton weight.

I took deep breaths, all the while chanting to myself, 'You can get through this. You can get through this.' I rubbed her shoulders and tried not to let my hand stray down to her arse. We sat for long minutes clasped together, two of life's casualties. Two dropped stitches of life's insane tapestry. I think I fell in love with her during those solemn moments. Eventually I forced myself to say, "There's more, isn't there?"

She pulled a handkerchief from her handbag, dabbed her eyes and blew her nose, and prepared for another onslaught.

"Eventually even Den tired so he tied you up and crashed out but the others took it in turns to keep an eye on you. It took another two days before you came down from all that acid. Then they had another idea."

"I can hardly wait."

"They got hold of Rafael and gave him a few slaps and sent him out to get a needle."

She was holding me by the arm as she said this, stroking me

gently, trying to soothe me.

"I told them how dangerous it was, that there was a real danger from getting air bubbles in the hypo so they got Romanov to do it."

"Why him?"

"He used to be a junkie. He used to inject himself. He was a bastard though. He was deliberately missing your vein, shoving it right through, out the other side... Really trying to hurt you."

"But what was in it?"

I closed my eyes and swallowed. It would be over soon. I saw the tear drop from her eye.

"It was Den's idea. He pissed in the syringe and they shot that into you. He said you were such a scumbag you were lucky to have his piss floating through your bloodstream."

I sat in crushing silence, too numb to speak or even to think.

"In the end I was hysterical and begged them to stop. The plane home was in a couple of days and they wanted you reasonably straight for that."

I stared around me. The glass in my hand, the puke on the coffee table and on the rug, the cans and bottles and food all over the floor, the split face, the bandage on my arm. Where had my life gone?

Eventually Dixie spoke, and what she said all but blew me away. She was still resting her head on my chest when she said, "You wanna do some crack?"

I thought I'd misheard her at first, thought that maybe she had said, "Do you want to shag?" Or something else, but no - that was what she wanted to know. Did I want to smoke some crack cocaine? I gave it some thought too.

"Actually, no darling. I don't think I will. Not tonight." There was even a hint of apology in my voice.

She lifted her head to look up at me. If I'd told her I had just copped a blow job off Prince Phillip she would have been less surprised. Then she said something else that amazed me further.

"Those traveller's cheques, Mick. Me and you. We could make it work. If you know something about it, tell me. You can trust me. I'm not with those animals anymore. We could make it work.

You see I've got access to a printer. We can run off as many as we want. Millions. No commission to anyone. We could be rich and I mean proper rich. We could do it. We could do it together. Me and you. We'll be the winners this time."

I looked down at her, into the honest wonder of her eyes, searching, scanning. What a thought. What a prize. Not only had I taken Denny Masters' scam, but his woman was now wanting to run away with me. I thought about his filthy, disgusting waste running through my veins. Then - just as I was getting excited, just as I was about to start making plans, like getting me and Dixie and Patsy together, I remembered something that brought me right back down to earth.

"You're welcome to stay, Dixie, but I've got to get some kip tonight. In fact, I've got to get some kip now. There is something very important I have to do in the morning."

The alarm clock sounded a few hours later and it was eight o'clock. Dixie was next to me, snoring like a tractor with a knackered engine.

Being asleep as opposed to being unconscious left me feeling noticeably refreshed. I got out of bed and had a nice hot shower, which made me feel even better. Then, my confidence bolstered by all the healthiness, I put the kettle on, found some instant coffee and made a big mugful. As I was doing that I noticed some things that I guess Julie must have bought. There was a loaf of bread and some bacon. Screw it, I thought, how difficult can it be?

As the clock ticked towards nine o'clock I found myself feeling rested, fed, alive and more together than I had in months. There was clearly something to be said for this clean living business. Then I rummaged through Dixie's handbag and grabbed the gram of coke powder she had on her, shoving sixty quid in its place.

I thoroughly cleaned the coffee table and racked out a quarter of the gram in one line. I could tell there was bundles of glucose in it, but it was the first I'd had in ages so it felt good. Then I was ready to pick up the phone.

I started out ringing each of the seven numbers I had for

Nigel. I was unsure of what to say, should I locate him, but as I was fairly sure he would not come to the phone anyway it did not matter too much. I just wanted him to know I was onto him. Unsettle him maybe. It was good abusing Nicolette's answerphone again, and that of the manageress of the one of the estate agencies I knew he was knocking off.

At one minute past nine I called the bailiff's office in Romford. There was no answer so I gave it another five minutes. I gave the case number and was put straight through.

"Perkins."

"Mr Perkins, the name here is Targett. You and your chaps called at number nineteen Clayton Avenue, Upminster, yesterday afternoon."

"Ah, yes indeed, sir. How can I help?"

He sounded like a man accustomed to people hating his guts. There was no pretence of nicety, no attempt at placation. He was professional and I was glad of it.

I had read accounts of some of the tens of thousands of repossessions that were taking place throughout the UK, as the recession bit deeper. I knew there was one thing they had to let you do.

"I'm Michael Targett. Number nineteen is my father's house. He's a little upset right now so he has asked me to talk to you. I understand we can go back into the house to get a few bits and pieces we might need in the short term. Is that correct?"

"That's right, Mr. Targett. One of our staff will let you in and help in whatever way he can. But you do understand that access is only granted this once. Thereafter it will be for the court to decide who has access and when."

"I understand. We shouldn't be too long. When may we be allowed in, do you think?"

"When would you prefer?" It was clear that in the eviction business a little civility went a long way.

"As soon as possible as is convenient for you, Mr. Perkins."

"Well how about this morning. Say ten thirty?"

"That will be fine. Thank you for your help."

"You're most welcome, Mr. Targett and may I offer you and

your family my sympathy. This recession is a terrible time for all of us."

"It certainly is."

I called the old man at the Rogers and told him what was happening. Then I called my mate Steve at the bike shop and asked if he could slip out for an hour. He looked like a bit of a handful, and I figured that might be useful.

Me, Steve and dad were sitting outside the house in my Granada when Perkins himself showed up. He was alone. I told him Steve was there to help us carry something heavy.

"Fine. I'll give you a hand where I can."

As we walked in I watched dad and saw the biggest grin I've ever seen split his face. Every second back in his home was a bonus to him. We all stood around in the hall.

"Would anybody like a cup of tea?" the old man said.

"Not for me, Mr Targett," Perkins replied. "It would help if we could make this as quick as possible."

"Well we can help in that respect," I told him. "We're not going anywhere and you are. We'd like you to leave straight away."

The weirdest thing was, it was like he knew. He knew it was no straightforward repo job.

"I see. And what are your plans, may I ask?"

"We are going to change the locks immediately and then we are going to call a solicitor. There has been a fraud perpetrated with this property. As soon as possible, we will apply to the court to have the possession order set aside. You'll probably see us over there in a few days. Hopefully this will have been sorted out by then."

He stared at me blankly for a moment, and then he smiled. Then it got even more surreal as he shook hands with all of us and wished us luck. Then he left. I couldn't believe it was that easy. Steve buggered off too. He hadn't been needed but he had been there for me anyway, and that was worth knowing. I pulled out the Yellow Pages and called an emergency locksmith. Dad handed me a cup of tea.

"I thought it was up. I honestly thought we'd never get back in, son."

"This is just the start Dad, and I think it's going to get a lot rougher. Let's relax when we're back in for good. There's court, the police, the bank and all sorts of shit to worry about first."

I grabbed the brief-case that Nicolette had bought him for all his bills and statements and stuff. I didn't really want to look but I knew that I had to. It was as bad as I thought.

"Dad. The money. All your money. It's all gone."

He sighed heavily and appeared to shrink before my eyes. "I know, son. I can't understand it. I had thousands in the bank. Then, a few weeks, I bought a new golf bag and trolley with a cheque from the shop at the club. They came to see me a while later and told me that the cheque had bounced. I told them that was impossible but, well, I suppose it had to be true. I called Nigel, but he is so busy he is never around. Then I called Nicolette but all she said was that Nigel was dealing with it all. He's so busy, I don't like to keep chasing him."

I looked through the statements.

"But the income. The money coming in from the investments. This stopped ages ago. What happened to that?"

He looked away from me. "I'm not very good with money. Your mother used to handle everything like that. I'm just a worker, boy. I didn't ask them what they were doing. He's my son and she is his wife. They told me not to bother with anything."

"Have you got any money on you?" I asked him softly.

"A few hundred quid or so. Why?"

I pulled a lump from my pocket.

"You don't have to do that, son. Don't forget there's my severance payment from the dock and your mother's life insurance from her company, and..."

"No there isn't!" I hadn't meant to shout.

"Dad I'm sure everything has gone. There's a couple of hundred quid left in the bank and that might be it. Do you have any income?"

"I've got my disability pension from the state and my dock pension starts in a couple of years, when I'm sixty-five."

I closed my eyes and tried to think. The doorbell rang. It was the locksmith. I put him to work. Then I looked at my money. I counted out two hundred and fifty and stuck that in my pocket and gave the rest, about five hundred, to Dad.

"Just... Just have that, Dad. Hang onto it. Don't spend anything you don't have to, OK?"

I scoured the Yellow Pages again and called up a local solicitor. Petrified to leave the house, I insisted on a home visit. Three hours later our new legal representative was lifting our spirits a little.

"A clear breach of intent. It was your father's intention to have the house in your names jointly, your brother clearly disobeyed those instructions. Presumably he placed the house transfer form in front of your father and asked him to sign it, giving the illusion it was something other than what it truly was. Therefore he obtained title to the house by deception. Furthermore, he has presumably applied for a loan against the house. Now, Mr Targett, tell me. Have you always lived at this property?"

"Well, no, Miss. We have only lived here since nineteen eighty two."

"No, I mean since you bought the house. You have lived here and never anywhere else."

"That's right. I've always lived here."

"Fine. Now your son, Nigel. Has he ever lived here?"

"No. He and his wife stayed here a few times. Michael used to live here before he moved on, but Nigel never has."

"Excellent."

I edged forward keenly. "Okay, so on the mortgage application form he would have been asked if the property was his place of abode and whether anyone else apart from him lived here. To get the mortgage approved he would have needed to lie in both instances."

"Correct," she said. "Sounds like it was a clear case of fraudulent application. What we must do is apply for legal aid without delay."

She unbuckled her briefcase and produced a form.

"What we also have to do is get the possession order set aside by a judge. Because of the urgency of the case I'm sure it will be heard by tomorrow. The court bailiff has obviously returned to the court by now, so not only will they know what you have done, but so will the mortgage company - and you can bet they won't be hanging around in getting the case heard. Now, Mr. Targett, the mortgage company will have legal representation at the hearing. It will be his job to discredit you. He will want to have you thrown out of the bungalow. Just be strong and tell the truth as you have told it to me. You will be under oath."

"I have nothing to hide."

"There's the possibility they will be thinking you and your son have cooked up this whole scheme together to perpetrate a deliberate fraud."

"I have nothing to hide."

I was so proud of him I started to cry.

Dad got through the hearing. Just. As our solicitor had envisaged, the opposition brief ripped into him like he had just murdered his daughter and it broke my heart to see him struggle for the words to fight off the smooth-talking bastard. Buggered by impotence I sat at the back of the court and squirmed and suffered as the legacy of my brother's unspeakable greed manifested itself before my bleary eyes.

Too honest to lie, I wondered where me and Nige got it from. His anguish was apparent for all to see, and the judge must have sensed that because he declared there was clearly more to the case than had been heard that day, and suspended the repossession order granted to the loan company pending further investigation.

Dad was back in the house legally, and I told him the next time he would leave would be when we carried him out feet first in a box.

Now that the whole ludicrous scam was out in the open, it seemed reasonable, I thought, to assume Nigel and Nicolette would be willing to volunteer all relevant information to the loan company and the police or whoever was involved. Thus the mortgage would be null and voided, the bungalow - and hopefully as much cash as they had left - would go back to Dad and we could attempt to rebuild what was left of our lives. Obviously this would leave the pair of them with one hundred and forty thousand pounds (the maximum they were allowed to borrow against the property) to find. Plus fees. If they weren't able to do that then they would, presumably, be in a lot of trouble. That was only right and proper, bearing in mind what a pathetically traceable crime they had committed.

I finally tracked them down together. I expected shame. I expected humility. I expected tears of pain.

"Ah, old son. Watcha." He swung the door of the mansion open. He was drinking, and clearly had been for some time. "Wanna beer?"

I walked past him into the hall and then into the stadium-sized lounge. Nicolette was there, ironing. She looked up and eyed me with terrible resentment. I said nothing to her and sat down. The television was on.

All the speeches, all the rehearsed, noble words and heavy threats vanished from my mind. I didn't know what to do or say, so we sat there watching the TV. Screaming jets, triple A fire, cruise missiles. Mad, barnstorming Americans.

"Can we turn this shit off and sort this out?"

It was as though he hadn't heard. I looked at him. He looked at me, picked his nose and burped.

"This has to be sorted out."

"What do you want me to do?" he asked casually.

"You might ask how the old man is."

"So how is he?"

"Devastated. Betrayed. For the first time in a long while he's talking about suicide again."

He looked through me, swilled from his can then his eyes drifted back to the television.

"So now I know."

I looked at Nicolette. She bashed and crashed her iron, hoping the noise would ruffle me enough to make me want to leave. The fact that my father was penniless, one step from homelessness, and suicidally depressed; the fact that many crimes that had been committed were traced directly back to them and the fact that there was a little outstanding matter of some two hundred thousand missing pounds, seemed only to be of fleeting interest. It was like it was all something they had done for a while and then got bored with, and didn't want to talk about anymore.

"Look. What do you expect us to do?" Nicolette demanded petulantly, slamming down the ironing."

I was aware I was making odd, gabbling noises. "Do? I... What do I exp'... What? Well that's it, what the fuck *are* you going to do?" I was boiling with rage and disbelief.

She sighed heavily. "I can't be doing with all this. I'm going to wash my hair."

"She's had a hard time of it lately." Nigel informed me as she stomped up the stairs.

"*She's* had a hard time of it!" I was screaming but my voice could only manage a strangled, tinny whine.

"Hey, here's one." he said. "Heard about the new film out? Honey I scudded the yids." He looked at me and smiled and I felt overwhelmingly awed to know that I was in the presence of true insanity. I stood up.

"I ain't listening to this. I ain't playing games, you cunt. The money. Where is all the fucking money?"

But I was quickly afraid. Afraid of my own feelings. Afraid that I couldn't do enough to help Dad and afraid that I would hate myself because I was so powerless. And, yes. I was afraid of him too.

His bloody eyes looked up at me. "Gone."

"Gone? Where has it gone?" What have you done?"

He shrugged. "All I ever wanted was to crack it like everyone else. Everybody was making it. All my mates, every other prat in the country. Even *you*. I needed... How could I be left behind? I had to do something. The cars, the shops, the investments, the poncing employees, the holidays, the flats, the lifestyle. Two estate agencies that I bought, just as the market was going into free fall. This place. He's not the only one. This place is getting repossessed next week. All I wanted to do was get ahead. I've only ever sold eight policies in my entire life. And now I've run out of Peters."

"Run out of Peters? What's that supposed to mean?"

"Peters. Peters to pay Paul. I've run out of them. I can't borrow any more money from anyone. All the money has gone. I'm a zero credit rating."

I gawked at him, paralysed by incredulity. Then with a look of vague puzzlement he said, "Hasn't anyone told you there's a recession on?"

The legal wheels, rusty and cumbersome and indeed unused to cases of such treacherous intensity, began to turn. The good news was that Dad would definitely remain in the bungalow until the case went to high court, which would be between three and five years hence. The outcome of that case - unless collusion could be proved which was practically impossible - would go in one or two ways. One, we would get a full result and title of the property would be returned to Dad. More likely however would be a judgement that would see Dad stay in the place until he died, at which point the loan company could legally take possession once again.

It was good to know that, for the time being at least, he was safe. I didn't feel so sure about me.

CHAPTER NINETEEN

Stock take.

I had nothing. No, not quite true. I had a few things and I considered them.

I had a gangster friend called Patsy Chetkins, who had used me to steal some potentially lucrative items from some ex-gangster friends of mine, Denny Masters and Pete Chalmers. However this potential would only be realised when Patsy found a sufficiently corrupt or greedy printer who would turn the items into something that was as effectively desirable as cash.

I also had another friend, Juliette Dixon. Allegedly *she* knew a printer. This was good. However to err on the side of security, as was now my intention, I decided to keep the whereabouts of said plates to myself. Perhaps Patsy had secured the services of his own printer and was already progressing the job. Problem was I couldn't find the dodgy bastard to give him the good news. He was abroad again. This was bad. It got bad to the point where I sometimes considered myself to have been ripped off. Frankly I didn't believe a face like Patsy would take so long turning up a dodgy printer. He'd nicked the plates from Denny and Pete and had then included me right out of things.

So what else did I have? I had a Ford Granada that was worth about six thousand pounds, although I barely had sufficient funds to fill it up with petrol. That was it. And *that* was the good part.

Everything else was a bloody nightmare. I had a beautiful flat, an aspiring yuppy's dream that had become a rope around my neck, costing me over two large a month. Even though I had shoved an obscene amount of money into the place I discovered that the term 'negative equity' now applied to me. I couldn't afford to keep it, but I could afford to sell it even less.

On the subject of craziness, I felt myself drifting into that bubbling cauldron once again, driven there by my appalling brother. Deep into each and every night I would drag the full horror of what he had done backwards and forwards through my tortured mind. I broiled with poison and powerlessness to the point where I felt that if I did nothing, if no revenge were exacted in some way, I would truly be driven insane.

So, while nobody was looking I did three sensible things. One, I put the Granada up for sale and two, I got a job.

I called Steve, who put me onto a bloke he knew who rented bikes. I scored a nasty old Honda CX 500 from him at forty quid a week and went despatch riding for a firm in Romford. My knee was sore and swollen at the end of every day, but what could I do? I knew nothing else.

Thirdly though, I bowed to the inevitable and rented out the flat. The DSS saw fit to house a family of Bosnian refugees in my gorgeous apartment and I moved back in with the old man. I didn't actually ask him if it was OK because I couldn't afford for him to say no. This all meant that I had to ride like a nutcase for twelve hours a day, with a leg that felt like it was hanging off half the time, to earn enough money to support a property I never saw which I rented out to people I didn't know. The world had surely gone mad.

I had friends though. I still saw Dixie. Every third weekend she would pack off little Wesley to his father's and she and I would hang out. She always intimated how she would love a crack at the Amex job, but it was just another dream that wasn't going to come true wasn't it? Patsy wasn't around. I could never even get to talk to Lauren. Even Barbara Chetkins got bored with me calling up all the time.

There was something else I had. When Denny had laid me out that time at my place, he and Chalmers had walked out leaving a sheet comprising just under three thousand double-dipped purple OMs. It was a few quid at least. Or rather, it would have been if I had anyone to sell them to. I had no alternative. I had to eat them myself. More accurately, I made my peace with Vicky and went down to see her most weekends and we ate them together. I told her about being used as a lab rat.

"I've been set up. I've been really fucked over. I was recently out in Lanzarote and I didn't even know I'd been there."

In spite of everything she looked at me with that cute grin, her head tilted over to one side. "Nice one."

"Not really. I was drugged."

"I should hope so."

"No, I don't mean that. I mean I was poisoned. I was nearly killed, and I'm pretty sure the same people grassed Ishy."

She looked at me sharply. I had no idea how she was going to take it.

"So how do they know him? How do they know about him?"

I looked across the room and to the window. The same window where I had seen the ghost, the ghost of Romanov past. What a sorry fuckwit I was. It was Paul alright, tailing me on Denny's orders, sniffing around.

"I guess they followed me one time. Traced me here."

"But why? Why fuck up Ishy? They don't even know him."

"It was me they were after. They take Ishy out of the picture, they cut off my supply and I'm out of business."

"So they called the cops? Even though you didn't know about it it's because of you that he got nicked?"

I sagged wearily and conceded, "Yeah, you could see it like that." I really hoped she wouldn't see it like that.

She did that thing of tucking her legs up underneath her again.

"Anything you want me to tell him? He gets sentenced soon."

"There's not a lot you can tell him that will do him any good, but for his peace of mind... You could try to convince him I had nothing to do with it."

"But you did."

"I know, but it wasn't my fault *as such*. It'll only do all of us harm if he thinks it was."

She thought long and hard. "He's got a record you know."

"For drugs?"

"Yup."

"Shit."

We looked across and then moved towards one another and embraced.

"Oh, babe," she whispered in my ear. "If only we were back on the beach. Me coming out of the sea and you offering me a drink. It all seems so long ago."

We held each other gently and both began to cry. We cried for the same reasons too. For our dear friend Ishy of course, but also for the vanished Utopia, for the lamented Mallorcan summer lifestyle and for dreams, long since lost and never to return.

Due his record and the prosecuting officer describing him as being part of an 'international drug dealing gang', Ishy was sentenced to four years on a charge of possessing controlled drugs of the class A category, with intent to supply.

There was something else I had that was good. There was another friend. Much neglected but much loved. I still had Julie. Julie, with her smile that could calm a storm and her heart as big as Essex. Soon though, I felt the friendship mutate into an uncomfortable dependence. One evening I was on the way over there. The A13 near Barking in the rain. An artic dragging a twenty foot container cruised past me on the outside. Then the entire rig began moving sideways. I touched the brakes and in skating rink conditions I lost control. Without hitting anything I did a swift one eighty, slammed into the kerb broadside and rolled the car onto its roof. The lorry driver kept going.

I managed to haul myself out and then stood at the side of the road without a single clue as to what I should do next. I called the cops on the 8000x.

"Been drinking, have we, sir?"

"Going a fair lick in these conditions were we, sir?"

I had cut my forehead and my back was really starting to hurt, so they breathalysed me and took me to Newham General. I was OK so I called Julie and she came to pick me up.

By the time we had eaten and were sitting by the fire I was in agony with my back, and with every drink I felt myself becoming more and more depressed. All the problems and all the sadness in the whole world were suddenly pressing down on me. I looked at Julie. She was so beautiful and trusting and honest and good. That was why I realised I had to tell her.

Even though I had drunk over a bottle of brandy I couldn't sleep. Every move she made massaged the mattress, which in turn pulled on the exposed rawness of the nerves in my back. I listened to her breathing until I could stand it no longer.

"Wake up," I said. I reached gingerly across and touched her shoulder. "Julie, wake up."

"Mmm."

"Julie, please." I felt myself choking up. I had to get it out before I changed my mind.

"Julie."

Thunder boomed in gothic splendour. The air hummed with terrible danger. My head was thick with worry and regret. It all seemed apt.

"Are you OK? Are you hurting?" she asked.

"No. I'm alright."

She peered, mole-like, into the darkness.

"What's the matter, darling?"

I stared up at the ceiling, my eyes swimming.

"I went with Jade."

Silence.

"Where?"

I sobbed at the comic ridiculousness. "No. We were lovers. We went to bed. I'm sorry."

I listened intently. I listened as she reached down to the carpet next to the bed for her T-shirt which she pulled on. Then she got up and walked in silence to the spare room. I cried myself to sleep and so did she.

In the morning she gave me a lift back out to Dad's. As we passed along the A13 I looked across at the Granada, adorned with Police Aware stickers. Someone was in it. A scavenger at work.

Julie did not get out of the car when she dropped me off. I dragged myself out, closed the door and looked at her through the open window.

"Don't phone me again, Mick." she said. "I won't be seeing you anymore."

As she pulled away I dropped the Cubs cap Franny had given me when I was on the up. It fell under the wheels. It was ruined.

I laid down on the living room floor and called our doctor. He came round and told me that if the hospital X-rays showed nothing, then it was simply muscular strain. He told me rest and relaxation were the answer.

I had never been on the dole or claimed sickness benefit, but the doctor then asked me if I needed a certificate to make a claim. It appeared I could still save the flat.

I couldn't call Nigel to make a claim for the Granada, so I phoned the insurers direct. They told me to go through my brokers. I told them that was impossible as they had gone out of business. No problem. They would ring me back shortly.

So I could still make it. A nice few grand from the car insurance, rent from the tenants and dosh from the DSS.

The phone rang.

"Hello."

"Mr Targett?"

"Yes."

"Hello, Mr Targett. This is Jason from General Mutual."

"Hello Jason."

"Yes, sir. It's regarding your car insurance."

"I thought it would be."

"Yes. Ah, you say that the policy was transferred from a Ferrari motor car to a Ford Granada, registration number F987 EMC."

"Correct. A few months ago."

"You say this transfer was carried out by your brokers at the time, Kent Insurance Brokers."

I suddenly began to feel ill.

"Right."

"The problem is, not only do we have no record of such a transfer, but the policy was actually cancelled at that time."

"Cancelled."

"I'm afraid so, Sir."

I tried to think calmly. "And the premium. Going from a Ferrari down to a Ford presumably left me with some kind of pro rata refund, Jason."

"Absolutely, Sir. I have that information here. A cheque for three thousand one hundred and twelve pounds was despatched some time ago."

"I see. Who was the payee?"

"Yes, Mr Targett. I have it here. It went to your brokers - Kent Insurance Brokers Ltd. They should have it in their client's account. They should have sent it onto you by now."

I thought of something.

"Jason. Would you not have needed written authority from me to cancel that policy?"

"Er, no, sir. The brokers would need written authority. They would then convey the client's wishes to us."

"I see."

So not only had the bastard done me out of my insurance premium rebate, which I had forgotten about, he'd had me driving around in an uninsured car. Which I'd just crashed. More importantly there would be no money back for the written off motor. I was cleaned out. Flat broke skint. How could I ever be a match for him?

I hauled myself to my feet, shuffled painfully to the kitchen and switched on the kettle. Whilst I was waiting for it to boil the doorbell rang. I opened the door to two uniformed policemen. I groaned audibly.

"Mr Targett?"

"More or less. You'd better come in."

They did and they gave me the dreaded producer that had been impossible to serve on me the previous evening but that wasn't the real problem. Compared to the real problem that was a piece of piss.

"Where did you buy the car from, Mr Targett?"

"Croydon."

"From a dealer or from a private vendor?"

"Private. Why? Some bloke it was."

"Do you have the receipt, sir? You'll know the address."

"Er, I don't know. I did get a receipt but I'm not sure where it is."

"How did you hear about the car being up for sale?"

"I saw an ad in the paper. One of the local rags I think, or maybe the Mart. The Exchange and Mart. Why? What's up?"

"When was this, sir?"

"Why?" I asked again in glorious innocence. "What is this?"

"Do you know what a ringer is, Mr Targett?"

That just about finished me off. Bamboozled. Suckered. Snookered. The two cops smiled knowingly at my protestations. What goes around, comes around. I had been sold a nicked motor. Then they arrested me for receiving stolen goods.

The worst part of it? The old man didn't believe me. I was my brother's brother. Nigel was a lying, cheating rat, and therefore I had to be one too. Guilty by relation. Tarred with the same vile, treacherous brush Nigel had so horribly used to taint and disfigure all our lives. But it was so ironic I had to laugh. What else could I do?

Throughout the rest of the summer and into the autumn I nursed my back carefully. I needed to - it was the only income I had.

My GP kept writing sick notes and I kept claiming. There was nothing else I could do.

I made another series of calls to the Chetkins household, all to no avail. Lauren wasn't even living there anymore. She had moved in with some Billericay Dickie, who, according to Barbara, was a bit of a jealous sort and wouldn't take to me calling her there. Patsy, needless to say, was away on business, splitting his time between Mallorca and South Africa. She told me she always passed on my messages.

As far as Nigel and the bungalow fraud was concerned, nothing seemed to be happening but throughout nineteen ninety one we found out what he had done and how. It was all paper, inspired by my mum's death and funded exclusively by my poor dad. When she died and there was suddenly a lot of money around, Nigel saw it as pay day. Suddenly he was rich. Then he didn't have to work, plan, sell. Maybe he saw it as his birthright or something. It was going to him anyway, why not reap the benefits sooner rather than wait until the old fella pegged out? So that's what he did. Fuck dad, fuck me, fuck everyone else. Fuck the risk too.

Maybe he had grand plans that were supposed to work out. Maybe he was going to make a mint and return all the money before anyone realised it was missing. But the dopey cunt just ended up pissing it all away, and the crowning glory was the purchase of two estate agencies, only a matter of weeks before the whole shithouse crashed in on itself. At the end he had something like three homes, four shops, nineteen paid employees and ten company cars to support, and I was probably doing more business than the entire group when I was working for Ali making cold calls in the City.

You could blame the times if you wanted. *Everybody* had cracked it. Nigel came from a time and a place that demanded success, and all around him that success prevailed and was displayed in the most ostentatious and unavoidable ways. Holidays in The Algarve? That shithole? A Porsche 944? Is that all?

All Nigel's peers were successful. Jesus Christ, *I* was successful. So he had to be too. Whatever the price and whatever the risk. I became a drug dealer, he stole his father's house. You had to do something, right? It's just a question of where you draw the line.

I'd been there a few times when the egotistical wanker had taken staff out to dinner. I'd seen him feed off the admiration. He'd visit the shops on rotation, like it was his own personal fiefdom. Dispensing largesse, extending favour, paying for everything with a flick of the gold credit card that bore his name, but was funded by our dad.

But Dad wasn't the only victim. For months after it all

collapsed we had friends, victims, employees - every bastard and his uncle calling up possessed of varying degrees of fury looking for blood and screaming for their money back.

My hatred was overwhelming and Dad sensed it. "Brother shouldn't fight against brother," he once laudably said.

"I haven't got a brother."

"He must have been so desperate," he would muse aloud.

"I'm sure lots of people are, mate," I would protest in slavering rage. "None of them steal every last penny their families have."

"I should have died instead of your mum." And he would turn his face away.

Our solicitor, Mrs Yardley, advised us to make a statement to the police. Dad reluctantly complied but, far from leading to the arrests I hoped would see Nigel and Nicolette languishing in jail, the investigation - lead by a succession of idiotic DCs fresh out of Hendon - went precisely nowhere.

Mrs. Yardley had obtained a copy of the original mortgage application form, and there for all to see were the false declarations of the treacherous, thieving scum that were my brother and his wife. And yeah, she was in on all of it with him, that superior, money-grabbing bitch. YES - they lived at the bungalow. NO - Nobody else lived there. Out and out fraud right there, and I looked forward to the gloating visits I would make to the prisons to see them.

Of course, they got away with it. They got away with it because the victim of the fraud was not my father. Can you beat that? The victim of the fraud was the loan company and they weren't prosecuting.

"Of course not," Mrs Yardley explained. "They have a charge over the bungalow, albeit a suspended one. That is all they want. If your brother and his wife are found to have acted fraudulently and the property is returned to your father, then all the loan company is left with is the prospect of chasing the two of them for the money, and I don't suppose there's too much chance of them seeing a penny. If they press charges they'll be shooting themselves in the foot. No, they are quite prepared to sit on the fence, wait until your father dies and then take possession.

Welcome to the real world.

"But we can still get him nicked?"

"What for?"

"Excuse me?"

"Well, what purpose would it serve? The fact is the law states that unless you are registered blind or certified as being mentally ill then you are responsible for what you sign. Of course we know that your brother tricked your father. It was a despicable thing to do, but he is responsible for what he signs. In the eyes of the law your brother legally owned the bungalow when he took out the mortgage. The victim of that crime is the loan company, and if they don't want to press charges then it's up to the police and the Crown Prosecution Service, and they won't press charges either because they basically don't care."

And that was that.

I hardly noticed the Christmas of ninety-one or the new year of ninety-two, but the period was remarkable for two things, both of them, in keeping with the spirit of the times, were tremendously awful. The DSS finally cracked onto the fact that I had an income (the one they had been paying me for the Bosnians) and suspended my income support with immediate effect. I hadn't given a thought to the possibility that the two departments would talk to each other. Not only that, they totalled everything they saw as being obtained via 'misrepresentation and false information'. It came to many thousands of pounds. I was urged to make contact to discuss 'suitable terms of repayment'.

Dad had sold his Micra a while before to raise a few quid, so I jumped into the shitty Fiesta he'd chopped it in for and trundled up to the flat. I'm not sure why. I think it was another of one those times when I felt the earth begin to move and I needed to do something - to be somewhere I had once been happy and secure. A kind of return to the womb.

I let myself in at the street door and caught the lift up. I knocked loudly. There was no answer so I let myself in.

It was one of those daft, double take moments. Wrong flat.

But then how had my key worked? I checked the door number.

I walked into the middle of the vast living room, my dragging footsteps echoing off the beautiful oak and the bare walls. As I made my way to the kitchen I looked out of the panoramic windows down onto the Thames. The writhing, silver snake which was now looking brown and dirty and unthreatening. Back out and across to the bedrooms. Then into the bathroom. They had even taken the mirrors, which was just as well because I don't think I could stand to look at my own reflection at that moment.

They had taken everything. Everything was gone. Stolen. Stripped. The way I felt. Every single appliance was gone. All the carpets. All the cupboards on the walls in the kitchen. The sink, the bathroom suite, the light bulbs, the handles on the windows, the internal doors. There wasn't even any dust. It was as hollow and as empty as I was.

It turned out the Bosnians were professional DSS scroungers, card users and con artists. They looted the place entirely. Shipped out, moved on, no doubt to change their identities and to repeat the process somewhere else.

I gave up on the flat. I didn't want it after that. I called up the building society and told them it was theirs. They told me to put it in writing and send on the keys, which I did. They would then auction the place and come after me for the inevitable shortfall between what it would go for and the ridiculously inflated purchase price I had paid, back when the world was a different place.

The second thing that happened was I made my appearance at Snaresbrook Crown Court. The Granada was indeed a ringer and because I had got it so cheaply, the CPS barrister implied that I must have known it was stolen when I bought it. The bloke that scammed me had rented the flat, but had presumably only knocked out the Granada from that address because there were no other poor suckers like me coming out of the woodwork. Therefore no-one else could corroborate my story. I was a convicted criminal. It was beautifully ironic. I was fined seven hundred and fifty pounds plus nine hundred costs. I had to get the bus home.

I had only brought a few things with me from the apartment when I moved out. As a special sentimental reminder, I made sure that two of them were the bottle of Courvoisier and the huge box of paracetomol. I pulled them out of my old suitcase and was surprised to see that some contents were missing from both. What was that about?

I set the pills and the bottle down on the small chest of drawers next to my old single bed and hid myself away. Every night I would peer up at the triumvirate of faded heroes looming over me: Mackay, Blackmore, Sheene. Some nights, when I knew the old boy was asleep, I would creep next door to my mum's room and sit on the edge of her bed. There I would whisper to her, call to her, ask her for help. Ask her to save me.

Ashamed, lonely and lost I came close to doing it a couple of times. One at a time, I placed a pill on my tongue and washed it down with a gulp of brandy. Cowardice normally kicked in after about eight or nine and I collapsed into a blithering, sobbing wreck and cried myself to sleep. It was dad who saved me. He didn't know it, but how could I kill myself while he was still alive? What would that have done to him?

The world had moved on and both of us had been left behind. Our memories were fading, just like that old photograph of his grandson. Nicolette had sent out a picture of the boy to all the family when he was eighteen months. That was all we had.

The thing about being screwed up in the head, is you don't know you are.

I went to the doctor to get some proper painkillers for my back. The doctor, who had known me for about sixteen years, started asking me loads of questions. After five minutes he stopped and wrote out a prescription for Citalopram. Then he quickly scribbled a note which he folded neatly and placed in an envelope. On the envelope he wrote: Emily Craven, Warley Hospital, Brentwood.

"Go there," he said. "See this person. You won't need an appointment. Just *get* there."

So, suspected of being a real loony by someone who ought to know, I toddled over to a real loony hospital and talked to people. I was on the lookout for some electrotherapy or maybe some drugs, but there was none of that. You know how they treat nutters these days? They talk to them.

"Why are you here?"

"My GP told me to come."

"Why do you think he did that?"

"I'm depressed."

"Why are you depressed?"

"My life is meaningless." I was serious. "I'm worthless."

"Why are you worthless, Michael?"

"Because I don't do anything. Nobody in the whole world benefits from my existence. If I was gone, nobody, except my dad, would know - and he'd get over it."

I didn't mean that last bit, I just threw it in for dramatic effect.

Dad didn't know. He thought I was going out twice a week for physio on the back. I let him. He had enough agro without having to worry about a clinically depressed son.

There was one practical reason why I couldn't shake off the suicidal thoughts. My only income was what I had coming in from that last sheet of Ishy's acid. Out of this I was paying off the money I owed to the DSS, and the fine to the court. Together that cost me fifty quid a week. I was giving Dad thirty. But soon the building society would bang out the flat at auction and take stupid money for it. After that their Shylocks would come looking for me.

I was down to five hundred trips. Those that me and Vicky weren't getting through, I was managing to knock out to a couple of Julie's old friends in Brentwood. I was getting near to the end and I was totally unprepared. But so what? How bad could it get?

One evening the phone rang. It was Lauren Chetkins. It had been so long I had to get her to say her name twice.

"How you doing, stranger?" she chirped.

"Ah, well," I wheezed, my throat burning from too much

cheap vodka. "Can't complain. Now that Princess Di has dumped Charlie, I'm being kept busy."

She laughed the glorious, girlish laugh I remembered from all those years ago. Almost eight years to the day. Back in time. Back in time. If only I could go back in time.

"Listen. Simon is away skiing. I've been meaning to call you, but you know how it is."

"Yeah, darling, 'course I do. Er, how is it?"

"Not bad, not bad. I mean things are going okay. I never thought it would be exactly like this but, well. I can't complain."

"Of course you can."

"What?"

"Complain."

"What do you mean?"

"You want to complain then complain. Stuff the son of a bitch."

"Mick!"

"What?"

"You alright?"

"Never better. So what you been up to? Hey, how's the kid? How is my little... Shit."

"James. He's fine. Getting ever so big. Mick, are you straight? I mean you're not on anything are you?"

"Life, darling. I'm high on life."

"You sound like you're having a time of it anyway. Listen, you up to doing something tonight?"

"Why?"

"Pardon?"

"Why do you ask?"

"I'm asking you out."

"Why?"

"What? Mick, what is it?"

"I don't hear from you in a year and whatsisname fucks off to the slopes with his Essex boy mates and you can squeeze me in. Is that it? Is that what it comes to?"

"Mick, please."

"Tell me I'm wrong. Are you a friend of mine?"

"Of course I am."

"So where you been? The number of messages I've left with your mum. She hates my guts she's so bored hearing my voice. I called so many times, Lauren, don't tell me it didn't occur to you there was something wrong."

"Wrong? What's wrong?"

"Wrong? Who said something was wrong?"

"You did. You just... Mick, what is going on?"

"Nothing is going on. Don't worry yourself. I'm alright. You don't have to worry about me."

"Oh, Mick. You should have said there was something wro..."

"I tried, Lauren. I tried. You weren't there."

The line went quiet. I could have bawled her out some more, but what would have been the point? She had her own life. She owed me nothing.

"Mick come out tonight. It would be great to see you. I've missed you."

It could have been two or three months since I had been out in public. I only ever saw dad at feeding times. Sod it. Let's see what's going on out there.

The trouble was I had just scoffed a couple of trips. In my room with a half a bottle chaser, it would have been a pleasant diversion. But out there? In the real world?

Dad gave me a lift down to the Hilton national: scene of many a romantic entanglement from a different era. In the bar-restaurant section there were loads of kids wearing really daft clothes. I sensed the acid seeping its way up the sensation barometer of my nervous system. Tickling fingers of paranoia, ghostly wisps of unreality - God bless them - were suddenly everywhere.

Then there was Lauren, looking pretty as a picture in some skimpy little number and even younger than I remembered her from that night in Magaluf all those years ago.

She walked over to me. Then she walked right past.

"Lauren?"

She turned and looked at me and then back the other way again. A gasp of recognition.

"Mick?"

Had I really fallen so far? Maybe it was just the beard.

"You look nice," I told her, avoiding her eyes. "Been a long time." Have you ever noticed there is never a crack in the floor to dive into, when you need one.

We ordered a drink but then I felt an urgent need to go to the toilet. I clocked the boat race in the glaring honesty of the mirror. What was the matter with her? I didn't look too bad. I felt pretty weary though, so I sat down on the lid of a khazi in one of the cubicles. As I was sitting there, my brain picked up an obscure and distant radio wave of a memory. It was to do with a time when I was in the Yeoman years and years ago. I had come out of the toilet and The Stomach had bollocked me about something. Being a fucked up druggy or something. Then I saw what he was getting riled about. I had been crashed out in the bogs and all the others were pissing on me.

These thoughts were then disturbed by someone calling my name.

"Yeah, mate," I answered.

The door to the cubicle was unlocked and I watched as it was pushed open by a seven foot penguin. This didn't faze me at all.

"You got a lady friend out here, sent me in to look for you."

I sniffed and tried to remember. "Oh yeah. Right," I replied as I stood up and flushed the toilet.

I walked past the penguin (at least he wasn't a Kraggenknaffer) and marvelled at the way he shape-changed back into a smartly dressed doormen. Lauren was outside. "Mick, what are you doing?"

"I've just been to the toilet."

"You've been in there for *half an hour!*"

She dragged me back to the table. We were supposed to be having dinner, and for some obscenely pretentious reason, we forced ourselves to do just that. The meal, with the drug taking a firmer and firmer grip, was archetypal acid madness.

We skipped starters, but for the main course I ordered a light fish job featuring loads of prawns in some exotic sauce or other. As soon as the waiter put the plate on the table I knew what was going to happen, but of course it only happened because I thought it would.

All those little prawns. Swimming. Now as an experienced acid man I was accustomed to eating live food - goes with the territory. But those prawns in that sauce. The mess they were making.

"Do you see this?" I said to Lauren.

"What?"

"I can't be expected to put up with this. Do they know who I am?" So then I called over the waiter.

"Listen, son, I'm a reasonable man. But kindly tell the cook to give the little bastards more oven time in future. We're not just talking undercooked here. These fuckers are still *alive*."

"Mick, do you want to go?" Lauren asked as the kid backed away.

"No, no. I'm alright. I'm just used to getting better service. When I think about the dosh I used to drop in here. Yeah, the old days. Do you remember the old days, Lauren?"

"I don't dwell on them."

"Yeah, we used to have some fun." I returned to the duel with my main course. Elusive little beggars they were and no mistake. Lauren was only too aware of the trouble I was having.

"Don't eat just to be polite, if you're not hungry."

"I think you're right. Guess I'll just have a bit of cake or something. I'm trying to get fit for next season. I've got a bit of trouble with my back and my knee keeps flaring up every now and then, but it's time for a comeback I reckon. Did I tell you I used to be a tasty fly half?"

Dessert was as much fun as the main course, and because I was onto the waiter he was now bold enough to show himself in his true colours. Yup, all sweetness and light on the outside, but I could see through that. I saw the scales on his neck and sensed his discomfort when he was up on his hind hooves serving us.

I opted for the spotted dick. Oops. Now there was this thing on my plate with all these black bits in it and the black bits looked just like... Yeah, right. Next thing there was a plague of flies buzzing around the restaurant.

I was aware of Lauren trying to keep me calm as I swatted thin air.

"OK, Mick," Lauren announced, standing up with unseemly haste. "I'll get this. I have to get back for the babysitter. I'll drop you off"

Then suddenly I was swaying around outside Dad's bungalow. There was no smooching. No peck on the cheek. In fact as soon as I was out of the car she burned out of there. I didn't blame her.

"Weirdo," I shouted as I watched her go.

I had trouble deciding which house I lived in but eventually I found it. Shuffling towards the door, I sensed something. Eyes on me. At first I thought it was the waiter come to freak me out some more. I stopped at the garden wall and turned to look down the road. Suddenly the night was all around me like a blanket. Thirty yards on the other side was a car. In the car was a man. Then the man started the car and drove slowly away.

CHAPTER TWENTY

The mental health therapy continued, but more importantly, the acid was running out. This meant two things. Firstly I would have to deal with the real world, and secondly, I would have to deal with the real world in prison for not paying of fines. Something needed to happen fast, and - for my sins - something did.

My mate Steve had been sacked from his job at the motorcycle shop for some scam or other. This turned out to be excellent and decisive news. He had been round to see me once or twice and had tried to get me out, but I think he'd been frightened off. Us recluses don't go in for personal hygiene much. I looked and smelt like Howard Hughes, but without the dosh.

Then he happened upon a dodge for which he needed my help. Smuggling. Nothing outrageous, not proper smuggling. Over to France, fill up with cheap booze and tobacco and then run it back home and flog it off. He was cleaning up. So much so that he couldn't handle it on his own. But it meant going out. It meant leaving the house. It meant dealing with people. And some of those people would be French.

"Nah, I don't think so, mate. Thanks for asking anyway."

"Ah, Mick, come on, mate. You can't hole up for ever. Besides, I need your help. There is a real gap in the market here, a few quid to be made. All you have to do is drive a minibus.

Nothing else I promise, and there is a oner in it for you plus a case of beer. Please. For me."

I hesitated. Since the debacle with Lauren two weeks before, I had left the house solely to go to the hospital. The more I stayed in, the more unnerving became the prospect of going out.

"Who's going to be there?"

"Well I'll be driving one bus, taking my parents and two of our neighbours. In your bus there'll be a bloke from the shop who got the bullet along with me, his girlfriend and two of her mates."

I thought about it.

"Listen. Can you tell everyone that I'm OK but they have to keep away from me?"

"What?"

"No. No don't say that. That sounds bad doesn't it. What I meant was...."

"Ah, Mick. What is it, mate? What's so wrong?"

He didn't know the half of it. I breathed deeply, feeling terrible sadness pushing at my door.

"Everything," I whimpered.

But somehow I did as he asked, and thus I became what was known as a booze cruiser.

UK tax meant that the price differential between beer, wine, spirits, cigarettes and baccy in France had become so chronic that there were battalions of people pouring across the channel into France, buying up oceans of booze and tons of tobacco products to consume and to sell to anyone who wanted to buy.

Once a fortnight I drove a minibus for Steve. The money essentially kept me out of jail, but almost as important as that I found a degree of confidence return. Amazingly, basic French - which I hadn't used since my A level year - was there at my disposal, and the joy of being able to use it to talk to shop assistants and sales people all but made my heart burst. All the others thought I was dead clever, and that made me feel good too.

Out of casual interest I called P&O and was surprised how little a channel trip cost. So I borrowed a few hundred quid from

Dad and did a run of my own in his Fiesta. I told Steve and he said that just so long as I left his customers alone, he thought it was a great idea. And so it was. It didn't take too long at all to knock out what I had bought to friends, family and chums of the old man down the golf club. Once again I had an income.

That was fine as far as it went. What I needed, I felt, was a big customer. Steve sold a lot of wine to a pub landlord in Romford. That gave me an idea.

I had only met him a couple of times, but that manager of Patsy's place, the Cock, had seemed like an approachable chap. What did I have to lose? I couldn't remember his name but I thought I could wing it. A woman answered the phone and I asked for the manager. She put me on hold.

"Hello?"

"Hi. I'm hoping you remember me, I..." Then I stopped, my heart in my mouth. It had to have been two years since I had spoken to him.

"Hello?"

"Is that Patsy?"

"It is. Who is this?"

I couldn't find any words. I had been waiting so long to have a conversation with the man. Now I had him on the phone I didn't know what to say.

"Listen, I'm going to put the phone down now."

"No, Patsy. Wait."

"Well well well. If it isn't the acid queen."

"Ah. You've spoken to Lauren."

"You think she's going to keep something like that to herself?"

"I suppose not. So, how you been? I've been trying to get hold of you, Pat."

"So I hear. Listen, son. I'm going now. One, because I'm busy and, two, because I'm bored. Have a nice life, sponge head."

"Patsy, wait. Listen. I know I've ballsed up. I've been out of my depth. That's no reason to shove me out is it?"

"That's not the reason you're out, Mick. The reason you're out is because you can't keep off the shit. Drugs make people stupid, stupid people are liabilities and liabilities we can't afford."

"How's your printing going?"

An opportune moment to ask such a question, it seemed, because he didn't have an answer. Furthermore, his hesitation told me that maybe the Amex job was still incomplete.

"Perhaps over the phone ain't the smartest thing, son."

"I need to see you anyway, Pat. Got something for you."

"I'm not buying"

"No. 'Ang on a sec'. I'm in the wine business."

The last of the acid finally went. I was completely out of drugs, but it was far from the nightmare scenario I had imagined. Apart from Dixie, I had no sources of drugs either. Coincidentally, after a break of some months, she started calling me up again. Asking if I needed any gear, if I wanted to go out. I was flattered, and I'd never forget what she had done for me out in Lanzarote. I told her things were looking up and that I'd be in touch.

I was doing a run with Steve. We were on the Pride of Kent on our way back to Dover, two groaning minibuses down on G deck. I was at the bar sipping a coffee when I heard a woman order a cappuccino in a scouse accent. I looked across and saw that she really was standing next to me.

"Hello, Julie," I said.

Her face was a picture. Mystification, recognition, warmth, resentment, indignation, acceptance. She did it all in about three seconds, but she ended up smiling and we went to sit down together.

"I'm over here on business. My boss and I are driving back from Amiens."

"I'm on business too."

"Really? What are you doing now?"

"I'm a smuggler." I roared as she gagged on her drink. "Nothing serious. Me and a mate are into the booze thing, you know?"

"No. What?"

You know. It's only booze and fags. The normal crap. Everyone's doing it."

"Are you sure that's all?"

"Sure I'm sure."

"Mick. Have you been away lately? You should get some sun you know. You look a bit rough. What's with the beard? You look like a demented disciple."

"Good to see you too."

"I'm only concerned." She touched my forearm lightly and my whole body tingled. "Has there been anything wrong?"

What to say to a question like that. I shook my head. "Don't worry yourself."

"I think about you a lot."

"I think about you a lot too, Julie, and the times that have gone by."

"Do you?"

"Of course."

Long awkward moments. Constriction in my throat. "I'm not very good at life. I see a psychiatrist now."

"Oh, Mick. Why?"

I couldn't face her. I felt so weak and useless. Ashamed of the failure I was.

"Because I don't like myself very much. I take anti-depressants too."

I studied my shuffling feet. I forced myself to look at her, and when I did I saw her beautiful eyes brimming over. How many tears, I wondered, had she shed because of me?

"It's OK, I've got you again," she told me. "I'm back."

It may have been not much more than a year since I'd seen her but it felt like a lifetime, and in some ways it was. For both of us. My world had collapsed. Hers had come to fruition in terms of her career and her relationships but in spite of the fact that she was engaged, she insisted on keeping in touch. She talked to me and advised and encouraged. She sent away for information about college courses, hinting, suggesting, helping.

It was an amazing, almost spooky time. Much as I was keen to let go of the past, it seemed less than willing to let go of me. Minus the beard and shaking with trepidation, I went down to the Cock to see Patsy Chetkins.

I took with me a carrier bag of samples. I wanted a foot back in the door and I saw the Calais runs as the way to do it. Once that was established we could talk about other things, namely, the ace of Dixie's printer that I had up my sleeve. Up in his office, though, I had that nasty feeling of inadequacy. Like I was an interloper. Like the world had moved on and I wasn't up to it anymore. Perhaps I never had been.

"Hello, son," Patsy said as I clanked over to his desk. The crunch of the hand remained a constant.

"In spite of everything it's good to see you. You don't look too bad. Keeping yourself together?"

I nodded as I sat down.

"Yeah. Yeah, I am." It was good not having to lie. I'd had a few honesty sessions over at Warley hospital and found that, once I'd got used to it, telling the truth wasn't the struggle I had imagined. Which was just as well, because if I thought going to see Patsy would be some quick route back to the top, then I was very much mistaken. He was looking at me with an air of a man who couldn't decide if he was amused or appalled.

"I expect you'll be wanting to speak to Lauren to apologise for embarrassing her that last time, eh?"

"I did leave a message with Barbara."

He regarded me with the cold scanners of his eyes, making me wait. He always knew so much more than me. They all did.

"You going to tell me about Jennifer Baddows?"

I was sure I had heard the name before. Then... then came the crush of realisation.

"That was a long time ago, Pat. In the past."

"In the past? A girl carrying a ton of drugs ODs in police custody. She makes one phone call and that's to you, and you say it's in the past. You've obviously done far more gear than I first thought, son. *In the past?*"

I was indignant with the need to understand.

"Pat, you've got to tell me. How the fuck do you know all this?"

"It's my business to know, you moron. If I'm to deal with the likes of you then it's just as well I can find this kind of thing out. Penny to a pinch of shit it was you who supplied that girl - and you are a personal friend of my daughter. There are people in this world who would pay a great deal for information like that. Now, tell me again, have you mentioned my name to Masters and Chalmers or to any of that lot?"

"No," I was able to say without having to stop and think.

"Are you sure?"

Frankly I wasn't. If a human being is able to talk with several pints of spirits, a dozen and a half acid trips and a hypodermic full of gangster's piss swilling around their bloodstream, then I suppose I could have said anything under those circumstances - but as far as I knew, I hadn't

"I'm sure."

He quickly softened, saying, "I believe you, son."

It was as if his flaring temper was all a show designed to unnerve me. Which it had. Next up from the Patsy Chetkins box of tricks came a real below the belt punch. A right kick in the nads, this one.

"So. You think you might be able to help with the printing?" he began, perking me up a touch. "That would be good. I have to say I've been so busy – I've spent so much time abroad I still haven't been able to address this properly."

Brilliant! I edged forward in my seat. "Yeah. Thing, is it's not someone I know. But there is this woman I know. Very close we are and I can trust her one hundred perc'..."

That was as far as I got. That was as far as I was allowed to go before Patsy Chetkins' palm flew up into the air, like he was a traffic cop slowing down a joy rider.

"Mick," he said with one of those dejected smiles you can only get when you have successfully tipped your favourite team to lose in the cup final. "Please. Please don't tell me that Dixie has told you she knows where we can get the printing done."

I should have known then. I should have sussed I would never be anything other than way out of my league. I would never be anything other than an innocent pawn in the games of these bloody tyrants. I was busy conjugating irregular verbs while they were all at Violet's funeral.

He sighed like a thirty ton truck releasing its air brakes.

"Look, Mick. Please. Don't worry about that for now. You're right in that I am still looking for a printer. Been on the back-burner long enough. You hear of anyone who may be up for the job then I am in the market, but take my word for it - Dixie ain't the one, OK?"

"No really. She's split entirely from Den and Pete, you got no worries about..."

"Enough!" His hand came slamming down onto his desk. "Don't insult my intelligence anymore. Now, there is one reason and one reason only why you are here. Show me what you got."

I delved into my bag. I had saved him around the million pounds mark with the Amex plate information, and here we were, talking about pouches of smuggled tobacco and a few ten quid cases of wine. It was quite surreal.

"Old Holborn is two seventy five for forty grams. Golden Virginia is in fifty gram pouches and goes for three pounds seventy five. They are the best known brands, but obviously I can price up anything they do over there."

"Uh huh. How do those prices compare to things over here?"

"The Holborn comes to you at about half price, the Golden a little dearer."

"Right. What about vino? My manager Ron wanted to talk to you about this but he's had to dive out, so I'll have a look myself. We'll have a little sampling session, eh?"

So we sat there for about half an hour, sampling all these French wines I'd brought in.

"Jolly good, son. I think we might be able to do a bit of business here. Tell me, how's your dad? You still looking after him I hope?"

The question exploded on his desk between us like a grenade.

"Mick? You alright, son?"

"Yeah. Yeah, I'm OK."

He looked at me curiously. "Well?"

I sighed. "He's not so good, Patsy."

Patsy had never even met the old man and most likely never would, so I suppose the reason I told him was because I just wanted the sympathy. Sure, Dad was the victim, but I was a loser too. So I told him. Everything.

Whatever my motivations, I never expected the reaction I got. He listened intently, not making a sound. Then, when I had finally finished talking, the glass in his hand spontaneously exploded.

"Excuse me," he said softly. "I've just remembered I have to speak to someone for a second." He got up and left the room. When he returned he was wearing glasses.

"Let's have another go at that Burgundy, young Mick," he suggested.

I uncorked the bottle and poured him a taste in a fresh glass. Then I poured myself one as well. We sipped in silence.

"Mm, I like that," he told me. "Barbara likes a red with a strong flavour too. How much for that one?"

"Thirty bob a bottle."

He smiled.

"Outrageous innit? Must be pumping it straight from the local refinery."

He smiled again and I could tell he was weighing things up. Calculating. He nodded like he had come to some kind of conclusion.

"You're a good boy, Mick. You're an unusual one, but you're alright. Keep going. Keep on trying and keep looking for that printer, you can do yourself some good there." He sipped the wine again, but his mind was somewhere other than his palate.

"Your father, he must be a remarkable man, and I can see that you've been troubled by it all yourself. But I reckon you're digging in. You've been hurt but you are trying to get back into things and I respect that. I never had a father as such and I'll never have a son. I can only wonder what it has been like for you and your pop."

Take advantage? Extract sympathy? Why the fuck not? I was sick of carrying everything on my own.

"I know I owe you and your Lauren an apology, Patsy, but now at least you have some kind of idea why I've lost my way. I'm not a spacehead. I'm not an idiot. I've just taken a bit of a kicking lately."

"You're a good boy, son. How can I help?"

"Er, well, how much do you want?"

"What? Oh yeah. Say six cases of each, two hundred packs of either on the baccy and as many duty free fags as you can get away with. That'll be at least once a week. I didn't mean that though."

The shock of the order and the attendant thrill of knowing that I was once again solvent scorched through me.

"What did you mean?"

He was holding a notepad and a pen across the desk at me.

"Your brother of course. I'll need description, address, number, work place, car details. All the normal. Whatever you've got."

It was what I wanted. I knew it wasn't right, but I was way beyond caring about that.

Being back at the cutting edge of mediocrity suited me. Walk before running.

Steve's idea and Patsy's order laid the foundations for a neat little cottage industry and I was soon up to hiring a Transit van once a fortnight, then weekly. Each run netted between five and six hundred quid. I stashed money away in the building society and made sure the fines would be paid, no matter what happened.

Dad came with me a few times too, enjoying not just the day out, but the fact that I was conversing ably with the locals and getting back on my feet at the same time.

In spite of new government guidelines regarding amounts of tobacco and alcohol brought into the country from abroad, customs never bothered us much. Back in the early nineties it was still a free-for-all and great advantage was taken of our united Europe. So much so that I often thought about how easy it would have been, running through a bit of gear in a van on the back of a beer run. No, stop it.

Patsy and I were spending time together, and whilst it was

only once a week to drop off his order and get paid, it was good to be in with him again. Stay with the money, I told myself. Take the money. Always be taking the money. Then one day, he said something to me that chilled me to the bone.

"Stay in on Wednesday. Stay by the phone. Have someone there with you too. Alibi." I saw gleaming intent and mad conviction in his eye. It was unstoppable. He was unstoppable.

"Things are turning around nicely for you, son. Soon you'll be rolling again. Earning a few quid on the France runs, you're off the shit and in a few days your head will be back on an even keel about this awful situation with your brother." He leaned forward and affectionately patted the back of my hand.

"I know how something - a problem hanging overhead, can affect the judgement. A problem like that has to be sorted out and fast. Like a cancer. Needs to be cut out." There was nothing I could do.

"Stay by the phone. Call me after you hear. There's a bit of work."

I wanted to be hard. I wanted to be the tough gangster. Why did it all hurt so much?

I got a call from an old friend. Dixie phoned up and asked me out. The diversion would be good. It was Tuesday evening. She looked a million bucks, and I was very pleased to be able to lay down a few quid on a restaurant table for her, courtesy of the Calais runs.

I kept it together and was mindful of Patsy's warning not to mention my association with him to anyone, especially as there was violence of some description about to go down.

I figured that the 'work' Patsy had mentioned had to be coke. He knew I had been knocking out the old devil's dandruff for Denny and Pete. Yeah, that had to be it. Wouldn't hurt to get Dixie primed. I could see her being my first customer.

Funny thing was, I felt no embarrassment in picking her up in Dad's old Fiesta. It didn't matter. After the way she had seen me? For old times' sake we slipped round to the Yaksak for kebabs but whilst I found the memories evocative they were not particularly warm. I suppose that place was literally where it had all begun. Sitting with Terry Farmer and the slippery burglar.

"Blimey, Mick, I can't believe how good you're looking. You're either on something special or you've given up for good. It's great to see you, and to see you smiling again."

Always a sucker for a pretty girl, that was me.

"Thank you, darling. I've got to say it certainly feels like I've come back from somewhere. I'm not too sure where it was I went, but I probably wouldn't want to know anyway."

"Good for you, my boy. Good for you."

"So," I said, feeling that I had to ask, "you heard anything of Denny and Pete?"

She shook her head as she drew circles in her soup with her spoon. "Nah. Don't want to neither. Not after the way they treated you. It all kind of fell apart around about that time. I also heard they gave up tearing the East End to bits, searching for their plates." Then she looked at me and I knew what she was going to say.

"Don't suppose you heard anything, did you?"

A question for a question. "Dixie, who's your printer?"

"What?"

"You said you've got a printer. You said if I turned up the plates you had a printer standing by and we could have a share out. A carve up between me and you."

"Well, yeah. That's what I said. So, what are you saying?"

"I'm not saying anything. I'm just asking you who it is, that's all."

I looked into her eyes and saw an unnerving defensiveness. Just being paranoid, I guess.

"Are you saying you know where the plates are?" Cat and mouse or what?

"No. I'm not saying that at all. All I'm saying is if those things do turn up, can you trust this bloke?"

She looked at me like she felt she had half been tricked, which I suppose she had.

"'Course I can. Jesus, don't worry about that. Mick, don't get my hopes up like that. Look don't worry about things my end. You just concentrate on turning those plates up, alright?"

We ordered the food and a bottle of wine. I wasn't sure what I was fishing around for. Patsy was so sure about keeping Dixie in the dark, but he hadn't bothered telling me why. Of course he didn't need the agro of a dust-up with Denny and Pete, but now that Dixie was off their firm, what did it matter? I decided to give her the good news about the Charles.

"Listen. I think I might have some real good bugle coming soon."

"Yeah?" The confident smile returned to her face. "Got yourself a new connection, eh? True what they say, you can't keep a good man down for long. Good on ya."

I flicked my eyebrows up and down. "Straight from the source too. It'll be some *righteous* shit."

"You old fox. Mick, who you in with these days? It might be embarrassing later on if it turns out I've shagged the geezer. You remember how it was when you took me around to the yard to see the chaps that first time."

I wasn't aware of the man walking along the main aisle of the restaurant until he gradually began picking up pace. Nobody ever ran in the Yaksak, except to the khazi obviously. Then in a flash I saw him reach into his inside pocket, and then his arm was out and in the air and he was suddenly level with our table. He reached across Dixie's shoulder and I saw his arm begin its descent in that classic, scything motion.

It was just damage limitation. I managed to ram my arm upwards in front of my face with my forearm horizontal to the ground. I felt the jarring impact as his wrist thudded into mine, but he had the weight and the momentum. Whatever was in his hand made contact with an explosion of napalm on the side of my head and face.

I'd flown sideways and was immediately gushing blood all over the girl who had been sitting on the next table to us. As he scrambled for balance I saw what was in his hand and I knew. I knew who it was. Then I looked into his boiling eyes and he looked into mine, but before either of us could react Dixie was screaming. A wild, high-pitched howl that froze the entire restaurant. Then she had our bottle of wine by the neck, and then it was up and coming down until it smacked flatly and horribly onto the back of his head.

It wasn't like the movies either. There was no spectacular shattering of glass followed by the painless, dazed look, followed by the gradual slide into unconsciousness. No, this wasn't a movie. This was real life, the life I had chosen.

His forehead thudded down onto the table, and then he was slithering onto the carpet, dragging the entire table load down on top of him, hollering like a klaxon all the way. I grabbed the swearing, fuming Dixie by the arm, paused to chuck a twenty over my shoulder and we were on the street.

Twenty-four hours later I was back in Patsy's office. It occurred to me, not for the first time, that this man was bad karma. It wasn't long before that things had been stable in my life. I was skint and clinically depressed, but things were stable. Since I'd been involved with him again, someone had taken to me like I was a sirloin that needed to be cut down to size. Not only that, but Patsy had organised some butchery for Nigel and Nicolette. I had been down to meet a man near the Dartford Bridge.

"What happened to you?" he asked handing me a man-sized gin and tonic.

I sipped long and slow. Boy did he know how to mix a stiff one.

"Jimmy Mulroney."

"Terry Farmer's oppo. You sure it was him?"

I nodded solemnly. "No mistake. The old-fashioned cut-throat razor. I'd recognise that mad bastard anywhere."

"Question is, why?"

"Well, first I thought it was some kind of set-up. You see, I was with Dixie last night."

"You ought to keep away from her."

"Don't worry. I was perfectly sober and didn't tell her a thing. My point being that it couldn't have been a set-up."

"What makes you say that?"

"Well, for one thing she could have got me to a much quieter, much more suitable place than the Yaksak in the middle of the evening. If it was planned then it was a terrible piece of planning."

"Good boy. You seem to learning."

"Not only that but she grabbed a bottle and smacked him over the head with it. I've heard of trying to make things look authentic, but that's ridiculous."

"So how do you read it?"

"I reckon it was just bad luck. I reckon Jimmy was in there, down the other end of the restaurant, and just happened to see me."

"So? That's not a very nice way to greet someone you ain't seen for a couple of years is it? He could've just said 'hello' like normal people do."

"It was for Terry wasn't it? For what you did to him."

"For what you *had* me do to him."

"Which was precisely what, Pat?"

"Mick you're going to have to trust me. Now, forget about Terry and last night and answer me this question. If you suddenly came into a load of money, what would you do with it?"

Talk about grab someone's attention.

"Pat, what is that supposed to mean?"

"Don't hesitate. Tell me the first thing that comes into your head."

"Easy. I'd buy the old man's house back for him."

He grinned at me like I was top of the form. "Good boy. Now I think you are going to like this one. Tell me, when you going to France next?"

"Tuesday."

"OK. Take a look at this." He reached down to the floor, clasped a case of beer between his huge mitts and set it down on the desk between us. "What do you think?"

"Case of Fosters."

"You're a pro. OK, try this."

He reached down again and dragged up another case.

"Two cases of Fosters?"

"Look 'em over. Tell me if you think there's any difference."

They were as I bought them on the ferry to and from France.

Twenty four 500cl tins of five percent proof export, sitting on their cardboard tray, tightly wrapped in transparent polythene.

"Pick them up," Patsy urged. "Shake them about. You're the expert. Tell me if there's anything strange about them at all."

A full minute of weighing, testing and shaking saw me no nearer to telling him what he wanted to know.

"You got me," I admitted. "Two ordinary cases of Fosters."

"Wrong," he said, smiling benignly. "This is a case of ordinary Fosters." He placed his hand on one of them. "Whereas this..." he indicated the second case. "This is the same but with a certain addition."

I instinctively began to feel uneasy.

"Four of these cans have been emptied, refilled, re*sealed* and the case rewrapped. It's impossible to tell them apart, isn't it?"

I knew what he was going to say. I was feeling sick, so my instincts must have been correct. I knew I had to say no to him but also knew that I couldn't. It was fucking horrible being a gangster.

"You go to the Continente supermarket, yeah?"

"Yes."

"OK. You buy the Fosters duty free on the boat, yeah?"

"Yes."

"How many?"

"Four or five each way."

"Fine. On Tuesday don't buy any on the way out. In the carpark of the Continente just sit tight. A man will approach you and he will give you four cases of Fosters. On the return journey buy your normal four or five on the ferry."

I looked at him and he looked at me. So, now I was going to be a cocaine smuggler.

Patsy was grinning. "You know, I think everything's going to work out alright. You'll have a chance to apologise to Lauren for your behaviour the other time too. She'll be going with you, plus a bloke called Frank. Nice lad. He'll help with the loading."

I relaxed when he said that. If Patsy was OK about Lauren going along, he had to be one hundred percent sure the scam would work.

I called in at the Cock to collect Lauren and Frank on the way to Dover, but was met only with disappointment. Lauren couldn't go. Young James had been taken sick during the night. It was just me and this Frank bloke. Shit.

Apart from my churning insides, everything went to plan. We went to the Place d'Armes to my normal tobacconist, and then to the Continente to buy Stella Artois and wine. We loaded all that on board and then we waited. We waited for fifteen minutes in complete silence. Then a man who had been sitting in a car next to us reading a paper looked up at me. He seemed familiar.

"Hi," he said.

"Afternoon."

"Been shopping?"

"Yeah." I was sure I'd seen him before. Maybe he was just a booze cruiser like me.

"You Mick?"

"Who are you?"

"You Mick?"

"Yeah."

"Got something for you."

I was hoping it would be a no-show. Hoping he had ripped Patsy off.

We got out of our respective vehicles and he opened the boot of his car while I pulled apart the rear doors of the Transit. Four cases of Fosters, as arranged.

"Good luck," he said and then he was gone.

The return ferry ride was a waking nightmare. I stood on the viewing deck of the P&O Pride of Burgundy and watched the white cliffs of Dover appear and then rush towards me, as if we were travelling in an off shore power boat. Ticking down. My hours of freedom were ticking down. Perhaps we would capsize and everything would all be alright.

What chance was there of a random search? As my trembling legs took me down to the car decks I comforted myself, as much as I was able, with the knowledge that smugglers only got caught if they were being watched or if they had been grassed. But then every drug runner thought that.

We waited in the gloomy, dank cave of the car deck, heard the buzzer sound and watched the mighty hydraulic rams force open the doors. I edged us forward when the deck marshal motioned me, and we rolled off the ramp and up onto the elevated section above the docks, then down the other side towards passport control and customs. I was looking forward to it now, because the sooner we got there the sooner we would be through.

I held two passports out of the window at passport control.

"Two of you in there?" the man called.

"Yes."

"Both British?"

"Yes."

"What's in the back?"

"Just some duty free, shopping, beer. That kind of thing."

"OK."

Just customs itself. Then up the hill, the A2 and freedom. What a party we'd be having that night.

I eased slowly over the speed bumps, not wanting to clank the bottles together too much. Not that we were in serious breach of any rules. I'd made sure we were within our EU 'guidelines'.

Ahead I could see the usual two customs officers seated on the island between the two exit lanes, scanning a clipboard that held registration numbers and descriptions of vehicles.

In addition, there were two or three others standing by, checking the drivers and passengers. What do their instructors tell them to look out for? Guilt I suppose, and its many manifestations. I employed the same system I always did and advised Frank to do the same: don't smile, don't talk, don't yawn, don't try to act relaxed. Don't do anything. Don't catch anyone's eye. Just look straight ahead and do nothing. Breathe.

Then we got stopped and pulled over.

CHAPTER TWENTY ONE

I thought of Dad more than anything else. First it was Nigel, stealing the bungalow and ripping off Dad. Then it had been me falling apart, ending up skint, in therapy and getting a criminal record. Now *this*. A convicted cocaine smuggler. A long term prison inmate. I looked to the far end of the search shed as a car was making its way out. Once it left, the massive roller shutter began its long descent, clanging shut as it hit the floor, and sounding the death knell on my life as it did so. No way out. What would it be for this? Six, seven years?

"Good afternoon, sir. Can you tell me how long you've been out of the country?"

Not the trainee I had hoped for. In his fifties, more experienced than the rest; he looked like he had seen every form of smuggling known to man and quite a few more besides. He had the measure of me and we both knew it.

"Just since this morning."

"Ah, a day trip, was it?"

"Right."

"What time did you sail this morning?"

"Ten. I have the ticket here. I rummaged in the door pocket and showed him the ticket for the outward sailing.

"May I see your passports as well, sir?"

Frank was holding the passports and he passed them straight

across me.

He studied the ticket and then both passports, and I knew I was dead.

For the same reason I used different vans, I used a different name to book the trip. A recurring name would therefore not appear on the list that the ferry operators showed to customs each day. This was fine, as no cross referencing was ever done to check that the name of the party leader who booked the trip was travelling in that particular vehicle. It was fine until that vehicle was pulled over at customs.

"You are Mr Targett, are you, Sir?"

"I am."

"Who is Mr Sinclair then? The ticket is in his name and he does not appear to be with you. It is just the two of you in there, isn't it?"

"Yes. Just us. Thing is Eddie was supposed to come too. He actually booked the trip but had to cry off at the last minute. He couldn't make it, so Frank came along instead."

"I see. Been shopping have you, sir?"

"That's right. Just a beer run, you know."

"Just beer, wine, cigarettes, that sort of thing is it?"

"That's it." Let me go. *Please* let me go.

"What shops have you been to?"

"Just the Continente supermarket and a tobacconist."

"Are you aware of customs regulations regarding the importation of firearms, drugs, animals and pornographic literature?"

"Yeah."

"And are you aware of the new guidelines regarding beers, wines, spirits and tobacco products?"

"Yeah. Roughly."

"Fine. Would you and your passengers step out of the van please, sir. We'd like to have a look at what you've got."

Then there was a bloke under the bonnet. Torch in hand, he was virtually sitting on the engine. Another was in the cab concentrating on the door panels. One was in the back of the van, handing out all the cases to a fourth, who stacked them against the wall in front of the old git who was running the show, his beady, all seeing eye running the rule over everything. There was no sign of any dogs but that didn't mean they weren't around

The Fosters was the last on and therefore the first off, followed by the bottled Stella and the wine with the tobacco at the front. I was more or less OK on the beer and the wine but we were way over the new guidelines for tobacco. This, of course, hardly mattered. When the old bloodhound sussed the several kilos of grade one Bolivian stashed in the trays of beer, I was sure he would be prepared to forgive the extra Old Holborn I was running through.

He pulled his pocket knife and sliced open the cartons of tobacco and checked each smaller pack within, casting an educated nose over proceedings as he went. Then he cut into each case of wine and checked those, and then each case of Stella. Then he turned his attention to the Fosters. I sat down on the bench at the side of the shed with Frank and waited.

I fingered the plaster on my temple. How easy would it be for Patsy to have me sliced properly in prison? Probably easier than on the outside. Where would I run to?

That was what I was thinking as I watched the old guy pick each pack of Fosters and shake them vigorously. Weighing, listening, comparing. Yes, he knew that little number alright. Did we really think we could fool an old pro like him? Who'd have thought Patsy was as much of a joker as me? Except Patsy wasn't here.

He had only checked six of the cases but that was clearly enough for him. He walked over, flicking through the passports that he held in his hands.

"Mr Targett, I feel I should ask you again. Do you know the government's new guidelines for what you bring into the country?"

What was this now? Did I know how much Charlie was allowable on each trip? But, no. He was just taking the piss now. I went through the motions.

"For beer and wine it's about a hundred litres each. For the tobacco I'm not sure, but we all smoke a lot, you know. We smoke a lot so we bought a lot." Let him have his little game. He and I would be seeing a lot of each other over the coming days.

"Oh, I see. You smoke a lot do you?" He chuckled and shook his head. Tut-tutted. What was the point of dragging it out? The other four had stopped work, now it was his call. Maybe they were worried about getting trouble from us and were awaiting reinforcements before giving us the bad news.

"You have to give me *some* credit, Mr Targett," he said, appearing to dispense with any niceties. "Don't take me or my colleagues for granted. We are fully aware of what is going on."

He let the words sink in. I nodded humbly and wondered if it would do me any good if I volunteered information. Give up Patsy? He was talking again.

"We're here all day long. This is our business." He shook his head with heavy seriousness and pulled a notebook from his pocket and took down details of our passports. Then he put the notebook back in his pocket and gave us our passports back.

"You are certainly not the first people to bring in tobacco and alcohol for resale purposes and I doubt if you will be the last, but you certainly won't do it again. I have your details and they will be entered in the customs central computer. We know what you are doing, Mr Targett. I don't expect to see you again. Smoke a lot indeed."

Then he turned to his boys. "Back in, lads. This one's okay."

We were on the A2 before we realised we'd actually got away with it, and then halfway back to London before we stopped howling. The greatest buzz I had ever known. I wanted to keep going to get straight back to Patsy, but Frank said he needed to pull over.

"I need the Khazi, Mick. Apart from that I haven't eaten all day because I've been so nervous. I'm starving."

It wasn't a bad idea. My shirt was soaked and I was completely dehydrated. We pulled over at the Pavilion services on the M2. Obviously we couldn't leave the van, so Frank went in first and then we swapped.

The soothing coolness of the motorway service station calmed me, and for the first time in a while I thought about money. Not what I had lost or needed to find, but in the positive sense: what I had coming. Patsy, the old soothsayer, had asked me what I would do if I came into a load of dosh. I understood, then saw why he had said it.

I went to the toilet, and with the flow it felt like I was unloading all the grief and the woes and the anxieties of the last year and a half. I really felt like everything was going to be alright.

I thought about buying some brandy but throttled back. Keep it together. So I wandered into a newsagent to score some milk and chocolate. What would Patsy pay me for the run? Should have squared that before. Never mind. He was like a kindly uncle to me. He'd be fair.

I noticed the queue at the till and opted for a pastie and a coke instead. The drink was pure nectar. I leant against a wall, relaxed. Breathed. As the adrenaline wore off, the fatigue hugged me ever closer. Better get moving. I took a bite of the pastie, looked up and saw Frank.

"Jesus, are you doing your Christmas shopping or what? You've been in here for twenty minutes. I'm sitting on all that and bricking meself."

Poor kid. We went outside.

I thought about Dixie as I followed Frank back to the van. She'd be psyched to cop some decent Charlie for once. What would I charge her? What would Patsy charge me? We stopped beside the van.

"No. Hang on." Frank said. "This is a Renault."

I looked at him and around. The place was mobbed. White vans everywhere.

"Ah, it's just there. We walked past it."

Maybe, if I gave him the run as a freebie, I could get Pat to front me a kilo at cost price, I mused. Would that work out better? But then how much could Dixie move?

Frank pulled the keys from his pocket as we approached the van and handed them to me. I thought about Ishy as I put the key into the lock. What a shame. I pictured his smile and his gold tooth as I jiggled the key. Crazy bastard.

"Mick."

Could do with him now, I thought. He'd go ape to see that much raw chop again.

"Mick, that's not it either."

I looked in through the window. There was a teddy bear on the front seat. Still, I checked the plate against the number on the key fob. I looked at Frank, then back at the number plate, then all around.

Then it came to me. The reality came to me with a slow, dawning of horror from which I would never recover. We combed every inch of the carpark. Twice. In the end Frank left me out there among the motors and the people, sweating, twitching and crying while he trudged back inside to phone Patsy to tell him that someone had nicked the van.

"Patsy, you know I would never screw you. Christ, this isn't happening to me." Patsy had sent out a car to bring us back. Me and him were in his lair at The Cock. The meeting had the air of an inquest. Or possibly an autopsy.

"Hey. This Frank geezer. This Frank," I blithered desperately. "What do you know about him? I wouldn't mind betting he would be the first place to start looking."

"Frank Junior is my Godson. His father and I are partners in South Africa. No, it wasn't him. The thing is, Mick, someone knew. Someone knew and well in advance. Someone had... information."

"Pat, listen. It was Frank's idea that we pull over. I wanted to get straight back here to see you. Ask him. I knew we shouldn't have taken the chance."

"Who said it had anything to do with you?"

I was so knackered. The fact that he did or did not suspect me didn't really seem to matter. A couple of hours ago I was looking at six or seven years for smuggling cocaine. Then I was looking at violent mutilation for losing Patsy's load. Then... It hit me at that moment. I may have been off the hook for losing the Charles, but I had spent just about all the money I had on the booze and tobacco I had bought in France. Patsy was just no good for me.

"I better get going, Pat. I need to call the hire firm to tell them

---

what happened. Bollocks, I should've phoned the cops too, I suppose." It seemed like I was collapsing in on myself, swirling helplessly in a vortex of bad luck.

"Forget that for now, Mick. You're up to your ears in some serious shit. There's maybe one way you can dig yourself out of it. Think back to your courier days. Think back to some of your old contacts. Things have taken on a sense of urgency. There is a potentially embarrassing, non-profit-realising situation developing before my eyes."

I was so tired. Or perhaps he was just in a different league to me. What was he *talking* about?

"A printer, Mick. I can't believe it has been this difficult." He looked up at me from his chair. "You sure you don't know any?"

Something began to stir. There was one brain cell in the deep recesses of my mind that knew something. It struggled to make itself heard above the furore of bullshit and worry that held sway in there. Then its mate joined in and started shouting too. They were jumping in the air, waving their hands around, trying to get noticed. A couple of times I felt they were going under, but they kept at it and more and more of their little chums hollered away too and then a kaleidoscopic rush of thought and energy nearly knocked me off my feet.

"Yes I do!" I shouted, as a wave of orgasmic knowledge and relief broke over me.

"Captain Francis' brother's gay lover!" I yelled at Patsy, and hit the ground running.

Finding Franny was pleasingly easy. I called him at the apartment and luckily it was his period off. Even luckier, Pascal the Frog was no longer dealing, so Franny was together enough to look in his little black book and read off Bill's number. I thanked him and told him I'd be in touch. Then I called Bill and within three rings I was talking to him. I had to describe who I was a few times, but eventually he remembered. Then came the first piece of bad news: Bill and his printer lover were no longer an item and it sounded like it had been messy.

"You know how some queens get when their looks start to go, Mick?"

I didn't like to admit that I had no idea whatsoever.

"Well, it was one of those. I couldn't go anywhere on my own. The green-eyed monster dogged my every move."

"Ah, I see, Bill. Sorry to hear that. Listen I need to get some printing done. Have you still got Jim's number?"

So, miraculously, within twenty-four hours of getting back from France with no cocaine, I was sitting with Jim Titmus in the office of his printing works down in Redhill.

I was overjoyed to hear that things were going terribly for poor old Jim. Behind it all was - what else? The recession. There was virtually no work around, and when they did pick up jobs the customer never wanted to pay or, in some extreme cases, folded their own company to avoid paying. Staff problems. Overdraft problems. Taxman problems. Suppliers were on the phone daily, hollering for payment. He was behind with the rent for the warehouse. In addition, he had made the monumental mistake of buying out his partner a matter of weeks before things began to turn nasty for them and consequently had an enormous private loan to service as well. Things could not have been worse, which meant that things could not have been better.

Not only did this mean that Jim was still a boring bastard, it meant that he was now a boring, *miserable* bastard. It was exactly what I wanted to hear.

"Good of you to give me a call, Mick. I can't believe you thought of me to do a bit of printing, after all this time." We were huddled in the cramped, chaotic confines of his office as his mighty Heidelberg clattered away on the other side of the flimsy wall.

"I appreciate every bit of work I get. Those machines aren't turning, then I ain't earning. And then I'm also having to pay blokes to stand around and do nothing. Then, when we *do* get work, my customers start giving *me* sob stories about how tough things are."

Aware of the value of timing, I let him ramble on. Then I

started talking.

"How long would it take to do a run of about ten thousand sheets of A3 on the Heidelberg?"

"Couple of hours."

"Can you print a water-mark onto paper?"

"Yeah. After a fashion it can be done. You mix a soft grey with some wax or oil. Print it on, the oil evaporates and the stain is left there."

"I think I came to the right place."

"What's the job?"

"Would you care if I told you your end was twenty-five grand? Cash on delivery."

He rubbed the side of his nose, looked down at the floor and then back up at me.

"Listen, Mick. People come to me every now and then with ideas like this for printing. It goes on."

"Does it go on here?"

"No."

"That's probably why you're skint and all the other print owners in the country are driving around in Mercs and Rollers. I bet your fat, lazy workers are earning more than you. Wake up, Jim. You're starting a hundred metre race ten yards back down the track. Give yourself a chance. Be like Ben Johnson."

"Ben Johnson got caught."

"That's because he was an idiot. I'm in with professionals. Everything is set. The job will even be put on special plates to suit your machine."

"It's been scanned already?"

"Yup. We'll even deliver a hot foil gizmo to do the silver strip. The paper will be supplied and delivered too."

"Silver strip? So you're forging bank notes?"

"Maybe. Think for a second. A man with your skills and experience. Weekend job on your own, do your stuff and for a couple of hours on the press there's twenty-five biggies in cash waiting for you. You deserve it, Jim. Soon enough we'll be back out on the terrace at Franny's. Poop deck time."

He thought about it.

"You're a bad boy, young Mick," he said jerking his thumb at the framed Printers' Guild certificate on the wall. "What do you think that is, a license to print money?"

"We're on," I told Patsy. "The Amex cheques?"

"No. That is now on hold. There is a new priority." He pulled an envelope from his pocket and laid the two notes on his desk.

"Deutschmarks?" I said.

"It's weird, Mick. Stealing the Amex plates from Denny and Pete over at Arthur Coltraine's place. Obviously it saved me a lot of money, but it didn't have to happen like that in the end. I've got a scanner man on the firm who actually approached me. Can you believe that? Not long after, an old friend from America got in touch and told me he needed this done. Two sides of the triangle: the order and the scanner. Now all we need is the printer. Weird the way it all works out, isn't it?"

Weird indeed. They rolled Arthur Coltraine, and all my troubles had stemmed from that, and now the ultimate irony was that they hadn't needed to do it anyway.

"Deutschmarks," Jim said as I laid the notes down, as Patsy had for me.

"Fifties and hundreds. Half and half in terms of value so twice as many fifties as hundreds."

"What's the face value of the order?" he asked as he fingered the notes, holding them up to the light.

"About three million quid's worth."

"Three million. Holy shit."

"It's not that much. It'll fit into a small van."

He looked at me and then back at the notes. "I could make a paper plate of the heads and reduce that for the water mark if it hasn't come out on the scan."

I grinned.

"What about payment?"

"What about it?"

"I'll need some up-front."

"What for? We'll supply everything. You won't be out of pocket a penny, apart from your time and the ink, and I'm sure you're willing to risk a little of those for twenty-five large, aren't you?"

"When do I get paid then?"

"When the job is completed I'll be over in a van, pick it up and deliver it to the customer. They'll pay me and I'll come straight back here with the cash."

"What guarantee do I have?"

"What can I tell you, mate? If I don't get shot or arrested I'll come directly here with your end. If that isn't good enough then you are quite welcome to come to the exchange yourself. That's how flexible these blokes are, Jim. They just want it to work."

"If there's no money up front I'll need more than twenty five."

"Steady, Jim. There is only so much in the pot."

He put the notes to one side and looked me over. Clearly I wasn't dealing with some stressed out, over the hill, law-abiding pushover.

"Three million quid's worth? The bottom line for that has got to be five percent and that is bare minimum. That's one fifty. Sounds like a third for the scanning, a third for the printing and a third for the bloke who's putting it all together. If the scanning has already been done, then a lot of money and effort has already gone into this, Mick. If you have tracked me down after all this time, I would guess you and your chums don't have too many printing options."

"Hypothetically, Jim. If I can pay you fifty grand - and I'm not saying I can, but if it's possible are you saying you'd do it?"

"I can have someone at the exchange?"

"Anyone you say. The stuff doesn't leave our sight until we get our hands on the real money, and you can rest assured about security. There'll be some muscle along and he'll be armed."

He was as shocked by this as I had been when Patsy told me.

"You're for real aren't you, Mick?"

"Nobody's fucking around on this one."

He smiled and said, "This is the chance I've been waiting for."

The iffy Marks were destined for the other side of what used to be known as the Iron Curtain. Eastern Europe was exploding and someone had spotted an opportunity. In truth, as he had confided in me, Patsy had haggled for ten percent of the face value, which was useful because then Jim moved the goalposts completely off the park by demanding one hundred thousand pounds. I was being pussy-whipped by a gay boy.

I was quaking in my boots when I gave the news to Patsy. His eyes blazed into me, searching. Scouring for finger-holds of information.

"I know what you're thinking, Pat. But I'm not behind it. I swear. You want to come and meet this wanker and negotiate, you're very welcome. He's starting to piss me off anyway."

"That's a good answer, Mick. It's good because you know I can't see him. I can't have my face out in the open."

"Then send someone else if you like. I'm not shafting you - he's trying it on with us."

He pondered that. "Okay. It's no skin off my nose. The scanner man is on fifty. I take a hundred. That leaves one hundred and fifty to be scratched over by you and lover boy. If he wants anything extra, it comes out of your share. Understood? Don't forget, this all goes well the easy money comes with the repeat orders."

At that time fifty thousand quid, irrespective of what I had to do for it, was more attractive than all the coke in Columbia. I called Jim and gave him the green light. He asked me if I could pop over again.

"Someone I want you to meet."

"Oh yeah? Who's that?"

"My man. The bloke who'll be going along for the trade."

I disliked Neil from the moment I met him. He was a big fellow and looked like he could handle himself, but had seen The Long Good Friday far too many times. I suspected he was a wally when he failed to crush my hand like any self-respecting gangster would have. Then he spoke.

"Thing is, Mick, we are going to need more than a hundred large for this gig."

I smiled and looked around Jim's office. He'd dragged me all the way over there for that? Even Jim looked embarrassed.

"Neil, that's all cut and dried. Originally it was supposed to be twenty five. Now you're getting a hundred. Negotiations are closed. We're too far down the road to change anything now."

"Yeah, but..."

"Yeah but I'm sorry. If you need more money, you're out of luck and if you're demanding more then it's all off and I need to use the phone to tell the big man. He insists on hearing bad news immediately."

"It's OK, Neil," intervened Jim. "Let it drop. Mick and me have had a chat about this and if that's all that's on the table, then we do it or we don't, and I say we do."

"But you said..."

"Never mind what I said. Thinking about it a hundred is fair for a couple of night's work."

"But we're not getting paid for the work. We're getting paid for the risk and if you think..."

"Yes alright, Neil, please. Not in front of Mick. If you are still not happy then I'm sure you can have some of my share."

Then I saw what was going on. They weren't so much quibbling about the pay-out. This was a power struggle and they were battling for who got on top.

"This was just a chance for him to get to meet you and for us to try to run through what might happen on the day in question." Jim explained.

"Night." This was Neil.

"Excuse me?" This was me.

"Night. Night in question."

"What makes you think it will be at night?" I was intrigued to know.

"Because it makes sense, and besides, I'm not doing it if it's during the day."

"Well you won't be going then, will you?" I'd had enough of him already.

"What do you mean?"

"If it's decided it's going to happen during the day and you don't want to come then fine. Don't come."

We all looked at each other.

"Neil is my man on this, Mick," Jim explained. "He has to go."

"Then he has to realise, as do you, Jim, that we have little

411

choice in this. The paying customer decides what happens and when, and we go along with it. If we tell the customer we aren't going to be doing any deal during the day because Neil doesn't want to, then it is entirely his prerogative to tell us to go fuck ourselves and take his money elsewhere. It's a free market. The customer has the money and it is our job to separate him from it by being as pleasant and as accommodating as possible. Basically, what he says goes."

"But it's safer at night."

"No it's not."

"Yes it is. It's darker, easier to hide. Number plates can't be seen so easily."

"And there's a lot less traffic around to blend in with. There's arguments for and against, Neil, but it's not our place to argue them. It's not our decision."

He slipped into a wounded, brooding kind of mode.

"When's all the stuff coming over, Mick?" Jim asked.

"The paper will be here on Friday afternoon and the plates during the evening. You still think you can get at it on the Sunday?"

"Yeah. There'll be one man in on Sunday but he won't be around long. What I can do is..."

"OK what about location? I'm not going anywhere North of the river." This was Neil again.

Why me? I was getting the short end of the money for the long end of the grief.

"You're what?"

"North of the river is out. I'm from down here and I don't know the turf over that way." He had his arms folded across his chest, staring me down. I looked at Jim.

"I've got to run. I'll call you tomorrow if I have any news." I stood up to leave.

"Mick. Easy. Don't go."

"Jim, you wanted me to meet your friend and I have. I cancelled a date tonight to come over here, but maybe I can still make it."

"You're not upset are you?"

"I'm not upset, Jim, I've just got a lot to do and I'm wasting time. Same rules apply with the location. If the customer wants to deal in a lay-by in South London at midnight, then everyone's a winner. However if the customer wants us all to meet up at the top of the Canary Wharf Tower at noon, stark bollock naked and holding roses between our teeth, then we call the florist and hope that it's a warm day. OK? Now I'll call you tomorrow with any developments. If not I'll be over on Friday with the paper "

I thought about giving Dixie a call to salvage our evening, but decided against it. I aimed the grumbling Fiesta back towards the M25, and once on the motorway I gave the old girl her head. On a downhill stretch I think we even broke the speed limit.

Through the Dartford tunnel and along the lanes, back towards Upminster. There were a few cars parked along the Clayton Avenue so I pulled up a couple of houses back from the old man's. They waited for me to kill the engine.

Not so long before, I would have had wits about me. No. Before I would have had no need to have wits about me, because I was a protected face. But as a Fiesta-driving pauper? My wits were fucking AWOL. They would have had more trouble knocking over a ten-year-old.

Movement to my right and from behind. Then the door was open. Then, shocking coolness on my face, like hard rain. Just for a couple of seconds. Even before the door had slammed shut again the agony hit me and I knew what it was.

I had brought back CS gas from France myself and sold it on to a mate who was working as a bouncer. He told me what it could do to you, but I didn't think anything could be as bad as he'd described. I was wrong.

In five seconds I could not breathe, my lungs had constricted to the point of failure, and my tongue was so swollen it had outgrown my mouth. In ten, my burning eyes were sightless. I scrabbled blindly for the door handle, skinning my knuckles and splintering my fingernails. I found it but I knew that it would do me no good, because one of them was doing the sensible thing, leaning against the door. I was being marinaded in gas.

The door flew open again and I was gagging and spluttering as they dragged me out. Stretched out on the grass verge, my only thought was damage limitation. I curled up into a ball and they stood in a semi-circle around me.

I couldn't tell how many there were, three I think, but I got the impression they were pros because they didn't say anything. There was no screaming and yelling, no wild blood lust that would attract any have-a-go heroes. I was so desperately short of air that I couldn't even cry out. So the kicking began and went on undisturbed. Then, at a given signal, they all stopped and somebody said something I really didn't want to hear.

"You want the cutters now?"

I heard him puffing, out of breath with the exertion. "Yeah."

Then they were all on their knees and I saw the jaws of the chunky bolt cropper waving around under my nose.

"Get his hand. Hold him down." Strong hands grabbed my wrist and I knew what they were going to do. I clenched my right fist.

"Open up his hand." They were kneeling on me. Lying on me. Pressing me down. To open my fingers the man freed my wrist and I instantly lashed out to feel the solid resistance of his jaw as my fist slammed into it.

"Cunt. Sort him out."

I heard a dog bark.

"Shit."

Then I felt the brutal heaviness of the bolt croppers slam into the back of my head and I knew it was all over.

"Mick? Mick are you OK? Can you hear me?" It was a soft, kindly voice. The voice of someone I could trust.

My hand, I thought. My poor hand. The fingers. Oh no! Bloodied, mashed, missing. I clasped my fist under my left armpit.

"Mick? What is it? What's wrong with your hand? Show me, darling."

I was safe. I was safe from them, but what had they done?

"Mick show me your hand. I can help you."

"My fingers," I whimpered.

"Show me and I'll tell you. Don't be afraid. I've got you."

My right hand felt riddled with spectre pains so I knew they had done a real job on me. With a massive effort I let her pull my right arm free. My eyes were clamped tightly shut. I waited for her scream.

"There, you see," she assured me. "Nothing to worry about You've just skinned your knuckles, that's all. Bad cut on the back of your head though. Christ, you must have really annoyed someone. Who was it this time?"

As a grubby, uncomfortable and terribly painful consciousness flooded over me once again, I opened my eyes and looked up into the face of an angel.

"Dixie?"

"Were you expecting someone else? This is my house you know."

"No, I didn't."

"Lie still now. I've got TCP."

This was something. They had me cold, and yet there I was in Dixie's little place in Walthamstow. She came back into the lounge with a bowl of hot water and some cotton wool.

"How did I get here?" I asked.

"You drove, I suppose. That nasty old motor is outside. Hold this."

I held the bowl of water on my lap as she sat next to me on the sofa. She poured the TCP on to lumps of the cotton wool, dunked them in the water and dabbed at my face and head. As she cleaned she dropped the used swabs back into the reddening water. I hadn't looked in a mirror and had no desire to.

"Drove?" Christ! You sure?"

"Yeah. Only you have the guts to drive a wreck like that, and there was no-one else with you. I guess you made it to the door, rung the bell and collapsed."

"Stroll on. But I can't understand why they stopped halfway through. They had me. The bastards had me."

"Maybe they got disturbed."

"Well, then Plod would be involved."

"Well maybe a car pulled into the street and spooked them and they took off. Then you woke up and got yourself here. You were at your dad's right?"

"How do you know that?"

She dabbed more TCP on a new swab. "You mumbled it when you were coming to."

Whilst I tried to focus my mind, and Dixie seemed to read my thoughts.

"So what do you reckon?"

"Well I've got it narrowed down to one of three. Either it was Jimmy Mulroney making up for his failed attempt in The Yaksak, or it was a bloke called Ishy. I think I mentioned him to you. He was the bloke I used to get the acid from down in Margate. He got it into his head it was me who grassed him and he's been swearing vengeance. If it wasn't one of them, then I think it might have something to do with Arthur Coltraine."

"Why do you think that?"

"Well it stinks of a revenge kick, doesn't it?"

"But Arthur getting rolled was nothing to do with you, was it?"

Shit. It was getting away from me. I was forgetting what she was supposed to know and what she wasn't.

"I don't mean him. I mean another printer, Jonesy. Me, Den and Romanov turned him over. He lost a finger and they tried to do that to me. Jesus. I ain't got a clue. What's it come to when you don't know who's trying to mutilate you?"

I thought it would be best if I stopped talking, so I tried to relax and closed my eyes.

"Tell you what you need. Help you chill out."

"Wassat?"

"Got some good smack."

I was too weak to resist. It was too painful to sit up and chase the dragon so she scooped some onto the corner of a card and I snorted. It was just medicine. The smell almost made me puke, but that soon passed as the greatest anaesthetic the world has ever known began to ply its trade in the sewage works of my

---

416

bloodstream. I sat down on those gloriously comfortable seats and the train pulled out of the station, soothing me to sleep.

"You should get out of the business," Dixie said. "You're not up to it. You're too nice. What's it going to be like if you *really* annoy someone."

Had to keep it together to deliver those Deutschmarks. The chaps were relying on me. Fifty grand. Buy Dad's house. I heard the roar begin in my ears and got ready for the first waves. Mother heroin, how could I ever be without you?

"What's that you say, Mick? You're mumbling," asked Dixie, dabbing at the shreds of my knuckles.

"Inside a week. My end is fifty grand." I chuckled and felt the pain in my head and back and knee and hands begin to ease. Why couldn't they put that stuff on prescription?

"You old dog. I knew you wouldn't be down for long. I hope it's a better prospect than the coke. That turned out to be a wild goose chase didn't it?"

"Not the Amex thing, but another bit of forgery. Ironic innit? Printed in a week and all we do is deliver and we're there." Clack clack. Clack clack.

My headache was gone completely and the relief of being out of pain and feeling *so* good was intoxicating. "Don't suppose I'll see much of the money because I have to give it to someone special, but thass okay. I suppose I've got something to prove. It's doing the right thing, innit? - Fuh someone 'pecial 'sokay. Do da right fing. Got to take care yeroan..."

There were sensations. Not so much dreams, not even nightmares. I wasn't in and out of sleep, I was in and out of life. The train rumbled on, further and further into the darkness.

"Fuck you." I told the man with the big gun. That was pretty brave, but by then I'd had enough. Dixie had been right, I was just no good at this business. What would happen if I really annoyed someone? Well, there I was in a field, staring down a man in a mask who was holding a big gun. I told him to fuck off

417

and spat blood all over him. I guess that made him annoyed, so we'd be finding out soon enough.

CHAPTER TWENTY TWO

Waiting.

This crime business. This villainy lark. How long had it been now?

When Neil was talking he annoyed me. When he was saying nothing it was worse. He eventually broke the silence.

"How long's it been *now*?"

"We've been here for twenty minutes, which means our man is ten minutes late."

He shuddered his petulant disapproval.

"Take it easy, Neil. He'll be here. This is Georgie Harper we're talking about."

Georgie Harper indeed. When all the Marks had been printed and Patsy had set up the meet, I knew I was definitely dragging myself out of the mire because he'd told me that Georgie Harper was in charge of security. THE Georgie Harper. Farmer knew of Georgie. Masters used to run with him and they had both talked about him in hushed, reverential tones. The one that Nipper Read couldn't put away. The survivor of capture and torture by a rival gang. The man who served eight years on bullshit charges when he could have freed himself by giving up just one name.

"Well, where is he then?"

"Haven't kept you girls waiting, have I?"

We both whinnied clear out of skins. There he was at the

window. More than that, worse than that, I saw that it wasn't the first time I had met him. I'd already met the legendary Georgie Harper and hadn't even known it.

"You," I said, like it was an accusation. "It's you."

A lopsided grin. "Micky Targett. Nice to see you again. That really your name?"

"Certainly is."

"Well, son. Let's hope you're a bit nearer the bullseye with this lot than you were with those tins of Fosters I gave you. Everything alright?"

I knew I'd recognised him outside the Continente. I'd seen his face in the papers many times over the years.

"Counted, loaded and ready to go."

I was star-struck by the gangster charisma, the stunning gunmetal grey eyes.

"Better let me have a look, son."

As I swivelled in my seat to open the side door of the Transit, I heard Neil.

"Look, it's all there. He's just told you. What about all this trust we keep hearing about?"

Keep cool. Show a united front.

"Neil, if George wants to have a look who are we to argue. He's going to make us rich soon enough."

"Only if you two ain't lying to me," he said as he hopped into the rear of the van.

For a guy who was well into middle age Georgie sure was fit and nimble. I observed him squatting down on his haunches next to the boxes and thought no way could I do that with my knees.

He ran a blade through the masking tape around one box and lifted a single note from the top bundle of fifties. With surprisingly elegant fingers, he held it to the light. Then, without a flicker from his gruff, ruddy features, he flattened it onto the top of one of the boxes and with a manicured fingernail chipped ever so delicately at the silver strip that Neil and Jim had managed to magically impregnate in each note. Again he said nothing. Then he pulled a note from his wallet and effected a millimetre by millimetre comparison.

He went through the same routine with the hundreds.

"What's the count here, Mick?"

I knew it off by heart. "There are seventy-two thousand fifties and thirty-six thousand one hundreds. That adds up to seven point two million Marks. At yesterday's rates, that comes out at three million quid, give or take a pfennig."

He put his notes back into his pocket and produced a slip of paper from his wallet, which he consulted briefly and silently.

"Let's go." He slid the side door open and hopped nimbly out. Before he dragged it shut he looked across at Neil. "Keep calm, son," he told him. "You're close to doing very well for yourself. I've no idea how you've come to be involved with real people, but there you are and here you are. Stay close but not too close. And don't lose me."

On the move, that magic old crime buzz was there for me again, like the first hit on a crack pipe. Exactly twenty three minutes later, we exited the M25 motorway and pulled into the carpark of a nearby motel. Mercifully it was in Surrey. Neil killed the engine and we watched Georgie slide from his car and with a flat, raised palm saw him motion to us to stay put. He went inside.

Waiting. Fuck me. Waiting.

I closed my eyes and thought how great it would be when it was all over. I heard Neil fidgeting. Heard him sweating.

"Christ," he blurted. "This is like sitting on a fucking time bomb. We're sitting ducks here. We could be IRA. Supposing a copper spots us and asks what we're doing?"

I couldn't answer that one, and I had to concede he had a point. Seconds became minutes, and the minutes trickled by with a crucifying heaviness. In a carpark full of unattended rep's Sierras and Cavaliers we stood out like... Well, like a couple of small time villains with a very big secret.

"And we still don't know if..."

"You girls really are making far too much noise." Bang on cue, he had us squealing in surprise once again.

"It's on. Now Neil, you stay with the van while Mick and I take in the boxes. Then..."

"Why? Why am I staying with the van? What's going on?"

How he hung onto his cool, I'll never know. "I need *someone* to stay with the van because I don't want any of the stuff left out here unattended. When there is one box left you pick it up, lock the van and we all go inside to conclude our business."

With his soggy brow and darting eyes, Neil thought about that. "Fine."

"Fine," Georgie said.

I was terrified Neil was going to say something like, "Let's have a look at your gun then."

I jumped out and me and Georgie grabbed a box each.

My faith in Georgie as a professional villain and ally was total. I was carrying something like half a million quid's worth of forged currency, and if he had told me to take them into the nearest police station because that was part of the plan, then I would have done it without question. I followed him through reception, past ordinary members of the public and felt vaguely hysterical. The words *I bet you can't guess what I've got in here?* barrelled through my head. I fixed my gaze to the middle of Georgie's broad back as I tracked him through the lobby and off down a quiet, cool corridor. Thirty yards along we swung right, and twenty yards further Georgie stopped and tapped his shoe against an unmarked door.

My trembling legs somehow got me into the room. Close to the far wall were two desks and a few chairs, and next to the desk was an easel, clipped to which was an A2 sized pad of blank sheets. Seven or eight other chairs were scattered randomly throughout the room. The curtains were closed and the lights were on. Seated on the desks facing us were three men.

As we advanced towards them with our boxes, they all stood so that we might place them down. I looked at who we were dealing with. The first was short and squat, a weight trainer, his pumped biceps stretching the sleeves of his blue T-shirt. He was blond and blue eyed and conveyed a rugged manliness that made me really hope he'd like what we had brought to show him.

The second bloke, I thought, actually reminded me a bit of me. Or perhaps he looked how I looked when I was happy and successful, and less beaten up. He was about six foot and had long dark hair, which was tied back. Jeans and a denim shirt covered his lean physique. He was assured with the confidence that came with money and success.

The clothes of both men were fairly tight and I noticed no bulges that might have been weapons. Which brought me to number three, Older. Old school. Late forties; shaven-headed, bull-like. Formidable. Forget about hand to hand with this bastard. If it came to it even Georgie would need a bazooka too bring this fucker down. It was warm in that room yet he still wore a zippered, leather jacket.

We dumped the first two boxes and as we hit the carpark again I expressed my concern.

"Georgie, maybe I should do all the lugging around. Is it wise to leave them alone with our stuff? Shouldn't one of us stay with it all the time?"

"Mick, do me a favour. Don't start behaving like soppy bollocks over there. These people are kosher."

We grabbed two more cartons and were off again. Halfway down the corridor, I thought of something.

"One thing, George."

He stopped and turned. "What is it?"

"I don't know how much space three hundred grand takes up, but I know that unless we have decided to take a cheque for this little lot our money wasn't in that room."

He was pensive for the briefest of seconds. Adjusting, calibrating, sifting information. "Good boy," he said.

Back in the room, the two younger blokes were busy with using torches, scalpels and a magnifying glass. The bull leant against a window sill, occasionally glimpsing out between the curtains. We dropped the next two boxes on the floor.

"That everything?" asked the taller of the two, with an American accent.

"No. Two more. Tell me, Charlie," Georgie began. I braced myself. "Our money..." He held his upturned palms in front of his body and looked around the room. "Not here, no?"

"It's safe, George. We're staying here in the hotel. The money is in the building. Don't worry. We just have to check and count, and then we can all get out of here. Why don't you bring it all in and we can get everything done in one go?" He smiled a worldly smile and I wondered how anybody got to be so cool, so young. I wanted to know this guy. Christ, I wanted to *be* him.

But Georgie Harper didn't move. He just stared. Then the bloke gave the most minute shiver of puzzlement, which said, 'Of course I'm not going to try anything.. Then, for confirmation, he asked, "George, how far back do you and big Charlie go?"

I watched George digest this and saw him allow the briefest and most respectful of nods before spinning on his heels.

Halfway along the corridor I spoke. "We cool, Georgie?"

He nodded. "We cool."

Now, I wanted to keep Neil out of there, if at all possible. Sure he'd be handy when it came to counting, but I had visions of him saying something daft, and then we would all be the next day's headlines. We got back to the van and the side door shot open and he leapt out. He handed me a box and the last one to Georgie, locked the van and marched in beside us like he was the Capo di tutt'i capi. I noticed Georgie's jaw muscles bunch.

Inside, Neil switched into full-on berk mode. First thing he did was introduce himself to everyone. In code.

"Hi. I'm Roger," he said, pumping the bull's hand. "Good to know you."

He then advanced upon the other two.

"Roger Peters. Hi." He offered his hand to the non-plussed American. "How's it going? I hope everything is to your satisfaction."

"Well, I'm sure," Mr Cool replied, at first shaking but then pulling his hand away with grave suspicion.

"If there is anything I can help you with, if you have any questions please..."

"Neil." Georgie's voice ripped clear across the room, blowing Neil's daft alias to bits without him even noticing.

"Hmm?" he said.

"Come over here for a second, would you?"

Fortunately he did as he was told because things were gathering pace. The American spoke, and I for one liked what he said. "Rudi, would you bring my case please."

And into the home straight.

In a silence that seemed to take on actual physical form, the three of us stood and watched the two of them pull random notes from the piles on the desk. The American checked the water-mark and then scraped carefully at the silver strip, before passing the note on to the blond geezer, who checked the serial number, the colours, the embossing and the general quality. The bull returned carrying a suitcase. A big one.

"Thank you, Rudi," said Mr Cool. "George, would you and your colleagues care to start counting? Problem is, and I can only blame myself for this, our counting machine has suddenly decided it no longer wishes to work. I guess we'll have to do it all manually."

"No problem, Charlie," said George, who took the case from the bull and lifted it onto one of the free chairs. He squatted in front of it and began to undo the heavy buckles, before tugging at the zip along three sides of the case. I heard a heavy, rhythmic breathing and turned to see Neil's enraptured, moon-like visage, inches from my shoulder.

I'd seen it in films of course - we all have. I remembered when those punters had brought around loads of folding for the rung motors, and I thought about the wads that Jenny and Ishy would hand over when I was knocking out the gear, but this... I closed my eyes and re-opened them and it was still there: that suitcase *full* of cash. Three hundred thousand pounds. George pointed at me and then to a space on the floor.

"Over there. Sit down." As I obeyed his order he scooped an armful of money out of the case and dropped it onto the carpet. I sat on the floor and got to it.

"You, over there." Thankfully Neil obeyed without murmur, and George made headway into the remainder.

All three of us counted, but occasionally halted to check for forgeries ourselves. "You never can be too careful," George explained to his amused and understanding contacts. "You wouldn't want us to be slipping any real ones into your lot now would you?"

So five of us counted and checked while the sixth stood and observed. Nobody spoke. The constant rustling sounded like a pack of rabbits enjoying a field of lettuce. The weirdness of it all was limitless. The whole scene was surreally entrancing, and whilst part of me wanted to say, "OK, fuck it, I've got enough," I felt as calm, focused and as satisfied as I'd been in years. If anyone was going to try anything, or if the cops were going to make an appearance, they would have done so by that point. So I knew we were all working with a common aim: that of making ourselves rich.

No victims to worry about either. No have-a-go shopkeepers, no car-buying punter with his life savings clasped in his white-knuckled mitt. These thoughts hummed in my brain as I sat, hunched over my stash, like some mad capitalist goblin.

Eventually we finished at roughly the same time. Georgie looked at me with raised eyebrows.

"One hundred and nine," I told him.

"Ninety-six," an exhausted looking Neil said.

"All back in," instructed Georgie.

We poured it all back into the case, which Georgie zippered shut. We stood up, and as I did so I felt my knee grind viciously. Over at the table the two blokes were still hard at it, steeped in their task, rubbing eyes, kneading foreheads. They seemed bored with looking for faults that were plainly not there.

"How're things looking, Charlie?" enquired George.

The American exhaled loudly and pulled his head violently to the left so that his ear nearly touched his shoulder. The resultant crack echoed around the room.

"Good, George. Good job. The money OK?"

"To the penny. Tell me, I think these boys need to be on their way. What do you reckon? You need to count all of it? You need to check everything?"

It was like waiting for your teacher to tell you school was over for the summer. I saw him eye his watch and look down at the sea of blue and green before him. He sniffed.

"Tell me, George. Exactly what is the count?"

Georgie dug into his pocket for the scrap of paper he had previously consulted.

"You have seventy-two thousand fifties and thirty-six thousand oners. That gives you seven point two million Marks. Three million Sterling give or take."

We hung on his word like he was a judge delivering a sentence. "The quality so far is fine, we haven't found a bummer yet. Trouble is, it's going to take us all night to count, let alone check."

Rush hour was on us. The M25 would be getting clogged. Cops would be on the road. I could see us being there half the night.

"Tell you what, George," the American offered. "Can you guarantee this? The amount and quality all the way through?"

Whoa. Tough one. There were literally millions on the table and here was one bloke asking another for a verbal okay. Talk about trust. Want to know what happened? What Georgie Harper did when asked by some big shit yank to vouch for the odd few million? He turned around and looked at me. All he knew about me personally was the botched coke thing for Patsy, but I guess Patsy must have approved me somewhere down the line, because he was happy to take my word as a working villain, even on a matter of such colossal importance. With a lump in my throat, I stared back into the lasers of his eyes and nodded my solemn commitment.

It was a religious experience. It was only later that I remembered how I'd only arrived at the printers as they were packing the boxes and that it was really down to Neil to guarantee the quality and the quantity. If Neil or Jim had opted for an unscheduled dip into the funds before I'd got there, then Georgie's name in the international criminal community, along with my head when he caught up with me, would have been rendered garbage. But I was centre stage and I had my moment.

"Our end is fine, Charlie," George answered. "It's down to me if it isn't."

The yank considered this for no more than two seconds and

then stood up. "Good enough for me, George," he said and offered his hand.

George strode forward and took it. Then he turned to me and pointed at the case.

"You OK with that, son? I understand you are taking care of things from here?"

We hadn't actually discussed the divi up and the transport of the dosh. I thought George would be nursemaiding us all the way, but it didn't matter. We were home free.

"Don't worry, George. I've got some real good ideas about how to take care of things." I grinned and picked up the case.

"Good boy. Now you take care. Don't lose anything this time. I'm going to stick around and help the boys tidy up. Watch yourself."

I felt tears not too far away. He was like my mentor. "Don't worry, boss man. I'm sorted. Thanks for making this easy."

I called to the others, "Thanks, fellas, and good luck with everything."

"Thank you and goodbye," the cool Yank said.

I turned to hit the road and noticed Neil fishing in his wallet.

"What are you doing?"

"I'm just going to leave my card with these lads," he explained. "Four colour presses, full litho and laminating capabilities. The entire printing process, under one..."

My hand shot out and grabbed his wallet. The thing was, he meant it. He was really touting for printing business. I died. Man I really died when he did that.

"Get the fuck out the door... Roger."

We spoke to no-one and no-one spoke to us as we scuttled along the corridor and through reception, barely resisting the urge to break into a wild stampede. Neil had the keys out of his pocket, and despite dropping them three times trying to unlock the van, we were soon on our way. Seat belts. Lights. Indicate. Nice, easy and legal.

Assuming our place in the flow of the motorway traffic and into glorious freedom, that moment of blissful success - of heavenly reward - that single moment was worth all of it.

Possibly. It was like losing your wallet, only to retrace your steps in a blithering panic to find it again. Multiplied a billion times. It made up for all the previous screw-ups and then some. A moment of triumph. One hundred percent pure joy. On the radio, ZZ Top were belting out Viva Las Vegas and we had to turn up the volume to drown out our whoops of joy.

Up to that time I don't think I'd ever seen Neil smile, much less lose himself in happiness. How could I not forgive him for being such a tosser, bless him? I had to slow him down a few times but that was okay. By then it was getting dark.

The plan was to meet Jim back at the print warehouse where we would settle up. From there I would jump in my car and take the remainder of the dosh back to Patsy at the Cock.

We turned off the M25 at junction five and headed in towards Croydon along the Godstone Road. A mile into the lane we got stuck behind a knackered out old Bedford van that was farting exhaust fumes all over us, and was clearly not long for the world. Thirty miles an hour became twenty which became ten which turned into what looked like complete engine failure. The bloke chugged to a smoky halt in the middle of the lane. Because of oncoming traffic we were unable to get by. The driver, a hippy looking sort, jumped out and attempted to shove the thing along from the steering wheel - an impossible task.

"I'll help him," I said.

I hopped out and leant my shoulder onto the rear door. We were picking up a little speed when the van exploded from the inside and the doors flew open. I landed on my back, practically under the wheels of Neil's Transit. Two dark figures wearing ski masks and what looked like big sticks leapt from the back of the Bedford and loomed over me. It was the classic nightmare scenario. They were lithe and powerful while I, tortoise-like on my back, could only scrabble like a comic cartoon figure, unable to simply stand up. Already one of them was around to the door of our van and had Neil out by the scruff of the neck.

"Into the bushes," I heard one of them yell as they bundled past. "Off the road or I'll blow you in half, right here."

Still helplessly sprawled, I watched as my caretaker paced

towards me and I noticed in the glare of Neil's headlights that he was wearing a pair of those heavy brogues everyone used to wear when I was a pretend little yob, back in the seventies. The thing about those shoes was... Oh yeah, they were really good for kicking people with. Taking a toe squarely between the eyes, I was dealt a perverse double blow as my body jack-knifed backwards and the back of my head smacked against the tarmac with dizzying force. I felt that I should have been unconscious and was deeply saddened to realise that I wasn't. I felt something on my face and had trouble seeing and knew I was bleeding heavily from the dent I was no doubt sporting in my forehead.

A mighty fist grabbed my shirt front and hauled me to my feet with such power I felt my feet leave the ground. I kept thinking, *Where are the police? Where were all the other motorists? Bystanders? Witnesses?* I was panicking for sure, but they didn't actually think they were going to get *away* with this, did they? Did they know who I was with?

"Off the road, son." Came the curt order and to back it up, if it needed any backing, I noticed... Oh yeah. In all my time in the game, I had never seen one in the flesh. Now here was a man, ramming the muzzle of a sawn-off shotgun into my cheek.

Peering groggily through my crimson curtain I was heaved bodily across the grass verge, through thick, prickly bushes and into a field where the other bloke already had Neil, sobbing with fear and panic.

"Please. I'm a married man. I've got a wife and kids. Don't hurt me. I'm only a van driver. Please don't hurt me."

I wiped my face in time to see his guardian flick his shotgun around and seize it by the barrels like a baseball bat. He brought the butt swinging through the air to land, with sickening force, on Neil's left shoulder blade. He flopped forward like a sack of potatoes, only to be dragged back up by his collar into the kneeling position.

"Hands behind your back."

Crying now, he clasped his hands behind him and the man was swiftly down on his own knees, produced a rope and had trussed Neil in seconds.

"OK back to the vans." This order came from the man who had rendered me as impotent as a schoolgirl. He was clearly in charge, as his subordinate obeyed without a word.

He came from behind to stand in front of me. "On your knees," he commanded.

There was a blithe feeling of detachment that had me feeling that maybe it was all happening to someone else. I really wasn't sure he was talking to me, so I just stood where I was.

"On your *knees*." He was fumbling with something as he circled behind me once more. Rope? Shotgun cartridges?

I tottered around in the furrows of the field there, on the ploughed ridges, and realised that this was how I had been for so long. Struggling, stumbling. Always trying to secure my footing on the ever-shifting sands that made up a life spent on the wrong side of the law and drugs. Yet there I was, it was happening and it was happening to me. I truly was standing in a field in England with a man who was going to kill me.

But I just stood there and figured that maybe it wasn't that bad. Dad popped into my head and I worried about him for a second or two. Mostly though, I pondered how a nice Essex boy could wind up trapped by such inordinately insane circumstances. All I wanted to do was get along. Keep up. I never meant to harm anyone, I just had trouble saying no sometimes. All I wanted was to be a bit special. Problem was, me being special was like the old square peg in a round hole syndrome: it didn't fit and neither did I. I was out of my depth and I always had been.

Was he talking to me? Was he?

"Bollocks," I heard somebody say, realising, after a few long seconds, that it had been me.

"You what?"

I peered down through the sticky redness. I saw Neil looking back up at me, the terror writ clear in his drowning, pleading eyes.

"Fuck you. I ain't making this easy for you." My dream. My beautiful dream was finally dying and dying with me, which I suppose is the only right and proper way for a dream to die.

There really was nothing left and nothing or nobody could hurt me more than that.

"Listen," I heard the snake hiss of his voice. "Get on your knees, or I'll..."

I spun quickly around and spat a gobful of blood all over him. "Fuck you," was all I said.

He flipped the gun around as his partner had done previously. I caught sight of the shadow looping down over my head and heard the crack of the polished Maple against my skull. Then, for a lulled nanosecond, I felt the strange warmth of the dark and the nothingness.

"Good boy." I thought I heard him say, as the lights went out.

CHAPTER TWENTY THREE

The good thing about the flight to Mallorca is it only takes two hours. The bad thing about it is... Yeah we know all that. Two hours in which to contemplate.... Yeah, yeah. As I undertook the ultimate Night Flight to Shoebury, I had zero interest in the view, as the big bird winged in over the mountains of the north and onwards down to Palma. Clack clack. Clack clack.

I had a little time left though, but that time presented more questions than answers. As I fingered the hardening scab that was smack in the middle of my forehead, I thought about my brief and remarkable recuperation in Mayday hospital down in Croydon. These old bones of mine, they just won't lay down and die. Two days after they finally kicked me out, I got two very interesting phone calls in the space of an afternoon.

Vicky was delirious with happiness for more than one reason.

"He's going to be out soon you see and we're already making plans to..."

"Who's going to be out soon?"

"Ishy of course, you dummy."

"Ishy? But they gave him years and years didn't they?"

"Yeah. So now he's done half of it and because he's been a good boy he's getting out. Christ, Mick, where've you been?"

Good question. It had been close on two years since Ishy had been nicked. Christ indeed.

"Thing is, he learned a lot about computers inside and it's the new thing. So he's got a brother who's got his own IT company, and we're going to move up north. Turns out he was from Doncaster all along, wherever that is. It's all going to be OK."

As frazzled as I was by the beating and the hospital stay, the mention of his name brought things into focus.

"So how's he feeling about me?"

"He's fine, Mick. I finally talked sense into him. He knows you had nothing to do with him going down. He's looking forward, not back. He wants to see you."

That threw me for two reasons. Firstly it blew out my theory that it was Ishy causing me all this grief. The kicking outside the old man's house. Then getting rolled for Patsy's three hundred large. Had to be Ishy putting a few of the chaps up to it. Didn't it?

What also upset me about Ishy's forgiveness was that I soon found out I wouldn't be around to receive it - wouldn't be there when they opened the gates to let the old bastard out.

Lauren Chetkins had called as well, telling me she had a one way ticket to Mallorca for me. Patsy wanted to have a little chat.

Then it came to me. I wish I could say that it had all been a dream, but it's not that easy. But it had all been a set-up. What if I never pulled Lauren out of that fight? What if I hadn't done that because there had never *been* a fight? Lauren had picked me out on Patsy's orders, and... Then he would owe me a favour, but once I'd collected that he would have me by the nads and then he could... Were some people really able to think like that?

Mechanically I went through the process. Disembarkation, onto the bus, off the bus, through passport control. I think I even recognised the guy who checked me through. I thought back to the times I used to walk into the country with thousands of pounds of drugs on me. How long ago it all seemed. Outside in the sun, I heard a voice.

"Hello, son. What's the scam?"

I stopped and spun around. Well, well.

"Georgie Harper in the flesh. How are you, sir?"

"Not too bad, boy. You look like you've seen better times

though. Jesus, Mick, you ought to get out of the business."

I never thought that the assassin sent to kill me would be so chatty, but it was about par for the course for my odd little life, so I paid it no mind.

"I think I'll probably be retiring soon enough."

"For the best. You got nothing with you?"

"I didn't figure on needing much."

He nodded. "I've got a car over here."

Azure blue, convertible top down to reveal a spotless white leather interior, the car truly was a work of art. I had ridden in Rolls-Royces before, but the new Corniche was too much.

"Patsy's," Georgie told me as the colossal motor breathed into life. "Wouldn't be mine on what he pays me."

I felt very moved. It should have been me. The sun belted down and we both donned our shades as the Corny cruised noiselessly away.

I wasn't afraid, just a little nervous. Fear of the unknown is what they say death is all about, and that sounded about right. I wasn't up for any pain though. I figured Patsy would spare me that. Gunshot to the head would do me, maybe from behind so that I didn't even know it was happening.

Denny shot a bloke a few years back - gave it to him in the temple with a nine mill. The bloke went down but hung on for a while and Denny, ever inquisitive, dived onto his knees to talk to him about it. You really need that don't you? Some animal plugs you in the brain and, not content with that, takes it upon himself to settle down with you and ask what it's like. You'd have to say something like, 'Well I'm a bit pissed off actually, mate.'

According to Den, the bloke was old-school about it, talked him through it. There were no visions of heaven or hell or his whole life flashing before him, or any of that old crap. Just a bit of a headache and heavy fatigue. The more they talked (he asked Den to make sure his wife and kids were looked after and he promised he'd see to it) the pain lessened and the tiredness increased, until he just couldn't keep his eyes open anymore and that was it. See you on the other side.

Unable to take my usual pleasure in the trip from the airport out to Santa Ponsa, I sadly observed the Las Rocas block where I'd stayed with Simon and his uncle. Past the turning for Preston Jack's family's place. It looked like we were going to take the sea road back towards Magaluf but at the last moment Georgie flipped a right up a narrow track I never knew existed. Out towards the cliffs. So *that* was it. An idiot tourist who had wandered too close to the edge. Make it look like an accident.

Then, as I was considering asking Georgie to knock me cold first, I saw a gate off to the left and the Rolls purred to a halt. He pumped the stately horn twice and the black, wrought ironwork swung open. We eased in and then down a tight, steep slope that opened out into the most beautifully manicured garden I had ever seen. Aside from the sweeping lawns there was a twenty metre pool, a huge gazebo, an aviary, a barbecue, patio and tables and chairs for around thirty people. Beyond the patio was the house which looked like some massive, suburban, mock Tudor manor house that had been transported magically from the home counties and thrown up next to the Mediterranean. A bougainvillea covered hacienda. A rock star's hideaway. A gangster's lair.

As Georgie was parking the car, I saw Patsy on the patio. He was wearing rather ridiculous khaki shorts that reached to his knees and a lemon coloured polo shirt that clung to his bulky form in a film of sweat. Then there were three. I stiffened.

"Hello, son. I'm glad you could come. How are you? You don't look so good, you know."

"Had a lot of bad luck lately, Patsy. I don't know what it is but people seem to keep wanting to hurt me."

"I'm sure there are explanations for that, son. It can't be because you are a complete spunkferret *all* the time."

I grinned. "I share your confidence, Pat. There must be something more to it than that."

He looked over my shoulder at Georgie. I had no desire to know what Georgie was doing behind my back. I just prayed that whatever it was, he would do it with all the swiftness, professionalism and attention to detail for which he was renowned.

Then Patsy asked, "What do you think of the house?"

I shrugged. "It looks like your place in Essex."

"To an extent it is. Barbara had a free rein and she included a lot of the features of the place back home. This is one of the reasons I've been away a lot. There's a terrific view. Come through and see, son."

With that he had his paw around my shoulder and was guiding me into the cool of the warehouse-sized hallway, then into the sixty foot lounge, and out the other side through floor to ceiling sliding glass doors to a view of the endless blue of the shimmering Med. The patio was about the size of a tennis court and featured another barbecue, more tables and chairs, several loungers and a Jacuzzi. The cream of the London underworld could hold a conference in secluded splendour right there. Patsy lead me by the elbow over to the far wall.

"Nasty drop, eh?" he observed, with classic understatement. "I'll have to have the wall raised. Anyone falls over it pissed..."

I held my breath and peered over the edge. Nasty indeed. A sheer plummet onto jagged rocks. I stayed there for long seconds, waiting for the jarring shove between my shoulder blades that didn't come. So I turned around and faced the house. It surely was a work of art. The pinnacle - the embodiment of English, Tory achievement. The summation of greed and tacky self-congratulation perched majestically on a cliff top on a Spanish island, where Patsy was king of this unassailable castle.

One hundred and eighty degrees of his view was the sea, and the rest consisted of dense thickets of trees and bushes impenetrable even to the most determined assailant or paparazzi. Privacy and privilege.

"See the little harbour?" He pointed down to the water's edge and I noticed that steps had been carved into the cliff side, all the way down to the sea. At the bottom there was a dock and harbour. Tethered and ready to go was a forty foot Sunseeker motor launch. Yup, the man had it all.

"I'm sorry, Mick. You must be gagging for a drink after the flight. Let's get a couple of cold ones." He took me by the elbow once again and lead me back towards the house. We took a table in the cool of the shade, under the awning that stretched out from the rear wall.

"What can I get you, son?"

"If it's all the same to you, Pat, I'd just as soon get on with this."

He fixed me with his solemn eyes, thinned his oddly sensual lips. "As you will, son. OK, that time on the way back from Dover. When the van got nicked with our coke in it. What happened? Who did it?"

"I told you at the time, Pat," I pleaded, suddenly annoyed we were going through it again. "Frank wanted to stop and it was Frank who left the van unattended. When we went out into the car park again, the van had gone."

"Yeah but the odds on that happening are just too much, aren't they, Mick? A random hit? Please."

"I don't know. Maybe someone just wanted a drink."

"Did you tell anyone about it?"

"No."

"You sure?"

"Absolutely."

"Who knows about you doing the France runs anyway?"

"Jesus, loads of people."

"So loads of people know you go to France, but you told no-one about that particular load?"

"That's right."

"I think you're wrong."

"Pat, I'm not lying."

"I didn't say you were."

Did I give a fuck what he thought and why? Did it matter anymore? Did I just turn down a drink?

"Let's lay that aside for a second," he continued. "Let's lay that aside and look at the other cock up. The Deutschmarks"

"Actually I *do* know what happened to that," I told him.

"You do?"

"Yeah. Someone stole it from me." I pointed to my raging, Hindu scar. "You try and kick yourself between the eyes. We got jumped by a bunch of blokes with shotguns and ski masks who knocked us about and had the dough away. I've tried to be a villain, Pat, but I'm not very good at it. Now that's as may be, but I've never been a liar and I've never taken from my own."

He considered this with stern deliberation.

"Tell you what, why not have a drink?" I said. "Dying man and all that. Shame I don't smoke."

"I thought you did, Mick. Crack and heroin, you smoke that stuff, don't you?"

Before I could ask him what the hell he knew about my drug habits, he called into the house.

"George, bring us a few tins out here, would you? And come out yourself. And bring the music player, me and Mick are having a gab."

Music? What was he going to do, seduce me? We sat in uncomfortable silence until Georgie appeared carrying a ghetto blaster - the kind with two tape decks. He also carried three tins of beer that glistened with their own coldness. Coincidence? Vindictive irony, more like.

"Recognise these?" Patsy asked, as George pulled up a chair with us.

I picked up the one closest to me. The bastard was really rubbing it in. Fosters Export. Five percent proof. Duty free.

"Open it," Patsy told me. "See what's inside."

My heart went straight into overdrive. They'd found the missing load! They'd tracked it down and got the gear back. A reprieve! I plucked feverishly at the ring-pull. I saw the jet, smelt the cloudburst of the hops. Cool froth dribbled down the can and onto my hand.

"Cheers," Patsy said, as he and Georgie popped their cans and gulped on the amber nectar.

Ha bloody ha.

"One more question, Mick, and I think we can put you out of your misery. You were selling acid to Rafael Martinez, weren't you?"

The hair on my head, down my neck and indeed all over my body stood on end. It was an unnatural experience. He was one jump ahead of me. Again. I took a slug of beer and shrugged.

What did I care what they knew?

"Actually, Mick, that wasn't the question. I know already about that. The question is do you know how Denny and Pete found out?"

I nodded and felt pleased with myself that I had an answer for him.

"Rafa was overheard taking a call from me about it. Den and Pete were informed. Dixie told me."

"So she's like you're spy on the inside of Den and Pete's firm?"

What was I supposed to do? Boast? I shrugged instead.

Patsy ejected the tape from the left side cassette player and checked the label.

"It's all cued up. They both are." This was Georgie.

"OK. Now Mick, three things have gone down recently. One, you got sussed selling acid in Mallorca. Two, you lost the load that came back through Calais. Three, you got rolled for the cash from the fake Marks. Now that is such a colossal run of bad luck, even you must admit there has to be something more to it."

I gulped more beer and breathed deep.

"You really don't know, do you?"

"Pat, just say it will you. Whatever it is. Say what you've got to say and then do what you've got to do."

He pressed play. It was a hollow sound. Cheap. The volume needed to be cranked right up.

The sound of a cigarette lighter, then a voice. A female voice. I heard her first and then him and I didn't like either of them. They sounded like a pair of skanky Essex druggies.

"There it goes, see? Chase it. Quick. It's going to waste. That's it. Keep it in your lungs. Hooold it!"

"Hang on," replied the man, clearly out of breathe. He sucked and sucked, then let out what was obviously a billowing lungful.

"Jesus. You okay? You look a bit pale. Don't worry it happens a lot the first time. Just be ready to...."

She broke off because there was a sudden flurry of activity. The smoker - the bloke was off and running and then that most unmistakable sound of them all, someone throwing up into a toilet bowl. The poor bastard sounded like everything including his spleen was coming out. I knew how that sucker felt. Then his trudging footsteps across the floor as he came back to sit with the girl, closer to the microphone.

"That's normal. Don't worry about it. Now you'll start to feel good." Her voice. Something about her voice. Then...

"So those plates turned up anywhere yet, Mick? You heard anything?"

It was clear to any fool what she was doing but that bloke, that berk stretching out on the Chesterfield? He didn't have a fucking clue. Not that it did her a lot of good. He was jammering and gouching and mumbling all kinds of nonsense. The smack had him already. But she kept on.

"So how are you making money, Mick? Where's it come from since you lost your drug connections? Surely not just from the Spain runs?"

"Been running acid out to Rafa. Secret. Shhhh."

That poor motherfucker. I hit the stop button.

"You bugged my flat."

"Fortunately, yes. The phone too. Shame when you moved. All we got after that was a bunch of foreigners jabbering away."

"Why? Why the fuck did you do that?"

"Think back. I got those plates from you in a pretty dodgy way. You could've run back to Denny and Pete and told them it was me that took them."

"Maybe I should have."

"Maybe, but Denny would have cut you to pieces. No, the smart play was to keep quiet and hope that you'd get in on that deal with me. Which you kind of did. But I still couldn't be sure of what information you were passing across. So Georgie got one of his boys to bug your place. Under the coffee table."

"What is this, MI5? What information? So I told Dixie I was selling acid on the side."

"That all?"

"Yeah. Dixie didn't necessarily pass that info onto Denny and Pete either. By that time she'd had enough of them too. No, Martinez caught Rafael with my gear and told Den and Pete. The only reason she wanted to know about the Amex plates was so me and her could go and work them together. She was only trying to help me out - and do herself a bit of good at the same time. "

"Mick, how would you know? You didn't even know you'd told her about the acid until ten seconds ago. The minute she used to leave your place, where do you think she went? George was parked outside, watching it all go on. You wanna hear some more? Yeah? You poor, deluded sap."

So then he reached for the start button to the right side cassette. I wanted to slap his hand back, and throw the piece of Alba crap over the wall and into the sea. But I knew that I wouldn't. Knew that I couldn't. I had to hear the absolute affirmation of my own stupidity, in all its pornographic detail.

"... What's that you say, Mick? You're mumbling"

"Inside a week. My end is fifty grand."

"You old dog. I knew you wouldn't be down there for long. I hope it's a better prospect than the coke. That turned out to be a wild goose chase didn't it?"

Then the man laughed, his voice beginning to slur.

"Not the Amex thing bu' nother bit of forgery. Ironic innit? Printed in a week and all we do izz deliver and we're there."

Then there was a pause. The man had fallen silent. He could have been asleep. All that was heard was the dripping of water into the bowl.

"Don't suppose I'll see much of the money because I have to give it to someone special, but thass okay. I suppose I've got something to prove. It's doing the right thing, innit? Fuh someone 'pecial 'sokay. Do da right fing. Got to take care yeroan..."

"Mick?" There then followed a ten second silence. Then two slaps.

"Mick? You awake darling?" Another ten seconds. Then the soft sounds of somebody struggling up from a sofa, taking care to do it gently and quietly, so as not to wake a baby. Followed by other sounds.

"Mick? You asleep, you useless, stupid, drug-fucked wanker?"

I clamped my eyes shut. Make it go away, make it go away,

make it go away, make it go away.

Then a few steps and the clear lifting of a telephone, the dialling of the number, the wait for the connection. Then something odd happened. The clarity of the sound improved beyond all recognition so, perversely, it was like the two of them were sitting around the table with us.

"'Ullo?'"

"It's me."

"'Ullo, babe. Any news?"

"Yeah. He's here with me now. Out of it again. But he's in bad shape. Someone's worked him over. I can't believe he made it here. Anyway, looks like you were right. He *has* got something on the go, but it's not the Amex job. Printing. He says it's going to happen in the next week and that his end is fifty large."

"*Not* the Amex job?"

"Well he *is* messed up and I smacked him too. He's crashed out at the moment but I'll carry on working on him when he comes to."

"The little fucker's up to something with a bit of printing, eh? Never mind what Pete says, it's got to be Patsy behind this. It's too much of a coincidence. Patsy has had a home in Santa Ponsa since they discovered the place and then little fuckwit there turns up and he's lived there too. No, I'm not having it. Besides, whoever knew about those stolen Amex plates must have known we were behind them, and who is going to steal them knowing that? There's maybe two or three firms in London that would have the balls."

"So what can we do?"

"Well what *can* we do? If we kill him or beat the truth out of him, then there's half a chance Patsy'll find out, and then we've got him and Georgie and the rest of those maniacs down on our heads. *Fuck it*! I'll get Romanov to follow him again. It's worked in the past. He'll lead us to his printing job and when he does we'll be waiting, and I'll make sure it's the last stunt he ever pulls."

"OK, fair enough. He's probably out for the count. I'll see what I can get out of him in the morning."

443

"Alright, Dix'. Nice work."

"Yeah, and just you remember that's what this is, work. Don't go taking it out on me again, alright. The grubby little shit stinks like you wouldn't believe."

"Yeah, but you love it like that, don't you?"

"Go fuck yourself."

Then we were left with nothing but the hiss - the stale, white noise of the empty tape.

I just wanted them to hurry up and shoot me. An end to my agony, that was all I wanted. I had told Dixie about the coke and I had told her about the printing and Denny and Pete had just waltzed in and taken both from Patsy. I had just heard the proof. But I didn't know what was worse: costing Patsy so dearly, or being so totally used by Dixie. Betrayed by a lover. Poor Dad. Poor me.

Patsy turned off the machine. They'd bugged Dixie too. I had my eyes closed. Eventually someone had to say something. It was Georgie. He was rubbing my shoulder.

"Son," he began. "What you must learn is that sooner or later, someone is going to do a number on you. If it doesn't happen to you, you've been luckier than you can imagine. What marks us out as men is the way we deal with it."

I wanted to keep my eyes closed forever. Patsy spoke again.

"Drugs is it, boy. That and naivety. You're a good kid, but selling or taking means you're in an unstable world."

I heard the canvas awning flutter in the breeze just above my head. If I tried hard and kept my eyes closed I figured I could have been anywhere. Anywhere warm and nice, where people I trusted didn't want to pump me full of noxious substances to take advantage of me and where evil, vicious men did not want to gloat over my last, agonised breath.

"So, Mick," I finally heard Patsy say. "Stay with it because I want this clear. You let slip to Dixie that we had the Marks deal up and coming, OK? So we can know they were involved in that in some way. Fine. But the coke from Calais. It's not on any of the tapes, from your place or hers, so we don't know exactly what it was you said to her about it. We can only assume that you said something, because she referred to that as being a wild goose chase. Why's that do you think?"

"Perhaps she doesn't rate your Charlie too highly, Pat. I don't know."

"I can see this isn't easy for you but I just have to get all this straight. Who do you think lifted the van?"

"Romanov?"

"Bingo. And what makes you say that?"

"He's a car thief, for one thing."

"Very good. Now here's something I know you'll like. We *know* he did, it because Georgie was there and he saw him."

"No he wasn't. He was in Calais. He gave me the stuff."

"Well, sure. But then he went back to the UK. He got there before you because he jumped on the Hovercraft."

"What? Why?"

"To look after you, of course."

"To look after me? You kidding me?"

"Mick, calm down. By then we had information and a chance to test two things at once. We needed to find out if Denny and Pete were onto us and we needed to know if stuffing beer cans full of Charles on a booze cruise would work. So we used you to find out both."

"I tell you what," I told them, as I felt tangy bile rise in my throat. "Being involved with you two has fucked me up much more than being in with Pete, Denny and Dixie ever did."

"That's a bit harsh. If you're going to play with the big boys..."

"Yeah, whatever. And you're so smart. So a load of coke came through and Romanov nicked it from under your noses. So where does that leave everything?"

"That leaves us *knowing* exactly what the opposition are doing. And knowledge is power. Christ, I can't believe you haven't got this. Did you go to a silly school?"

A thrilling bolt of enlightenment shot through me.

"There never *was* any cocaine on board."

They exchanged their knowing glances again. "Of course not."

"You just needed to see..."

"By George, George, I think he's got it."

How brilliant. How absolutely, perfectly, symmetrically brilliant.

"You just needed to see if customs would pick up on it, which they didn't, and you needed to see if Denny and Pete were onto you, which they were. And Frank was onside, too."

"Naturally."

So this was how it worked at the sharp end. My heart was pounding with both joy and indignation.

"So if there was no coke on board then... I didn't lose any. Well excuse me for asking, Pat, but was there no chance of me being included in on things? For fuck's sake, do you know how much sleep this has cost me?"

"You were too much of a liability. With a headful of gear you could have said anything and that's without the possibility of you working with them to set *me* up. At least now I have the full picture, and thanks to you, the wheels grind on. Pioneering work, I suppose you could call it. In between then and now we've brought three major loads through that way. Good on you, son."

You would think I must have been used to speechlessness by that point.

"I would have loved to have seen their faces when they opened up all those cans," Georgie snickered. "They must have got everything out of that van and opened every single container and every single pouch of tobacco. Must have been a party. Shame we weren't invited."

Then they both laughed.

"So there we were, Mick," Pat finally said. "In possession of certain facts, but unable to make a move in any direction, because something weird had happened."

"What?"

"Denny and Pete had disappeared."

"Do what?"

"I reckon they gave up on the plates, heard about the gear coming through in the back of the van via you, and decided to sell up everything and fuck off and nick my coke all at the same time. They sold the Road Rats, their houses, all their interests, everything. They must have figured that with all of that, plus the money from the coke, they would be set for life, wherever in the world they chose to go."

"Jesus Christ."

"May he help them. They know I usually move at least fifty kilos at a time, and I guess they reckoned the income from that was worth burning their bridges for."

He must have seen me trying to work it out.

"Fifty kees at twenty-five a time is one and a quarter million quid, Mick. That's just wholesale."

"Right."

"Cheapskate bastards," Georgie said.

"Thing is, that gave us a problem. It would be a matter of hours before they knew they had been duped. Our problem then was the up and coming Deutschmark deal. Since you'd given up your Wapping place we only had coverage of the pair of you at her place. Then we had some luck."

I was fascinated. "What?"

"You got beat up outside your dad's house."

"And that was lucky, was it?"

"Well it was clear that you weren't using drugs as much as you used to. A good kicking and a bit of sympathy would loosen your tongue."

"Look, I'm sorry. Are you saying you organised that?"

"Of course not, Mick. Christ, do you think we're nasty men? Like I say, that was just a stroke of fortune we were able to use. George was tailing you. Watching over you."

"Watching over me? That's a laugh, what those fuckers did to me was way over the top."

"Not compared to what they were going to do to you." Georgie had a meekness to his manner that almost made you forget he was there. And he was right. I looked down at my fingers.

"Who do you think it was did that, Mick?" asked Patsy.

"Well at first I thought it was a bloke called Ishy. He got it into his head that I'd grassed him a while back. But I now know it wasn't him so I reckon it was something to do with Arthur Coltraine. Or it could have been from a bloke called Jonesy." I hung my head in eternal shame. The pain I had caused.

"It was neither," Georgie said with his calm authority.

"How do you know?"

"Because I was there, you idiot. I'd followed you from the printer's in Redhill. They were waiting for you outside your father's place. They had the bolt croppers out when I got there."

I looked into the granite of his face. "Thanks, George," I told him.

"Part of the job," he shrugged.

"So if it didn't come from Arthur and it didn't come from Jonesy, who was it?"

"I caught the number plate as they belted off," George said. "The car was registered to a bloke called Richard Stephen Baddows."

I squinted through the setting sun. "Richard Stephen Baddows? Who the f..." I caught Patsy's eye and I knew.

"Little Jen's brother, Ricky."

"Adds up, don't it?" Patsy concurred.

"So George flicked those blokes away from me and then saw that as an opportunity to get me back with Dixie, to carry on learning what the others were doing?"

"That's it."

"Wouldn't it have been smarter to have kept me away from her? If I hadn't seen her I wouldn't have told her about the Marks scam and we'd still have the money."

"That's a good point, Mick," Patsy told me. "But you must have heard of keeping your friends close and your enemies closer. By that time they'd risked their all on the coke grab and gone to ground. We needed to flush them out and end all the tit for tat nonsense. The only way we could do that safely was to deliver you into the tender care of Dixie. George drove you there."

I held my hand up to stop him again. "Pat, why the fuck couldn't you tell me any of this? Am I really that untrustworthy? Never once did I tell anyone that you nicked those Amex plates."

"I know you didn't, son. But we also know that Dixie could get information from you. I believe you to be a very loyal person.

We've just heard on the second tape you telling Dixie the fifty grand you would have copped from the Marks scam would have gone to someone special. I'm assuming you mean your father?"

I nodded. "But you still couldn't tell me?"

"Couldn't take the risk, boy."

We broke off and all drank in silence for a while.

"So you reckon it was just a case of Denny and Pete tailing me from the printers, all the way over to the hotel off the M25, and then back with the real money, where they rolled me and Neil in the field?"

"Kind of looks that way."

"I *knew* it was Den in that field. Knew I recognised his voice."

"Listen, if Denny Masters had got you in a field, in the dark, with a shotgun and no witnesses apart from a scared poof he was going to kill too, then believe me, you would not be sitting here enjoying the view today."

Surprises. I was just so sick of surprises.

"And if they had nicked three hundred grand of our money, do you really think we would be sitting here enjoying it with you?"

"I have a confession to make, Mick." Georgie's voice cut into the conversation like a buzz saw. And the confession? Talk about save the best until last.

"It wasn't Denny who donked you over the head in that field. By the time you got hit, Denny, Pete and Romanov were trussed up like chickens in the back of their own van - the one they were planning on using for the snatch. I had a couple of ex-para pals of mine in on the gig and we hit them even before they had cleared the carpark of the hotel."

More tingling. It started on the top of my head and travelled down through my skull and swamped the rest of my body, better than any E rush.

"It don't take a lot of working out, Mick. Our plan went down a treat. Denny and Pete were onto you but we were onto them. We clobbered them before they clobbered you. No, it wasn't Denny who whacked you in that field." He drew on his can of beer and made me wait for the coup de grace. "It wasn't Denny

… it was me."

I stared into the solid flint of his face for twenty, thirty seconds and knew I wasn't going to die. I knew that I was going to live and even though I had nothing and I was nothing I was going to see my dad again. And Julie and Vicky and Ishy.

"It was just about money, Mick. Nothing personal. George told me what a total liability that Neil fella was, and I knew they'd hiked their end at your cost. Neil saw you get clouted and robbed. Wasn't your fault. Terrible. Money gone. George, would you get that case for me and another round of beers, please."

I felt my senses reeling, but the big man was still talking.

"I told you a little while ago that the big money, the easy money in this particular scam was with the repeat orders. Now these blokes anticipate needing upwards of twenty million quid's worth of Marks and they are prepared to pay a decent rate all the way through. I'm in the big seat for that so I can waive my cut on the first lot. George needs about thirty for him and his boys, and the scanner man was on fifty grand but I have a question to ask you, Mick, and I need you to answer it without hesitation. What would you do if you came into a lot of money?"

He was going to let me live. That was all I could think of. I wasn't going to die.

I felt myself shrug. "I'm the last person you need to ask a question like that of, Patsy. Where the hell am I going to get..."

"Answer the question."

"I'd give it to my dad. You heard me tell Dixie the same thing on the tape. That's what I was going to do with my fifty from the Marks deal."

I saw him smile broadly and nod as if giving me his rich approval. Then Georgie reappeared. Clasped in one mighty hand were three more cold ones. In the other was a suitcase which he slung onto the table.

"Thanks, George," Patsy said. "Tell you what, mate, would you mind leaving me and Mick for a bit? There's a couple of things I want to run by him."

"Sure," said Georgie Harper. He set two of the beers down and walked back into the house.

Patsy and I picked up a can each and he faced me again, searching both me, it seemed, and himself, undergoing the final throes of some internal conflict, before his mood lightened and he smiled.

He popped his can, took a slug and I did the same. I still didn't have a clue what was coming.

"I know you don't know too much about it, son, but here are the reasons. First, there was the time all those years ago over here when you pulled my Lauren out of trouble."

"I really did that, didn't I?"

"Well of course you did, you berk. Now I know I said we were even when I flicked Terry away from you, but that was before I knew you. I'll always be in your debt for that because there is no way a father can repay something like that. And this thing with your dad and your brother... You're a good boy. I knew you'd give me the answer you just gave me. I never had a son and I never will and I'm certainly not about to say that if I had one I'd want him to be anything like you, or any of that old crap. What I will say is that if I'd ever had a decent father I think I would have liked to have been as good a son to him as you've been to yours."

I couldn't stop staring at the case.

"On top of that, I'm doing OK financially out of you. Three loads of Charlie through Calais already, thanks to you. The Amex cheques lined up, thanks to you. And you indirectly introduced me to Jim the printer."

"Jesus, Pat. Do you really think he's going to work for anyone again after what happened to Neil and their end of the money the other day?"

"No way will he. Of course not. But his disappointment at losing all that money and his ongoing financial problems lead me to play a hunch. I approached him through a third party. I don't know why I never thought of it before."

"Thought of what?"

"I bought him out. I don't suppose I'll have any trouble getting anything printed in the future now that I've got my own printing works."

"Hooolyyy shiiit!"

"So you actually could say you have been a successful villain, Mick. You just didn't know anything about it. But thanks for everything you have done for me. I'm sorry you were kept in the dark for so long and I'm sorry you have suffered so much recently. I hope this makes up for it." He patted the suitcase.

He was talking as I ran the zip around, but I barely heard him.

"Three hundred exact, minus fifty for the scanner man, and thirty for Georgie and his boys. It sounds expensive and even though he bashed you up he's worth every penny. Leaves you with two hundred and twenty large in folding. Congratulations, son. I truly believe you deserve that."

How did I feel? Difficult to say really. I bawled my eyes out through sheer relief for ten minutes, for one thing. When I'd done that I fell victim to all manner of emotions, outrage and indignation foremost amongst them. Not unhappy at being handed my life back *plus* a suitcase full of cash, yet I still felt like speaking out.

"You have no idea what I've been through, have you?"

"Hey, you got treated like an idiot because...? Right, because you *were* an idiot. Why would anyone respect that? Taking Lauren out on acid, blowing everything you earned on cars, bikes, flats and drugs. You got used - get over it. And you had some bad luck, get over that too. Happens all over the world. And there's two hundred and twenty with no tax to pay. Life's a bitch, right? Walk my way."

He stood me up and ushered me to the wall near the edge. We looked down at the glorious Sunseeker and beyond, as the sun danced eye-popping spangles off the points of the gently rolling sea.

"One thing, if I was just a wind-up toy - a means to an end for you, like the bug under my table, then why pay me? Why not just leave me in that field and not tell me any of this?"

"Me and George talked a lot about that. Thing is with you, you *mean* well. You ain't got a nasty bone in your body. You worked hard for Den or Pete, and you trusted Dixie all the way, because it wouldn't occur to you not to. You're a nice man. Do you have any idea how refreshing that is? You just stumbled into the wrong way of life and got tarred and feathered. And that thing with your dad, that really got to me. Loyalty. And not only that but you've been bashed up by Cut Throat Jimmy Mulroney, Terry Farmer, Den Masters, some other bunch of yobs *and* Georgie Harper - and you're *still* fucking standing! Now that deserves some recognition."

We sat down on the wall and I tried to take in what he was saying. Deserved? Interesting word.

Nobody deserved what I had been through, the sights I had seen, the feelings I had felt. Maybe I deserved to get nicked driving a ringer that I had bought in good faith - what a hoot that was - but I hadn't deserved everything that had come my way. Even Nigel and Nicolette hadn't deserved that. Patsy had meticulously pointed out that he needed to lose something he would miss the most, and that's why his left eye went, because his great love was cricket and he batted right handed. Not anymore. Nicolette deserved to lose all the toes from her left foot because she would then be deprived of the long walks in the country, of which she was so fond. More than that, they would live the rest of their lives in ignorance and fear. They deserved all that - but even *they* didn't deserve what I had been through.

And the others? What did they deserve?

"Denny and Pete are gone, son. We let them go and they've moved away from London, warned off in a way that means they won't be back. Leave it at that. Romanov, or Dimitri Costas as he was christened, has gone home to Greece. To die."

"What? Jesus what did you do?"

"He did it to himself. He's got AIDS."

I was truly stunned. Deep breaths. Keep calm.

"Terry Farmer?"

"What about him?"

"What did happen to him?"

"Terry's back in the gulag."

"Blimey. But you told me you sorted him."

"So I did. He's in Durham, doing a seven for possession with intent to supply and for unlicensed possession of a loaded firearm. He got caught outside the gates of his local school. He hasn't got a clue how it happened because he doesn't know you know me. He was actually arrested by someone in my employ. DC Black. Remember him?"

"You're *joking*. You planted a gun and drugs on Terry and bribed Black to nick him?"

"I didn't plant anything. Blacky does all that. Timed it just nicely too. Terry was picking up his son from school and Blacky and his boys swooped. Made it look like he was knocking out smack to school kids. Must have put another couple of years on the sentence."

"DC Black," I said. "He came round my place the morning after... That's how you knew about little Jen isn't it?"

He nodded.

Jimmy Mulroney. What did he deserve?

"What about Jimmy?"

He laughed and swallowed more beer. "Thing is, Mick, I do have things to do, other than stop all your enemies from attempting to murder you. But don't worry about him. Someone spoke to him. He wasn't touched but he knows. He may be insane, but he's not stupid."

That only left...

"Dixie," announced my omnipotent benefactor. "You want to know what happened to her?"

I wasn't sure if I did. Out of all of them, she probably deserved the worst. Maybe she was the only one who deserved to suffer as much as I had. The betrayal. The treachery. I couldn't bear it.

"You better tell me."

"She's back down Walthamstow market, flogging fake Lacoste shell suits."

I wanted to ask him why he had been so soft, but I bit my tongue.

"The word's out on her. Out that she's a grass, out that she's trouble. It's a life down the market dodging the trading standards people and the Old Bill, with no protection whatsoever. Don't bear a grudge against her, Mick. She's just a pawn, just a victim. A bit like yourself."

It was all so sad. The things people did to each other.

"She came to me. She came to me when I was at my weakest and we went to bed together, and it was all a lie"

"Let me guess, she never calls anymore? Mick, it was hardly true love was it? It was all part of her game. Forget it. She's forty-five this year."

"*WHAT?*"

"Here's the thing, you have two hundred and twenty large ones at your disposal and I'll help you with the mechanics of it... But you need to give up drugs."

I railed automatically. "If it's my money, I should be able to do what I like with it."

"No, son. Ordinary rules do not apply. This is personal. For what I owe you for Lauren and for what you and your family have been through, I am involved personally. You owe it to them to give it all up, but most of all you owe it to yourself. You have another chance. Don't blow it."

Life without drugs? Jesus. What would that be like? Especially now I was holding serious folding.

But we imbibed nothing more powerful than five percent lager as we strolled the massive, scorched expanse of Patsy Chetkins' patio, with him casting chunky arms of declaration and explanation before him as he walked, and me tottering in his wake on legs of runny jelly, all the while marvelling at yet another staggering sub-plot in the screenplay of my ridiculous life. I got over the initial indignation of having my life threatened by understanding that it never had been. Far from it - Patsy and George only wanted to clue me up and give me lots of money. The possibility of being murdered, like a lot of things that had come my way, had existed only in the flooded, marshy, no-go area of my head. In my dreams and in my nightmares.

Then, to cap it all, Patsy Chetkins started talking to me about dreams. When they come true and when they don't, knowing all about it in the same way a travelled man might know of the customs of a strange land, or how to choose the correct path at a a forked road.

"Perhaps you need a goal, Mick. Something to aim for. A

dream towards which you can strive and work."

I smiled. "Dreams, Pat? I've had enough to last me a lifetime and beyond. They always seem to get me into trouble."

"But I bet they helped to see you through. Like most things, it's a question of balance. We can all wish for Rolls-Royces and helicopters and early retirement, but it doesn't work like that, does it? You're always going to come up short, and I can tell you that when you have a dream you have clung to, cherished and loved like a child and it doesn't come true, then the sense of defeat and loss can become almost intolerable. I've lost close friends and grieved less."

My heart soared. He knew what I'd been feeling all my life.

"The thing is, if you don't mind taking advice from an old git like me, you got to temper your dreams with some rational visions. Look at it like some kind of competition. Our dreams and our intelligence are our ability in the race, but reality represents the rules. You can have all the ability in the world, but if you break the rules then life ain't going to let you win. Make sense?"

It was so beautiful and made such perfect sense, my mind was swimming.

"Look around you." He jerked his square chin back to the house, to Santa Ponsa, to his life. "This, all of this, has only happened because of dreams. My dreams. The car, the home, the boat, the location. All of this was in my head a long, long time before it was visible to anyone else, but I suffered to get it. I paid my dues. You can't break the rules all the time and still expect to win. That's what you were doing."

"Example?"

"Well, there are drug rules, company rules, common sense rules. You had things sweet with Den and Pete, but you got greedy and started dealing on their runs. You knew you shouldn't have done that. Broke the rules. You can't take from the table and not put back. Common sense is all it is. I'm not giving the key to the universe. Do the right thing, that's all."

I felt strangely calmed, yet excited at the same time. It felt like a mystical insight, even though I knew he was telling me nothing

I did not already know.

"You stand in front of a mountain and you look up. What do you think? You think, shit, there's no way I'm ever going to get up that thing. But what you do is get ten per cent of the way up and tell yourself, 'Yeah, I can handle that'. Then you just do that nine more times, that's all. That's the way mountains get climbed. Real ones, as well as the ones that ordinary people find shoved in their way, every single day of their lives."

Nobody - not my teachers, my parents, my friends nor anyone else had ever managed to explain these points to me as lucidly and as easily as the big, bear of a gangster I then realised I hardly knew. I marvelled at the strength and beauty of his simple logic. He may not have known about everything, but he sure knew about me. Then he said something even weirder.

"Ever thought about getting a job?"

I giggled out loud until I saw he wasn't joking. "Got a problem there, Pat. I can't actually do anything. I ain't riding a bike again and my back and knee stop me from doing any real work. No excuses, but I am a bit restricted."

"You can do bar work, right?"

"Hey, I'm the best."

"OK then. I'm going to be buying a restaurant and bar, or building one. I could do with a manager or, if you're interested in investing some of your new found wealth, I may be approachable for risk spreading offers, should you wish to buy in. Up to you. Think about it."

Work like an ordinary schmo? Brave new world? We ambled back to the wall and plonked our backsides down.

"Any ideas how I might break all this to me dad? He's not gonna believe I found two twenty in the street."

"I can sort that out. I own a couple of betting shops and I know a man who has an interest in a casino in London. You are about to have the most incredible run of luck. Tax paid. Don't worry, we'll justify the money."

I grinned. All things seemed possible.

"Hey," he said, jovially poking me in the chest with a porky finger. "I've never met your dad. You'll have to bring him over. "

Suddenly, from somewhere, there was an enormous lump in my throat.

"You'd like him, and he'd like you. Yeah, I'll sort that."

"How much is owed on his place?"

"The initial debt is about a hundred and forty, but with the interest that is probably up to around a hundred and sixty or so."

"How much is it worth?"

I blew out my cheeks. "Probably two hundred, what with the slump. Maybe less."

"Offer them a hundred and I bet they'll bite your hand off. There's a recession on. Then, if you and your dad fancy it, sell up. You get your hundred grand back, your pop gets a hundred in his pocket. Move out here and buy a palace. You'll live like kings. Be right handy for you if you are in with me, won't it?"

It sounded certifiably brilliant but, employing my new found wisdom I knew I was running before I could walk and of course he sensed that.

"Tell you what. Take it easy for a bit. Summer is coming. You deserve a break. Phone your dad and tell him things are going your way – you've just had a mega win at the casino and that you'll be staying on for a couple of weeks."

I nodded enthusiastically. "Right, yeah. It's been a long time since I had a holiday."

"Fine. Did I tell you that Lauren is coming out here in a few days with young James? She'll be here for the rest of the summer. Don't tell her I told you, but it was her idea that I only got you a one way ticket over here. Stay at least until she gets here, eh?"

I grinned some more. "That's nice. 'Course I will."

"Good boy. Well listen. This has taken a lot longer than I expected. Some local worthies have apparently objected to my dinky harbour. It's not a planning permission thing, they are just concerned Morocco and Algeria are the next stop that way." He waved an arm in the general direction of the shimmering horizon. "I mean, did I design the planet?"

"What on earth can they be worrying about?"

"What indeed? Mr Mayor is bringing said citizens over shortly, just so they can get a chance to meet me and appreciate what a decent, law-abiding, tax-paying expat I am."

"Doubtless you'll be making a generous donation to civic funds, as a mark of respect and of your commitment to the island."

He was smiling now. "You're a natural, son. I'm so pleased you are here and that things have worked out for you." He offered me his hand and I was intrigued to feel no pain whatsoever when I shook it. Back at the table, he patted the suitcase.

"Now take this upstairs and try not to lose it. Either of the four bedrooms on the left at the top of the stairs will do you. Make yourself comfortable."

"Thanks, Pat. Thanks for everything. Listen. I think I'll freshen up and take a stroll around town, get out of your way. I need to do a bit of shopping if I'm going to stick around for a while." I splayed my arms out wide and looked down at my sweat-stained clothes.

"Sure. Whatever's best. Hey, don't get too pissed - dinner is at nine. Georgie is staying for a while and there'll be another couple of interesting types turning up too. We'll talk some more business."

In a dream, I floated up the sweeping staircase and chose my palatial quarters. If I had closed my eyes and flapped my ears I would have made my way there just as easily. I showered and tried to relax.

I redressed in my dirty clothes, flopped the laden case onto the bed, unzipped it and looked inside. It was true. There really was a case full of money in front of me. Know how, bottle and the right people. Maybe Nigel had been right, all that time ago.

I'd shoved about a grand into my pockets before I caught myself. Patsy's calming reason was there for me, and I hoped it always would be. Nothing in particular, just all the things he had said that made such perfect sense. Throttle back sometimes. Easy does it.

I replaced all but a couple of hundred quid. Maybe I would start by buying a wallet.

I knew the road into town well, and even though it was a

couple of miles I opted for the walk. When my knee started to give me a little trouble I just slowed down. Easy.

I felt like I had felt all those years ago when I was a young, silly tourist, out for a holiday in the sun with my mates. An eventful evening was stretched out before me, and would be followed by a hot, lazy day, which would be followed by... I felt like a chosen one.

I scored some pesetas at an exchange bureau then bought a new pair of jeans, some light loafers and a plain white, short-sleeved shirt, all of which I kept on. Then I walked outside and dumped my old clothes in the first bin I saw, revelling in the ceremonial shedding of skin.

Happy and comfortable, I hiked up to the old town centre, took a seat on the terrace of Tom's pub and ordered a beer. Just a beer - no tumbler of gin, no Kamikaze shooter - just a beer. Then I looked up and saw that Tom's pub was no longer called Tom's pub. It was called Pat's Irish bar.

I sat there for long, lovely, soulful minutes as the sun began to dip and the day cooled, watching the early season tourists make their way from the beach to their rooms. As I sat, a wondrous peacefulness and tranquillity fell over me, with the realisation that I had finally achieved what I had *really* been looking for: I was ordinary. I was a face in the crowd. OK, I had a couple of hundred thousand in cash back in my room, but if I managed to forget that, if I appreciated that all the hard work had been done and all the sacrifices made, I knew that I was the same as the happy, chattering crowds in the street. The joy of that discovery thrilled me more than drugs or money or power ever had.

Then I heard a voice.

"Ah, Commander Targett."

The voice seemed to know me well.

"It is way after five, but I believe cocktails and refreshments are still available on the poop deck."

Acknowledgements

Of all the people I've met in my life half of them seem to be represented in these pages. I'm not going to thank (or blame) anyone by name. For good or bad you will know who you are. And if you don't then you must have been even more smashed than I was.

On a practical level I need to thank the following: Caroline Keefe for the early read and all the encouragement. Rose Lock for the final edit and all the suggestions. Heather Temple and Nathan Church, not just for their help with the cover and getting this thing ready to publish, but for all their generosity and kindness with everything, and for the perennial availability of the twin's room.

Finally my parents. To say that my mother, Eileen Taplin, is in a better place and is better off for not having to read what I needed to write, would be to miss the point. If she hadn't died when she did, I know most of what took place simply wouldn't have happened. I miss her every day. And what can you say about the old man? Teddy Taplin, last of the Wapping hard men, the toughest bloke I ever knew. To them this book is gratefully dedicated.

DT. Essex. June 2017.

About the author

You know far too much already.

Printed in Great Britain
by Amazon